ALL THE FUN OF THE FAIR

It's the 1950s and Grundy's Travelling Fair arrives in town with a bang. When night falls, the local town is drawn to the fair. The troop who run Grundy's Travelling Fair know they can always rely on each other to put on a great show and hold things together through the long hours and backbreaking work. Gemma married into the lifestyle, her reliable husband Solomon making the work worthwhile. Solly's dad Samson is still the boss, but his other son, known as Sonny, is getting a reputation... Times are changing. Can the family – and the fair – survive?

ALL THE FUN OF THE FAIR

ALL THE FUN OF THE FAIR

by

Lynda Page

Magna Large Print Books
Long Preston, North Yorkshire,
BD23 4ND, England.

British Library Cataloguing in Publication Data.

A catalogue record of this book is
available from the British Library

ISBN 978-0-7505-4707-9

First published in Great Britain in 2018 by Canelo

Published in Large Print 2019 by arrangement with
Canelo Digital Publishing Limited

Magna Large Print is an imprint of Library Magna Books Ltd.

Printed and bound in Great Britain by
T.J. (International) Ltd., Cornwall, PL28 8RW

Chapter One

Late March, 1955. On a large slum-clearance site surrounded by a maze of dilapidated back-to-back terraced houses, factories and other industrial buildings, in a rundown area of a south Yorkshire market town, colourful flashing lights lit the dark evening sky and thumping rock and roll music blasted the air. Grundy's travelling fair had arrived.

Inside the surrounding crumbling dwellings and in a progression of more prosperous streets stretching way beyond, a frenzy of activity was underway. Evening meals were being gobbled down, then a rush to wash and change out of school and work clothes for best. Tonight was not one to linger, all occupants desperate to be ready for the off. Every second of the next few hours was to be spent enjoying the thrills and excitement with money saved, stolen, begged or borrowed.

Leaning against a lamp post at the edge of the site, drawing deeply on a rolled-up cigarette, was thirty-seven-year-old Solomon Grundy, a ruggedly handsome, muscular man of five foot ten. He was dressed in a pair of black trousers, the sleeves of a white shirt worn under a black waistcoat rolled up to his elbows, and a black pork-pie-style hat that covered short dark hair beginning to grey at his temples which gave him a distinguished look, he felt. His wife teased him that it was a sign he was just getting old. He smiled, gratified to see the never-ending stream of excited-looking people being drawn, Pied-Piper-like, towards the entrance. The evening was the sort you'd usually find people behind closed doors, huddled around a blazing fire, but the hordes of animated punters streaming out of side streets and hurrying over the waste ground didn't seem to notice, the lure of the good time to come all they could think about.

It was never possible to predict how lucrative any session was going to be but, judging by the number of people already arriving this early in the evening, it looked set to be profitable.

Solly took a last draw from his cigarette before throwing it down, grinding it out with the heel of his shoe and joining the snaking crowd. He might have been on the go since five this morning doing his share readying the fair for opening tonight, the same as everyone else connected with Grundy's, but along with a couple of gaff lads, he was also in charge of the dodgems tonight. As an expert in all the tricks of the trade, he knew he had already left the youths for far longer than he should, leaving them at liberty to supplement their meagre pay by wrong-changing or tapping, as they called it, the general public. Although it was known this practice went on behind the owner's back it was not condoned and, if the culprits were caught red-handed, it was an instantly sackable offence.

Using centuries-old tricks of the trade to make a living was one thing but, as in all walks of life, there were those that were out for themselves who felt no shame in doing whatever it took to feather their own nest, illicitly or not. The Grundy family, same as all the other fairground operators up and down the country – from the huge outfits to the very small – always had to be on the alert for those blatantly thieving sorts that had infiltrated their fair for fear of tarnishing their reputation. But regardless, deep down, Solly couldn't blame the gaff lads for lining their pockets by short-changing the odd threepence or sixpence as the pay they received for their hard labours hardly kept them in the basics of food, rolling tobacco and drink. After all, a fairground job was seen as a last resort for those unable to secure themselves anything better through varying reasons; mainly because they had no fixed abode or were ex-prisoners. It was far better than living rough. The job did have its perks for the gaff lads though, as a certain type of female was dazzled by any man connected to the fair, seeing them in the same light as a knight in shining armour and praying to land one and be whisked into what they believed was a glamorous, thrill-a-minute life, far removed from their mundane one, governed by their parents' rules and regulations. They didn't realise that, apart from an isolated occasion when a fairground employee did lose his heart to one of these girls, their only interest in them was for sex.

All the main rides were in the middle of the fair area, several circular stalls such as hook-a-duck and hoopla dotted between them, the rest forming a horseshoe shape around the boundary edge, the entrance being the gap in the middle. The living caravans were sited a few yards behind the stalls and rides before a tangle of dense undergrowth that edged a rundown part of a canal. The dodgems where Solly was heading were towards the back of the rides area and, to avoid having to fight his way through the crowds at the entrance, he skirted the back of the stalls and was just about to sidle through a narrow gap when above the noise coming from the fair itself, the sound of an angry voice along with someone else yelping in pain reached his ears. It was coming from the edge of the waste ground several yards away where a high wire fence separated it from a building site where the council was building new houses to replace slums. The lights from the fairground didn't reach that far so Solly couldn't see what was going on, but it seemed to him that someone was getting a savage beating.

He groaned inwardly. He really needed to be supervising the two gaff lads on the dodgems, the most popular ride at the moment; certainly Grundy's most profitable one. He not only needed to be on hand to keep a watchful eye on the lads, but also to manage troublesome sorts who didn't like waiting their turn and started making a nuisance of themselves. But apart from the fact that his morals would not allow him to walk away from someone who was in trouble, whether they deserved it or not, should a member of the public happen upon this and call the police, it would be enough excuse for them to close the fair down for the night. Off duty, the police enjoyed a visit to the fair with their families as much as anyone else did but, on duty, some of them regarded being called to deal with incidents at the fair as an extra burden they could do without on top of all the other everyday crimes and would therefore treat fair-related matters far more harshly. Without further ado, Solly spun on his heels and hurried over the uneven ground in the direction the commotion was coming from.

His guess that someone was being thrashed was a correct one. Due to the darkness and the lack of any man-made light in this part of the ground, Solly was on top of the scene before he could actually make out what was going on. A middle-aged, thickset, shabbily dressed man was beating someone with a sturdy walking stick. They were scruffily dressed too, curled up in a foetal position on the ground, hysterically screaming for the attacker to stop. Solly noticed a large tear in the sleeve of his thin brown jacket.

The man had his arm raised, ready to deliver the stick down again on his victim, but, without further ado, Solly grabbed his wrist in a vice-like grip, demanding, 'That's enough of that now, unless you want to land in prison for murder.'

The attacker was stunned by Solly's intervention and stood staring at him for several moments before he gathered his wits and tried frantically to free his wrist from Solly's hold. 'Get the fuck off of me! I'm only giving me son what he deserves. Now get off me, I said.'

This incensed Solly. Grown men beating each other was one thing but an older man beating a child, and his son at that, was not right to Solly. As a father of two strapping sons himself he knew only too well that at times during their adolescence they had tested his patience to its very limits, but to beat them half to death by way of punishment, to use manly strength on a juvenile, was totally despicable behaviour to him. He abhorred any man that did this. He hissed, 'I'm sure whatever your lad's done doesn't warrant being beaten to death. I'll not let you free until you calm down.'

The man responded, 'I'll bloody calm down when me son promises to do as he's told. He knows the score should he disobey me.' He again desperately tried to free his wrist and kicked out a shoddy workman's booted foot, aiming for Solly's shin, but Solly pre-empted what he intended and, whilst still gripping the man's wrists, jumped out of the way. At his failure to free himself, with his free hand the man then aimed a punch at Solly's chin. Solly wasn't quite quick enough this time and the fist caught him square on the side of his face. Regardless of the pain from the blow, he was going to be sporting a good bruise shortly, Solly still managed to keep a grip on the man's wrist but he was angry now that the man had turned his wrath on him and told him, 'Hit me again and you'll regret it, man. It'll be you I'll be calling an ambulance for, not your son. Now, either drop that stick and calm down or I'll drag you with me to find a bobby... I'm sure you know there's never a copper far from a fairground ... and I'll have you charged with assaulting me as well as your son. Now, what's it to be?'

Solly was having to control such a deep urge to give this bully of a man a taste of his own medicine. He saw the wisdom in dropping the stick, which clattered down on the ground between his and Solly's feet, and he snarled, 'I did what you asked so now get yer hand off me.'

Solly released his grip, then immediately bent down to snatch up the stick and throw it javelin-like across the high fence into the builders' yard the other side. 'Judging the kick you tried to aim at me, I doubt you need that to actually walk with.' He looked hard at the man for a moment, then added, 'Bit of advice, mate. You need to think long and hard on the fact that sons grow into adults. If you continue thrashing him like I saw you doing every time he does something you don't agree with, then he'll more than likely grow up to hate you, that's if he doesn't already, and before you know it it'll be him beating you.'

The man snarled, 'How I raise my son is none of your business.' He looked down to the figure on the floor. 'Get up, you little runt. I'll deal with you when...' His voice trailed off when he realised he was talking to an empty space. Whilst his attacker had been otherwise occupied he had seized the chance to make his getaway. He looked furious for a moment before he smirked nastily. 'Ah well, he'll have to come home sooner or later and I'll be waiting for him. *You* won't be there to save him from the thrashing he's gonna get then.'

With narrowed, icy eyes, Solly watched as the man hurried off, very quickly, to disappear into the darkness. Solly had been right; the man didn't need the stick to aid his walking. As he turned and made his way back to the fair to resume his duties, he was deeply worried that instead of stopping the lad's beating by his father it was only going to resume at a later time and, riled by

Solly's bettering of him in front of his son, the thrashing the lad was going to get then was going to be far worse for him. He wondered just what it was that the young lad had refused to do that had fuelled such fury in his father but, as matters stood, he would never know.

As soon as Solly entered the actual fairground encirclement, the encounter with the brute and repercussions for his son left him as the charged atmosphere created by the punters' high spirits, their determination to have themselves a good time, enveloped him, cloak-like. Hurrying his pace, he made his way over to the dodgems to do his bit to help make sure that happened.

Solly's family connection to travelling fairs stretched centuries back to the days when street performers, jugglers, musicians playing hurdy-gurdies and fiddles, fire-eaters, puppeteers, actors, game tricksters and suchlike entertained the crowds and used their tricks to get the public to part with their money at yearly town and village annual gatherings. In the early 1900s, Solly's father Samson Grundy, fed up with the paltry living he was making from his two side stalls, made the monumental decision – much to the horror of his wife and children – to sell the two stalls in order to buy his first ride, a set of dilapidated gallopers needing a vast amount of mechanical and cosmetic repair. Thankfully his decision turned out to be a sound one as, once repaired and repainted in its original bright colourful traditional style, the popular ride brought in far more profits than both his stalls had between them. Over the next few years Samson bought more rides and eventually became his own ring-master. His fair quickly became the main attraction at numerous towns and villages annual festivals from the Midlands and up and around the north.

Grundy's fair was considered a medium affair compared to the likes of the giants; amongst them Collins, Harris or Codona. Grundy's fair did not afford a luxury lifestyle as it did the bigger outfits, enabling them to live in their modern caravans with every amenity available, drive fancy vehicles and send their children to private schools, but the business kept his family housed, clothed and fed, along with a number of other families and casuals who worked for him too. He was content with that.

Since the late 1800s, fairs were run on a strict set of rules and regulations put in place by a group of showmen calling themselves The Van Dwellers Association, later changing the name to The Showmen's Guild, which had been formed to protect the rights and safety of all travelling showmen. Any grievances between individual showmen that couldn't be resolved between themselves would be put to the guild for them to adjudicate. The same went for problems showmen faced with council officials and the general public. Individual fair owners, though, were still at liberty to run their businesses in their own particular way. It was the same as in all other walks of life; there were good fair owners to work for and the not-so-good. As the owner of his stalls, hard-working family man Sam Grundy had worked for some very amenable bosses but had also been at the mercy of the bullish, controlling type, having no choice at the time but to pay the extortionate rent they charged for a space for his stalls, even though guild rules prohibited such a practice. Sometimes he had no choice where he was sited and would be treated like the dregs of the earth; should he dare speak out about his treatment that particular ringmaster's attitude would be that if you didn't like it then leave, plenty more where you came from. In consequence, when Sam found himself faced with the upper hand as ringmaster himself, he operated in a firm but fair manner and, as a result, established himself a reputation as being a decent type to work for so was never short of stall holders wanting to rent pitches or casuals applying for jobs as ride operators or labourers.

Life as a fair owner or for those associated with it in any capacity was not the glamorous existence most outsiders, or 'flatties' as the show people called them, believed it to be. Providing the public with their few hours of thrills and excitement required long hours of back-breaking labour dismantling the rides and stalls at the end of one session, packing up living accommodation, transporting it all to the next event on their calendar, then reconstructing it. And all to strict timescales, often battling atrocious weather conditions and at times obnoxious or even corrupt council officials and locals, who believed that fairs were dens of iniquity, operated by dishonest sorts who drew even more unsavoury types to their towns and villages.

Living conditions for the casual fairground workers, or gaff lads as they were known as, was far from luxurious; several bunking in together in old caravans with no electric or water facilities, heating obtained from smelly paraffin heaters or oil lamps, sometimes no heating at all. Stall-holders and ride operators' accommodation was marginally better, usually with generators and wood-burning stoves. The caravans themselves came in varying states of repair depending on the owners' financial situation.

Sam and his two sons, Samson junior known as Sonny and his younger brother Solomon, Solly, each lived in large, old-style curved-top wagons, all passed down several generations and kept well repaired with funds allowing modernisation where possible. The walls of the living area, kitchen and number of bedrooms, ranging from one to three, were partitioned off by curtains. Much of the interior was lined in highly polished oak or mahogany and were a devil for the womenfolk to clean. The cast-iron stove in the kitchen was heated by wood and, although small, was adequate enough to cook meals on for a large number of people. There were plenty of cup-boards and spaces under beds and seating for storage and also outside, running along the undersides of the van too. Solly's wagon even had a rudimentary bathroom. The wagons were made homely with knitted throws, cushions and shelves and lead-paned window ledges were filled with fairground glass, ornaments and trinkets, all keepsakes collected by past and present occu-pants. The wagons were no longer pulled along by horses but by motor power – old Land Rovers or lorries – so transporting them from place to place now only took hours, not days. These were much larger inside than the more modern types and also, in winter, extremely warm and comfortable. This was why, along with nostalgia, the Grundy family still opted to live in them.

Fairfolks' lives were hard as they battled to make themselves a living but they did it because it was the only way of life they knew; the same as their ancestors had done for hundreds of years before them.

Chapter Two

Over the other side of the fair, having gotten her helper of the night to man the fort while she nipped back to the living vans to use the make-shift toilet facilities, Solly's wife of twenty years, thirty-six-year-old Gemma Grundy, was making her way through the crowds to retake her position in the pay booth of the House of Fun. Suddenly she stopped short, staring in disbelief at the scene she had happened upon.

By the candy floss and confectionary stall, laughing hysterically, three youths were vigorously rolling around a wooden barrel between them. No harm in that to Gem, just a bit of fun which is what the youths had come to the fair to have themselves, but not when a pair of legs was sticking out of the open end of the barrel and a torrent of muffled expletives was emitting from inside, courtesy of the legs' owner. Knowing the owner as well as she did, Gem was absolutely outraged that these youths were treating that person in such a way. A small crowd had gathered to watch, some laughing, others in obvious disapproval but, regardless, not doing anything to halt the proceedings.

To ensure the lads would hear her over the rest of the din the crowds were making, and the blaring music from nearby individual rides, she launched herself over to the rolling barrel, bringing it to a stop by using her weight against it. 'Oi, stop that now. What the hell do you think you're playing at?'

She was a shapely, attractive strawberry blonde, with humorous violet-blue eyes and dressed in a full apple-green skirt with layers of netting underneath. She wore two-inch black stiletto court shoes.

A thick black belt was around her trim waist, a scoop-necked white, sleeveless blouse and short red cardigan with black embroidery down both sides of the front completed her outfit.

The three teenagers stared at her, stunned for a moment at the abrupt interruption into their fun and it was the lankiest, spottiest one of them that finally answered her, in a cocky manner, more to impress his other two mates than actual bravado. 'Just having a laugh, missus, no harm done.'

'Yeah, that's right, just having a laugh,' the two other lads parroted.

She sneered at them and snapped, 'That's your idea of having a giggle, is it? Risking hurting someone by putting them upside down in a barrel and rolling them around!' She wagged a finger at them. 'Like me to get some of the gaff lads to do it to you and see how funny you think it is then?'

The three boys looked horrified at the very thought and, before she could carry out her threat, they kicked up their heels and shot off to be lost in the crowd, gesturing with their fingers as they went. Show now over, the gathered crowd dispersed too.

Gem addressed the person in the barrel. 'It's me, Mrs Grundy. Those louts have gone, so stop thrashing your legs about so I can grab hold of them and get you out.'

The response was too undecipherable for Gem to translate but it was apparent that her message had gotten through as the legs stopped flaying. Grabbing hold of the ankles, she pulled until the body they belonged to slid free. As they scrambled upright and straightened their clothes, Gem said, 'You alright? Did those clots hurt you at all?'

Renata Shawditch glanced down her body, all four foot three of it, before lifting her head and bringing smiling hazel eyes to rest on Gem. 'All me bits and pieces still seem to be in place and, apart from a few bruises, I'm fine. It could have been worse had you not come to my rescue, so ta very much, Mrs Grundy.'

'Glad I happened to be passing.' She then eyed the tiny woman, confused. 'What on earth got into those idiots to do what they did to you?'

'I caught one of them red-handed, trying to help himself from the penny dip when I was serving a customer. I threatened to bash his thieving head with me trusty tennis racket that I keep under the counter to protect meself with from such brain-dead sorts if he didn't put back what he'd stolen or pay up. He didn't like being bettered by a woman and, to boot, one half his size; especially not in front of his mates or the other punters as I'd a queue at the time. Next I knew, him and his mates had upended the barrel of its sawdust and prizes and forced me into it and ... well ... you know the rest.' Her face then screwed up with annoyance. 'And not one of those in the crowd came to me rescue, did they?' Then her face crinkled good-naturedly. 'Must have thought it was part of a side show. If anything like this should happen again, I'll stop the proceedings until I've gone around the crowd and collected money from them first to watch.'

Gem couldn't help but chuckle at that. Trust Ren to see the funny side. But then that was Ren all over, always seeing the humour and positive side of life. She eyed the woman fondly. Twenty-four years ago Ren's parents, both from showmen families who had travelled with Grundy's for years operating their hoopla stall, had welcomed their daughter into the world with all the love and protection anyone would shower on their most precious possession. Both in their mid-forties at the time, they had long ago given up on being blessed with even one of the dozen or so children they had planned to have when they had gotten married over twenty-five years before. Ren's arrival one bitter winter's night in early February had come as a bolt out of the blue, Ren's mother having no idea she was pregnant. In fact, she was convinced she was on the change of life when her periods had suddenly stopped nine months before. She had thought the pains she was experiencing were caused by a dish of potted shrimps she had had for her tea and it was an aged crone who had helped to bring many fairground babies into the world who was to put her straight; that she was in labour.

Ren had been physically perfect in every way and achieved every milestone that all other children did as they grew and developed, except that height-wise she was always many inches shorter. Before she was a year old it became apparent to her parents and everyone else that, by a freak of nature as there was no family history on either side of this happening before, Ren was a midget. This could have devastated other parents, but not Ren's. Whether she grew to six feet tall or only reached three foot was of no consequence to them whatsoever. They raised her to be confident and proud of herself and to ignore completely any slights aimed her way from others. She was encouraged to view any as the culprit's show of jealousy for the fact they were not so petite and pretty as she was. She wasn't at all the sort of woman that won beauty contests or that men did a double-take at, just pleasantly attractive, but what drew people to her in droves was that she had a great sense of fun and an extremely kind and caring nature and could always be relied upon to do whatever she could for those in need of help.

Gem had a great respect for her and she knew, without doubt, that Ren would make a wonderful wife to a special kind of man who would not let her lack of height blind him to the array of other qualities she possessed. Gem knew Ren had had her fair share of boyfriends over the years; most had ended because, when all was said and done, the men in question could not cope with what others threw at them for being involved with someone they deemed not normal. Gem believed though that one day a man worthy of her would see her worth and Ren would then get the happiness she deserved.

What Gem or anyone else of the Grundy community did not know was that it was doubtful that even if any of those men had been enamoured enough to turn a blind eye to the taunts and ridicule of others, the relationship would have gotten any further than friendship in respect of Ren herself.

Her heart belonged completely to another and had done since she had first clapped eyes on Donald Douglas, or Donny as he was known. Both had crawled upon the grass together as babies whilst their mothers sat on stools outside their living vans and shared gossip over cups of tea and chunks of homemade cake. The pair had been close friends since that time. Indeed, so much did he think of Ren that friendship might have turned to love for Donny as it had for Ren on her reaching an age when she recognised just what love actually was, had not another girl arrived on the scene and set her cap at the then fourteen-year-old Donny, using her good looks and wily ways to turn his attentions away from Ren onto herself. And all because to Susan Potts even at that young age, in ordinary-looking, gangly Donny, whose parents owned their own ride which as the eldest male child he would one day inherit, she saw a good prospect for a future husband. She reckoned he'd give her a better life than the one she had with her own family, who scraped a living from a stall selling cheap penny-type toys and trinkets that broke not long after the purchasers bought them. Before Donny was aware of what was happening to him, at the age of seventeen, he was married to the then sixteen-year-old Suzie and was living with her in a modern, two-bedroomed caravan bought for them as a wedding gift by his family.

Despite her own heartache that the man she loved more than anything in the world would now never be hers, generous-natured Ren would have been happy for Donny had she been convinced that this marriage was a good one. She was far from sure about it as she had seen with her own eyes how Suzie had systematically manipulated him up the aisle and, right from the start of their marriage, it was very apparent from passing comments Donny made just how lazy Suzie was. It was Donny who did most of the cooking, cleaning and other chores, as besotted with her as he was, accepting Suzie's never-ending excuses for her laziness.

But as if watching the man she loved being made a fool of by his wife was not torture enough for Ren, when no one else was around to witness it, Suzie wasn't the amenable, helpful young woman everyone believed her to be. She was jealous of Ren's friendship with her husband, rightly guessing that Ren felt more for him than friendship; out of pure spite she would taunt and belittle Ren. Ren usually managed to brush Suzie's nasty remarks off but occasionally, after a particularly nasty onslaught, they did get the better of her. Never would she allow Suzie the satisfaction of knowing it; she would always nurse her upset in private.

Ren kept her knowledge about Suzie to herself as she knew the truth about his adored wife would break Donny's heart and she cared far too much about him to ever do that to him. For Donny's sake though, all Ren hoped for was that one day Suzie would wake up and realise what a good man her husband was – one she would find it very hard to better – and start treating him the way he deserved to be.

Through the crowds Ren's nemesis, dressed in a tight pair of bright green capri pants, a waist-length box-style red blouse with a short bolero-style cardigan over the top, flat black pumps on her feet and long brunette hair tied up in a high ponytail, suddenly materialised. She was breathless from running and with her pretty face screwed up, clearly annoyed, she blurted out, 'Oh! I missed all the fun then.'

Gem looked at her incredulously. She had always found Suzie such a pleasant, helpful young woman whenever she had had dealings with her since she had arrived with her mother and father ten years ago and secured a pitch from Sam for their toy and bric-a-brac stall, that this show of acute disappointment that she had missed out on the humiliation of one of their community greatly shocked her. 'Surely you can't think that was funny, Ren being shoved in a barrel and rolled about? She could have been seriously hurt.'

Suzie stared stupefied at Gem, mouth opening and closing fish-like. She had spoken her thoughts out loud without considering just who was present. When she had overheard what was happening to Ren via two gossiping women happening to pass by Ren's stall at the time and who then had stopped by Suzie's parents' stall to have a peruse of the goods on sale, she had pelted over in order to witness Ren's humiliation. She planned to use it later to make the woman look foolish and belittle her in the eyes of her husband. Donny was so blind and stupid not to have realised, or have an inkling even, that Ren was head over heels in love with him and in truth although Donny was besotted with herself, deep down it was Ren he really loved. Had Suzie not manipulated him into it, it was Ren he would be married to now, not herself. Suzie cared for Donny but didn't love him as a wife should and never had. But being married to him was a damned sight better than the life she was living with her parents and two younger brothers in their ancient, damp four-berth caravan surviving on the paltry amount their stall brought in. Until someone with better prospects than Donny came along – something she was working hard at finding herself – she meant to keep him, never give him a chance to question his feelings for her or especially those she knew were lying dormant for Ren. Except for Ren, every other member of the Grundy community believed her to be a devoted wife to her husband and a thoroughly helpful and caring woman to have around. And that was the way she intended to keep matters until she was ready to let them know her true colours. With a look of deep concern on her face, she spoke earnestly. 'Oh forgive me, Mrs Grundy, that didn't come out as I meant, really it didn't. As soon as I heard two women giggling about what they'd seen, I told me mam I had to come over and put a stop to what those lads were doing to Ren. Mindless idiots.' She looked at Ren then in feigned deep concern. 'Glad to see you're not hurt.'

Ren just looked back at her blankly. Suzie deserved the lead in a play for that performance. She might have sounded sincere but she certainly wasn't one iota. Ren was in no doubt that Suzie was fuming she had missed the actual show because it was just the sort of incident she delighted in coming across so she could use it to torment her with. She would certainly use it to make a fool of her in Donny's eyes in a continual effort to erode their friendship which, despite numerous efforts up to now, she had failed to do. Now, same as always in such situations, she smiled at the malicious young woman and said sweetly, 'It's very thoughtful of you to come to my rescue, Suzie, but Mrs Grundy beat you to it.'

Just then, a loud voice rent the air. 'Is anyone serving or do we just help ourselves?'

Ren turned around to see a crowd queuing at her stall. She spun back, smiling at Gem. 'Best get back to it.'

'Yes, I must get back too. Muriel will be wondering where I am,' said Gem. Then, patting Suzie's arm in a gratified manner, she said to her,

'So good of you to put your own safety at risk to come and help Ren when you heard she was in trouble instead of alerting some of the men to deal with it. You should be proud of yourself.'

Looking like butter wouldn't melt in her mouth, Suzie waved a dismissive hand and said, 'You don't think of your own safety when you hear that one of your own is in trouble, do you, Mrs Grundy?'

'You certainly don't and God forbid that anything like this should happen to me, but then should it, I just hope that you're around at the time.'

Now she was alone with Ren, Suzie's whole demeanour changed in a flash. Gone was the sweet smile, replaced with a malicious smirk. She sneered at Ren. 'What a laugh me and Donny will have over this tonight. I'll make it my business to let everyone else have a good laugh about it as well.' She then took a look around to make sure no other fairfolk witnessed what she was about to do and, satisfied there wasn't, stepped over to the pile of sawdust and prizes that Ren had been left to put back into the barrel and spitefully kicked her foot through it several times scattering it all about, then turned back to Ren and laughed at her before she went on her way.

As she watched her go, Ren heaved a deep sigh and sadly shook her head. She had a terrible feeling that one day Donny would have a very rude awakening as to the real person his wife was and not the one she showed to him and everyone else. When it did happen she would be there to help him pick up the pieces as a good friend would.

Seventy-year-old, wiry, silver-haired Sam Grundy, dressed in a 1920s-style red-and-yellow striped jacket and black trousers – his trademark outfit as ringmaster – sported the battered face of a fist fighter; damage he had received over the years from defending his people and business from outsiders hell-bent on bringing down the fair for whatever reason they had at the time. He was leaning against the safety barrier that circled the big wheel, smoking a pipe and watching his youngest son skipping expertly between the racing dodgems to help a punter who had gotten themselves stuck onto another after crashing into them.

He saw Solly's good humour and easy-mannered banter with the punter in the car defuse their annoyance at not being able to unlock one car from the other, which was eroding into his time on the ride. Solly lived and breathed the fair, would wither and die if the life was taken away from him, just the same as it was for Sam himself, his own father too and back down the line of Grundys. It was a pity that the same couldn't be said for his eldest son, Sonny, who would inherit the business in the not-too-distant future when Sam's own life came to an end. He couldn't fault Sonny for the way he never failed to pitch in and do what was necessary in keeping the business running, but it was his way to boss others around, to assert his authority against Solly's opinion, which in fact mirrored his own. They all worked together for the same end, and he should ask instead of command.

Sonny hadn't always been like this; up until his

twentieth birthday he had been very much like his brother in nature but then suddenly, overnight in fact, he had changed into a surly individual that gave the impression he felt the world was against him. No matter how much his family tried to get to the bottom of why Sonny's personality should go through such a sudden, dramatic change, either Sonny didn't know himself or wouldn't disclose what had happened to him to bring this about; they had no choice but to accept him as he was now and hope that someday he had an equally sudden change back to being the affable young man he'd been before. That, though, had never happened and after all these years didn't now seem very likely to.

Sam sighed, a frown furrowing an already deeply lined brow. Now the end of his life was getting closer, the future of the fair was becoming more of a problem for him. Fair tradition dictated that the eldest son of fair owners inherited the main business and the next male in line a ride each or whatever the owner thought suitable; nothing in some cases where there was discord between father and son. Sonny was his eldest living offspring and therefore should be the one to become its ringmaster when he died. The trouble for Sam was that he felt Sonny hadn't the right temperament for the job itself or for keeping harmony amongst the Grundy community, which was equally as important to him. Solly, though, did. Sam felt that, under Sonny's management, there was a great danger that Grundy's would not flourish and prosper in the way he had striven for it to. Whereas under Solly, Sam knew, without doubt, it definitely would. Did he then break with tradition and make Solly his main heir or follow fairground tradition and leave it to Sonny? Showmen traditions were cast in stone to Sam but, as Solly had proved to him over his marriage to outsider Gemma, there are occasions when traditions need to be ignored.

He ran a gnarled hand through his profusion of wiry silver-grey hair. Time to make a decision over the fair's future leader was not on his side. He was three score and ten now, in good health apart from arthritis riddling its way through him, but any time now he could be struck down. Only a few weeks ago Harry Sparrow, a robust-looking, energetic man in his late fifties who had worked for him for years, an all-rounder who could turn his hand to anything, suddenly dropped dead as he'd been helping to unload a lorry after arriving at a new site. He needed to discuss the problem. Nell, his beloved wife, had always been his listening ear, whose advice and judgement he had trusted beyond reproach, and she would have helped him arrive at the right conclusion, but now she was gone and her wisdom along with it. Luckily for him though there was one person amongst the Grundy community whose friendship over the years he had come to value highly, especially since Nell's death when without her to turn to he doubted he'd have managed to get on with his life without her in it. Nell had thought very highly of her too. Maybe it was time he took her into his confidence and asked for her guidance on his problem. He would do that at the first opportunity so he could put this worrying matter to bed and enjoy what days he had remaining to him without it hanging over his head.

He felt so proud though that through his hard work, at times literally shedding blood, sweat and tears, he was leaving his sons a business that was in a far better state than when he had himself taken over. Before he did die, though, he wanted to see Sonny happily settled with a good woman, same as Solly was. But, if he ever did have any relationships with women, he kept them very much to himself. He never actually knew what his eldest son got up to after working hours; in fact, as far as he was aware, he spent his time on his own, inside his van that was parked far away from any of the others. His son's need to keep himself to himself puzzled him and, considering that Sonny was now thirty-nine, a change of temperament back to the easy-going, kind young man he had been before his sudden, abrupt change didn't seem likely.

Just then Sam spotted Gemma weaving her way through the high-spirited crowds, heading for the House of Fun. He went to shout a greeting to her but then changed his mind as she would never hear him over the din the punters were making and the reverberating music. Sam and his wife Nell had been furious when Solly, at only sixteen years of age and she only fifteen, had out of the blue introduced Gemma to them as his future intended. Furious not only because she wasn't one of them and they were well aware of the flak they would have to deal with from the rest of the showmen community for their son's breach in traditional values, but because Solly had deceived them, carrying on a serious relationship they'd had no idea whatsoever about for over a year.

It transpired that the pair had first met when the then thirteen-year-old Gem had come along with her friend when the fair had been in her town. She had gotten talking to Solly, who had been helping on the ride they had chosen to go on. For both of them it had been instant, all-consuming love. They weren't to see each other again though for over a year until the fair came back again and this time they vowed not to lose touch. Solly would call Gemma at prearranged times from a telephone box near where the fair was at the time. When the fair was within travelling distance of Gem's town, she would make excuses to her parents and visit him.

When the relationship was finally revealed – when the pair could not bear to be apart for any longer and decided to get married – Gem's own parents were equally as outraged as Solly's were at the proposed union of two people from such differing backgrounds. They warned their daughter that if she went ahead, without their blessing or permission, they would disown her. But, no matter what was thrown at them, the pair were adamant that they were destined for each other and marry they would. Not prepared to wait until they were both of legal age, they did the only thing they could and ran away to Gretna Green. By the time both sets of parents found out it was too late as they were man and wife.

His wise wife knew that if she did not accept Gem into their lives then she would lose her son;

another ringmaster would jump at the chance of having someone with Solly's knowledge and background work for them. After many arguments on the matter, Nell managed to get through to Sam and he grudgingly agreed to accept Gem into the family. After a shaky start, eventually Nell and Gem enjoyed a close mother-and daughter-in-law relationship and Gem was as grieved as Nell's blood family when she died five years ago at the age of sixty-four. Gem might be an outsider, initially ignorant of showpeople's ways, but it quickly became apparent by the way she got stuck in not only in her wifely duties but also her eagerness to learn how the fair was run so she could pull her weight, that Nell and Sam's fears that Solly would regret his choice of partner were unfounded. The rest of the Grundy community, although wary of this unknown incomer at first, soon found themselves warming to Gem's easy-going nature. Not that she suffered fools gladly! When Nell died, Gem naturally took her place in the care of her husband, making it her business to be sure his living van and clothes were clean and he ate three good meals a day.

Sam couldn't deny that Gem had weathered well over the years, despite being the mother of two grown-up children and now approaching middle age at thirty-six. She still had a shapely figure and very good legs; apart from a few crows' lines around her eyes she was still as pretty as she had been when he had first been introduced to her over twenty years ago, although it was now a mature prettiness. Like the men, today she had been up and working since the crack of dawn, cooking a hot meal for the fifteen labourers and twenty gaff lads helping to erect all the rides and safety test them in readiness for opening tonight. Then she'd cleaned their van, updated the business accounts and was now doing her bit manning the pay booth for the House of Fun. Even when the fair closed for the night she would not stop until her family had been fed their supper and everything was ready for when they rose the next morning.

Sheer stubbornness and an amount of still-harboured grudge that he couldn't seem to let go of, for his son going against showmen tradition and marrying an outsider, prevented him from openly admitting it, but secretly Sam felt Solly had made the right choice in choosing Gem as his partner for life. The pair were perfectly suited and rubbed along very amicably together. They had given Sam two wonderful grandsons who now played their own part in keeping the business flourishing. When all was said and done, Gem must have loved his son very deeply, without any reserves whatsoever, to have given up the future she could have had for the tough one showmen lived.

As he was thinking of his two sons, a momentary wave of sadness washed over Sam. Memories of the three he had lost pushed their way to the surface. Him and Nell had had five sons altogether. Two had died of childhood illnesses then thirty-year-old Joshua had died serving his country in the war, blown to bits by a German Panther tank out in France in 1943. He left behind a wife and two young girls of six and eight, now both teenagers. Nita, sixteen, and eighteen-year-old Rosanna, along with their mother Francine, who they all called Fran. They earned their keep running whatever ride or stall they were assigned to at the time on Sam's behalf. Solly had been out in France at the time of Joshua's death, in the same unit in fact, but thankfully had come home safe and sound, the only scars mental ones from the horrors he had witnessed which had taken him a while to learn to bury but, with unwavering support from his family, he had been able to pick up his life again. Sonny had volunteered too. Just how he managed it was a mystery Sonny was keeping to himself as, despite him being a very fit and able-bodied young man at the time, he'd spent the entire war working in the stores at various army camps around Britain. Thankfully, like Solly, he had come home safe and sound.

Losing children, no matter how old, was a terrible happening that was never gotten over. Over time you just learned to live with it and Sam knew that despite the fact that Nell superficially appeared to put all three of her children's deaths behind her and got on with caring for those living, she never got over their loss. As Sam would, she went to her grave grieving for them.

Just then his musings were interrupted by a tug on his jacket and he looked down to see a scruffy young boy of about nine looking enquiringly up at him.

'Eh up, mister. You the fair boss?'

Hiding a smile, Sam took his pipe out of his mouth and answered in his usual polite but gruff manner, looking at him like he'd a cheek to be accosting such an important figure. 'I certainly am. And what would you be wanting to speak to the boss about?'

'A job. I wanna be a fair man.'

Being asked for work was a daily occurrence and it wasn't the first time by someone so young who believed that running away to work for the fair was a good way of getting out of going to school. 'You do, do yer.' Sam looked the boy up and down, then said matter-of-factly, 'Well come back when you're fifteen and I'll see what I can do.'

'Fifteen!' the boy exclaimed. 'Why that's ... that's...' Not being able to do the calculation in his head whilst still realising that, regardless, it was many years he'd to wait to reach that age, he then lied, 'I *am* fifteen, mister, just small for me age.'

Remembering a comical quip his mother used to make whenever she saw anyone who was on the short side, Sam put his pipe back into his mouth and sucked on it before he said dryly, 'Your mother obviously didn't put any horse manure in your shoes to help you grow when you were little, then.'

The boy gawped at him blankly for a moment before he shook his head, dismayed. 'No, she didn't. Is that what your mam did for you and why you've growed so tall?'

Again Sam hid a smile. 'She certainly did but I wouldn't recommend it as it doesn't smell nice and you can forget having any friends. Best way to grow tall and strong is to eat all your greens. Now you go home, son, and do as I advise. When you've shot up another couple of foot or so, then come back and see me and I'll see what I can do for yer. Now you'd best get back to your mam and dad before they notice you missing and raise the alarm.'

The boy nonchalantly shrugged. 'Ain't got no dad and me mam don't care where I am. She's gone down the pub with me new Uncle 'arry. When she went out she just told me to behave meself till she got back. She's always telling me that she wished she'd never had me as I get in her way so I thought if I got a job she wouldn't have the bother of me no more.'

Sam looked sadly at him. He wondered how many 'uncles' this poor lad had had over his short life and, more to the point, how they all actually treated him, which he didn't expect was in much of a parental way considering how he gathered his own mother did from what the lad had told him. He didn't look at all well fed and his clothes had seen much better days. Sam's eyes darkened angrily. He himself might not have been the best of fathers compared to some, but he had done his best; loved, nurtured and encouraged all three of his surviving children and him or Nell always knew where they were, morning, noon and night, until they were both satisfied they were mature enough to take care of themselves. Some people didn't deserve to have children and it was his opinion that this lad's mother certainly didn't.

He looked at him. 'Had a go on any of the rides, boy?'

The lad shook his head as he took a longing look at the rides nearby before back down at his feet and shuffling uncomfortably on them. He muttered, 'Nah. Ain't got no money. I asked Mam if she would bring me but she said she can't afford it.'

But she could afford to go to the pub, thought Sam. He shoved his hand in his trouser pocket and pulled out two half crowns, went to hand the boy one of them, then changed his mind and held out both, telling him, 'Go and enjoy yourself and get a hot dog from the stall too, eh. Then get yourself off home as I don't want you wandering about here without an adult with you when the big boys start rolling in after a visit to the pub.'

The boy looked in awe for a moment at the fortune being offered him, then quickly snatched it before his benefactor changed his mind. 'Oh, ta, mister.' Before he dashed off to follow Sam's instructions he said, 'Soon as I'm fifteen, I'll be back.'

With that he shot off and instantly disappeared amongst the crowds.

His pipe had gone out and as Sam relit it his thoughts were all on the young boy. He so wished he could have offered the dreadfully deprived youngster a home here at the fair. One of the families would have taken him in; fairfolk were generous people when it came to opening their arms to anyone in desperate need, especially someone like that young boy. The life they gave him in comparison to the one he had now might have lacked in certain quarters such as regular school attendance and easy access to medical aid when needed but, overall, it was a damned sight better than the one Sam suspected he was living now.

As he journeyed around, Sam was gratified to note that most of the stalls had people at them, playing the offered games of chance, accuracy of aim, physical strength or buying confectionary, cheap toys, bric-a-brac or fairground glass. All the attractions, amongst them the carousel – or gallopers as the fairfolk knew them – Hall of Mirrors, House of Fun, helter-skelter, waltzers, Wall of Death, the big wheel, boxing booth, sky chairs and several kiddies' rides. The favourite with the punters at the moment, the dodgem cars, although not full to capacity as it was still early in the evening, were whizzin' about, generating shrieking and laughing. Even Gypsy Velda Rose – although it was doubtful she actually *was* a gypsy and just where she did come from no one knew as Velda was very private person, extremely tight-lipped on her past history, but regardless her customers seemed very happy with her predictions – had a queue beginning to form at her red-and-yellow striped, dome-shaped tent with boards outside advertising her talents and announcing, whether actually true or not, that those from the royalty and stars of screen and stage were amongst her customers. Tonight looked set to be a profitable one, not just for him but for all the Grundy community. Sam hoped this was a good sign that the rest of the week here would be too, along with the rest of the season so that they would all be warm, well-fed and have enough funds to repair and re-decorate stalls, rides and living accommodation over the winter break.

Nearby, thirty-eight-year-old, tall, muscular, snake-hipped Sonny Grundy, his skin darkly tanned from his years of working out in the open, was lolling in a chair in the small room in the centre of the Sky Chairs, one foot up on the panel as he operated the controls and changed records on the record player that relayed music through the tannoy system blaring from the speakers outside. Getting a signal from one of the gaff lads that all the customers wanting to ride were strapped into their seats, Sonny pulled the lever for the ride to start. As the chairs started to slowly rotate then lift up, he reached behind his ear to retrieve a half-smoked roll-up which he lit with a battered old brass petrol lighter, a relic from his army days. The lighter had a deep dent in the middle which had happened after he was demobbed when he had accidentally dropped it onto a metal strut of a ride he was helping to erect at the time, squashing it against another. He would brag to women he wanted to impress, amongst other well-practised, persuasive charms that he used on them, that the lighter saved his life in the war as luckily it was in his breast pocket when a German sniper decided to take aim at him. It was a blatant lie as, during all his six years in the army, he never saw active duty; had managed to completely fool a gullible young, newly qualified doctor, and the powers-that-be after, that he suffered epileptic fits. Even he marvelled at how he'd gotten away with it for six years, but he had.

Combing long fingers through his thick thatch of black hair – no grey yet that he needed to disguise with hair dye – Sonny looked at his watch and his ruggedly handsome features twisted in frustration. It was only seven-thirty and he had thought it was at least an hour later than that. He couldn't wait for closing time so he could make his escape and take advantage of the night life this town offered.

Sonny was far from content with his life and hadn't been for an extremely long time. It hadn't always been like that for him. Up until he was approaching his twentieth birthday he had been a happy-go-lucky young man, content with a nomadic lifestyle that his ancestors had lived for hundreds of years, immensely proud of his family. He was especially proud of his father for his hard work in building on the legacy his own father had left him of two stalls, and transforming the business to what it was now. Sonny had willingly worked long, labour-intensive hours doing a diversity of work, from fixing machinery to operating the rides, doing his bit to keep the fair successful.

But his view of life and the future he then envisaged for himself had completely changed.

Even as a teenager, Sonny had always been aware of his good looks and, as his mother was always telling him, he had a charm about him of the sort that attracted the birds from the trees. He took advantage of it when he did have a fancy for the girl concerned, one willing to share their body with him. Regardless, he was in no rush to settle down despite an amount of envy for his two brothers having found themselves good women to share their lives with and enjoying all the comforts a good marriage brought. Deep down he wanted that for himself, so he was always on the lookout for that someone special.

Then, one evening, completely out of the blue, there she was. She was riding on the waltzers with her friends. The most beautiful creature he had ever seen with a very shapely figure; long colt-like legs, large breasts, cornflower-blue eyes and a mane of golden blonde hair that cascaded down her back. She had an invisible aura that drew Sonny to her like a magnet did metal. For him it was instant, unadulterated love. The world around him suddenly faded into oblivion and all he could see was her.

All he could think about was making contact with her. He immediately abandoned his post, shot over to the waltzer ride, ran up the wooden steps and, whilst the ride was still speeding around, expertly timed a jump to land on the back of the carriage the girl was sitting in, unmindful that his foolhardy actions could have killed him.

Right from the off she made it apparent that his flirtations were not offensive or unwanted; she giggled at his suggestive banter as she batted her eyelashes at him, openly encouraging him to carry on. By the end of the ride she had agreed to meet him alone at closing time around the back of the Cake Walk.

Wanting her to know that he thought her special to him, that he wasn't with her only for one thing, he asked her if she'd like to go to a club or somewhere that opened late that served food, but she refused. She just wanted to go for a walk down by the canal. He was happy to oblige. He would follow her to the ends of the earth if that was what she wanted. As they talked he learned she was a few months younger than he was, lived a few streets away, which he knew to be a slum area of town, in a rented two-up two-down terrace with her parents and two younger brothers. Her father was a drunken wastrel, her mother a cleaner and she herself worked as a machinist in the same factory her mother worked for. She was funny, intelligent and very sexy. Her name was Belinda.

For the first time since he'd been sexually active he was nervous around a woman and worried witless he was acting more schoolboyish than grown man in his efforts to show her he saw her as more to him than a one night-stand. To his relief, if she noticed he was over-anxious to impress his good qualities on her, she made no reference to it. He was, though, most shocked when she stopped by a clearing on the tow path, encouraged him to sit down with her, then made it abundantly clear she wanted him to make love to her. Usually it was him leading the way in that respect. But, again, he was happy to oblige. Anything Belinda wanted that was in his power to provide, he would give her. He was putty in her hands.

For the next five nights, as soon as Sonny finished work, he would find her waiting for him and she would lead him to the secluded place down the canal tow path and, after a short time making small talk, she would lead the way to them having sex. The more time he spent with her, the more their partings grew ever-increasingly difficult for him. She was like an intoxicating drug and the more he had, the more he wanted. His life had no meaning whatsoever without her by his side. As far as he was concerned she seemed as besotted with him as he was with her and she didn't give him any reason not to believe she didn't see her future with him.

Usually, by the last night of the fair, Sonny was ready to move on to pastures new, but this time the thought of leaving Belinda behind – having a long-distance relationship with her, maybe not seeing her for weeks on end and the worrying possibility of some other man snatching her away from him in the meantime – did not appeal at all. He wanted her by his side permanently. He would ask her to marry him. Joshua had married a showman's daughter and his parents had been extremely happy with the union, but he knew they would play merry hell with him as they had when Solly had announced he was marrying a flattie. But, same as Solly, it was his right to choose who he married and his parents would just have to accept he'd picked Belinda.

They had just made love and were lying, exhausted, in the secluded clearing, looking up at the stars. Knowing it was now or never, Sonny propped himself up on one arm and, looking down at her adoringly, blurted, 'I love you, Belinda. Please marry me? Come with me when we leave tomorrow and I'll go to the nearest registry office and get a special licence. We'll run away to Gretna Green if you want to. One of my brothers did that when he married his wife and said it was very romantic. My folks will get us a nice van to live in as a wedding present like they did my brothers when they both got married. We'll be so happy together, Bel; you, me and our kids, I know we will. You'll love the fair life. Travelling around, not being tied down to one place.' And, wanting her to know that one day he might be more than just a worker on the fair, he told her, 'My family own the fair. When my father dies my elder brother, Joshua, will inherit the business but Dad will also leave me and my brother Solly one of the rides each. So you'll be the wife of a ride owner,' he said proudly. 'So what do you say, Belinda?'

To his utter shock an immediate expression of delight and her acceptance of his proposal did not come but instead she started to laugh. Frowning in confusion, he asked, 'What's so funny, Bel? You do want to marry me, don't you?'

She scanned his face and mirthfully snorted. 'My God, you're serious, aren't you? I thought you were just having a laugh.'

He frowned, even more confused. 'You think I would ask you to spend the rest of your life with me just to give you a laugh?'

She sat up and started straightening her clothes. 'What on earth makes you think I would lower myself to tie myself to the likes of you. You're just a traveller, gypsy–'

Sitting bolt upright he indignantly exclaimed, 'I damned well am not a traveller or gypsy. My family are showmen.'

She sniggered. 'Same difference. All thieving lowlifes to us. I half expected to find my purse emptied every night I've left you and was quite surprised it wasn't, to be honest, knowing well your lot's reputation for pinching anything that moves. And you're all illiterate because you don't go to school. I bet you sign your name with an X.' She gave a violent shudder. 'Oh, just the thought of living in one of those damp, cold huts on wheels fills me with dread. I can't imagine for the life of me how you survive living not much better than cavemen did.' She then eyed him incredulously. 'I can't believe you would ever think that *I* would ever want to live like that! Cooking meals over an open fire outside with no running water inside or proper toilets. This week with you has been fun, but that's all it's been for me, so if you thought there was more to it on my part then more fool you. Anyway, even if I had fallen for you, I could never take you home. My parents would have a dicky fit, would disown me if they thought for a minute I was thinking of marrying a *fairground* worker. Sooner me marry the local gangster. They'd never hold their heads up again. The neighbours would have a field day. I'd never dare tell my friends I've been seeing you as they would be disgusted with me for having anything to do with someone like you.' She paused for breath and gave him the once-over, smiling at what she saw before adding, 'I couldn't help myself, though. You're a hell of a good-looking man, Sonny Grundy, and I've had the best sex with you I imagine I'll ever have. Be something to look back on, won't it, when I'm bored with my husband after being married to him for years.' She then eyed him regretfully. 'If only you weren't a gypsy and had a good job that would keep me in the style I want for myself, then me and you... Well... Let's say things might have been entirely different.' She grabbed her handbag, jumped up and looked down at him, shooting him a winning smile. 'Next time your fair comes here I'll stop by and say hello and if we're both free...' She left the rest of the words hanging in the air, knowing he would know what she was insinuating. Then she turned and swanned off down the tow path to disappear into the darkness.

He stared after her blindly, the wonderful future he had planned with her shattered into smithereens. The pain of hurt and devastation flooding his entire being was immeasurable. Whilst he had fallen head over heels in love with her, had been planning their future together, all she had seen him for was to use him for sex and a memory to look back on when she was old and grey. A vice-like grip clamped his heart, like an invisible hand had ripped open his chest and was tearing it out. Now he realised just why she had turned down his offer of going to a nightclub or having a meal in a public place as she didn't want to risk being seen with him by anyone she knew. She didn't want them to look down on her for associating herself with an illiterate fairground worker.

Whilst growing up he had witnessed many situations of outsiders acting hostile towards the fairfolk community and had suffered them himself. The children at the array of schools he, his brothers and other fairfolk children had attended, had made fun and mercilessly bullied them, sometimes the teachers too. Numerous times he'd witnessed his mother and other fairfolk women being refused to be served in shops, glared at like they were dirt, even spat at, but he had always believed what his mother had told him; that flatties were jealous they had the fair facilities permanently at their own disposal so could have fun whenever they wanted, not have to wait for a year in-between. She also told them flatties were jealous of their travelling way of life; riding through beautiful countryside, sampling life in different towns and villages every week when they themselves were permanently stuck in one place in a grim street surrounded by factories whose chimneys blotted out the sky with their belching black smoke. But now, thanks to Belinda, he knew his mother had lied to him. Outsiders saw showmen as scourges of society, only to be tolerated for a few hours every night for a week once a year while they enjoyed the entertainment they were offering. Otherwise they most certainly didn't want them mixing amongst them in their own communities.

A deep-seated need to make Belinda pay for her callous treatment of him ignited, then began to overwhelm and consume him. But not just her; all outsiders.

And there was his brother too. He resented Solly for achieving something he hadn't. Solly had obviously got a special something about him that he himself did not possess. Gem was an outsider and came from a far better background than Belinda did, yet Solly had worked that magic he had to make her want to leave her life behind and live the one he was offering her. Why hadn't he got that quality that would have made Belinda want to turn her back on her own life for the one he was offering her? The love, respect and admiration he had always felt for his younger brother was swept away like a tidal wave and replaced with deep bitterness toward him. It wasn't fair that Solly had got the woman he wanted and he hadn't.

So just how was he going to make Belinda and all outsiders pay for their unjustified, superior attitudes towards him ... because this was all about him as he didn't care about other fairfolk now. If they were willing to keep turning a blind eye to how outsiders felt about and treated them just because they needed their money to survive on, then that was up to them, but he wasn't prepared to. But how could he make them pay? As it was he hadn't at this moment any idea how he was going to come face to face with any of them in future and not stop himself from being civil. But the money they spent at the fair paid his own keep so, regardless what he felt about them, he would still have to act congenially towards them by way of encouragement to spend that money in his father's fair. What an impossible situation to find himself in.

Then an idea struck. He could act hospitable towards flatties in future if he himself knew that he was reaping his vengeance from them for their undeserved opinions of him. It was just a pity that what he had in mind as a way to do it, they themselves wouldn't know. Still, he would, and until he thought of something better, for now that would suffice for Sonny. Outsiders believed him to be a thief living a debauched life, so he would be. It would no longer be just the gaff lads that fleeced them of their money as he would too. And he would then use his stolen gains to fund his fun in their pubs, clubs and gambling dens. He would use his looks and charm to bed their women and then cast them aside like they were trash – just as Belinda had him. One thing was for certain though; he would never give his heart to another woman and risk having it broken so callously again, whether she be one of his own kind or an outsider. The pain he was suffering, the devastation and humiliation; he was never putting himself through it again.

From that moment gone was the happy-go-lucky, affable Sonny to be replaced by a sullen, surly young man, harbouring a deep grudge against life.

At the first opportunity he rounded up the gaff lads and warned them that in future he wanted half their tapping money every night and if any should try and hold out on him, then not only would they be out of a job but they should expect to get a long stay in hospital in intensive care. With the money he made from them and by short-changing the customers himself, he also fleeced his father by withholding some of the ride money he'd taken each night. He was clever enough never to arouse suspicions in the shrewd older man of what he was doing and persuaded his parents it was time for him to live on his own. He knew, deep down, they would offer to pay for a van for him; the same as they had for his brothers. As soon as he finished work of a night, he rid himself of all traces of his showman's life to become a smart young man about town seeking fun for himself in the local community, socializing with all those that would never voluntarily breathe the same air as him outside of the fairground.

Then Britain declared war on Germany and, as a result, all places of entertainment – including travelling fairs – were ordered to close and men of his age called up to join the Forces. Before Belinda had caused her damage on him, Sonny would have been amongst the first, standing proud by his brothers' sides in the queue signing up to fight for his king and country, but now he was putting off the deed until he had no choice, as he was adamant: why put his own life at risk to protect people that thought so disparagingly of him?

But, as matters stood, it seemed Sonny would have no choice but to risk life and limb for those he had no care for. A man had to have a serious illness or deformity to have any chance of being excused. He was fit and in good health. He could always claim he was a conscientious objector but that meant he could land in jail or be sent down the mines and, regardless, he fancied neither. After the war ended he wouldn't be welcome in either the outsiders' community or that of the showmen as neither would accept a traitor to their country living in their midst. The only life facing him then would be that of a vagrant.

But just when he had begun to accept that there was no justifiable reason he could use to avoid joining up, a possible way to at least avoid being sent to the frontline presented itself. It was the day before he had been ordered to register to serve and he was helping his father. Joshua and Solly had both already volunteered and were at training camp awaiting their postings by then. Sonny, along with three other men from the Grundy community who were too old to join the forces, was storing all the fairground equipment in a large storage facility. One of the storage yard's employees, a young man around Sonny's own age, suddenly collapsed to the floor, his body wildly jerking, eyes rolling around in their sockets. As they all stood helplessly looking down at the man, not having a clue what was wrong with him or what to do to help him for the best, the wife of the storage yard owner came running over. She threw herself down beside the convulsing man, whipped off her cardigan, balled it up and placed it under his head, loosened his tie, then spoke soothingly to him until the jerking stopped. Then she immediately rolled him onto his side. She looked up at the men looking worriedly down and told them he would be alright now. She asked if they would carry him into the house to rest on the sofa for a while until he was well enough to return to work

Not at all out of concern for an outsider but purely out of curiosity, Sonny asked the woman what had caused the young man to convulse like that. She explained that he'd suffered an epileptic fit which could come on at any time. His illness had resulted from when, as a young boy, he had been struck by a falling roof tile from a house he was passing at the time. It was such a shame for him too, as he was desperate to do his bit for the war effort, but his illness was severe enough to exempt him from actual fighting. Regardless, the authorities were looking to see what else his illness wouldn't prevent him from doing towards aiding the war effort.

Sonny was elated. This was the perfect excuse for him to avoid putting his own life at risk for people he had no allegiance with. A safe job, away from harm, would suit him fine. Convincing a doctor of his disability was another matter though.

After reporting to the recruiting office and filling out forms, the next stage was a doctor's examination to determine that he was fit enough to fight. Praying that the doctor would fall for the act he was about to put on, it was with great trepidation that Sonny walked into the doctor's office. As luck would have it, the old stalwart of a doctor that usually did the examinations was off sick and a newly qualified doctor, who looked like he was still a school boy to Sonny with his slight frame and boyish face, had been called in to cover his duties.

The examination was just about concluded and the doctor about to inform him, Sonny knew, he had passed with flying colours, when Sonny decided now was the time to put his plan in action. Copying exactly what he'd witnessed happen to the young man at the yard, he suddenly fell into a dead heap on the floor, wildly jerked his body and rolled around his eyes, carrying this on for at least a minute, then pretended to pass out, lying dead still as the young man had done. During his act he felt the doctor put a pillow under his head and, as soon as he'd halted his jerking body, he rolled him over on his side.

A while later, now sitting on a chair, the doctor perched on the edge of his desk looking at him concernedly. Sonny said, faking a worried tone, 'It happened again did it, doc? I passed out?'

The boyish-faced doctor solemnly nodded and said, 'This has happened before, then?'

Conscious that the doctor would question why he hadn't been to a doctor about this condition already, he responded. 'It's happened once before, just after I got knocked on the head by a metal strut when we was dismantling a ride the other week. I was on my own in my living van so I didn't know what had happened to me until I came around and noticed time had passed so I knew I'd passed out.'

'And you never went to see a doctor about it?'

'I'm a fairground worker, doc. Not easy for us to get to see a doctor, not that I've got the money to pay his bill either. I didn't think it was serious anyway.' He then looked at him worriedly. 'Why, do you think I have got something serious?'

'How serious, I'm not sure. But from what happened just now I'd say you have been experiencing epileptic fits caused by the bump to your head you told me about. This might not happen again but, if it does, you'll need to go and see a doctor immediately and be properly examined. You might be given treatment to control the seizures. In the meantime I can't pass you as fighting fit and while we wait and see whether this happens again and whether you are epileptic or not, the army will assign you to a desk or stores job or suchlike.'

Sonny feigned dismay. 'So I won't be allowed to fight?'

'I'm afraid not, Mr Grundy.' Then he added

optimistically, 'If you don't have another fit for a good period of time and it transpires you aren't epileptic after all, then that's a different matter. But just thank goodness you had a seizure whilst you were here and not whilst you had a gun in your hand or you might accidentally have shot yourself or one of your colleagues.' He smiled at Sonny sympathetically as he stood up and went around the desk to complete the paperwork.

Sonny hid a smile of triumph, thinking: *Thank God it was you I saw and not the older, far more experienced doctor that might not have been so easily fooled.*

He did have several more fits at necessary intervals when it seemed he was being looked at by those above as medically sound to join the fighting force. So, whilst Joshua and Solly were risking life and limb with thousands of others in France and Italy, Sonny was risking nothing helping to run stores in several different camps in the north of England. He had himself a ball in his spare time; dancing, gambling and drinking his pay away and having sex with any of the local girls willing to give their bodies to him. Some of Sonny's peers made themselves nice little nest eggs through being in league with local black-market racketeers. Much to Sonny's rancour, he was working alongside very patriotic types that wouldn't entertain the idea of betraying their country by being involved in such activities, so his chances to make any money on the side was very limited and extremely risky. So, when he was demobbed, he did not have an illicitly gained wad of bank notes in his pocket but just a few pounds above his allowance he'd managed to put by.

His family never learned the truth of just how it was that Solly was pronounced unfit to fight when, as far as they were concerned, Sonny was as fit and healthy as his elder and younger brother, who both passed their medicals with flying colours. Regardless, he was welcomed home as much a hero as Solly was, and all mourned together the loss of Joshua.

Sonny was sad his elder brother had died; he had loved him very much. That said, his death would prove very fortunate for him. Now he was the eldest living son and that meant that when his father died, he would be his heir and the fair would be his. With the kind of money at his disposal from the sale of it, he would find himself in a far better position to come up with a superior plan for getting outsiders to suffer for their untoward ill feeling against him. He had plenty of time to come up with an idea as his father was still hale and hearty and had a good few more years in him yet, but patience was a virtue – or so he had heard. The longer he waited for vengeance to be reaped, the sweeter it would be. Until the time came, he was content to carry on getting it the way he had before the war had disrupted him.

Sonny ground the tip end of his roll-up in an overflowing astray and looked disinterestedly out the window of the small, central operating room. Through the whizzing chairs he spotted his father in his trademark striped jacket, hobbling amongst the crowds and checking all was well. For a moment he felt a flicker of guilt over what he planned to do with his father's beloved fair once he was dead but that quickly passed. His father could have sold the fair at any time and done whatever he wanted with the proceeds but, instead, he had chosen to keep it running to support his family. Sonny had no family to support and no children to leave the business to when he passed on so, as far as he was concerned, he had no need to feel any guilt for what he planned to do with it once it became his. His lip then curled sardonically and he sniggered to himself. Solly was under the false illusion that all his labour was in order to keep the business profitable to provide him and his family a living and for generations to come. He couldn't wait to see Solly's face when he discovered that all his effort had been purely to fund his brother's future, not his own. But, far more importantly, how would Gem cope? She had given up a very privileged lifestyle to marry Solly, but would she be prepared to live the far more frugal one as the wife of a mere fairground worker? Hopefully she wouldn't be prepared to and would leave Solly to return back to her old way of life. To lose the love of his life, Sonny knew, without doubt, would devastate his brother far more than the loss of the fair would. Then Solly would know just what it felt like to have his life shattered at the hands of a woman, just like he himself had.

Chapter Three

At just after eleven-thirty that evening, Gem was looking at her two sons, annoyed. James, Jimmy, the image of his father; ruggedly good-looking, dark-haired, six foot. He was the eldest at nineteen and was sitting on a chair in the lounge area of the living van taking off his shoes. Taking more after her own side of the family was fair-haired seventeen-year-old Robert, Robbie, narrowed-shouldered and slim of build. Not so tall as his brother at five foot ten, he had already taken off his shoes and was tiredly lolling back on a comfortable, well-worn red velvet-covered horsehair sofa waiting for his mother to serve him his supper. The first day of a fair arriving and setting up and the last day, packing up and moving on, were the two busiest of the week and at the end of both days even the youngest and fittest members of the community were too tired to have the energy for much else but having a bite to eat and crawling into bed.

'Did you two gannets have to eat all the leftover apple pie and not save some of it for your dad and grandfather? What am I going to give them now for their supper?'

Both young men looked up at her, puzzled. 'I haven't eaten any pie, only what I had at dinner. Anyway, I walked in tonight the same time as you did, Mam, so you know I haven't eaten any,' Robbie told her through a loud yawn.

'And I came in just after you both, so the same goes for me,' said Jimmy. 'Maybe Dad slipped back earlier and scoffed it.'

'Dad came home earlier and scoffed what?' said their father, taking off his jacket which he hung on one of three hooks on the wall beside the barn-style van door.

Gem spun to face him and snapped, 'Oh, you didn't, Solly? You greedy so-and-so. You could have left some for your sons and father.'

As he walked into the room and sat down on a wooden dining chair at the table in the kitchen area and began to take off his shoes, Solly looked at them all bemused. 'Would someone kindly tell me what I'm supposed to have come back earlier and scoffed the lot of?'

Gem enlightened him. 'The remains of the apple pie I was going to give you all for supper.'

He shrugged. 'I never came back here at all tonight so I couldn't have eaten the pie.'

Gem eyed him blankly. 'Well, it's all gone, hardly a crumb left in the dish, so if it wasn't any of you three that ate it, then who on earth was it? Your father never eats between meals these days and Sonny... Well it's hardly likely to be him that's the culprit as he never eats with us except for high days and holidays and hardly pays us a social visit when we're here let alone when we're not and, besides, he never eats puddings.'

Robbie looked knowingly at her. 'Well someone obviously did, Mam. But, more to the point, I'm starving so if we're not having pie, what are we having?'

At that question the other two men in the room looked at her expectantly too.

Big Sam then arrived, rubbing his hands and proclaiming, 'It's getting nippy out there. The sky is clearing so could have a frost.' He looked at Sonny. 'Might be wise to put a tarpaulin over your van genny or you might have a job to get it started in the morning if we do.' As he sat down next to Robbie on the sofa he looked at Gem enquiringly and grumbled, 'No cuppa or supper on the go yet.' And not being able to resist a chance to remind her of her non-blood showwoman status, added, 'If you was a true show woman it'd be on the table by now and the kettle on the stove ready to refill the pot for a second cuppa.'

'That's enough, Dad,' Solly shot warningly at him.

His father eyed him innocently. 'Just stating a fact, Son. Our womenfolk would never stand idly by while they had starving men around.'

So used to jibes of such nature after twenty years of them from her husband's father, knowing there was no maliciousness intended and that it was just his way of reminding her that she was only a show woman by default, Gem responded, 'For all a true red-blooded show woman she was, I doubt Nell could have filled your belly from an empty plate, Mr Grundy.' Gem had long ago stopped wondering whether if she had been a true-blood show woman she would have been allowed by Sam to call him Dad. Perhaps it was old-fashioned respect that he had never allowed her to address him in any manner but by his full title. After her marriage, however, Nell had insisted Gem call her Mother.

Sam looked confused. 'Eh?'

Jimmy laughed. 'We've had a visit from the pie thief, Granddad.'

He looked even more confused.

Robbie enlightened him. 'Some kind soul let themselves in while we were all out working and ate the leftover apple pie Mam was giving us for supper.'

Sam's face darkened thunderously. 'I'll skin the buggers alive if I catch whoever did it. There's no one who has such light pastry hands as my Nell did, but you come a close second, girl.' And before he realised that he was paying his daughter-in-law a compliment added, 'As apple pie's not on the cards, what *is* then?'

Gem sighed. She really didn't feel like cooking this time of night and, besides, she hadn't anything to cook except for what was intended for breakfast tomorrow morning. She hadn't had time to shop today, having been busy enough playing her part in setting up the fair for opening this afternoon, along with all her other chores she'd had to fit in. So all that she could offer her hungry brood right now was toast and jam. A choice between that and going hungry, they all readily accepted her offering.

It didn't escape Gem's notice that Sam seemed in a hurry to finish his supper and make his leave. It was no secret that, since Nell had died, when the evening was a dry one, he had taken to visiting Velda to have a nightcap with her and these chats, talking mostly of Nell to a woman outside the family who knew her well, had helped ease his grief. But lately Gem felt that something within Sam had changed and these visits were no longer just to have a friendly chat with Velda. She suspected that he had developed feelings for her and wanted more from her now than just friendship. She had never broached the subject with Sam. Sam was definitely not the kind of man that easily divulged his feelings; he kept them very close to his chest and would only have gruffly told her that she was imagining things and to mind her own business. Neither had she mentioned her suspicions to Solly as he had idolised his mother; her death had hit him hard. If his father was to take up with Velda or any other woman, in fact, it was best coming from him. But, even so, that didn't mean she couldn't try and quash her curiosity over the matter by carefully probing Velda herself though, did it?

Secretly, she hoped that Sam did find someone to share the rest of his life with and knew that the big-hearted Nell would be happy about that too. Gem also thought that if that woman *was* Velda then she herself – and Nell too – couldn't be happier for him. Nell had thought a lot of Velda, valued her friendship greatly. Gem herself owed Velda a great debt of gratitude. She had very much been Gem's ally when she had first joined the Grundy family and faced the backlash of Solly's decision to marry an outsider. If it hadn't been for Velda's support and encouragement, she and Solly might not still be happily married now with two strapping sons. She would more than welcome Velda into their tight-knit family circle as her stepmother, should her suspicions be correct.

A while later, Jimmy and Robbie in their separate bunks, Gem was snuggled comfortably into Solly in their small bedroom at the front of the van. She was just dropping off into a peaceful sleep when, all of a sudden, she was jerked out of her slumber by Solly exclaiming, 'Oh, hell!' The covers were then thrown back, he jumped out of bed and began to pull his clothes back on.

Yanking the covers back over herself, she looked over at his shadowy form moving around in the darkness and demanded, 'What on earth is wrong, Solly?'

He responded in a frustrated tone. 'I forgot to cover the genny when I turned it off before I came to bed. Best go and do it as a precaution in case Dad is right and we do have a frost.' He leaned down, kissed her cheek and tenderly told the love of his life, 'Won't be long. You go back to sleep.'

She snuggled back down. 'Don't you dare put your cold feet on me when you come back and wake me up.'

He just smiled as they both knew he would.

Millions of stars twinkled down from an almost cloudless sky and an icy nip in the air made Solly shiver as he stepped down the wooden van steps onto the hard ground below. His father's prediction that there would be a frost seemed very likely, he thought as he made his way round the back of the van to fetch the tarpaulin generator cover. Enough light from a three-quarter moon alleviated Solly's need for a torch. When not in use, he always kept the tarpaulin cover folded up and secured for safekeeping under straps on top of the large tool box fixed to the back of the van.

He was surprised though to find it wasn't there. He frowned. On arrival at any place, his first job was always to set the generator up and running so Gem could have electricity in the van to aid her in getting food on the go. Yesterday evening, as soon as they had arrived here, he distinctly remembered removing the tarpaulin that he had covered the old generator with when they had left the last place in order to protect it during transportation, folded it up, put it on top of the tool box and secured the straps over it. But then, as it wasn't here, he couldn't have, could he? He walked back around to the side of the van to where the genny was sited and looked around it. No sign of the tarpaulin. Had it somehow been kicked under the van itself then? To discourage vermin fairfolk were very vigilant that nothing food-wise or anything they could nest in was left lying around. If the tarp was under the van and rats had already made a home inside then Solly would be very cross with himself for being lax.

It was almost pitch black under the van but, to save him going back inside to fetch a torch and his rummaging around possibly waking the others, Solly took a chance that if the tarp was just under there then there was enough light for him to see it. If it was further underneath he would have to fetch a torch. Running around the two sides and back of the van between the four wheels were storage cupboards leaving only just over the wheel width between the bottom of the cupboards and the ground so Solly had to flatten himself on the ground to see underneath it. At first glance the space under the van didn't appear to have any darker shapes indicating something was under there but on a second look around he spotted something beside the inside of the wheel nearest to him. It appeared to be a bundle of some sort. Was it the elusive tarpaulin cover? But just how had it come to be under there though...

Crawling under the van, Solly reached out and grabbed hold of an edge of the bundle. He knew by the feel of the material that it was tarpaulin he was clutching, but it appeared to be caught on something. He gave another hard tug of it. At this, and to his own shock, a surprised yelp resounded from under the tarp and something inside it began to move. Solly froze. Was it a rat? But then rats didn't yelp, they squeaked! Whatever was hiding in the tarpaulin was human. Had his own unexpected appearance disturbed a burglar? Perhaps he found the length of tarpaulin and hid himself under it until Solly himself had gone back inside and he could carry on with what he was up to. That or he was a vagrant using it as a place to sleep for the night? Whoever it was, though, was fighting to free himself from under the tarp and it was Solly's guess that, as soon as they did, they would make their escape out of the other side and be long gone before he could get around there to catch them. Solly's reactions were quick. Like an attacking snake he slithered further under the van and, as best as he could in such a restricted space, flung himself on top of the tarpaulin, pinning down the person under it who was still flaying about in their efforts to free themselves from its folds.

'I've got you. Come out now.' But the thrashing

about still continued so Solly commanded in no uncertain terms, 'I'm warning you, don't make me use force. I've a hammer in my hand and I will use it,' he lied.

At that the flaying abruptly stopped and, after a moment, a timid voice stuttered, 'Please don't hurt me, mister. I wasn't doing nothing bad, 'onest I wasn't. I was only sleeping. Oh, you're heavy. I can't breathe–'

The tone of voice told Solly that the person was a young lad. Twelve or thirteen, certainly no older. Doubting he posed a threat, Solly eased himself off the top of him and wriggled back, but still keeping within grabbing distance should the young man try a bid for escape. Slowly the outline of a body started to emerge and the more that revealed itself, the further Solly inched back out from under the van until, a few moments later, they were both sitting by the side of it.

The intruder was a young boy of around ten. As Solly studied him for a moment a flicker of recognition struck but for the life of him he couldn't place just where he had seen him before. Then it came to him. It wasn't the boy himself he recognised but the shabby brown coat he was wearing. It had a tear in the sleeve, the same tear he had seen on the coat being worn by the figure huddled on the ground who was being attacked earlier.

Head bowed low, arms wrapped around himself, the boy was violently shivering and Solly was of the opinion that it wasn't from the cold but from fear as to how his captor was going to deal with him for trespassing under his van. He placed a reassuring hand on his knee and said, 'Stop worrying, you're not in trouble, lad. I'm just glad I found you alive tonight and not in the morning frozen to death.'

Recognising Solly's voice, he lifted his head and eyed him hero-like. 'You're the bloke that stopped *him* from beating me, ain't yer. Thank you, mister, thank you so much. I really thought he was going to kill me this time.'

It seemed from that comment that the boy's father thrashing him was a common occurrence. Solly heaved a sigh. 'Look, I don't know what you did to make your dad give you such a thrashing but I'm sure he'll be worried where you are. You really need to go home.'

A terrified look flooded his gaunt face and, grabbing the sleeve of Solly's jumper, shaking it wildly, he frenziedly cried out, 'Don't make me go back, please, mister, please. Please let me stay here. I won't cause you no trouble. I'll do whatever you want me to do. I know I don't look it but I'm strong, honest. Just don't make me go back.'

His desperate pleas tore at Solly's good nature. He sadly shook his head. 'But you're not old enough to leave home without your parents' permission. If your dad comes looking for you and finds I've been allowing you to stay here, I could get into serious trouble with the police.'

Tears filled the boy's eyes and he hysterically cried out, 'But I can't do what he makes me do no more. I'm so frightened that I'm going to get caught. I nearly have been so many times and I'll get slung in jail. I heard what jail's like and I can't go in there, I just can't.'

Solly looked at him for a moment and,

although he had an idea, he asked him, 'Just what is it your father makes you do?'

He sniffed back snot before he uttered, 'Robbing. It's my job to get people's attention while he picks their pockets or bags or he stands lookout while I go into houses and steal stuff he can sell.' He looked at Solly through miserable eyes. 'But it ain't right, mister, is it? He should get a job to pay for his booze and bets down the bookies, not steal it. Me mam taught me that you work for what you get. She'd be so upset if she knew what he'd been making me do.'

Solly had been about to ask where his mother stood in all this and now he had his answer. 'Oh, by that I take it from what you just said that your mam is no longer around?'

A fresh flood of tears rolled unashamedly down his face and he blubbered, 'She's dead.' There was a slight pause before he added, 'It was *him* who killed her.'

Solly gawped, stunned by this announcement. 'What do you mean, he killed her? And if he did, why is your dad not in prison for her murder then?'

'Cos he managed to fob the police off with his lies. He swore blind to them that we were out at the time me mam had her accident, that he'd taken me to the park and when we got back we found her dead at the bottom of the stairs. He got one of his friends to back him up... I think he paid him to. But I knew it was *him* that killed her because I saw him push her. I was hiding in my bedroom and watched what he did through the crack in the door. Mam was telling him to leave and packing up his stuff as he wouldn't pay the money he owed her and he got angry as he'd nowhere else to go. When she wouldn't change her mind he shoved her out of his room and she stumbled and went down the stairs. He threatened he'd kill me too if I told the truth and I was so scared of him I didn't dare. I was only seven at the time. I had no other family to go to so I had to stay with him.'

Solly was desperate to offer to help this boy escape the clutches of his fiend of a father but was worried about the repercussions if he was caught doing so. Heaving a deep sigh he said, 'But he's still your father though.'

The boy vehemently cried out, 'No, he's not! My dad died in an accident at work when I was just a baby. Archie Cox was me mam's lodger. There was never nothing between him and me mam. Along with the three cleaning jobs she did, his lodging money helped keep us going until he lost his job when he had a row with his foreman because he was caught stealing stuff from work. After that he couldn't get another job and just used to laze around the house expecting me mam to keep him for nothing. When he couldn't steal anything to buy his booze and fags, he'd rob money from Mam's purse and hit her. He threatened her he'd batter me if she tried to stop him. This went on for months. That night he'd emptied Mam's purse and gone to the pub and while he was gone she was going to pack his stuff, leave it outside and lock us inside; she thought that would show him she meant business and he'd go away then and leave us alone. But he came back while Mam was packing his stuff and when she heard him coming in she told me to get in my bedroom and not come out until she told me to, and...' His voice trailed off, the rest of the story obviously far too painful for him to continue on with out loud. 'The police were going to get the authorities to put me in a home but Archie lied, made them believe he'd been living with my mam for years and treating me as his own son and wanted to keep me so they let him. He told me he did that cos I'd be useful to him. Yeah, I was that alright. I hated what he made me do but I was so scared of the beating he'd give me if I refused. If I ran away I'd nowhere to go and no money cos he never gave me any. We got thrown out of me mam's house not long after she died cos he never paid the rent and he sold all our stuff. Since then we've lived in that many different rooms. I hardly went to school so I've never had any friends...' His voice trailed off again and he gave a deep, shuddering shiver before he added, 'Tonight, though, well I don't know what got into me but like what happened to me mam that night he pushed her, I'd just had enough and told him I wasn't doing what he made me do any more. And, if that meant he killed me then I didn't care. And I really didn't, mister, cos I can't live like this any more.' He then buried his head in his chest and wept.

'You can't send him back to live with that monster, Solly, you just can't.'

At the unexpected sound of his wife's voice, Solly spun his head around to see her standing at the bottom of the van steps, looking deeply distressed. Under the pretty scarf wrapped around her head her hair was pinned with clips and under a long blue belted dressing gown with white piping around the edges of the collar and wide cuffs, she wore a long rosebud-patterned nightdress. Solly jumped up and placed his arm around her, pulling her close and whispering, 'You heard what he told me?'

She nodded. 'I heard someone cry out, thought you'd hurt yourself or something, so I came out and saw you come out from under the van with the young lad.' Her bottom lip trembled and she said chokingly, 'Poor little mite. I can't imagine how it's been for him having to do what that man made him and knowing he was responsible for his mother's death. He looks like a bag of bones to me under that baggy old coat he's wearing so obviously not much of the stolen money went on food for him, did it?' She then eyed Solly knowingly. 'I don't think we need look any further to find our apple pie thief and I don't begrudge that boy one crumb of it. Bring him inside, love. I'll find him something to eat while we decide what's best to do for him.'

She turned then made her way back up the steps and disappeared inside the van.

Solly went back over to the boy, leaned down and took his arm. 'Come with me.'

The boy jumped up, clearly terrified. He blurted, 'Are you taking me back to *him?*'

Solly shook his head. 'My wife is going to make you a bite to eat while we decide what best to do for you.' He clapped his hand on his shoulder. 'I promise that whatever it is we won't be forcing you to go back home.' He sincerely hoped he didn't have to break that promise.

Having rekindled the stove, two thick slices of bacon which had been intended for her own breakfast the next morning beginning to sizzle in a pan on top of it, Gem was at the table cutting slices of bread off a loaf. As soon as the boy stepped in she wrinkled her nose. While he stood just inside the doorway looking in awe around the comfortable, homely interior, she motioned Solly to come over to her. Once by her side she told him, 'I dread to think when the last time was that boy had a wash, his clothes either. I doubt his clothes would stand a laundering. While I finish his sandwich send him in the bathroom, there's hot water in the kettle so use that and I'll reboil it for tea. See if you can find a pair of Robbie's old trousers and a pullover for him to wear. There're piles of their old clothes in a box under our bed. I keep meaning to sort them out and give them to mothers of kids on site but just never seem to get around to it. Glad I didn't now. Even something Robbie wore when he was the boy's age will be far too big for him even though our Robbie was a skinny clothes prop then ... and still is for that matter. But for how skinny he is at least Robbie had some meat on him at his age. That poor boy looks like those photos we saw of all those poor prisoners rescued from Belsen. Put his clothes in a bag, chuck them outside and we'll burn them in the morning.'

A few minutes later, having done Gem's bidding, Solly returned to her and said, 'If I doubted his story that he was regularly beaten by Archie Cox, then I certainly don't now from what I saw when he stripped off his clothes for his wash. Oh,

Gem, his back is covered in old scars and fresh ones he got tonight before I stopped that monster beating him to a pulp. You're right, we can't send him back. But then I doubt he'll go back but will end up living on the streets. He's such a nice lad too, well-mannered, obviously his mother did a good job in raising him before she died. When I gave him Robbie's clothes, grateful for them doesn't go anywhere near expressing his response. You'd have thought I'd given him the most precious gift ever.' He heaved a deep, worried sigh. 'What do we do, Gem? If we let him stay here and Archie Cox or the police come sniffing around and find him then I don't need to tell you what trouble we'd be in for harbouring a juvenile. This was the last place Archie Cox saw him so it'll be his first port of call to find him, won't it?'

The young lad appeared out of the bathroom then, Robbie's old clothes swamping his slight, undernourished frame. Gem smiled over at him. 'Make yourself comfy in a chair, tea's just mashing and your bacon and egg sandwich is ready. Would you like tomato or brown sauce on it and sugar in your tea or not?'

Large sunken brown eyes looked back at Gem in utter shock; it was obvious that it had been a long time since he'd been asked such questions. He blustered, 'I don't mind, anything. Thank you, thank you so much.' A guilty look then filled his face. 'But I ... well ... I do need to tell you something.' He anxiously twisted his bony hands together. 'You see...'

Gem cut him short. 'Did you enjoy it?'

He looked at her blankly. 'Eh?'

She smiled. 'The remains of apple pie you found in my larder cupboard.'

He swallowed hard, eyeing her warily, not sure where this was leading to. 'I did, missus, it was scrumptious.'

'Then that's the main thing. Now, tuck into your sandwich before it gets cold.' He didn't need another telling and snatched it up and took a large bite. As he swallowed the first mouthful he proclaimed, 'Oh, this is ... this is...' It was apparent he couldn't at that moment find the words to describe how delicious he was finding the food and just enthused, 'Oh, thank you, thank you so much.'

Sat on the sofa alongside Solly, Gem's smile was a warm one towards the waif, but her eyes brimmed with sadness. 'It's all my pleasure. We haven't been introduced properly, have we? I'm Mrs Grundy and this is my husband, Mr Grundy. What is your name?'

He went to tell her it was 'boy' as that was how he'd been addressed for so long by Archie Cox he'd almost forgotten what his real name was. 'Colin.' He gave a wistful smile. 'Me mam always called me Col. I like to be called Col.' He took a gulp of his tea and another bite of his sandwich.

'Well, we're pleased to meet you, Col.' She then whispered to Solly, 'Over the years I've lost count of the number of youngsters that have begged us for a job because they're desperate to leave home or, most times, think a job with the fair is an easier life than the one they have but this time, if ever I've seen anyone who genuinely needs rescuing... Well, he's on an even pegging with the desperate situation we found Kathy Folds in and we helped her. And it's not like you haven't seen first-hand what that maniac that calls himself Col's dad is capable of, is it? Whatever we decide to do with him it won't be to send him back to that man, Solly, like we never sent Kathy back to that butcher she was living with. I'm adamant on that.'

When Gem was adamant about anything Solly knew there'd be nothing he or anyone could do or say that would make her change her mind. He was though, on this occasion, as adamant on that as she was. 'There must be an orphanage around these parts and if we explain to them that Archie Cox is not his real dad and how he...'

Solly was cut short by Gem's vehement shake of her head. 'Putting him in one of those places is hardly better than sending him back to Cox and I'll not do it, Solly. We can't just give him some money and send him off to fend for himself either. I'd never sleep at night for worrying what has happened to him and you, you big softy, I know the same would go for you too.' She sat in deep thought for a moment before she announced, 'There's nothing else for it. We're only here for another six days and after that we'll be miles away so, in the meantime, we hide him.'

He nodded in agreement. 'In the same place we hid Kathy. It worked before, didn't it? I'm sure Col won't mind a bit of discomfort for a few days if he knows at the end of it he'll be free from Cox for good.' His frown then returned. 'But what then for him, Gem? Are you thinking we keep him? You know I would if that was what you wanted but we have to be realistic. There's no room for him to bunk in with our boys and it wouldn't be right for him to permanently sleep on the sofa. And you've already got your work cut out for you with all you do as it is, let alone taking on the extra care of a young boy.'

All Gem's maternal instincts had come to the fore and were screaming at her to care for Col. She could never replace his mother, but wanted to do her best to give him all the love, care and nurture he deserved. Regardless of Solly's reminder of the lack of room, she decided that they would somehow manage; larger families than theirs managed in smaller accommodation than they had. Still, now that her own sons had grown up and she was no longer just a wife and mother helping out on the fair when time allowed, she was now playing a major role in the business and thoroughly enjoying it. She didn't really want to give that up and go back to being more of a full-time mother again. She though had a better solution to solve Colin's dire situation. She told Solly, 'I know just the people who'll take him in and treat him as their own. The lad will thrive under their care.'

Solly looked at her blankly for a moment until just who she was referring to struck him. 'Iris and Bert.'

She smiled. 'Yes. I've no doubt they'll fall in love with Col as soon as they meet him and not need any persuading from us to give him a home. Iris was only telling me the other day, and not for the first time either, that since their three have grown up and moved away to work elsewhere, they've both sorely missed having youngsters around. She even said that if she wasn't too old now, at forty, she'd have more. With a few of Iris's good home-cooked meals, her fussing over him and fatherly guidance from Bert, even Cox himself wouldn't recognise Col in a few weeks. I'll go and visit Iris and Bert now and put this to them. If they're asleep I'll wake them as this is important.'

She came back less than ten minutes later and whispered to Solly that the pair had needed no persuading; they were more than willing to take in the boy and treat him as their own, really excited about the prospect but not at all happy that they'd have to wait a few days first whilst he was hidden from Cox but in the meantime would get everything ready for him to welcome him into his new home.

Col had now finished his food and was licking the last of the crumbs off his fingers, sporting the sort of satisfied look on his face of someone who'd just eaten the most sumptuous banquet. Gem said to Solly, 'Let's see what Col feels about our plan, shall we? Do you want to tell him or shall I?'

He affectionately patted her knee. 'Being's it's all your idea, I'll let you do the honours.'

A few minutes later, Col was staring at them, dumbstruck as he tried to process what Gem had just told him. Finally finding his voice he stuttered, 'But ... but ... are you sure these people ... well, really want *me?*'

Sonny and Gem both realised that he'd been so demoralised by Archie Cox's cruel treatment of him that he believed himself worthless. It was Solly that responded, in a voice loaded with reassurance, 'And why wouldn't they? You'd be a credit to anyone that takes you in. You do fully understand though that the next six days, while we are still in this place, will not be very pleasant for you.'

'In that hiding place you told me about just in case *him* or the coppers come looking for me?' He eyed Solly and Gem earnestly. 'If it means I don't have to go back and can stay with the fair and live with those people then I'd hide away for years if that's what I have to do.'

Gem got up, saying, 'I don't think we need to worry about any visits tonight so I'll go and fetch some bedding to make you comfortable on the sofa but, first thing in the morning, we'll show you where you'll be spending your time until we move on next Sunday morning.'

He looked at them worriedly. 'And I won't be found?'

Solly told him. 'For good reason, we've hidden a couple of people in this place in the past and they were never found. Anyway, to my mind from what you've told me about Cox, I doubt he'll want the police involving. You told him you weren't doing what you were for him any more and didn't care if he killed you, so if the police do find you and you tell them just how he's been treating you, then he's taking a huge risk. You're far too valuable to him for him to easily give up on you so I expect we'll get a visit but, don't worry, by the time I've finished with him that'll be the last we see of him.'

He said that with such conviction that Col visibly relaxed. 'I ... I don't know how I'm ever going to thank you for all you're doing for me.'

'We don't need thanks, Col. Just knowing we

got you away from that brute is enough for us.'

A rush of mixed emotions washed through Col, ones he had not experienced for so long he had forgotten what each felt like. Excitement, optimism, expectation, hope, amongst others. He had woken this morning dressed in the only clothes he possessed, in a dingy, damp room on an old, thin, stained, lumpy mattress. Breakfast was the remains of a stale loaf and cold water out of the green, mould-encrusted brass tap protruding over a pitted, discoloured sink. There was no money to put in the meter to heat the blackened, battered kettle over the ancient gas stove or heat the room with the equally antiquated gas fire. Cox had still been asleep, snoring pig-like on a mattress close by, and would be for a few more hours thanks to the amount of alcohol he'd consumed the previous night, paid for from the proceeds of an old woman's purse Col had helped him to steal. Suspecting that Col would try to escape his clutches while he was out or sleeping, Cox would shackle him with ropes to a water pipe by his mattress. The future facing Col this morning at the hands of the selfish, nasty bully Cox had been unbearably bleak, the only ending of it that he could see was when death finally released him – either Cox's or his own – and, regardless of his lifestyle, Cox was only in his forties so his death might not be for many long years yet.

That evening Cox had told him he was expecting great rewards as the fair had come to town which meant rich pickings were to be had for types like him. Dragging Col across the waste ground towards the fair entrance, Cox spotted a mother and excited-looking young daughter of about six. They were both cheaply dressed so obviously not well off. Cox told Col they would be their first target and ordered him to bump into the child and knock her over. While the woman was picking her up and scolding him for his clumsiness, he himself would relieve her handbag of its purse.

A vision of his own mother taking him to the fair when he had been that young girl's age had risen before him. The money for the rides Col knew had been hard saved for and could have been used by his mother for much more necessary things. But she'd wanted to give him some fun, the same as he expected the mother Cox had targeted wanted to give her daughter and was willing to go without to do so. Something inside Col snapped. He just couldn't do what Cox was ordering him to do purely in order for that stolen money to be wasted on drink, cigarettes and bets. If this meant that Cox carried out his promise to beat him senseless, even to death, for refusing to do his bidding, then death would be a blessed relief from this purgatory as far as Col was concerned.

But thanks to fate, or just pure luck for Col, Solly Grundy had happened along and put a stop to Cox's retaliation. He'd given him an opening to escape his clutches, to be free of him for good and, although he'd been racked in pain from the thrashing he'd already received, weak from lack of nourishing food, he hadn't waste a second – acutely aware a chance like this might never come along again. So, whilst Solly Grundy had been keeping Cox otherwise occupied, Col had scrambled away like a cat on hot coals, hiding himself under a caravan and covering himself up with tarpaulin, praying Cox wouldn't find him. He had no idea where he went from here or how he fended for himself in future but at least he was free from that wretched life. And, if that wasn't enough, his hero and his wife were now offering him a chance of a good future with people who would welcome him into their home and take care of him.

He suddenly felt terrified that all this was a dream which soon he'd wake up from. That he'd find himself in that desolate room on the thin smelly mattress again, arm and leg both badly aching and stiff from him being shackled all night to the water pipe. But, if this was a dream, he would have woken up by now, like he always had done before when dreaming of wonderful things happening to him. Always, just when he was about to experience those wonderful things – as if the Devil was playing games with him, giving him a taste of what he longed for, only to snatch it cruelly away when it was within his grasp – he'd be whipped out of his dreams back into reality. But this time that cruel awakening hadn't happened and he was going to grab hold of those wonderful things being offered him and not let them go. He would forever owe his saviour and his wife a debt of gratitude; the amount would be impossible for him to even make a dent towards repaying but if, in the future, he saw a glimpse of a chance then he wouldn't fail to seize it.

Chapter Four

In a modern two-bedroomed caravan was Suzie Douglas. She was dressed in a pink, long satin nightdress which exposed a good amount of her high, rounded breasts. Her long brunette hair was tied back in a matching pink ribbon and she was propped up against frilly-edged pillows in bed, idly filing her fingernails. Her husband Donny – not a tall man at five foot nine and a half and not particularly good-looking but, regardless, with a very pleasant, kindly face that matched his disposition – was at the kitchen sink having a wash down. The water for it had been fetched in a bucket from the council-provided standpipe and heated up in the kettle on the stove.

'She must have felt so stupid having an audience witness her embarrassment of being stuck in a barrel and rolled around in it. Worse that Gem Grundy saw it too. Ren tried to joke it off but, even so, inside, she must have been dying of shame. I do feel so sorry for her.'

Donny arrived in the bedroom, wiping his torso on a towel, looking at her bemused.

'That was terrible what happened to Ren, but why would you feel sorry for her?'

His immediate jump to Ren's defence raised her hackles. 'Well ... just for what she has to put up with looking like she does. She's not normal, is she? I'm surprised she has never applied to be in a panto to play one of the dwarves when we shut down over the winter.'

Donny shot her a look of shock. 'Ren's not a dwarf, Suzie, she's just little. That's all. That was not nice of you saying that.'

She feigned hurt. 'I was just stating a fact.' She realised that Donny was putting his clothes back on. 'Where are you going?' she demanded of him as if she didn't know.

'To check Ren's alright.'

The fact it was Ren he was abandoning her for was not what fuelled a surge of jealous rage within her but the fact that her conceited nature wouldn't allow her to play second fiddle to any woman. She blurted, 'She's fine. She thought the whole thing funny. This sort of thing is like water off a duck's back to her. Anyway, it's after twelve so she'll be in bed by now and your place is in bed beside me.'

He looked over at the alarm clock. 'Yes, she probably will be in bed, so I'll pop and see her first thing in the morning.' He began to take off his clothes again. 'But you're wrong that this won't have affected her, Suzie. She might not have shown it in front of you and Mrs Grundy but I've known her since we were babies and she does her crying behind closed doors, does Ren.'

'Huh.' Then her face crumpled and, forcing tears to her eyes, she blubbered, 'Sometimes I think you think more of her than you do me.'

A look of utter astonishment filled his face. 'What! Oh come on, Suzie. Ren's my friend, that's all. It's you I love.'

'Well, why is it then you always put her before me?'

He looked astonished as to why she would make that statement. 'I don't.'

She squeezed out more tears. 'Yes you do. You were leaving me tonight to go to her.'

'Only to check on her after that terrible thing happening to her. She'd have come to see me if something like that had happened to me.' He looked at her closely for a moment before heaving a deep sigh. 'You've really got a bee in your bonnet about Ren tonight. In fact, you're always having a go at me about my being friends with her. You know we're just friends and nothing more so why don't you like me being friends with her? It's like...' He raked his fingers exasperatedly through his hair and sank down on the edge of the bed. 'Well, if I didn't know better, I would think you saw her as a threat.'

She clambered out from under the covers, crawled over to cuddle into him, resting her head on his shoulder. 'Of course I don't see Ren as a threat. I love you, Donny, you love me. Our marriage is happy and strong, the sort no one can break. It's just that...' Her thoughts tumbled for a plausible reason to placate her constant grief to him over his friendship with Ren. The truth was that she was terrified he would realise his true feelings for Ren and leave her before she had found someone to give her a better life than Donny was. When she had, they were welcome to each other.

But, until then, her life with Donny was far superior to the one she'd had with her parents and she meant to keep it. She thought she had found someone several times since her marriage but each man either turned out to be married themselves and were just using her for sex or she, thankfully, found out just before she burned her boats that they were no better off, worse in a couple of instances, than Donny. Then an idea came to her. She lifted her head and kissed his cheek before saying in a feigned reluctant tone, 'Look, darling, I've never told you this before because I knew how much it'd hurt you but Ren isn't the woman you think she is. Well, she's certainly not the true friend to you, you think she is.'

He turned his head and looked at her quizzically. 'What do you mean?'

She heaved a deep, forlorn sigh. 'Oh, God, this hurts me so much to tell you but since we started going out together she's been making nasty digs at me. Such as: what is a very pretty girl like me wanting to be seen dead with a ... er ... gormless lump like you?'

He gawped. 'Gormless lump? Ren called me that?'

'And worse. Village idiot. Chump. At first I thought she was jealous and wanted you for herself and I told her so. She just laughed and said she might be on the short side ... you know how she's always making jokes about her height ... but even she could do better than you. She said she wanted herself a real man, not a plodder like you who'd never make anything of himself in life. She joked once that Frankenstein's monster was better-looking than you. But I used to take no notice of her, Donny. To me you're the best-looking man ever. James Dean could try and sweep me off my feet and I wouldn't trade him for you. Anyway, tonight, she really went too far and I can't keep this from you any longer. Wives and husbands shouldn't have secrets, should they? When Mrs Grundy left this afternoon I said to Ren that it was a pity you hadn't heard about what those lads were doing to her as you'd have come haring over and sorted them out, made sure they never showed their faces in our fair again doing something like that to one of us.'

'And I would have done,' he said with conviction. Donny never shied from protecting those he cared for.

'I couldn't believe what that ... that ... woman ... said.'

Quizzically he asked, 'What did she say?'

She made him wait a moment, pretending she was reluctant to hurt him with what he was asking her to divulge before she finally answered. '"Huh! A wet lettuce would give more of a slap than one from Donny's limp hand. Thank God it was Mrs Grundy that came to my rescue because if it had been Donny I'd still be stuffed inside that barrel being rolled around." She said she was glad I'd come along as it meant she hadn't got to pretend to be your friend so much now you were spending more of your time with me. She said you bored her silly and she would never have picked you as a friend but had been forced into it by both your mothers being such good friends then expecting you two to be.' She then eyed him sorrowfully. 'Now you see why I didn't want to tell you.'

He couldn't believe what he was hearing. The

nasty-mouthed woman his wife was describing was nothing like the one he knew Ren to be. His first thought was that Suzie must be lying but he couldn't come up with a valid reason as to why she would. He felt so utterly stupid for unreservedly believing all these years that Ren valued his friendship as much as he did hers when, all the time, she was just pretending that she did because of the friendship their mothers had shared and, in truth, thought very little of him as a person.

Suzie was stroking a finger down his cheek and said, 'It's not nice the way you found out how Ren feels about you, Donny, but at least you know now.'

He was still reeling from this, such an unexpected revelation, that he felt like he'd had the stuffing knocked out of him. He solemnly nodded. 'I'll not go where I'm not wanted. I'll keep out of her way as much as I can in future.'

A smug glow filled Suzie. She had no care whatsoever that her deviousness had just devastated her husband. She had achieved just what she wanted and that was all she cared about. Now Donny thought Ren despised him. Even if he did realise his true feelings for her, he would now never tell her as he believed they'd be laughingly rejected. Her marriage was safe until she was ready to end it.

A couple of vans away from Donny and Suzie's, sixty-five-year-old fortune-teller Madam Velda May was relaxing outside her small, wooden gypsy-style van, painted traditionally in bold bright colours. It used to be pulled by a horse but was now moved around by a battered seven-year-old Land Rover. She was sitting in a comfortable but shabby Lloyd Loom wicker chair padded with cushions. On a small black Chinese lacquered table at the side of her was an empty tea cup and plate that had held a cheese sandwich before she had eaten it, a bottle of malt whiskey and a tumbler. Another wicker chair ready for visitors, should she receive any, was at the side of that. She was a tall woman at five foot nine and a half and, as usual, was wearing long, flowing tent-like robes over her rotund body. Tonight, to ward off the icy chill in the air, she had added a black gypsy-type heavy shawl around her shoulders. Her homely-featured face was always heavily covered with make-up, in particular darkening around her eyes to give herself a gypsy-ish, mystic look. She always wore a black scarf too, pulled tightly around her head and knotted under her chin. As she'd been working earlier she had the traditional fortune-teller's small silver discs dangling across her forehead. Her greying hair was long and worn in a braid which hung over her shoulder and down her chest.

Clasping thick hands over her stomach mound, she gazed distantly up at the millions of stars twinkling down from the clear sky above. This was her favourite time of day, when all the noisy crowds had gone home and the loud music switched off. All the Grundy community children were in bed fast asleep and, apart from the odd raised voice from arguing couples coming from open windows in surrounding vans, silence reigned. Not that Velda's hour or so tonight had been all peace and quiet for her as it had been broken several times by visitors and passers-by. Not that she minded as Velda was a very warm and welcoming woman who never turned anyone away from her door. She was much loved by the Grundy community and, especially in respect of the other women, one of the first they turned to in troubled times for help and advice. No one really knew where Velda came from or anything more than a scant knowledge of her background that she had travelled around a lot until she had settled down with Grundy's nearly thirty years ago. She was a very private person and, no matter how hard anyone quizzed her, her past, as far as she was concerned, was her business alone.

One of Velda's visitors tonight had been Ren. In fact it was a rare night when Ren did not call by just for a quick catch-up, to check on the older woman she had come to look on as her second mother since her own had died. She always made sure she had had a good day and that there was nothing she wanted Ren to help her with, before she retired herself. Velda loved and cared for Ren as much as had she been her own daughter. She'd fill her coal bucket from the sack she kept in a box under the back of her van to fuel the small cast-iron stove inside and topped up her water bucket from the council standpipe. These were both jobs Velda was still capable of doing herself but she knew it gave Ren such pleasure to do for her. Tonight Ren had regaled her for the ten minutes she stayed with the incident with the barrel and, as always, Velda inwardly marvelled at

– and was somewhat in awe of – how the tiny woman always chose to see the humorous side of such wicked happenings. She never wallowed in self pity over her situation but, regardless, deep down, Velda was well aware that such incidents greatly upset Ren and if she did shed a tear over them it was always done in private behind her closed van door.

A few minutes after Ren had left, Glenda Kitchen had stopped by to ask Velda for a quick tarot card reading. It was something she did quite frequently, as she was desperate to learn that her domineering bully of a husband, one of the dozen labourers Grundy's employed to do the heavier types of work and also help drive rides from place to place, would meet someone else or die. Either way, to leave her and their five children free of his tyranny to live in peace. Despite Velda being very much in sympathy with her plight and feeling very helpless as there was nothing she could do about it personally and wanted therefore to give Glenda some good news, unfortunately, the cards – as usual – showed that nothing in her life was set to change drastically in the near future. All Velda could offer Glenda was her own belief that, sooner or later, everyone got their just deserts so she should have patience until her errant husband got his. Glenda left Velda no happier than when she had arrived. After a couple of dogs walkers had stopped and swapped a few moments of pleasantries with her and another near neighbour called on the cadge for a cup of sugar, her last visitor of the evening was Sam Grundy. She had been expecting him as he always called by on a dry evening after having supper with his family before he retired to his own living van, knowing he'd find her in her usual spot.

Easing his ageing body down into the empty wicker chair, resting his walking stick against the side, he smiled at her warmly and asked her, 'How goes it, gel?'

She smiled. 'It goes well, thank you. Made enough tonight to keep me in bread and marge for the rest of the week.'

As he helped himself to a large tipple from the whiskey bottle, knowing he didn't need to ask as Velda purposely put it out for him just in case he fancied one should he call upon her, he chuckled. He knew from the steady queue of customers he'd seen at her tent that evening on his rounds that she'd made herself enough tonight to pay for all her groceries for three days at least. 'We had not a bad night too but then the first and last nights are always the best, profit-wise.' Taking a sip of his drink, for a moment savouring the taste and the warming sensation as it hit the back of his throat, he then looked up at the sky. 'Likely we'll have a frost tonight. Got plenty of coal in to keep yerself warm?'

She knew that this was his way of offering to help her if she hadn't. She nodded. 'Ren came by earlier and filled up my coal and water buckets.'

'She's a good gel is Ren.' Then he scowled darkly and said gruffly, 'I heard what happened to her earlier. Bloody toe-rags. Good job I wasn't around or I'd have seen 'em off with a few whacks of me stick.'

Velda stifled a chuckle. Had it been four or five

years ago it would have been with his fists, she knew. She surreptitiously glanced him over. He might be knocking seventy and somewhat debilitated by arthritis but, in her eyes, he was still a fine figure of a man. She liked men that were strong-minded, weren't afraid to stand up for themselves and those they cared for – any underdog, in fact, faced with adversity – and that had a bit of a wicked sense of humour, but still had a compassionate, caring side to their nature. To her, Big Sam Grundy was just that kind of man. She had liked him the first time she had met him thirty years ago when she had turned up at the fair in the town they were playing in at the time, enquiring after a pitch for her fortune-telling tent. He'd told her in his gruff, matter-of-fact way that they'd never had a clairvoyant travel with them in all the fair's history as it was more of a circus or seaside attraction and, to make matters worse for her, she was an outsider. She had done her best to persuade him that she would prove an asset to the fair and she had been kept on tenterhooks for several long moments as he had hummed and hawed over the matter. She had been overjoyed that his open-mindedness had forced him into at least giving her a try.

From the start, her tent was the most popular, visited mainly by women. Never in all her thirty years with Grundy's, even during lean times, had she not been able to afford her rent. The war years were hard for her, as they were for the rest of the community when fairgrounds were forced to close, but she had kept her head just about above water plying her trade in several seaside towns along the south coast. She had been as relieved and delighted as the rest when word arrived to her that Grundy's was reuniting. Over the years, as she had gotten to know Sam well, her liking for him had grown and eventually turned to love on her part. Futile love though, as he was extremely happy married to his beloved Nell. Velda had liked Nell, a good and solid woman she thought her just like her husband, and her and Velda had got on well together. But now Nell had passed these last five years and, although Sam would never completely get over his loss, he had come to terms with it. Along with that, Velda had recently become astutely aware, by the whole way Sam acted when with her, that he was developing feelings far deeper than just friendship for her and that it was only a matter of time before he got the courage to approach her over it.

This state of affairs should have been a dream come true for Velda, that finally the man she had secretly admired so deeply for nearly half her life could eventually be hers. That the pair of them might spend what days they had left to them together, caring for each other, sharing life's up and downs. But, in fairness to Sam, Velda had no choice but to nip this fledging love he was developing for her in the bud before it went any further. She had to blatantly lie to him in a way that wouldn't cause damage to their friendship, something that was very precious to her. She must pretend that she wasn't interested in a relationship – not just with him but with any man – to save him from the pain and humiliation of her rejection.

Velda had a secret so shocking that she could never expect any woman, let alone any man, to either understand or accept. Should it ever come to light she knew it would see her immediately expelled from the confines of the small community she had come to consider her family. She felt so safe amongst them all that to face a solitary life travelling the roads alone was, to her, a fate worse than death.

Sam had grown quiet and she instinctively sensed that he had something on his mind that he wanted to talk over with her. Under normal circumstances she would have encouraged him, as she would anyone who seemed in need of a listening ear, to open up. And, if encouraged by them, she might offer her advice on the matter. But she greatly feared that the topic that Sam had on his mind tonight was the one she did not want him to discuss with her so, in an effort to stop him, in order to give her chance to plan how to let him know that she wasn't interested in taking their friendship any further without hurting his feelings and damaging to their friendship, she forced a yawn and said, 'Oh, forgive me, Sam. I think I might call it a night, if you don't mind. I'm really tired tonight.'

A surge of disappointment filled him. Since Nell had died, weather permitting, he had fallen into a routine of calling to see Velda for a nightcap and chat before he went to bed. Until a few months ago all he had wanted to do during these visits was talk about Nell to another woman who had known her well as he'd travelled through his varying stages of grief and eventually learned to carry on without her by his side. But recently, and with great shock to himself, he had realised that although he still missed Nell and always would, these nightly visits to Velda were no longer for him to reminisce over his life with his late wife. They were to spend time with Velda herself because, quite simply, as he had come to know her more intimately as a person, he had fallen in love with her and now he wanted to be far more than just her friend. It was apparent to him that Velda liked him, enjoyed his company; she never discouraged his visits or seemed in any hurry to see him go and they shared so many likes and dislikes. He saw no reason that his proposal to her would insult her in any way. How his family would react to him taking up with another woman he wasn't sure but, as far as he was concerned, they could like it or lump it. Nell had left a huge void in his life and if ever another woman could fill at least three-quarters of it, that woman was Velda. Although she might never have married and, as far as he knew, had never had a relationship in all the thirty years he had known her, there was still the possibility that some other man could suddenly materialise and snatch her away from him and that he didn't want to risk. After giving himself numerous headaches trying to come up with a way to approach Velda with his proposal of stepping up their relationship in some romantic setting or other, it had hit him that there was no more romantic setting than when the both of them were sitting together late in the evening under the stars as they were now. As desperate though as he was to begin a new future with Velda, a more pressing problem needed to be resolved first, and that was the future of the fair once he died. That was what he in fact wanted to discuss with her tonight, get her wise advice on, help him decide what was best for him to do. And then, with that matter satisfactorily resolved, he would be free to concentrate all his efforts on wooing this very dear woman sitting next to him.

He leaned forward and clasped his hands together, then looked over at her with a troubled look in his eyes. 'Could you just spare me a few minutes? I've a problem, you see, a big one to me that I could really do with a bit of help on?'

She momentarily froze. The Sam Grundys of this world were men who saw it weak to ask others for help, therefore they only seemed to when desperate. How could she call herself his friend if she turned him away, no matter how frightened she was of the subject matter he wanted to talk to her about. Subconsciously she reached over for the bottle of whiskey, poured herself a good measure of it into her empty tea cup, lifted it to her lips and took a large gulp by way of affording her some Dutch courage to help her deal with the awkward situation she feared she might be finding herself in. Then she spoke encouragingly to him. 'Just what is it that's so troubling for you, Sam?' Then, filled with trepidation, she steeled herself to hear words she really didn't want to and, at this moment, had no idea how to respond to whilst keeping intact the close friendship they shared.

He took a drink of his own whiskey before beginning, 'Well it's like this, you see, Velda. I'm sure over the years you've been with us you've learned some of our showmen's ways and traditions.'

She had, and there were some very wise ones but also some that seemed totally mystifying to her. Still, no specific tradition over how a man asked a woman to become on more intimate terms with him jumped to mind. As far as she was aware, in all cultures when a man fancied a woman, he simply asked her to accompany him out for dinner or suchlike by way of making his feelings known. She said cautiously, 'I've, er, learned a few, yes.'

'Well I don't know whether this is one of them but when a ringmaster dies, his eldest son inherits the business, less bequests to any younger sons and other family members and friends.'

She was confused. What did bequests have to do with telling a woman you have romantic feelings for her? Then it hit her and tremendous relief followed. It hadn't. At some time in the not-too-distant future she knew Sam would broach her over their relationship but not tonight, thank goodness, as it seemed a problem over his last will and testament was taking precedence. Heaving a sigh of relief she smiled at him and responded, 'Yes, I did know that.' She then eyed him shrewdly. 'Are you having doubts about leaving the fair in Sonny's hands when the good lord comes to collect you?'

'That's exactly it. You're a very perceptive woman, Velda.'

She laughed, one of her deep, throaty chuckles. 'Couldn't do my job if I wasn't, Sam.'

He laughed along with her. 'No, course not.' He then grew serious again. 'I am very worried about handing the business over to Sonny when it's my time to go.'

'You don't think he's up to the job?'

He shook his head, sadly. 'I don't think he's got the right way about him.' He sighed. 'I love my son, can't fault that he does his bit as much as the rest of us towards keeping the business running, but he's very...' He paused, trying to find the right words. 'It's hard for me to describe ... but ... well ... he doesn't get on with people in the way a ringmaster should, in my book. The people who work for us look to you as their leader, someone who'll keep them safe, there to turn to to help sort their problems out. You have to be fair but tough and that's not easy to be sometimes when someone is crying on your shoulder after you to help them out of a terrible predicament when, deep down, you suspect they're exaggerating their situation or just blatantly lying about it and taking you for a mug. When I was younger and had just two stalls which I rented pitches for at other travelling fairs, I worked for some decent types but also some downright bullies. It was their way or no way. If you had a problem, you sorted it out yourself. They weren't interested. All they cared about was you paying their rent. I fear Sonny is very much like those ringmasters. He never used to be like he is now though.' He looked at her enquiringly. 'You must remember, Velda, when you first joined us, that Sonny was such a different young man then?'

She nodded. 'I do. Very helpful and pleasant he

was, the same as Solly. Both asked you if you needed any help with anything before you had to ask them. Always getting up to a bit of mischief, weren't they, only silly pranks though. It was never anything at all malicious. Yes, Sonny was a lovely lad back then, there's no denying that.'

Sam was smiling at the happy memories of his eldest son that Velda was conjuring up in him but then his smile faded and he sighed again. 'But then, for God knows what reason me or Nell could ever get to the bottom of, he changed.'

She nodded again. 'I remember. All of a sudden it was, wasn't it. Like someone had flicked a switch. Nell talked to me about it often. The change in him was so drastic and it worried her sick. She couldn't understand it and neither could I. I did the cards for her, read her palm, consulted my crystal ball, but all they came up with was that she had trouble with a child. It wasn't *her* cards or palms I needed to read though to get to the bottom of it, it was Sonny's himself but there was no approaching him for a sitting, the mood he was in. And, after a while, Nell gave up asking him because she knew what the answer would be.'

Sam sighed. 'It came as such a relief to me and Nell when Sonny announced he wanted his own van which we gladly helped him buy. Well, we paid for all of it, same as we had for Joshua and Solly when the time came for them to leave home. That way he could mooch around inside like a bear with a sore head and we'd no longer have to put up with it. Him and Solly used to be such good friends but they became like strangers to each other and it was all Sonny's doing. It was like he suddenly deeply resented his brother, but for what, we could never work out. We thought ... hoped ... he'd grow out of it, go back to being the old Sonny we all loved and missed, but he never did.'

'And your worry is that Grundy's will fall apart when Sonny becomes ringmaster.' It wasn't a question but a statement.

He slowly nodded, his face screwed up with worry. 'It certainly won't be the happy community it is now, that I am sure of. Part of a ringmaster's job is to keep the council officials, landowners and local police on our side ... there's a diplomatic way of dealing and negotiating with them or they have the power to refuse us opening in their town or village despite our age-old charter rights. Sonny hasn't got a diplomatic bone in his body, whereas...' His voice trailed off and he lifted his glass and took a large swallow.

Thoughtfully Velda watched him then take out his pipe, tap out the old ash in the barrel, refill it then light it with a tarnished silver petrol lighter, a present from his late wife on their first wedding anniversary. Once he was puffing on it she said to him knowingly, 'You were going to say ... whereas Solly is everything a ringmaster should be in your eyes.'

He looked at her for a moment before he admitted, 'Yes, I was.'

'You could leave it between them in equal shares?'

'That's a possibility I have thought of but that could cause problems if they can't come to an agreement over decisions needing making and the fair could suffer as a result.'

She leaned over and patted his hand. 'So then that's your answer. Leave the business in Solly's capable hands.'

His face screwed in anguish. 'But tradition dictates I leave it to my eldest son.'

She shrugged her meaty shoulders. 'Traditions can be broken if they aren't right for the occasion. It's tradition for outsiders like me to eat turkey on Christmas Day but when I was little my mam couldn't afford one, chicken neither, so we had sausages. Several years in a row, in fact, until our finances improved and nothing bad happened; we never had a worse year than the one previous or any of us struck down with the plague and died.'

'I can appreciate what you're saying, Velda, but expecting turkey for dinner and getting sausages can't be compared to expecting to inherit a fair but actually getting a ride, along with the blow that his father favoured his younger brother over him.'

She shrugged. 'I grant you it can't be compared but I was still terribly disappointed and it's one I had to get over, same as Sonny will if you decide to favour Solly over him as your heir. Look, Sam, he won't like it, that's for certain, but he'll have to appreciate the reasons why you decided to do what you did and accept it. No court of law will overturn a will unless there's a damned good reason, like there's a doubt you were sound of mind when you wrote it. If Sonny tried that then everyone here, including me, will vouch that you might be getting old and crotchety but there's nothing wrong with that sharp mind of yours.' She paused to think for a moment before she offered, 'If you do decide to leave the fair to Solly then you could always write Sonny a letter of explanation as to why you have done what you have.'

He thought about that for a moment. 'Yes, I could. Coward's way out though it would be.' Then the red of embarrassment tinged his aged face. 'But, er...'

She immediately realised what he was going to say and cut him short. 'I would be delighted to help you write it.' Sam, like many showmen, had never had any schooling as such so could not read and write well enough to compose a letter.

He shot her a quick smile of gratitude.

'Anyway, there's no rush over this, Sam. I mean, it's not like you've been given a death sentence by the doctor, told you've only days to live. It's my opinion that you've still got a good twenty years left in you yet. So take your time and think carefully how you want to leave matters when your time finally comes and, if you still want me to help you write that letter, I'm always happy to oblige.'

He didn't want to take his time over this matter, wanted it resolved so he could concentrate all his efforts on getting his personal life in a much happier state. He looked at her searchingly. 'You're a wonderful woman, Velda.'

She waved a dismissive hand at him. 'Ged away with yer. Just being a good friend to a good friend, that's all.' Then fearing Sam might just decide now was the time to divulge his feelings for her, she downed the remains of the whiskey in her teacup, shuddering as the fiery liquid hit the back of her throat, then eased her comely body out of her chair. 'I really need my beauty sleep now, Sam.'

He then also downed the remains of his drink in his own glass, grabbed his walking stick and stood up, saying, 'Fine weather permitting, I'll see you tomorrow night, then, eh?'

She smiled and nodded. 'I'll have your nightcap ready for you.' *And by then hopefully the right words ready to tactfully refuse your advances towards me.*

A mile or so away from the fair site, standing at the bar of one of the town's better class of hotels, Sonny, looking forward to an evening of the sort he liked to enjoy, took a sip of his large gin and tonic. His preferred drink was best bitter but that was what Sonny the fairground worker drank and tonight he was Raymond Goodman, successful businessman, who wouldn't dream of partaking of such a common working man's beverage and especially in such surroundings as he was in at the moment. He was surreptitiously looking around for a likely candidate to aid him in making his evening a successful one for him, funded by the amount he had creamed off the top of the ride money and his share of the gaff lads' tapping of the punters. Plus what was also left from his winnings from an illegal game of poker he'd managed to get himself a seat at.

Had his father or anyone close to him walked into the hotel bar they would have had to look at him at least three times before they recognised the man at the bar to actually be Sonny. Gone was the fairground worker of earlier, in black trousers, white shirt – the sleeves of which were rolled up to his elbows – black string tie kept together with an American-style silver-plated bull's head tie fastener, hair slicked up in a trendy quiff, sporting a five o'clock shadow and a permanent roll-up hanging from the corner of his lips. Now he looked very much a man of means, wearing a smart wide-shouldered, broad-lapelled, double-breasted dark blue suit under a long mohair camel-coloured coat, quality leather shoes, hair parted down the side and smoothed neatly with hair oil, clean-shaven chin, aftershave by Chanel, a gold cigarette lighter case and crocodile-skin wallet holding his illicitly gained money.

As he sipped on his drink, his good mood began to darken. This hotel bar was as unproductive as the last one he'd tried when all the clientele seemed to be elderly couples or old military types, one or two tartily dressed women obviously prostitutes on the prowl for clients, all of whom would never frequent the sort of place he was after help getting into. Then his spirits lifted as he spotted a man of around his own age, dressed similarly to himself, confidently weaving his way through the tables towards the bar. If there was any action of the sort he was after in this town then, to Sonny's expert eye, this was the sort of man who would introduce him into it. He waited while the man ordered his drink, then struck up a casual conversation with him.

Putting on his perfected refined accent he said, 'I'm a visitor to this town, here on business, any idea where to go for a bit of fun?' He offered the man his hand. 'Raymond Goodman. Ray.

Pleased to meet you.'

Taking a sip of his rum and black, the man accepted his hand and they shook. 'Charles Hillman. Charley. Good to meet you too. So what sort of business are you in?'

'Cars. Buying and selling. Not your old bangers, mind. High-class models is all I deal in. Have you heard of Goodman Elite Cars? I've several garages across the country, mainly around the London area. I'm looking to expand up north and am here for the week to check out a few properties.'

The man looked thoughtfully at his swarthy companion. 'Goodman Elite Cars?' he mused. 'Yes ... yes ... I think I have heard of your firm. I've friends in London and I think they bought a car off you a while back.'

Sonny thought, *No they didn't, because the firm doesn't actually exist.* He said, 'Well maybe it's time they renewed and came back to see what I can do for them. Mention it to them the next time you see them. What line are you in yourself?'

He looked a little cagey at that question. 'Oh, this and that to do with finance, mostly business insurance.'

'Well, when I'm looking to renew any of my business policies I'll have to give you a call. Have you a card?'

Charley fished in his inside pocket and pulled out one which he handed to Sonny, who put it in his own inside pocket, then asked him, 'Have you one in case I'm ever in the market for a decent jalopy myself in the future?'

Sonny fished around in his pockets and, of course, never found one because he hadn't got any. 'Ah, seems I've left them in my hotel room. Same again?'

'Yeah, don't mind, thanks.'

Their drinks refreshed from a well-stocked bar by the black-and-white-attired, polite bartender, Sonny prompted, 'So ... what has this town got to offer fun wise or is this it?' He looked disdainfully around.

'Depends what kind of fun you're after, exactly. There're a couple of dance halls where most of the youngsters go, a folk club, skiffle one too, or there's a strip joint if that's more to your taste.'

He eyed the man meaningfully. 'Oh, I was thinking of somewhere a little more higher end.'

He looked Sonny over before he offered, 'If you've the money ... and I ain't talking loose change here ... I might be able to swing you entry into one I am off to myself after I've finished my drink.'

'I've the money,' Sonny assured him.

Charley downed his drink. 'Then let's go.'

From the outside the place looked similar to other clubs Sonny had gotten himself inside of; it was in the basement of the building, housed in an old and rundown part of town. They were met at the door by a bruiser type who looked him over suspiciously before his companion vouched for him, then let them through a heavy security door into a small, dingy anteroom. As soon as they passed through another door, that was where all similarities ended. The room was at least twice the size of any of the other clubs Sonny had been to before and the decor far more opulent, from the sparkling chandeliers hanging from the ceiling, red-and-cream flocked and Regency-striped wallpaper lining the walls to the gilt chairs at the matching tables. The bar was manned by white-shirted, black-trousered barmen, drinks and meals served by scantily dressed pretty women with model-type figures. Sonny didn't like to guess the price of the drinks or food and worried now that he'd enough in his wallet to cover the cost of an evening here as he'd already parted with five pounds to get in. Sitting at one end of the bar on high seats were four women who, it was apparent to Sonny, were high-class call girls. A couple of equally scantily dressed usherettes were weaving through tables selling expensive brands of cigarettes and cigars from trays strapped around their necks. Three brutish-looking, suited men were stationed around the large room ready to deal with any trouble. There were thirty or so tables, several of which were filled with parties of wealthily dressed twenty- to late thirty-somethings. It was evident by their demeanour that the price of the food and drinks were of no consequence to them ... would most likely be paid for by their affluent fathers. Other tables had obviously married couples seated at them as they were barely speaking to each other, and there were other tables with older men and far younger women who were definitely not their daughters. A slinky-looking platinum blonde, dressed in a long figure-hugging sparkling evening dress was belting out a popular song, accompanied by a five-piece band on a stage at the back of the room. The singer and musicians were all very accomplished. There was a wooden-floored space before it for dancing, which several couples were taking advantage of. Charley had already informed Sonny that in another room there was a mini casino should he fancy a gamble and also in another room a strip show.

A man sitting at one of the tables caught Sonny's eye. Others were dancing attendance on him. He was a small, rotund, ugly-looking gnome-type man of obvious foreign origin; Greek, Turkish or a mixture of both – it was hard to tell – dressed immaculately. He was accompanied by a young, stunning-looking woman in a very becoming evening gown, the type of woman that normally wouldn't have given the man she was with the time of day had he not had money, judging by the wad he'd just pulled out of his pocket and peeled a few notes off to give to one of those pandering to him. It became apparent that this man was the owner of the club.

A sense of exhilaration filled Sonny then as it hit him just what kind of business he wanted to build himself with the proceeds of the sale of the funfair. A high-class club such as this was one that attracted the sort of clientele who didn't need to worry one iota how much they spent on their leisure time. But he wasn't going to stop at just having one club, he was going to have a string of them; one in every major town and city up and down the country. What better revenge would that be for him, knowing that the cream of British society were all kowtowing to him in order for them to be members of his clubs. And wouldn't he have a field day letting it be known that the man they were having to ingratiate themselves with was just a lowly fairground worker from a group of people their sort despised. When Belinda saw just what sort of life she had thrown away when she had so callously turned down his offer to marry her, wouldn't she then be spending the rest of her life deeply regretting it?

As he followed an usherette to a table with Charley, Sonny inwardly smiled to himself. He wondered if all these outsiders would be so accepting of him being amongst them should they learn the truth of his heritage, how he lived and worked. No matter how smart he looked, how much money he had in his pocket, they would have him unceremoniously thrown out before he could blink and warned never to return or risk physical harm. But now he knew what line of business he wanted to be in, in the not-too-distant future, that would no longer be the case. That day couldn't come quick enough for Sonny but, until then, the revenge he was reaping for outsiders' misguided opinions of showmen that had resulted in the loss of the only woman he had ever loved and wanted to spend the rest of his life with, would continue to be reaped in secret.

The audience were clapping after the singer on-stage had just finished a number when Charley leaned over and told Sonny he was going to the casino and was Sonny going to join him? He declined, as he'd a better offer. He'd caught the eye of a very attractive woman. He had noticed her immediately as he had first arrived at the club, sitting at a table amongst a party of her friends looking quite bored. It was apparent that the male companion sitting next to her was failing in his attempts to ingratiate himself with her; but her eyes had immediately sparked with interest when they had settled on Sonny, which they were still doing now. She was definitely giving him an invitation and it wasn't to have tea and cake with her. Was a quick exit out of the tradesman entrance of a hotel on the cards for him tonight, leaving her to settle the bill? But then she wasn't the only woman whose attention he'd attracted. The other woman was older than him, middle forties round-about, and in good shape for her age. She was sitting at a table with a man he had seen her dancing with when he had first arrived. The way they were together he was obviously her husband, who she would be leaving with at the end of the night. Evidently her husband was lacking somewhat to have his wife looking elsewhere for some excitement in her life. It would be very gentlemanly of him to give it to her, wouldn't it! He mused over matters for a moment, then decided he would have the older woman first, then have himself some fun in the casino and, after, watch the strip show for a while. Then he would make the younger woman aware this was her lucky night ... but not so lucky when she discovered he'd slunk away from the hotel room whilst she was asleep and left her to settle the bill!

He shot the older woman a look by way of telling her that her invitation was accepted and to indicate to him where she wanted them to meet.

Chapter Five

The next morning at just after eleven, wearing old brown overalls caked in grease and rubbing dirty hands on a grubby piece of cloth, Solly was making his way back to his living van for a wash, change of clothes and to have his dinner after overseeing the morning maintenance checks of all the rides Grundy's owned personally. He'd also been lending a hand to several other ride owners who had need of it to ensure all were safe for the afternoon opening at two o'clock, when he spotted a figure skulking around the fairfolks' private residence area; Solly instantly recognised the figure as Archie Cox. As he went over, he steeled himself for the confrontation he knew was to come.

Cox had just righted himself after fruitlessly crouching down to search under a van when Solly joined him, trying to keep his utter distaste for this bully of a man from outwardly showing. The man looked filthier and smelt far more disgusting than he had yesterday evening, if that was possible. He spoke evenly. 'The general public aren't allowed in the fair until opening time at two and this area is off-limits. You have to leave.'

Cox grunted. 'Ain't doing no 'arm. Just looking for me son.'

'We're closed so he won't be here, will he.'

Cox glared at him darkly. 'I can see that, you

ignorant gyppo. He didn't come home last night and the last place he wa' seen was coming in here yest'day evening at about six.'

Solly stared stonily back at him, squashing down a surge of anger for him assuming what the majority of outsiders did; that showmen and gypsies were one and the same when, in fact, they were an entirely separate society of people with their own rules, regulations and traditions. He knew he would be wasting his time trying to educate this uncouth man, though. 'We have a thorough check around after we close for runaways or vagrants thinking they can use any of the rides as a place to sleep and we make them leave so, if your son was hanging around after closing, he'll be long gone now.'

Cox's lip curled in a sardonic smirk. 'The wily little bugger might have sneaked back when you wa' all asleep.'

Solly shook his head. 'He might have tried but our workers have a dozen or so dogs between them. Just one of them sensing an intruder anywhere on the site would have woken all of us up. The dogs would have all been let loose and if your son was here they'd have soon had him running, believe me.' He then narrowed his eyes and looked at Cox coldly. 'If...' He just stopped himself in time from saying 'Col' as then Cox would question just how it was that Solly knew his son's name, not that Colin was actually his son anyway. '...your son has any sense, he'd be miles away from you by now, somewhere you'll never find him.'

Cox looked at him quizzically for a moment

until a memory struck, then he stabbed a dirty finger at Solly and angrily blared, 'You're the bastard that stopped me chastising me son last night for disobeying me and gave him the chance to give me the slip.'

Solly pushed his face into Cox's, recoiling at the foul smell of his breath and furiously hissed, 'You're lucky I didn't knock you into kingdom come for what I found you doing to that boy.' He grimaced disgustedly at the man. 'Your type doesn't deserve to be fathers.' Not being able to suffer his bad breath any longer, he took a couple of steps away from Cox before telling him, 'Me and my maintenance crew have been all over the place this morning checking the safety of the rides and if your lad had managed to escape the notice of the dogs, which is doubtful anyway, we'd have found him. You're wasting your time looking for him here. Now I'll ask you politely again to leave.'

Cox was glaring at him, clenching and unclenching his fists, desperate to lay into Solly, seeing him as being ultimately responsible for his loss of his lucrative asset in Colin. But, whereas he might have the upper hand with weaker types than himself, from his experience of last evening he was no match for this muscular man. He still wasn't about to leave until he was absolutely convinced that he was not lying and Col was, after all, sheltering here. He scowled menacingly at Solly. 'I know your fucking game. You're hiding him yerself. In your van now, is he? Having a cup of tea? Plan to use him fer cheap labour or as part of yer gang when you go out on the rob, eh? He's a good little tea leaf is Col and we all know what thieves you gyppos are. The fair is just your cover. Earn most of yer living robbing off good folks like me. Anyway, if yer ain't hiding him inside your van you'll have no objection to me having a look, will yer?'

Solly's temper exploded to fever pitch then and how he managed to control it was all credit to himself. Cox had made it clear that he wasn't going to leave until he was absolutely convinced they were not hiding Col and, in order to get rid of him once and for all, he had no choice but to do what he had asked and pray he wasn't that vigilant. He walked over to his own van, stood at the bottom of the steps and said, 'Be my guest and search my home.'

Cox went over, climbed the steps and walked inside.

Gem was in the kitchen attending to pans bubbling on the small cast-iron stove, humming away to a popular tune being played by Billy Cotton and his Showmen over the crystal wireless set. She looked shocked at the dishevelled stranger that stepped in, wrinkling her nose at the nasty smell emanating off him. Turning down the sound on the wireless, she went to demand who he was when Sonny appeared and told her.

'This man is looking for his son and has got it into his head we've kidnapped him and propose to use him as cheap labour and as a member of our gang when we go out thieving.' He held up his hand to stop her responding and said meaningfully, 'We've nothing to hide have we, love, so let the man nose around all he likes.' He then addressed Cox, 'I'll accompany you on your search as we don't want to find any of our valuables gone when you leave.'

Cox inwardly fumed as his intention had been to swipe anything that he viewed would make him a few pennies, something he was desperately short of now he'd lost the help of his sidekick to line his pockets. He snorted nastily. 'Huh! A junk shop sells better stuff than the crap you have in here.' He then rudely pushed past Solly and began to nose around.

Although Gem was inwardly panicking that although the place they were secreting Col inside might have escaped the eagle eyes of a bully of a husband on the search for a runaway wife, that didn't mean to say it would the beady ones of Archie Cox, she appeared to be unconcerned about the search and continued preparing their meal.

It didn't take Cox long to hunt inside and under places in the van that might conceal a small boy and there was one instance when Solly held his breath whilst Cox took more of an interest in one particular place than he would have liked him to but, thankfully, Cox's quest to find Col proved fruitless.

Back by the outside door, Solly said to him in no uncertain terms, 'Now we've proved we aren't hiding your son, I want you out of my home and off the site. If I see your face around here again I warn you you'll be getting the same treatment from me that I caught you dishing out to your boy last night. Is that clear?'

Cox went to respond in his usual offensive manner but obviously thought better of it and hurriedly scuttled out.

Solly stood on the doorstep and watched him go before he returned back into the kitchen area where both him and Gem let out great exhales of relief.

It was Gem who spoke first. 'What a thoroughly unpleasant man. I could tell by his face that he took your threat to him seriously so I think we can safely say we've seen the last of him. Let's go and tell Col the good news.'

They went along the narrow corridor off the living area, one side of which was their sons' shared bunkroom, the other the tiny washroom, pulled aside a floor-to-ceiling curtain and entered their bedroom together. The bed itself filled three-quarters of the space at the back under the deep-silled leaded bow window. At the bottom of the bed on one side was a curtained-off space for hanging up clothes and opposite a narrow long-shelved cupboard, with a long mirror on the door, held underwear, woollen wear, shoes and such-like. A foot or so below the bowed ceiling ran a continuous shelf which held all sorts of Solly and Gem's personal possessions. Gem took off the bedclothes and piled them on top of a row of their shoes in the makeshift hanging wardrobe, then together they pulled off the thickly filled feather mattress and piled it in a heap behind them. This left them both looking into the empty box base of the bed.

To the untrained eye the base of the box appeared to be the bottom of the van itself. At the front in the right-hand corner though was a tiny knob of wood which, using a thumb and index finger and pulled on, lifted up to reveal another box-type space underneath, roughly four feet wide by five feet long, originally created by the maker of the caravan as storage space, which is what Gem and Solly usually used it for. But on occasion, as with the case of Kathy Folds desperately trying to escape her violent husband and now with Col from the clutches of the bully Archie Cox, it could conceal a body. For the person hiding inside, it was cramped, uncomfortable and claustrophobic, time crawling by in the pitch black, apart from the light from a torch whilst the battery lasted. But to them it was more than worth enduring the suffering to escape their miserable lives at the hands of their persecutors.

Col's terrified face greeted them, worried that Cox had taken control of them somehow and were forcing them to reveal his whereabouts. Col was blinded for a moment as light flooded into the box but, as soon as his eyes accustomed themselves to it, he saw Solly and Gem smiling down at him and he visibly relaxed, heaving a huge sigh of relief.

Extending a hand to aid Col out, Solly told him, 'I suspect you won't be sorry to say goodbye to our hidey-hole, Col.'

Standing upright now, he looked at them blankly for a moment before he hesitantly ventured, 'Does that mean he's ... he's gone for good? I really won't ever see him again? When I heard the noise of the mattress being taken off and then his voice I was so frightened he was going to find me I daren't breathe. Any second I expected the lid to lift up and see his face ... and ... and ... him force me to go back with him.' With great pleasure Gem laid a reassuring hand on his bony arm and emphatically assured him, 'You won't ever have to see that man again, Col. Not after Solly warned him what would happen if he ever caught him nosing around our fair again.'

A great flood of tears filled Col's eyes and gushed down his face. He leapt on Solly and hugged him crushingly, blubbering. 'Oh, thank you. Thank you. Thank you, thank you. Oh, thank...'

'I think we've got the message,' laughed Solly as he prised Col off him.

'Although you don't have to hide inside the hole any longer it might be wise to stay out of sight until we move on Sunday morning, just as a precaution in case Cox didn't believe us. He might lurk outside somewhere, hoping to catch us out. After the fair closes tonight, we'll sneak you over to Iris and Bert. They're desperate to meet you and welcome you into their family. Every time I see either of them they want to know how you are and if you're looking forward to coming to them as much as they are. Iris has got your bed all ready and has sorted out some clothes for you. I'm going to give her some of my boys' clothes for you too.'

Col was too choked to speak.

Chapter Six

A while later, having fed her family and cleared up afterwards, leaving Col happily sitting on the sofa wading his way through a pile of her sons' old childhood comics they'd refused to part with, Gem was just leaving the van to go over to the helter-skelter when she frowned, perplexed to see a policeman entering the living van area. Immediately, a great worry filled her. A visit from such officials usually meant they were in trouble of some sort. What they could be in trouble for, she had no idea though. As far as she knew, they'd had no problems of any sort at the fair during this annual visit here so she just hoped that one of the fairfolk hadn't caused any bother while they'd ventured out into the wider community. If serious enough, the fair could be ordered to pack up and leave and their revenue for the rest of the week would be lost to them all. Then she noticed that trailing subduedly behind the policeman were sixteen fairfolk children, ages ranging from five to thirteen, that had been seen off to school by their individual parents earlier that morning.

Confusion written all over her face, she bounded down the van steps and rushed over to meet the policeman.

Before she could ask him why he was here with the children he asked, 'These yours?'

'Well not personally, officer, but they all belong to fairfolk here. Why are you here with them when they should be in school?'

He was a middle-aged, portly man with a large walrus moustache and bushy eyebrows. Although he was acting stern, Gem couldn't fail to notice a twinkle of amusement in his hazel eyes. He breathed deeply in, then puffed out his barrel chest before he responded, 'Should be but that's not where I found them.'

All the children were looking guilty, shuffling uncomfortably. She demanded of them, 'And just where did this nice policeman find you all?'

They all looked at each other. It was the eldest, Tommy Dawson, whose father worked for Grundy's as an all-rounder – labourer, driver and helping to man the rides, his mother helping out also wherever needed at the time – that finally elected himself as spokesperson. He was a tall, well-made boy with a shock of jet-black hair well overdue for a cut. He raised his chin in the air and said in a defiant manner, 'Playing on the bomb site the other side of the canal.'

This was not the first time the children had been caught playing truant. Secretly she couldn't blame them as she knew that attending a different school every week during term times, most times, was a very unpleasant ordeal. Except for the isolated occasion when they had a compassionate teacher that encouraged the rest of the class to be accepting towards them and at least tried to actually take the time to teach them something. She heaved a sigh and shook her head at them before saying to the policeman, 'I'm so sorry, officer, the children know they're not supposed to leave the school without permission. I promise this won't happen again.' The promise was a hollow one; whilst certain teachers perceived fairground children as they did, the children would retaliate against their unwarranted treatment by disassociating themselves from it.

He took her aside, his eyes twinkling humorously. 'Can't say as I blame them wagging school. I hated it too and got a thick ear many times from my parents for being caught doing it. One of the local women reported them to us. She told me she hated to spoil their fun and, believe me, they certainly were having that when I arrived to round them up, but she was worried they might hurt themselves as the site is dangerous. It's been cordoned off by wire fencing but some bright spark cut a hole in the fence. I'm always being called to herd local kids off from playing on it.'

Gem eyed him, surprised. It was a rare occasion for an outsider to show compassion towards fairfolk, not seeing them as the dregs of the earth. 'Please thank the lady for me.' Then she asked him worriedly 'Are the children in trouble?'

He smiled kindly at her. 'Not this time but if I catch them again...'

'You won't, officer,' she assured him.

He looked towards the main fairground. 'I'm looking forward to tonight. Bringing my wife and six-year-old granddaughter along. It's her first visit to the fair and she's so excited.'

'In that case I'm on the House of Fun tonight so I'll make sure you all get a free pass. My way of thanking you for being so understanding about the kids.'

He accepted her gesture with great pleasure and, after reiterating his warning to behave themselves to the children, he made his leave.

With hands on hips she sighed with frustration as she scanned them, still looking guilty. But, before she could say anything, Tommy spoke up. 'Please don't send us back ter that school, Mrs Grundy. It's 'orrible, it is. The teacher don't like us, said we were dirty tykes that hadn't the brains to learn nothing and shouldn't be allowed in the school with decent kids. She told the other kids to have nothing to do with us in case they caught lice.'

Gem stared at him, horrified. 'She said what?'

'She did, Mrs Grundy, 'onest,' he declared. 'She made us all sit in the cloakroom and gave us some tatty old books. She told us if we made a sound we'd get the cane.' He put his arm protectively around a young boy standing next to him. ''Arry was so scared of that 'orrible teacher he daren't ask to go to the toilet and he wet himself.'

Gem looked down at the young lad's crotch area, appalled to see the dark stain on his grey short trousers and her heart went out to him for the embarrassment this must have caused him.

Eight-year-old Molly Adkins, whose parents owned the rifle range stall, spoke up then. The hem of her dress had partly come down; Gem assumed she had caught it on something jagged when playing on the bomb site as her mother would never have sent her to school looking anything but immaculate. She had lost one of the ribbons securing her long fair hair into two bunches, so one side was hanging down. 'At breaktime one of the older kids pinched my sandwiches and threw them on the bike shed roof. I sawed the teacher had seen him do it but she just turned around and pretended she hadn't. Tommy was mad when I told him what the boy had done and started to climb the bike shed to get them for me or I'd have had to go hungry at dinner time but the teacher sawed him and came and dragged him off and started whacking him with her stick, screaming at him he was a vandal. That's when we decided to leave.'

'It was my idea to skive off, Mrs Grundy, and I made the others come with me,' Tommy told her boldly.

Gem saw another child go to speak up then and the warning look Tommy shot him to keep his mouth shut. It was obvious to her that it wasn't Tommy who had been the instigator of them all playing truant, it was a unanimous decision, and she couldn't at all blame them. As the oldest he was taking the responsibility for it by way of protecting the others from the possible backlash from their angry parents when they found out what had transpired. She admired him for that.

Anger was bubbling away inside her. She had known all of them from the moment they'd been born and, same as any children, they all got up to mischief at some time or another and didn't always obey their parents but, on the whole, they were well-behaved and well-mannered. Had the teacher allowed them to sit in her class and given them some encouragement they could have learned a lot during their week there and even enjoyed it. Gem did appreciate how frustrating it must be for any teacher to suddenly find their class swelled by an extra dozen they'd to accommodate for a week; the time-consuming task of finding out what level of education each were at and advance that in some way. Most didn't bother, just gave them books to look through or paper to draw on to while away their time. But this particular teacher had deliberately done what she could to make their time at her school as miserable for them as she possibly could. No child deserved to be treated so appallingly and especially by a teacher whose job it was to educate, nurture and protect those under their charge, no matter their own feelings on the society those children belonged to.

It wasn't Gem's decision as the children were not her own but when she explained to them how their children had been treated, she doubted the parents would be sending them back to that school again. Nevertheless, as a member of the family the children's parents all worked for, she felt a deep responsibility for their welfare and an overwhelming need to confront the teacher over her despicable behaviour towards them.

She sent the children off to find a parent and explain to them why they were home early. Then she asked Tommy to go and find Solly and tell him she had a sudden urgent errand to go on and could he find someone to man the pay booth of the helter-skelter during her absence. She returned back into her living van to collect her outdoor coat and handbag, then set off for the local school.

The school was a one-class, one-teacher type, a remnant of bygone times when the area used to be a village a mile or so away from the town but had been swallowed up inside its boundaries when the town had slowly expanded. Like all such small schools dotted around the country, it was to be closed when the construction of a modern school was finished and all the pupils from several smaller schools surrounding it were amalgamated. Gem arrived just as the pupils were heading back into their classroom after dinner hour was over. Gem expected the teacher to be an elderly, bony, pinch-faced, humourless woman, based on her behaviour. It was the image of a formidable, spinster-type governess she had conjured up whilst reading novels and portrayed by actresses in films set in Dickensian times. Therefore she was utterly shocked, on enquiring from the caretaker of the teacher's whereabouts, to be pointed out a young, pretty, slim, fashionably dressed woman with a happy smile on her face, arms filled with books, jauntily heading down the corridor towards the classroom they were all heading into.

Gem went over to waylay her.

Looking enquiringly at the smartly dressed woman exuding an air of confidence about her, assuming she was something to do with the school board or council education department, the teacher asked politely, 'Can I help you?'

'Yes you can. You can help me understand why you treated the fairground children so despicably this morning?'

The younger woman looked at her, taken

aback. 'I beg your pardon?'

'It's not my pardon you should be begging, it's all of those children's.'

The woman said with conviction, 'I had to be firm with them as they started to cause trouble from the moment they arrived, wouldn't do as they were told. Anyway, what is it to do with you how I manage the children? I am the headmistress. Just who are you?'

Gem cut her short. 'Firm! Is that what you call making the children sit in the cloakroom by themselves and turning a blind eye to an older boy bullying one of the younger fairground girls? Her sandwiches were thrown onto a roof and when one of the fairground boys tried to get them back for her so she wouldn't go hungry at dinnertime, you personally dragged him down and thrashed him with your cane. That is more than being firm, that is pure cruelty. And I dispute that any of them were causing trouble from the moment they arrived. They have all been raised to respect adults and know what the consequences are if they're sent home for being disobedient.' Gem then shot her a look of disgust. 'You have no right to call yourself a teacher. A teacher is someone who wants to impart their knowledge to anyone who is willing to listen and to nurture and encourage that learning in them. You did none of that for those children today. You never even tried. You should be thoroughly ashamed of yourself. They might not be able to read and write as well as your pupils and that is simply because teachers like you never bother to take the time to teach them how, but the fairground children could have taught you and your pupils so much if you had encouraged them to. They could have talked about nature, all the places they have visited up and down the country, about how to navigate by the stars as their parents have showed them and so much more, but that is you and your pupils' loss. Anyway, I expect you'll be delighted to hear that those children will not be returning to suffer any more of your unjustified tyranny towards them.'

She made to turn and walk away, but the teacher stopped her by asking, 'Just why is an educated, well-bred woman like you so interested in such dirty low-lives? Are you just some do-gooder with nothing better to do?'

Gem took great delight in informing her, 'Yes, I do come from a decent family and had a good education. When I was a young girl I was as narrow-minded and bigoted as you are. But then I met a man that introduced me into a community of people I was taught were scum and it was proved to me I was so wrong to make judgements based on what others had told me. I saw for myself how hard-working these people are, just trying to earn their living in the way their ancestors have done for hundreds of years so they could look after their families the best they can, the same as the people I come from were doing and those you live amongst too. They take pride in their homes and raise their children to have good manners and morals. The only difference is that they have to travel around to make their living so don't have the benefit of having some of the modern facilities that you have at your disposal. I am no do-gooder. Those people you feel so beneath you are my people. I have been married to a showman for the last twenty years, very happily. I have never once regretted swapping the wonderful life I live, travelling through the beautiful countryside, staying in a different place every week and meeting some lovely people along the way for the drudge of a life I could have lived had I not met my husband. For the one you live, in fact, in your little rented flat or house with only other brick buildings to look at through the windows, the condition of your place dependent on whether you have a good landlord or not, trudging the same treeless streets every day and nodding a good morning to the same miserable people off to airless factories or offices, breathing in smoke-filled air. The only thing for you all to look forward to is a few days at the seaside every year if you can afford it and having yourselves a few hours of fun once a year when the travelling funfair comes to town, which I will remind you is provided for you by those people you think so little of.' She paused for a moment to take a long breath after her long tirade before she added, 'Maybe now you might take the trouble to find out first whether gossip and rumours are true, such as the ones you hear about fairfolk and their lives, before you take them for gospel. Then you won't have to face the embarrassment when you find out you were so very wrong to. Good-day.'

With that, Gem spun on her heels and stalked out, leaving the teacher gawping in stupefaction after her.

Neither woman noticed that their whole

conversation was being overheard by someone further back along the corridor, having hidden themselves in the recess of the doorway leading into the caretaker's room.

Back at the fairground the parents of the children accosted Gem as soon as she arrived back. None of them had had much schooling because of their lifestyle; most, if not all, were not able to read or write and the rest only rudimentarily, having painstakingly taught themselves enough to get them by. They all wanted better for their own children. So yet another teacher in a long line refusing to at least try to teach their offspring something and, not only that, this particular one treating them so despicably, had greatly angered them so much they were ready to form a lynch mob and tackle the teacher themselves. Gem had no doubt this would see them all being arrested for whatever offences the police could pin to them and see them jailed for a good length of time; most of the police's opinions about fairfolk mirroring that of the teacher. It took great effort to calm them all down with a promise that this situation could not go on and a solution to the children's education would have to be found. She would speak to Sam Grundy at the earliest opportunity on the matter and let them know the outcome.

She was dreading the conversation with Sam as from what she could see there was only one answer to this problem as matters stood and she didn't like the thought of it one little bit.

She spoke to Solly about it though. She was

putting the evening meal together at five that evening before they all went out at six to join the rest of the Grundy community to have all the rides and stalls fully manned for when the public would start to arrive en masse from six onwards. Jimmy and Robbie had arrived with their father and were both in the living area waiting to be called through for their meal. Jimmy was having a doze in an armchair and Robbie was looking through that day's edition of the *Daily Sketch*. Solly was sitting at the kitchen table listening to his wife rant on over the problem of the children's schooling. He too could only think of one solution and, knowing his wife as well as he did, knew it wasn't at all a palatable one for her, so was dreading her asking for his opinion on the matter.

After taking time out to visit the school, Gem was a few minutes behind serving up the evening meal. Throwing chips into a pan of hot fat on the stove which spluttered and spat, reflecting her mood, she gave them an agitated stir with a large metal spatula blackened with age whilst blurting, 'I can fully understand they all want their kids to be able to read, write and add up a simple column of figures if nothing else, but it's not fair they're looking at me to volunteer to teach them. And, yes, I know I'm the only one that has the skills to do it so it makes common sense but, call me selfish, Solly, I don't want to be a teacher. I haven't got the patience for a start.'

'You can say that again, Mam,' piped up Jimmy from the living area. 'Always shouting at us you were when you was putting us through our paces.' He mimicked: *'Sit still and concentrate, Jimmy.*

Robbie, you should be copying those letters on the paper not picking your nose and looking out of the window. Jimmy, stop flicking your brother with the end of that ruler. Now I don't care how many times I make you both say your times tables, you'll keep doing it until you get them all right and same goes for the alphabet. I used to dread them lessons.'

'Yeah, me too,' mirrored Robbie. 'Pure purgatory they were.'

Solly remained silent. He had never learned to read or write, although like others in his situation could recognise enough words to get by in life and anything more than that he relied on Gem for. As it became apparent that it was hit or miss whether they would succeed through any schooling they got and Gem decided to take on their schooling, she had tried to encourage him to join in. But, out of pure embarrassment, he had declined and this was something he had always regretted as he would now like nothing more than to be doing just what his youngest son was; reading a newspaper. He would now love the opportunity to gain information about what was transpiring in the outside world, or through reading books, instead of having to rely on being informed verbally by anyone willing to impart the information he was after to him.

Had Gem not been so disconcerted over the matter troubling her she would have belly-laughed at Jimmy's imitation of her as he had got her down to a T but, instead, she scowled crossly over at both her sons. 'Do you regret those lessons then when you're catching up with the news in the paper or, more likely, looking at the entertainment advertisements to see what's on that you fancy going to after the fair closes for the evening?'

They both looked sheepish and shook their heads.

She looked at her husband. 'Our sons are right, though, those lessons were purgatory and not just for them both, me too. I only persevered because I didn't want them growing up illiterate. But my days are filled enough already with looking after my family and the fair business work I do, so how on earth could I fit in teaching the kids for however many hours a day, even just a couple? It would be impossible for me.' She heaved a sigh. 'Trouble is though, I've promised the children's parents to speak to your father on the matter and find a solution and I know he will tell me that being as I am the only one in the community with an education then it falls to me.'

Solly nodded solemnly. 'Yes, that's just what Dad would say.'

'Oh? And what is it I would say, then?' said Big Sam as he arrived, expecting his dinner on the table. He immediately sat down to eat and was clearly put out that it wasn't, so couldn't help himself but add, 'Oh, twice in one week food's late getting to the table. Nell would be turning in her grave. Can't ever remember a time in all our forty-odd years of marriage when our meals weren't on the table on the dot. So is anyone going to answer me then? What it is I would have said, then?'

Solly looked at Gem by way of an apology that he would have to answer his father's question as he wouldn't let it go until he had. He steeled himself and explained what had transpired this morning.

As soon as he finished, Sam began to laugh; a deep, rich belly type. His family all looked at him, bemused as to what he was finding so funny. Finally drying his eyes on the handkerchief he kept in his jacket pocket, he chuckled. 'When you were giving the boys their lessons we all kept clear, believe me. We could all hear you shouting at them from the other side of the fairground for not paying attention or playing their tricks to get out of those lessons. You'd no patience with them whatsoever. After each one was over, Nell used to swear blind she could see steam coming off the top of your head. We all knew you hated giving those lessons as much as the boys hated having them. The fairfolk that were with us at the time obviously have short memories and the others no idea of what hell both you and the boys went through or they wouldn't be looking at you now to teach their own kids their... What is it called?... Their three somethings, anyway. I'll give yer yer due though, gel, through your bullying and persistence my grandsons can read and write as good as if a proper teacher had taught 'em and I can't fault yer for that.'

Gem's mouth dropped open in shock. Had her father-in-law just given her a back-handed compliment? If so, then this was a first and one for the record book.

Sam was continuing but now the laughter had left his voice and his tone was a grumbling one. 'Don't know what all the fuss is about myself. I can't read or write and I've done alright for myself. Whether they can read or write isn't what is going to make any of those kids successful. A quick brain and the will to succeed but, most importantly, being prepared to work damned hard is what will.'

Gem clamped shut her lips, forcing herself not to voice out loud to Sam that no one could deny that he had an eye for a lucrative business deal and excellent negotiating skills which had seen the business he'd inherited expand massively but, regardless, he seemed to be conveniently forgetting the fact that it hadn't all been achieved without his ability to read and write. When official forms had needed to be filled in, letters read or composed, he had sought someone with literacy skills to do the honours, which had been Gem herself since she had married his son. She knew that her husband was thinking exactly the same as she was but both harboured too much respect for Sam to speak out.

Solly said, 'Not many people are the same as you, Dad, and do need to read and write to get on.'

It was apparent that Sam was pleased with the compliment as he puffed out his chest importantly and replied, 'I appreciate they ain't. But, when all's said and done, it's my job to keep the business running so that those that work for me can feed and clothe their families, not to educate their kids.'

Gem and Solly thought that Sam had a point. So although he hadn't actually said it, it seemed that, as far as Sam was concerned, if the parents did want their children to better themselves then it was a matter of continuing to send them to the nearest school in each town they performed in with the hope that the teacher was the sort to show a welcome and a willingness to teach fair-folk children.

But then she saw the frightened faces of all those children today, and of her own promise that they wouldn't suffer that treatment again. She had meant at that particular school, but their young minds had more than likely interpreted her words to mean at *any* school. Her conscience got the better of her. She had made those children a promise and her morals dictated that she must honour it. Not that she at all wanted to, but maybe an hour of her time once a day in the week to try and help them learn their alphabet and some simple words, also the times tables, she could manage.

She spoke up before she could change her mind. 'I'll do it. Just for an hour or so a day which doesn't sound much but it's more than they're getting. Ten to eleven and I'll do the lessons in here. I'll fit in with my other work. But this is only until a better solution regarding the children's education is found.'

Sam looked thoughtfully at her for a moment. It was unclear by the bland look on his face whether he thought her a fool or heroine for making her offer. 'I'll spread the word. I'll make sure the parents send them on the dot tomorrow morning.'

Gem paled. 'Oh, I was thinking of starting next Monday, give me time to prepare.'

Sam looked nonplussed. 'No time like the present, gel. According to you, the kids have missed enough learning as it is without any more.' He then looked over at the pan of chips sizzling away on the stove. 'Them nearly done yet? I'm famished. And what are we having with 'em? Sausages and egg, I hope.'

Gem shot her father-in-law a dark stare. To him, throwing her into the deep end with little time to prepare, to tackle a job he knew she wasn't at all happy doing, tickled his sense of humour. She felt like telling Sam she hoped the meal she was about to put in front of him choked him, but then her better nature took over. Sam was right; the children *had* missed enough learning through those unwilling to teach them already without losing any more. 'Right, seems like I'm the community teacher from tomorrow morning.' And she added, meaningfully, 'For now, that is.' But then, as Sam had made it clear, he wasn't seeking another solution as he didn't feel that the children's education was his responsibility. So for how long 'for now' was, Gem dreaded to think.

From the living area two voices were heard to mutter in unison, 'God help the kids.'

At ten-thirty the next morning Gem was on the verge of literally pulling her hair out. Before she had gone to bed the previous night, she had gone around the Grundy community and scrounged enough paper and pencils for the children to use for their first lesson and then painstakingly written out the alphabet on twelve sheets, leaving a wide space underneath each row in order for the children to copy those letters by way of a start to them learning their alphabet. But getting them all to sit quietly and concentrate on what, to her, was a simple task was proving frustrating, to say the least. As soon as she had sat them down and explained what she wanted them to do, one had announced they needed the toilet, so then four others announced they did too. Then one child complained that another kept nudging them with their elbow as they tried to form their letters on the page, so others complained of the same thing and downed tools. The space they were all crammed in was small; six of them were sitting around her kitchen table, the rest squashed together on the sofa and in armchairs in the living area with books on their knees as a surface to write on. So, in order to provide each child with more elbow room, she asked four of the children to sit cross-legged on the floor, so those seated could spread out a bit. For a few minutes this seemed to work and the children did start to concentrate on the task she had set them. But just when Gem was thinking this was going to work and the children might actually learn something, one of the youngest children suddenly burst into tears because she couldn't form the letter to mirror that of Gem's and so several of the others joined in out of sympathy. Then, to make matters worse, an older boy called them babies for their crying and so one of the crying children's brother, out of protection for his sister, punched him on the arm. Out of retaliation, the lad punched him back and a fight then broke out between them, which took Gem several minutes to break up. It then took her a few more minutes to soothe the crying children, move others around so the two boys were sitting apart, and get them back to copying their letters again.

The hour lesson was halfway through by this time and she'd only just gotten the children to actually settle down enough to attempt some work. She could sense that this harmony between the children would not last for the rest of the lesson, as the end of one child's pencil had snapped off and that child was clearly on the verge of snatching their neighbour's pencil to replace the broken one. Quickly, she went over and took the broken pencil from the child in question and offered to sharpen it for them before they caused mayhem.

With her back turned, she did not see one child glance over at her neighbour's work and, seeing they were doing better than they were, jealously snatch the paper they were working on off them, screwing it up. The first she knew of the incident was when the victim jumped up, screaming that she was going to tell her mother what the culprit had done. The peace amongst the other children was completely shattered and all hell broke loose as some commiserated with the victim and others banded together on the side of the culprit; they all started yelling at each other.

By now, Gem's patience was non-existent. She slammed down the knife, spun on her heels and shouted crossly out, 'Stop this nonsense! Sit down and get on with your work.'

None of them took any notice of her, all carrying on as though she hadn't spoken. Now Gem had had enough. If this was a prelude for all the lessons to come...

She went to the door, let herself out, shut it behind her and, closing her ears to the bedlam coming from inside, she sat on the steps and cradled her head in her hands. The children in the van had always treated her with the utmost respect and with politeness whenever she had come across them, so why now were they all being so naughty? The noise the children were making inside the van invaded her troubled thoughts. She needed to return back inside and quiet them down, get them back to working again, but the thought filled her with dread; she'd sooner have faced a dozen rampaging bulls than twelve squabbling children. But she was going to have to and somehow get them to behave and do the work she set them or otherwise she would be breaking her promise to their parents.

Her despair deepened; she felt as if she was in a deep, dark hole with no way of escape. She lifted her head and looked skywards. *Lord, I know I haven't exactly been a good disciple of yours. Well, in truth, not a good one at all. I can't remember the last time I went to church as my parents weren't at all religious and so I'm not either, but if I could just ask you... Well, if you do exist, that is... Just this once, if you could see your way to helping an unreligious person and send me one of your miracles, not your loaves and fishes kind but grant me the gift or whatever it is that teachers possess to get children to sit and behave themselves while I try and teach them their ABCs. If you do, I promise...*

'Are you Mrs Grundy? I was told you were the person I needed to speak to.'

At the unexpected intrusion into her thoughts, Gem's head shot down to see standing before her a thin, plain-faced woman. In her late fifties or early sixties was Gem's estimate, smartly but cheaply dressed in a brown coat, sensible shoes and a brown handbag hung over her arm. Her salt and pepper hair was scraped back from her head and knotted in a tight bun at the base of her neck, accentuating her sharp features. She looked exactly as Gem had pictured the teacher she had expected to find at the school yesterday.

She eased herself off the van steps. 'Yes, I'm Mrs Grundy. I'm rather busy at the moment dealing with some of the fair children so if you need to speak to someone about fair business, then Mr Sam Grundy is about somewhere.'

The woman looked at Gem's living van, then eyed her knowingly. In a pleasant tone of voice she said, 'The children seem to be causing you a problem by the sound of it. Excuse me a moment.'

Before Gem could stop her, she marched past, letting herself inside and closing the door behind her. Whilst Gem stared at the closed door, wondering what on earth the woman was up to, to her absolute shock the commotion from inside stopped. Seconds later, the woman returned to stand before Gem again, saying, 'At least we can hear ourselves speak now. The children are all busy getting on with their lesson.'

Gem gawped in amazement at her and stammered, 'How ... how on earth did you manage that? Quiet the kids down and get them to get on with their work?'

She smiled. 'I just asked them to.'

Gem felt affronted that this austere-looking woman had managed something she had hopelessly failed to and said defensively, 'Well so did I but they just ignored me and played up even more.' She sighed. 'I can't understand it. The children are usually so well-mannered and polite to me, yet today they are acting so naughty. I wish I'd never offered to act as their teacher now.'

'Children are very perceptive; they would have sensed your reluctance which would have made them feel awkward and unwanted. And so, by them being naughty, they were allowing you the opportunity of getting rid of them.'

Gem stared at her, having difficulty digesting what the woman had just told her. Then it suddenly registered and a surge of utter guilt rampaged through her. It was herself that had evoked this bad behaviour within the children today because they had picked up on the fact that she resented having to spend her time with them when she would far sooner have been elsewhere. How on earth though did she put this right, put the children at their ease, when in fact her resentment of having to teach them when she'd sooner not, was still as virulent?

'Look, while the children are quiet, what can I do for you?'

'I'm hoping it's what I can do for you.' She paused for a moment before she ventured, 'I heard what happened yesterday at the school with the fairground children. I was horrified by the way the teacher treated them and felt it was very admirable of you how you put her in her place. I suspect that the teacher's behaviour with the children isn't an isolated case either.'

'No, no, it's not. The children are very lucky if, during our season on the road, they receive any schooling at all because of teachers' attitude towards us fairground folk. The local children don't always give them an easy time either.'

'And I doubt very much that will change unless people's attitudes to travellers do. I feel it's wrong that any child from any walk of life be denied learning for any reason.' She then shocked Gem to her core by offering, 'I could teach the children for you.'

'You would?' Gem exclaimed, most surprised.

'I'd really like the opportunity to, if I'd be allowed.'

The way she said it left Gem in no doubt of her sincerity. She couldn't believe that this was happening, that an actual teacher was volunteering their services to them. 'Oh, this is wonderful news. At least the children will receive some learning while we are here.'

'I was thinking for longer than that. Of being their permanent teacher.'

Gem gawped at her, stunned. 'Joining our community and travelling with us, you mean?'

'I'd very much like to.' She held out her hand. 'My name is Emily Dunn.'

She was speechless that this prim-looking woman – the sort of woman that was usually found amongst those that banded together to petition those in authority to ban the fair from coming to their towns and villages, deeming them dens of iniquity – was offering her services! Before she changed her mind, she accepted the proffered hand and happily shook it. 'Gemma Grundy. Gem. I'm very pleased to meet you, Miss Dunn.'

Emily Dunn said, 'I wish I could offer my services for free but I'm afraid I am not a woman of means and would therefore require some remuneration.'

Of course she would as she had to live. Gem felt foolish for thinking that this woman was offering her services for free.

Emily Dunn was continuing, 'I'm not asking for a lot, just enough of a wage to keep me in the basics I need. Three pounds a week would be sufficient.'

Gem had no idea how much a teacher earned but was aware that it was usually far more than three pounds weekly. For what she was offering, this amount sounded very reasonable to Gem. 'After the time I've had this morning, I would snatch your hand off for you to take over the responsibility of the children's education but, unfortunately, the decision isn't mine to make. I'll have to speak to Mr Grundy.' Sam didn't easily part with his money so it wasn't going to be an easy task to persuade him to go ahead with this but Gem was determined not to give up without a fight as she doubted an opportunity like this would ever come this way again. But then another problem presented itself. 'Oh, but of course there is the question of living accommodation? People who work for us provide their own, you see.'

'I am in a position to fund a small caravan adequate enough for me that I can tow around with my trusty old station wagon.'

That bridge was crossed then but yet another problem presented itself and she frowned in thought. 'It's where we would hold the lessons, though? Continuing using my living van wouldn't work.'

'I have given thought to that problem and I came up with the idea that a military tent would more than do the job. They are not expensive to purchase from an army surplus store and, in the winter, it can be heated with a wood stove.'

Emily Dunn had obviously given this all a lot of thought, so it was not some idle gesture on her part but something she really wanted to do. Despite struggling to accept that someone so prim and proper, the type Gem pictured residing in a Victorian terrace littered with dust-collecting ornaments and an aspidistra plant in the window – the complete opposite of the usual runaways, ex-prisoners and those that believed a life with the fair was a glamorous one – was so keen to join their community and live their nomadic lifestyle, she was worried this answer to her prayers might just change her mind and vanish as suddenly as she'd arrived. 'I'll just check on the children and, if you wait here, I'll find Mr Grundy and have a word with him. If he's keen on the idea I'll bring him to meet you.'

'I would be delighted to check on the children for you while you go off and find the owner.'

Gem looked towards her van, amazed that the children were obviously still working away as no noise could be heard. Emily Dunn's magic was still having its effect on them, it seemed. Accepting the woman's offer, she went off.

She found a not-too-happy Sam having strong words with one of the teenage sons of a ride owner. He had been despatched that morning to the printer's to collect a parcel of pre-ordered leaflets advertising the arrival of the fair in the next town they were due to visit, which he and two other workers had been going to travel to tomorrow to hand around to the general public and also put up in shop windows. Trouble was though, the lad had returned with someone else's order, advertising the opening of a new furniture shop. The repercussions of this meant a return journey for the lad using valuable time. Knowing Sam as well as she did, this would normally not be a good moment in respect of his bad mood to tackle him on spending money paying for a service he didn't feel fell to him to provide, but then the costly mistake the lad had made was all down to the fact that he couldn't read the name on the front of the package to realise the mistake the assistant had made, so maybe this moment was the perfect one for Gem to put her case to him.

His first response was a flat no, along with a reminder to her that, as far as he was concerned, the education of the fairfolk children was the responsibility of their parents.

As they were discussing this matter, a disinterested Sam was hobbling along as he wove his way around the stalls and rides on his way to the boxing ring to have a catch-up chat with the man he employed to run it so Gem was having to trot alongside him to keep pace.

Despite his flat refusal to even to consider it, Gem was not giving up. 'But, Mr Grundy, this woman ... Mrs ... Miss ... Dunn is offering her services so cheaply. At least we should consider it.'

'We!' he snapped. 'It's me that pays the bills, not you, so there's no "we" about it. The answer is still no.'

'Well, what about the money it cost you this morning when Trevor came back with the wrong order from the printer's and had to go back again. That was all down to the fact he couldn't read.'

'Well he won't be making that mistake again after the bollocking I gave him. Whether he can read is neither here nor there as he should have checked with the assistant who gave him the order that he'd got the right one before he left. Anyway, I take it that this teacher woman is an outsider? We've got enough outsiders in the Grundy community already without any more invading us.'

Gem was well aware that this wasn't Sam being bigoted, that he was purely using any excuse not to lay out money he didn't need to if he could help it. Sam had many friends that he deeply respected amongst outsiders he had met over the years in different towns and villages. She snapped, 'If I wasn't here and doing your books for you then I dread to think how much it would cost you to employ the services of a book-keeper when you don't pay me anything, nor do you for all the other jobs I do around the fair either, come to that.' Stabbing a finger into her chest, she added, 'This outsider is worth her weight in gold to you and you know it. And may I remind you that Velda is an outsider and you are such good friends with her. Or had you forgotten that? And don't forget the money you make out of her? And most of the gaff lads are outsiders too and the fair wouldn't function without them.'

He made no response but, regardless, Gem knew that her words had hit home.

'So will you take her on or not?' Gem asked him.

He suddenly stopped his pacing to look at her stolidly. 'I ain't daft, you know. You didn't want to teach those kids in the first place so you only want me to take this woman on so it saves you having to.'

She readily admitted, 'Yes, it is. But not entirely. I don't enjoy teaching the children, I haven't got the patience, but mostly I want you to take this woman on for the children's sake. Because their parents want better for them ... and there's nothing wrong with that. Didn't we all want the best for our kids when they were young and still do, in fact. But you know what those poor children face each week when they have to go to a different school and is that fair to them, not knowing what awaits them? When they've been treated badly knowing they have no choice but to face it again for the next four days, the only saving grace they have is the hope that the next school might be nicer to them.' Despite her reminding him the trauma the children faced every week during school term times in the hope it might prick his conscience, she could still see that what it was going to cost him was the principle reason Sam was not receptive to this idea. She understood why. She did the business accounts and knew that the profits at the end of the year were not that much and usually ploughed back into the business, buying new rides and replacing old equipment no longer repairable. Three pounds a week might not be a huge amount but, over a year, it was a large chunk of money that could be used to replace a clapped-out old lorry or put towards a new attraction to pull the punters in with.

Then an idea came to her that might help change his mind. 'Just think how much good this is going to do your reputation amongst the rest of the showmen community up and down the country. You will go down in fairground history as the ringmaster that was the first to provide proper schooling for his workers' children.'

He looked at her blankly and she could see the cogs in his brain whirling. To her great delight it seemed that the thought of his name gracing the pages of the history books, alongside the other great showmen such as P.T. Barnum and Tom Norman, was enough to sway him. He gruffly said, 'Alright, you win, I'll pay for the bloody teacher.'

She blurted, 'Oh, and, er, a tent as well to hold the lessons in. They don't cost much. We'll have to consider getting tables and chairs for the kids to sit at, but they can sit on the floor for now. And also a stove to heat the tent in winter.' Before he could change his mind she spun on her heels, calling behind her, 'I'll go and tell Emily Dunn she's hired and welcome her into our community.'

To say Emily was delighted with the acceptance of her proposal would have been an understatement as she was positively overjoyed. Having made arrangements to arrive that coming Sunday in time for their collective departure for their next venue, she left. As Gem returned to tell the good news to the children and release them from any more lessons until their very own teacher took up her duties the following Monday morning and then on to inform their parents of this turn of events, it was then she began to wonder just why a woman like Emily, and especially at her mature age, would want to leave her old life behind? It was indeed puzzling to Gem.

Early that evening, holding his wife in his arms, Solly was looking at her with unadulterated love and awe. 'I can't believe you got the old man to agree to put his hand in his pocket and pay for something he doesn't think is his responsibility to pay for.'

She chuckled. 'It wasn't easy. Your father can be a stubborn old cuss, as you well know, and I seriously didn't think I was going to until, thankfully, I had the brainwave to convince him that he would stand beside the greats in showman history as a pioneer for the education of fairground workers' children.'

Solly's love and admiration for his wife radiated all the brighter. In all their twenty-odd years of marriage, never a day went by when he didn't bless the day he met her. He still marvelled that, considering his young age at the time, he'd summoned the courage to go against his parents and their staunch belief in fairground traditions and married her. He never forgot the fact that she gave up a very privileged life with her prosperous parents and that with her good looks and personality would not have failed to attract a man of her own ilk that could have provided for her handsomely. She had given him two wonderful sons, raising them to be decent, honest, hard-working young men any father couldn't fail to be proud of. Even after all these years they still giggled over private jokes together, same as they had as teenagers, never kept secrets between themselves, and their lovemaking was still as frequent, rampant and satisfying. Despite the numerous times he had seen her in conversation, even flirting with male punters as part of her job to entice them on rides or stalls she was manning, never did he question her loyalty to himself. She never gave him reason to worry over her straying from him, so complete was his trust for her. He did indeed bless the day she came into his life and decided to stay.

In turn, Gem's thoughts mirrored her husband's as she felt the love and protectiveness from his hug enveloping through her. Never once in all their years of marriage, even through difficult times – and there had been too many of those to count – had she ever regretted going against her parents' wishes. Being disinherited from her family and giving up a privileged future was worth it to be with the man whose arms she was now wrapped in. He had been a loving, supportive, completely faithful and devoted husband and there was nothing she would change about him in any way whatsoever. All but one thing though. Solly believed that he and his wife had no secrets between them, were totally open and honest with each other, but Gem hadn't been so with him. She had a secret that she knew would devastate her husband. The chance to tell him had come and gone many years ago and she had chosen not to inform him purely out of her love for him and unwillingness to cause him the pain it would bring him over something he could have done nothing about at the time. She herself was already suffering enough for the both of them. So, rightly or wrongly, it was her intention that this secret would go to the grave with her; she felt some secrets were kept secret for the best of intentions.

Solly now whispered in her ear, 'The boys won't be back for a bit so shall we take advantage of having the van to ourselves?'

Her eyes twinkled wickedly and she grinned.

Chapter Seven

Ren, Jimmy and Robbie, their cousin Anita (known as Nita) and her sister Rosanna (Rosa for short), along with several other Grundy community members in their teenage years and early twenties were gathered outside Ren's caravan. Some were sitting on upturned wooden crates, others on the hard ground, some were drinking pop, others beer, and they were eating various snacks they had each brought along with them. It was just after eleven and most fine evenings, same as some adults did, the friends would gather together for a catch-up with each other before they each retired to their sleeping quarters for the night.

Rosa, a thin, sharp-featured eighteen-year-old with waist-length black hair, which today was plaited and hanging down her back, was wearing a red full skirt with a white short-sleeved, Peter Pan collar-style blouse and an old-fashioned black, heavily fringed gypsy-style shawl around her bony shoulders, and was saying, 'I saw that woman you're on about, Robbie. God, did she think she was Marilyn Monroe with her bleached-blonde hair and wearing that dress that was so tight I thought that huge chest of hers was going to burst out the front of it. She was swanning around with that little gnome of a bloke who looked like Al Capone with all them gold rings on his fingers and that fur coat he was wearing. I was worried that at any minute him or any of them men that was with them was going to whip out their machine guns and spray us all with bullets.'

Nita, in complete contrast to her sister, was chubby and homely looking with a mop of short brown curly hair framing an oval face. She chuckled. 'You're just jealous of that woman's chest, our Rosa, cos you ain't got one. Not like me, eh?' she said, cupping her own ample dumpling-like breasts in her hands and giving them a jiggle. While the rest of the gathering laughed at her humorous actions she went on, 'One of them cheeky buggers tried to get me to go for a bit of hanky-panky around the back of the Fun House, offered me five bob, and him old enough to be my dad 'n' all. Our mam saw what he was up to and sent him packing with a threat of the rolling pin she keeps under the counter. Good job Granddad, Uncle Solly or Uncle Sonny weren't passing at the time or they'd have made mincemeat of him.' She ruefully shook her head. 'Flatties think all us fair women are easy, don't they? I don't think he still thinks that now though after Mam said what she did to him. I've heard Mam swear before but I never knew she knew language like that.' She then said to Ren, 'I heard what those morons did to you earlier today. Are you alright?'

Ren took a sip from her bottle of pale ale. 'Could have been worse had your mam not put a stop to their antics,' she said, nodding at Jimmy and Robbie. Then she added, 'Just a couple of bruises, that's all, thanks for asking, Rosa, and all in a day's work.' She smiled. 'Apart from what those lads did, it's been a good day for me. A never-ending queue for my candy floss stall from almost when we opened to when we shut and I sold a lot of sweets too. *And* all my customers were nice ones. Hope the rest of the week is as good then I might be able to afford myself some material to make myself a new dress and the shoes to go with it. I might be able to have it ready for when we go dancing in Leeds when we take the fair up there next month and won't the lads all be after me then?' It then struck her that Donny was late dropping by tonight and she wondered what was keeping him. At the same time as thinking this, she turned her head and looked over in the direction he would come from after leaving the main fairground to enter the living van area. Then she spotted him as he appeared in the light of a living van he was passing and her heart soared, only then to crash back down when it appeared he was heading straight for his own van and not over to them all. She called out to him, 'Not joining us tonight, Donny?'

Since his wife had devastated him by telling him the true feelings of the woman he believed was his lifelong friend, unable to face her, he had done his best to avoid her. That had been easy enough during the day considering the size of the fair, the amount of people milling inside it and where his parents' ride was located on the other side of the site from Ren's candy floss and sweet stall. But to get to his living van, though, he had no choice but to pass by Ren's and, knowing she and all the rest of their fairfolk friends would be gathered together outside on a fine night and would be expecting him to join them as he always did, he'd been praying he could keep to the shadows and slip past without any of them seeing. He was still having troubling accepting that the Ren he knew, the kind, caring, loyal and funny person she portrayed to him was, in truth, spiteful and callous. Donny was not the sort of person that could feel one way and act another; he wasn't two-faced as his mother would deem such types so, to excuse himself, he just called back, 'Got to get home. Suzie's waiting for me.'

As he hurried off Ren frowned, bewildered. His manner had been abrupt, bordering on the rude, in such contrast to his usual easy-going nature. Something must have greatly upset Donny for him to be in such a foul mood. And now she came to think of it, Donny never failed to call by her confectionary stall at least once during the day and she hadn't seen him once. Neither could she remember an evening since she had lost both her parents and had been living on her own, no matter the weather or how urgently he needed to get back to his own van, when Donny hadn't called by to check on her welfare, offer to tackle any heavy chores for her, her diminutive size prohibiting her from doing herself. And, weather permitting, to have a quick catch-up with the rest of their friends over a bottle of beer or pop. Something wasn't right, she could sense it. It couldn't be between herself and Donny as never had they fallen out and, besides, nothing had happened between them to fall out over. She had seen Suzie from a distance that day, and at a distance was near enough for Ren considering how the woman treated her. She had spoken in passing to both his mother and father, his brothers too, and they hadn't seemed to have anything troubling them that she had detected. Since Ren could remember, should either herself or Donny have a problem they had always turned to each other to mull it over with and help resolve it. Even his marriage to Suzie hadn't changed that, so why had he changed tonight? It then struck her that maybe it was because she was surrounded by friends and whatever was troubling him he didn't want to discuss in earshot of others so would seek her out tomorrow.

She joked to the others, 'Seems Donny's on a promise tonight and desperate to get home, so he won't be joining us.' She then looked around them all enquiringly. 'So, are we all going out then on Friday night after work and, if so, where to?'

The group usually went out together once a week on a Friday to the local dance hall. On occasion, some of the locals knew they were fairfolk and didn't hold back in making it clear their types weren't welcome, issuing threats of bodily harm if they didn't leave promptly. But, on the whole, the majority of the locals, especially the young women eyeing up the influx of handsome young men from the fairground, stood up to the bigoted few and made it clear that for them the fairfolk were welcome. The bullies were usually seen off and a good time was had by all.

Robbie shook his head. 'I can't afford to go out this week as my wages are going towards a new pair of shoes. I want a pair of winkle-pickers and they ain't cheap either.'

Jimmy said, 'I've got a date after work on Friday with a girl I met last night when I was working on the carousel so I won't be joining you all this week.'

His brother accosted him. 'You never told me?'

Jimmy cheekily smiled. 'Didn't want to rub the fact in that I've got a date when you haven't and remind you that I'm the best-looking out of both of us. Ouch!' He cried out from the hefty punch on the arm he received from his brother at his self-aggrandising.

'Me and Nita are grounded for the next week cos we got back home late last Friday night. I wouldn't mind but it was only by ten minutes and I pleaded with Mam that it was only because one of the gaff lads that came with us was sick as he'd had too much to drink and we all stayed until he'd finished filling the gutter. Us all were following fairground rules that we all stay together when any of us go out but, even so, once Mam's made her mind up there no changing it,' she grumbled.

As several others also pleaded poverty, it seemed that their night out on Friday was not going to happen so Ren suggested, 'Well surely we could all afford a few bottles of beer between us so we could have a party. You could bring your guitar, Mal, for music for us to dance to,' she said to a tall, well-built twenty-year-old who was one of several riders on the Wall of Death.

Just then Jimmy noticed a huge, handsome black man, his arms and legs resembling tree trunks, walking past on his way to the van he shared with a couple of other boxing booth fighters, carrying a small brown paper bag in his meaty fist. ''eh, up, Willy, fancy a beer?'

William White, whose stage name was Basher Bill, had never yet been beaten in the ring since he'd joined Grundy's two seasons ago. William loved working for Grundy's; he appreciated the boxing booth manager treating him as a human being, not just a commodity to abuse and line his pockets with whilst paying him a pittance.

He smiled, showing a row of big white teeth and in a thick Jamaican accent responded, 'Not tonight, man, tanks. Got a date with dis.' He held up the brown paper bag they all knew held marijuana. 'I'll come to yer party though. I'll bring me bongos.'

'And spread the word!' Ren shouted over to him. 'If we're having a party we might as well make it a good one, so the more the merrier.'

A while then was spent discussing arrangements for the party and then, gradually, everyone made their way back to their own vans, leaving Ren alone with her thoughts. It wasn't the excitement of the forthcoming party that was occupying them though, but what could possibly be troubling Donny for him to have acted so out of character with her?

But when he neither called by her stall the following day or at her van on his way home that night, it was then two days since she'd spoken to him. Never before had that lapse of time passed without them speaking, even only for a moment or two, so it was a very worried Ren that delayed setting up her stall the next morning to seek Donny out.

His parents' ride, which Donny helped them operate, had been safety tested and was all set up ready for opening. So she found him lending a hand to one of Sam Grundy's labourers repairing one of the cars shaped like a boat with the head of a swan. It glided through the winding track in the Tunnel of Love, which was ironic given how she felt about him. The head of the swan had come loose thanks to a succession of punters pushing against it with their feet and, spanner in hand, Donny was in the process of tightening the bolts that secured it.

He had his back to her when she said to him, 'Hello, Donny. I haven't seen you for a day or two so came to see how you are?'

She was absolutely stunned to note that at the sound of her voice he physically jumped and it was several long seconds before he slowly turned around to face her. Her shock turned to abject confusion to notice that when he responded to her he refused to look her in the eye, like the very sight of her was repellent to him. His tone was gruff. 'You can see I'm fine. Excuse me, I must get on.' He turned his back on her and continued with his task.

Now she was positive that something serious was bothering him but just what it could be that could make him act towards her as he was, she couldn't fathom. 'Donny, what is the matter with you? I know something is. Whenever you've had a problem before you've always turned to me to help you with it, so why aren't you now? I don't understand?'

The same thing happened again. He slowly turned around and, when he did, his eyes – that usually held the spark of deep affection for her – were filled with hurt. She was astonished even more by what he said to her. 'I know, Ren. Now please leave me alone.'

He made to turn his back on her again but she dashed over and grabbed his arm. She blurted out, bewildered, 'Know what, Donny?'

He shook free his arm like her hand was burning him and went to tell her of his discovery that their friendship, something so very dear to him, was just a sham on her part, but his kind nature prevented him causing hurt to Ren, despite the distress she had caused him when he learned the truth about how she really felt about him. With a deep sense of sadness filling him for the loss of a friendship which, in truth, he knew now thanks to his wife, he never had in the first place he told

Ren in a dismissive tone, 'My wife is my friend and she's the only one I need. Please don't bother me any more.'

He abruptly turned away and continued on with his task.

Ren stared at him, utterly stupefied. Had Donny really just ended their friendship? After all they had been to each other since babies? And to do so with no reason that Ren could fathom? This didn't make sense to her. And what did he mean by, *I know?* Know what? At least if he afforded her the reason for his decision it would help her understand and come to terms with it, but he had made it clear to her that he wasn't prepared to so she had no choice but to accept it and do as he asked; not to bother him any more. She had thought she couldn't possibly suffer any worse pain than that she had when watching the love of her life marry another woman but this she was experiencing now, losing her best friend completely, was immeasurable. She would miss him dreadfully. With a heavy heart she turned and dragged herself to her stall.

The party on Friday night was a great success; all the attendees thoroughly enjoyed themselves. There were a few bloodshot eyes and hangover sufferers amongst the younger members of the Grundy community that arrived to start work the next morning. All except for Ren though. For her the party was an emotional trial that she would sooner have not participated in. What she wanted to do, instead, was curl up on her bench sofa on her own in her van to nurse her heartache and try to come to terms with her devastating loss, but as the organiser and as it was her van the party was being held outside, she had no choice but to put on a brave face and appear to be enjoying herself as much as the rest.

Chapter Eight

The rest of the week passed without major incident and, from the minute the last punters left the fair on Saturday night until it was all set up and ready to open at their next venue the following Monday afternoon, which was the small market town of Barnsley, none of the Grundy community got much sleep. In a frenzy of activity, whilst the men set to dismantling the rides and stalls, loading them on the various lorries and then transporting it all to the next destination for it to be resurrected again, the women packed up their living vans. Once deposited at their next venue, they unpacked all their belongings again and made it all homely, all the while making sure their families were well fed and looked after in all respects. It was unusual for any move to proceed smoothly without any hitches but, much to everyone's relief, this one did. This was to be a two-week stay as Barnsley was a larger town with many nearby surrounding villages.

The site on the outskirts of Barnsley was at the end of a road called Summer Lane, on a large area of common grassland surrounded by trees and hedgerows, a small stream running down the boundary. The children were delighted with the paddling and swimming opportunities. Although the surroundings on this site were far pleasanter for the fairfolk than the hard, stony ground of the cleared slum site at their last venue in a poor area, the downside was that there was no source of electricity so generators had to be fully relied upon to power all the fair's electrical needs. There was also no running water supply so the womenfolk had the extra task of boiling up their water needs collected from the stream. But then the area came under the control of a local parish council and the fee they charged was nominal compared to what the larger councils did for their sites in the middle of a town. As soon as they arrived and had set up, it was Sam's first job then to go along to the parish council's office and settle up.

On moving days the task fell to Gem to provide a hot meal for all the Grundy labourers and gaff lads Sam employed as well as her own family so, as soon as Solly had sited their van and fired up the generator, out came her pots and pans and with the aid of a couple of the other women she cooked up an enormous cauldron-sized pot of nourishing meat and vegetable stew, along with chunks of thick crusty bread. They would all sit together and eat at long trestle tables off their plates and cutlery each had brought with them.

Despite having no idea why Sonny acted so distant with his family, it had been long ago accepted that he preferred to cater for himself and eat alone. It was apparent that he harboured nothing more than contempt for Gem, going by the off-hand manner he always displayed towards her whenever they had dealings together. Out of respect that he was Solly's brother, on moving days, Gem would always send one of his nephews over to his van with a tray of food and did likewise on Christmas Day and any other occasion the family had a special meal together such as Easter Sunday and birthdays. Whether he ate the food, let alone enjoyed it, she had no idea as he neither complimented her on it in any way nor thanked her for her thoughtfulness.

Shopping was never a chore that fair women looked forward to because they never knew how they were going to be received in any shops they ventured into once the proprietors and other shoppers realised just who they were. It all depended on their individual perception of fairfolk. Verbal abuse was commonplace and, occasionally, fair women had been physically attacked. Consequently, groups of friendly fair women usually shopped together. Gem's shopping circle included her sister-in-law, Fran, fortune-teller Velda May, a couple of younger show women who had joined Grundy's on their marriage, along with a couple of elderly widowed Grundy matriarchs whose sons or daughters had inherited their stall or ride from their deceased fathers. They shopped and cooked for their families by way of paying their keep while they were still mobile enough to.

That first Monday morning of their stay on the outskirts of Barnsley it transpired that only Velda and herself would shop together as the other members of their group had either opted to go with others on this occasion or were going another time as they were otherwise busy.

It was about a half mile down a winding country lane from the field the fair was sited on to a row of shops that included a butcher, bakery, general grocery, bookmaker and cobbler's, with just the odd cottage and row of workers' two-up two-down terraces in between. Velda did offer to drive them in her old Land Rover, to save them lugging the shopping back, but they decided to walk as the spring morning was such a lovely one. The sun was shining down from an almost cloudless sky and, having not seen anything green except for weeds the previous week having been completely hemmed in by grimy brick buildings and breathing in the thick smoke-filled air from the belching chimneys of the surrounding houses and factories, they both wanted to savour all the delights the countryside afforded.

Gem was dressed in a pair of black capri pants, pretty pink blouse and blue belted woollen jacket, blue pumps on her feet, and Velda was in her usual voluminous robe-type dress which, today, was a black one edged in red braid around the cuffs, neckline and hem. Her long hair was parted down the middle and coiled in plaits around her ears. As she wasn't plying her trade on this occasion the scarf around her head was a plain black one, and she wore a thick tassel-fringed red shawl around her shoulders, sturdy well-worn shoes on her large feet. Both were carrying several bags to hold their shopping in.

It being just the two of them together in such

pleasant surroundings, Gem thought this a unmissable opportunity to probe the older woman on her feelings for her father-in-law, who she was instinctively aware had romantic feelings for the older woman. But veering Velda towards her instigating this conversation was proving very difficult though for Gem as Velda herself was consumed with her own worries for Ren.

'Since the lass's parents both died, you know, Gem dear, how I took her under my wing and become a second mother to her. I felt very honoured that she allowed me to do that. Just a pity her parents aren't still around to see what a wonderful job they did with their daughter.' She paused for a moment to reach over to a hawthorn tree in the thick hedge by the side of her and picked a bud from it, along with a couple of newly sprouting leaves, which she put in her mouth and chewed on. 'Just delicious. Have a taste of nuts. Chopped up and sprinkled on potatoes adds lovely flavour to them. I shall pick a handful on my way back to put on boiled potatoes to go with the pig's trotter I plan to have for my dinner. Now, what was I saying? Oh, yes. I was telling you my worries over Ren. So getting to know her as she's allowed me to, I know that these last few days she most certainly hasn't been herself. Oh, she appears to be on the surface but ... well ... there's a sadness in her eyes I haven't seen since she lost her parents. Oh drat, it's so hard to describe ... it's like the heart has gone out of her.'

Gem grimaced thoughtfully as she sidestepped a pot hole in the rutted surface of the country lane. 'What those three louts did to her week ago was nothing short of nasty. She seemed to take it on the chin and was joking about it in a typical Ren way so I happily went away thinking she was alright. But do you think that it upset her more than she let on?'

Velda shook her head. 'She's had worse done and said to her. Still, when all's said and done, she's only human so in private I've no doubt she would have shed a tear or two, but affect her in the way whatever it is that I feel is now? No, it's something else that has completely knocked the stuffing out of her is my opinion.' She lapsed into silence for a moment as they continued their journey before she offered, 'You know how close friends her and Donny are ... not that I'm nosy but with us all living so closely together you can't help noticing things, can you? And, given how special Ren is to me, I do tend to take an interest in her. Well, I have noticed these last few days that Donny seems to be avoiding her.'

'Avoiding her?' Gem said, bewildered. 'But those two are the best of friends and I can't ever remember a time when they haven't been, which I've always thought unusual for a boy and girl to be so close and not romantically involved. What makes you think he's been avoiding her?'

'When I'm not busy in my tent sometimes I take a break outside and if there's not too many crowds I can see Ren's stall and, a couple of times this week, I've seen Donny purposely taking a longer route to his parents' ride instead of a quicker way past Ren's stall. And, at night, when I've been sitting outside my van on a fine evening which we have been lucky to have this past week,

I've seen Donny ... well I can't describe it in any other way but *sneak* past Ren's van on his way to his own. Before, Donny always dropped by for a quick chat and to check if she needed his help with anything on his way home, same as Ren does to me.'

Gem looked thoughtful for a moment before she ventured, 'Maybe they've had a falling out over something trivial that's been blown out of proportion and that's what's upsetting Ren so much. I'm sure they'll soon make it up. I have to say that, considering how well those two got on, I did think they would end up getting married until Suzie came along.'

Velda pulled a grim face. 'Ah, Suzie.'

Gem frowned at her. 'What about her? She's always come across as being a very nice girl to me.'

'Yes, I agree she does, but... Well, I'm not sure if she's as nice as she makes out she is. Just a feeling, that's all.'

Gem eyed her knowingly. 'This your extra-sensory perception kicking in.'

Velda looked at her, confused. 'My what?'

Gem laughed. 'That gift you have for sensing things.'

'Oh, my sixth sense. I've never heard it called that. All us women have it, Gem. Some listen to it and some don't. I've seen you use yours many times over the years, especially where your family is concerned.'

And sensing that my father-in-law has romantic feelings for you, thought Gem.

Velda was continuing, 'Yes, it is what I sense

from Suzie as a matter of fact. I just feel that she's not all what meets the eye, so to speak, that lurking under that smile is a wicked sneer. I wouldn't be surprised to find out that whatever had caused the rift with Ren and Donny, Suzie has got something to do with it. It was bad enough for Ren witnessing Donny marry Suzie so to lose his friendship will devastate her.'

'What do you mean by that, Velda? Why was it bad enough for Ren watching Donny get married?'

She heavily sighed. 'He's the love of her life, that's why, and no other man will ever measure up to him in her eyes. I can see you're wondering why you've never noticed but she kept this well hidden, even Donny himself has no idea how she feels about him. She's not clever enough to hide it from me though.'

Gem said, aghast, 'I really hadn't a clue and I thought I knew everything that went on in the community. I feel it's part of my job as a member of the ringmaster's family to keep an eye out for anyone I suspect is struggling in any way and offer help. I've fallen down badly on this one, haven't I?'

Velda affectionately patted her arm. 'Don't be so hard on yourself. As I said, Ren has kept her feelings well hidden. It was just the way her eyes lit up whenever his name came up in conversation and the occasions I've caught her looking at him when she didn't realise anyone was watching her that gave her away to me. He might be head over heels in love with his wife but there's no getting away from the fact that Donny is extremely fond of Ren in return and more than I think Donny realises himself. I've never raised a word of this to her as it's obvious this is not a matter to be discussed and I've respected that. I would never have talked to anyone else about this but you, Gem. As the honourable woman you are, I know you will keep this information to yourself. Ren suffers enough from her affliction without the humiliation of gossip over being in love with another woman's husband.'

Gem looked at her companion reassuringly. 'Of course, that goes without saying. I think far too much of Ren to say or do anything to cause her trouble in any way.' She turned her head and looked through a gap in the hedgerows across a vast expanse of fields, at a herd of Friesian cows grazing contentedly and said softly, 'I can't imagine how it must be to love someone and know that person will never be yours.'

Her words reminded Velda of her own situation with Sam; that regardless of how much she loved him, he could never be hers in the way she would dearly like him to be. She lied, 'No, neither can I.'

Gem heaved a deep sigh and said sadly, 'There's no cure for a broken heart, is there, Velda? Just time passing that helps you learn to live with it. I admire her for managing to see Donny on a daily basis and accepting that he'll never be anything more than a friend to her.'

'Only now it doesn't appear he is her friend any longer from what I can see,' said Velda worriedly. 'All we can hope is that whatever has gone off between them is just a temporary rift that will sort itself out. And at least she gets him back as her friend which, to her, it's better to have him in her life as her friend than not in it at all.'

Just then a postman rode up and stopped his bike outside a row of three workers' cottages they were passing on the other side of the lane. Over his shoulder hung a large bag full of post he was delivering. As the young man climbed off his bike, he looked over to the two women, settled his eyes on Velda and, making his judgement on the way she was dressed, said, 'You two with the fair?'

Just then a middle-aged woman, wearing a faded floral-print wrap-around apron over a shabby day dress, curler-ed salt and pepper hair covered by a scarf tied turban-style, came bustling down the path to meet the postman at the gate. Spotting the two women across the narrow road she looked expectantly at them and mirrored what the postman had asked. 'Oh, you two with the fair?'

Not knowing just what their reaction would be towards them when they received their answer it was a guarded Gem that said, 'Yes, we are.'

The postman's whole face lit with a happy smile. 'Seems like an eternity I've been waiting for you to come since I made my plan. I'm bringing my girlfriend on Friday night and I'm going to propose to her in the Tunnel of Love.'

The woman told them, 'It's a whole family outing for my lot on Saturday night. My husband and me, my two daughters and their husbands, three sons and their wives and twelve children between them. The kids can't sleep with excitement. I've been saving in my jar since Christmas for this.'

Relief rushed through Gem and Velda that for these two outsiders, at least, the coming of the fair and the folk running it were welcome. They hoped that the rest of their community felt likewise, which would make for a trouble-free stay here. Gem fished in her handbag and took out a strip of free ride tickets she always carried for such times as this and ripped off two. Stepping over to the postman she handed them to him, telling him, 'Have your ride in the Tunnel of Love on us. I hope your girlfriend accepts your proposal.'

'So do I,' he said worriedly at the thought that she might not. Then his face brightened. 'She's made enough hints so I'm sure she will. Thanks for the free tickets.'

Gem then ripped off another twelve which she handed to the woman. 'For your grandchildren to have a turn on one of the kiddies' rides.'

The woman accepted with great delight. 'Oh, ta so much. This means my savings will go further. The kids will be beside themselves.'

Leaving two happy people behind, Gem and Velda continued on their way.

As they walked along together Gem's thoughts returned to her finding a way to raise the relationship between Velda and her father-in-law. Then an idea came and she broke the silence by saying, 'Ren is such a pretty and good-natured young woman so I'm sure another man will come along and sweep her off her feet. Er, never met a man you felt enough for to marry yourself, Velda?'

Velda froze. Yes she had, Sam Grundy, but to come clean to Gem would mean questions being asked that she didn't want asking. Her reply was short. 'Not anyone I felt enough for to commit myself to.'

'So you never wanted children, then?'

There was silence for a moment before she replied, 'Can't lie and tell you I never yearned to be a mother when I was younger, Gem, but I knew it wasn't meant to be for me.'

'You knew? Oh, you mean your intuition told you you'd never have children?'

Velda wistfully smiled. 'Something like that.'

Frustration swept through Gem. Getting information out of Velda was like blood from a stone. If she wanted to find out what she did then she'd have to be bolder. She took a breath and said bluntly, 'You and my father-in-law get along very well together.'

Velda spun her head and eyed her sharply. The way Gem had said that implied that she knew, or suspected at least, that Sam felt more for her than just friendship and maybe she sensed that she herself had more feelings for Sam than she had said she had. To her relief Sam had not, as yet, broached the subject of furthering their relationship. He was currently far too consumed with making his decision on how to leave his affairs when he died and that was, at the moment, his main topic of conversation. He would repeatedly go over the whys, wherefores and repercussions when he came to visit for his nightcap on fine evenings. Still, she feared it was only a matter of time before he resolved his will problem and the subject of their relationship was raised. She was ready for it now though. She had pre-prepared just what to say to refuse his proposal whilst not in any way causing damage to their friendship. To lose the friendship, the same as Ren over Donny, would absolutely devastate her. She said, 'As you know, it broke Sam's heart when Nell died and having someone who knew her well to talk to about her has helped him come to terms with it. I was only too glad to be his listening ear.'

'Nell's been gone now for over five years and I've no doubt he will always miss her but er ... have er ... you ever thought that you and Sam might become more than just friends, Velda?'

Velda responded vehemently, 'Absolutely not. The thought never crossed my mind. I'm happy with our friendship as it is and wouldn't want it any other way. I'm sure the same goes for Sam too.'

Then it seemed that Sam could be heading for a huge disappointment if her suspicions on his feelings for Velda were correct, Gem thought. And it was obvious that that particular subject was closed as far as Velda was concerned, as she completely changed the subject to ask her how Colin was settling in.

'I can only liken him to a pig in muck, Velda. Considering it's only been a couple of weeks since he joined us, anyone who didn't know he was an outsider would automatically think he'd been born a showman, he's settled in so well. I shudder to think what kind of life he had with that awful Archie Cox, but he certainly couldn't be with better people than Iris and Bert now. They treat him like he was their own son. He looks a different boy with the weight he's put on and is already calling them Mam and Dad. He's made himself friends with other community kids. The only thing he's not happy about is that Iris has insisted he goes to lessons with the other children when he'd sooner be helping Bert on his stall. He's not alone there though as most of the other kids would sooner be doing anything else than going to school.'

Velda chuckled. 'I certainly did anything I could to get out of going. My mother used to despair of me at times.'

Gem grimaced. 'I daren't not go. My parents are not the type to defy.'

Velda turned her head and eyed her knowingly. 'But you did when you married Solly.'

'Mmm,' she said ruefully, 'And they certainly made me pay dearly for going against them.'

'But Solly was worth it.' This wasn't a question but a statement.

'Absolutely. I couldn't have wished for a better husband.'

Velda didn't need to ask if she had regrets over the loss of her family as the price she'd been made to pay for her choice of husband, as that oozed off her. Over the years she had been friends with Gem, Velda had learned that her relationship with her parents, both the stiff, unyielding kind of people whose main focus in life was what others perceived of them, had not been easy for their warm, easy-going, fun-loving daughter. She'd had to temper her persona to suit theirs; when she wanted to run around singing and dancing, she'd been made to sit quietly and read a book. She was told who she could be friends with and who she couldn't. But then they were her parents and she loved them regardless. Their loss to her, along with her siblings, was a pain she would have to endure for the rest of her life. She understood this so well as she herself had suffered the same fate when, many years ago, she had gone against *her* family's wishes and followed her own path in life.

It was obvious that Gem didn't want to talk on this subject any longer as she completely changed it by saying, 'I poked my head inside the...' She laughed. 'I went to say "school" then, but tent is what it is. I poked my head through the flap to see how things were going on the first morning before I came to join you for our shopping trip.'

'And it's going well?'

She nodded, looking pleased. 'So far it seems. Miss Dunn...' She laughed again. 'Isn't it funny that I'm calling her that instead of by her Christian name? Still, she's a teacher and out of respect I will always address her as such, the same as I did my teachers when I was at school. Anyway, Miss Dunn had written the alphabet on the blackboard and all the children were singing and clapping as they sang a song...' Gem sang out in the tune she'd heard the children singing: 'A is for Apple, B is for Bread, C is for Cat and D is for Dog ... and so on. It was more of a game than a lesson.'

Velda looked impressed. 'A much more fun way to learn it than how I did when I was at school writing out the letters in order over and over again on a small chalkboard our parents had to buy us ... we never had pencils or paper in those days. Woe betide us if we got a letter in the wrong place because out came the stick.'

'I suppose I was lucky as I did have paper, pens and pencils to write with but that's how I learned too. Not one of the children that I could see wasn't joining in this morning, even the older ones, and they all looked like they were enjoying themselves. I dread to think that what happened to them last week they could be suffering again right now had Miss Dunn not come along and offered her services to us.'

Velda chuckled. 'What's more of a shock to me is that Sam agreed to pay her to teach the kids and for setting the school up. Not one of Sam's qualities is putting his hand in his pocket to pay out for what he sees as unnecessary. The times I used to listen to Nell's gripes that she needed something new and he would tell her that there was nothing wrong with the old one and buying new would just be throwing good money away. She used to call him a stingy old bugger, to his face as well, but then Nell did realise that they would still be stallholders working for another ringmaster had Sam not been careful with his money.'

'Sam has no idea yet how much it has cost him for the officer's tent as I do the banking and the accounts, remember, so it's not until I update him on financial matters that he'll find out. I do need to choose my moment to ask him to fund some tables and chairs for the kids to sit on as, at the moment, they're on the floor. And, as winter comes, we'll need a stove for heating. Miss Dunn brought the blackboard and other bits she needed with her which she told me were just old items stored in the basement of the school she'd been working in that just hadn't been thrown out, so that saved a good bit. The blackboard was broken so I got Solly to fix it. Anyway, Sam's basking in the thought that he's going to get the equivalent of a knighthood in showmen's terms when it gets around that he's started a school for his workers' children so I'll remind him of that to soften the blow when I do tell him how much it has all cost him. No money is too much to pay to stop our children having to face what they have each time they went to school to my mind and, more importantly, they've all got a proper chance to learn to read and write and that alone will make their lives so much better for them, along with all the other stuff Miss Dunn will teach them.'

Velda said, 'I haven't met Miss Dunn yet. When she arrived yesterday to join us before we all set off to come here I did make a point of calling on her van to welcome her to our community but there were several mothers of the kids she'll be teaching already crowded around her door with their homemade cakes and bottles of home-brewed concoctions. By the time I'd sorted my living van out and erected my tent ready for the fair opening this afternoon, it was late, after ten, and I didn't want to disturb her in case she was in bed. I intend to call on her this evening. What is she like?'

Gem took a moment to formulate a description of Emily Dunn before she responded. 'She looks like a prim, dried-up spinster woman, the sort usually leading a campaign of locals to get us ousted out of their community by branding us all thieves and child stealers. In Miss Dunn's case her looks defy belief because I found her to be just a lovely person and she's got a way with the kids that I can only say is magical; one word from her and they're all sitting quietly paying attention. Even Tommy Pope who can't sit still for a minute! I read a book once when I was a child called *Mary Poppins*. She was this mystical nanny that appeared out of the blue to look after children whose mothers had died. She possessed magical powers and got the children to behave and do all the things they should do but didn't, just by a look or a word. Miss Dunn, to me, is a real, live version of the fictional Mary Poppins.' She paused for a moment before she added, 'I do wonder what brought Miss Dunn to ask for the job and to travel with us in the first place? I mean, at her time of life, it's such a huge thing to do, isn't it? Change your life for a completely different one.'

Velda said sharply, 'She must have her reasons and it's up to her; it's not our business to pry.'

Gem looked taken aback at her companion, who had been unusually terse of manner. In fact, it had come across as more of a warning to Gem than a comment; not to poke her nose uninvited into another's business. But Velda knew her well enough to know that it wasn't in her nature to interfere unless she was invited to, so why did she feel the need to caution her? Then it occurred to her that she knew next to nothing about Velda's past. Was it then that Velda's comment had nothing to do with prying into Emily Dunn's reasons for joining the fair but was instead a warning to

Gem not to pry into her own? But why? She supposed it could be that Velda just didn't like revisiting the past because, like it was for Gem herself, it was too painful to but then could it also be because she had something to hide? Whatever though, Gem was never going to find out as Velda had made it very clear that the past was the past to her and it was only for her to know.

But then all thoughts other than those associated with the feeding and care of her family were swept from Gem's mind as they arrived at the small row of shops.

The area was bustling with activity, women of all ages going in and out of the various shops, weighted down by their purchases. The first shop they came to was the butcher. Several women were already queuing, awaiting their turn to be served by a fat, florid man, a bloodstained apron straining over his wide girth. His equally plump wife was also behind the counter. To their relief, all the other queuing woman were too engrossed in talking between themselves or immersed in their own thoughts to take any notice of the two new arrivals behind them. The butcher did a double-take at Velda, whose style of dress did nothing to hide what community of people she belonged to, but then he continued to serve her in the same friendly manner as he did his local customers while his wife did likewise with Gem. And when both were done, they told them they looked forward to seeing them the next time they called. *So far so good,* they both thought as they left the shop to enter the next one, which was the baker's. Again they left with their purchases, both having received the same friendliness from those that served them. This time even a couple of customers smiled a greeting and told them they were looking forward to visiting the fair as they waited their turn.

Their last port of call was the grocery shop. The shop bell clanged as they opened the door and automatically the queue of waiting women all turned their heads to see who the newcomers were. Realising they were fairfolk, several woman ignored them, turned back their heads and continued to await their turn; it was obvious they were not pleased to see just who the interlopers were but choosing to keep their feelings to themselves. A couple of others smiled a brief welcome at Gem and Velda before resuming their wait.

There were two old women, dressed from head to toe in black, sitting together on chairs by the counter, clutching capacious handbags on their laps. They both glared darkly at Gem and Velda when they arrived and, as they joined the queue, one old crone gave a disdainful sniff and said loudly to the other, 'Oh, I see the *tinkers* have arrived in town so I hope everyone is aware to keep an eye on their daughters and lock up their valuables. Filthy creatures shouldn't be allowed to mix amongst decent folk.'

The other woman said equally loudly, 'Last year when they was here my 'arry's prize pigeons went missing and we all know where they went ... in a gyppo's cooking pot.'

Most fairfolk perceived pigeon or rabbit stew or pie as part of their staple diet. Hunting for wild fare in woods and fields was one thing but stealing from the local community's hutches or lofts, Sam would not condone and both Gem and Velda knew – without doubt – that none of the fairfolk would consider it worth their jobs to have done such a thing. Both women went to defend themselves but then, just as quickly, thought better of it, having long ago learned it was best not to respond at all to derogatory remarks aimed at them, that way avoiding the fuelling of trouble. Instead, both pretended not to have heard what the two old women had said, Gem apparently studying the sides of bacon, cooked meats and cheeses on the marble slab inside a large glass container one side of the counter and Velda a shelving stand just by her holding an array of household goods; several of the items she picked up in succession and pretended to read the labels of.

The shop owner, though, wasn't prepared to ignore the rude remarks the two woman made. He had a living to earn and was far too grateful to see anyone in his shop intent on buying any of the goods he offered, whoever they were. Ernest Flinders was a middle-aged, pleasant-faced, stick-thin man with merry twinkling blue eyes. He finished wrapping a pound of streaky bacon that he had just cut on the slicer for the customer he was serving and, his voice stern, addressed the two old women. 'Now then, ladies, while yer in my shop I'd ask you to respect my other customers and keep your thoughts to yourselves.'

The oldest of the two crones scowled and wagged a gnarled finger at him. 'Well I'm picky who I shop with, Ernie Flinders, but it's obvious you ain't at all particular who you sell your goods to or you'd be asking them to leave. Make sure you check their persons before they go as no telling what the big woman has hidden in false pockets under her dress whilst she's been in here. Gyppos are all thieves, we all know that,' she snapped, nodding her faded black felt-hatted head, which was covering a bob of thin grey hair, in Gem and Velda's direction.

Ernest puffed out his chest and responded, 'Now then, Mrs Crabbitt and Mrs Dane, you're both welcome to shop elsewhere if you're not happy with the way I run my shop.'

They both gawped, aghast. Mrs Crabbitt spat, incensed. 'You know fine well that the nearest grocery shop to here is at least a mile away.'

'Well then, either wait outside until the two ladies have bought their needs and left or sit comfortably where you are until it's your turn and I'll ask you again to keep your thoughts to yourself.' He then returned his attention back to the customer he was serving. 'Anything else I can get you, Mrs Jenkins?'

A young woman in the queue was shifting uncomfortably on her feet. It was obvious she was undecided on whether to speak up about something she had on her mind or keep it to herself. She decided to speak up. 'It's not fair of you accusing the fairfolk of stealing your husband's pigeons when the fair was last here, Mrs Crabbitt, as I know for a fact that you arranged with the Youngs' eldest boy to take them when your husband was out as you were fed up with him spending all his spare time with them and cleaning up the mess they made in your yard. You did it when the fair was here so you could blame them for it and your husband would never know it was you behind it.'

Another woman then piped up, 'Oh, so that's where Mrs Young got all those pigeons from to make those pies. When I asked her, she was very cagey and I can understand why now. I did buy one off her and my old man said it was the best pigeon pie he's ever had, very tasty.' Then, with a wicked twinkle in her eye, she said to Mrs Danes, 'Cora, didn't you meet your husband at the fair when it came to town just after the First World War? He was collecting the fares for the man who owned the swing boats. Me and a few other girls were with you at the time. We'd all sneaked off to the fair behind our parents' backs, you can't deny it. If I remember right, he'd managed to get a job with the fair after being released from Borstal for robbing the local off-licence where he came from. So really you married a dirty, thieving fairground worker, didn't you?'

Aged face screwed up furiously, Cora Danes grabbed hold of the coat sleeve of her companion and pulled her up along with her as she stood up. 'Come on, Martha, we'll come back later as there's a bad smell in here that's making me feel sick.'

After the two venomous women had left, Ernest said to no customer in particular, 'People should really check how clean their own house is before they complain of dirt in someone else's. Now, was it a quarter of cheddar you asked for, Mrs Jenkins?'

A while later, Gem and Velda left the grocery shop weighed down with all their purchases, triply so for Gem as she had a family to feed whereas Velda just had herself.

As they arrived out into the street, Gem said, 'Well, apart from the two nasty biddies, the rest of the locals we've met today seem very happy the fair has come to their town and were very welcoming to us, so hopefully that means we're in for a trouble-free stay.'

Velda smiled. 'We can live in hope, dear, we can live in hope.'

As they turned in the direction of the fair-ground and began their journey, Gem sighed and moaned, 'These bags weigh a tonne. It was a lovely walk here but now I'm seriously regretting not coming in your car.'

Just then they heard a vehicle horn blare out. Looking in the direction it came from they saw Jimmy beckoning to them out of the driver's window of a flatback lorry. As fast as the heavy bags she was carrying allowed her to, Gem hurried over, exclaiming, 'I've never been so glad to see you, Son. What are you doing here?'

'Dad sent me. He knew you'd regret walking when it came to carrying the heavy bags back so he told me to give you an hour or so then come and pick you both up.'

Velda had joined her now and, having heard what Jimmy had told his mother, she said, 'If he was here now I'd give Solly a big wet kiss. What a wonderful husband you have, Gem.'

She smiled. 'Yes, he does have his moments. But you keep your eyes off him as he's all mine.'

Five minutes later, all the shopping loaded next to Jimmy in the front cab, the two women were perched on the back of the lorry, their legs dangling over the side, both clutching the side boards so they didn't fall off. Gem shouted out, 'Right, let's get back as the fair is due to open in a couple of hours and you men can't manage without us women.'

They both chuckled together as they pictured the look on Jimmy's face at his mother's quip as he revved up the engine and set off.

Chapter Nine

It was now Saturday evening and the Grundy community were gratified that the fair had been busy every day, apart from yesterday afternoon when the weather had turned miserable; a blustery wind whipping persistent rain in all nooks and crannies and soaking everything it fell on. Regardless, there were still those determined types who descended on the fairground dressed in their waterproofs and wellingtons, hell-bent on having their entertainment whatever Mother Nature threw at them. The Grundy community, dressed likewise, did their best to provide it with a welcoming smile on their faces, glad of the money to add to their coffers. Thankfully, just after tea time, the grey clouds drifted off to reward other areas of the country with their cargo and the spring sun that shone down was sufficiently warm enough to dry the grass and muddy puddles ready for the hordes of workers to flood in that night to have themselves some much-looked-forward-to enjoyment after a week of hard labour inside their factories and offices.

For the locals their day and a half of freedom from their paid labours began at one o'clock on Saturday afternoon. Fairground workers though were lucky to get a few hours on a Sunday afternoon and evening as although the fair was shut on a Sunday as it was only places of worship that were open for business, there was still work to do in respect of keeping the stalls and rides in good repair and living accommodation too.

Despite what work awaited them on Sunday, some members of the Grundy community had special plans after the fair closed on Saturday night and couldn't wait for the time to come so they could instigate them.

It was approaching nine o'clock and the fairground was heaving with people queuing at all the rides and several deep waiting their turn for a play on the many games of chance offered at the stalls or to buy the wares sold. Big Sam was, as usual, patrolling his way through the crowds on the lookout for potential troublemakers but also for any of his workers acting in any way that wasn't in keeping with his rules of operating and could bring disrepute to his business. At the moment he was making his way through the main ride area; on one side of him was the carousel, its barrel organ in the centre blaring out in one ear, on the other side of him was the waltzer, spinning and twisting its squealing occupants around. 'Rose

Marie' was blaring out from speakers in Sam's other ear and, along with the din the crowds were making, he could hardly hear himself think.

After being consumed with his problem of how to leave his estate for the past couple of weeks or so, struggling deeply with his conscience, he had now made his decision and was ready to cement it with the help of his dear friend Velda. And with that out of the way, he was free to pursue matters in respect of his personal life with her. He meant to speak to her tonight. Before then, though, he had work to do.

Aided by his sturdy stick and puffing on his pipe, as he walked and looked observantly around, his eyes fell on a young girl of about five who was sobbing hysterically into the folds of her mother's skirt by the hook-a-duck stall. *Just some mardy child throwing a tantrum because they can't get their own way,* he thought and made to continue on, but then it struck him that this child's crying was the upset sort, not the foot-stamping temper kind. People's first impression of Sam when they saw him, especially that of children, was of a gruff, fearsome-looking old man and, for the most part, they would be right; his life had been a tough one and he'd had to find a toughness within himself to deal with it or he'd have withered under the strain and wouldn't now have a successful business to be worried over how to leave it when he left this world. But he also had a soft side, especially where children were concerned, and it distressed him greatly to see any child suffering grief like that little girl was now. Besides, to him, whilst in his fairground, all children should be laughing not crying. So he made his way over to find out why the child was so upset in the hope that he could reverse the situation. On arriving up to the child and her mother, who was trying her best to calm her daughter, he leaned over and said 'What's the do, lass? Lost a shilling and found a tanner or did yer drop yer candy floss in the dirt?'

The child was unmoved and it was her mother that responded, somewhat embarrassedly. 'Milly saw the rag doll on the hook-a-duck stall, fell in love with it and set her heart on winning it. She's spent all her pocket money and another couple of shillings I gave her besides on seven or eight goes altogether but she didn't win the doll or anything else for that matter. I've tried to explain to her that it's just bad luck, but...' Her voice trailed off and she gave a helpless shrug.

Sam straightened up, lips tightening, and his eyes narrowed into two thin strips as he looked across at the young man running the hook-a-duck stall. Cyril Bagshaw, or Ducky as he'd been nicknamed by the rest of the Grundy community for obvious reasons, had been with Grundy's since he'd arrived to join them around the same time that Velda had, thirty years before, with his then wife and five young children. On his death four months ago from his body failing to fight off a severe bout of influenza that had swept through the community and also caused the death of two young children, his eldest son had returned to the fold to claim his inheritance. His other siblings, like himself, had gone off several years before to earn their livings with other fairs. Cyril

Bagshaw had been a very congenial man and had a way with him that had people flocking to his stall and he'd made a reasonable income from it. Along with his equally likeable wife, he had been highly regarded by the rest of the community. His eldest son, though, was a different matter. Sam had never had a liking for Micky Bagshaw, a thirty-four-year-old man, big of build with his arms and torso covered in an array of garish tattoos of naked women, some hidden under the American-style black T-shirt he was currently wearing. He'd been a surly child that hadn't made friends easily and was somewhat of a bully, and lazy too. Consequently, none of the other children had at all liked him and had outcast him from their friendship groups.

Time had not mellowed Micky and Sam had a feeling that his father's death had not come at a better time for him as, through the showmen gossip grapevine, he had heard that several fairs he had secure work at had fired him for his ability to look as though he was busy when in fact he was doing very little. Among other things. Sam had hoped that the responsibility of running his own stall would teach him a lesson and he would change his ways for the better. He watched him; his face was a blank mask as he snatched the money from his customers' hands without a smile or a thank you, a wish of good luck. His mother, who had used to stand by her husband's side, bantering jokingly with the customers, cheerfully handing over a prize when they hooked a winning duck, was now sitting on a stool looking thoroughly miserable, a defeated air about her. She looked much older than her fifty-eight years.

Going over to the stall he said to Micky, 'Got a minute, son?'

Micky looked over at the owner of the fair through indifferent hazel eyes. 'Bit busy at the moment as you can see fer yerself, Mr Grundy.'

Sam's eyes narrowed and he snapped, 'It wasn't a request, lad.'

Micky gave an irritated sigh. 'Hold the fort,' he said off-handedly to the woman who had given birth to him as he put the fare he'd just taken off a customer in the money pouch around his waist. Then he bent to crawl through a small door in the skirt of the stall, under the circular water trough holding the gliding ducks.

Sam fixed his rheumy eyes onto the nonchalant ones of his companion and asked, 'How many ducks have you got swimming around?'

Micky shrugged beefy shoulders. 'You can see for yourself, boss, a few.'

'How many is a few?'

He shrugged again and snapped, 'I dunno ... fifty?'

'And how many of that fifty are winners?'

Micky looked at him warily. 'Why yer asking me that, boss?'

'Just answer, Micky. How many?'

'I dunno. A few.'

'How many is a few?'

Micky frowned, bothered. 'Why yer asking me that?'

Sam hissed, 'How many, Micky? Or do I count them myself?'

He hung his head and shuffled uncomfortably

on his large flat feet before muttering under his breath, 'None.'

Sam's eyes darkened, thunderous, and he growled, 'Repeat that, Micky, and just a bit louder as I'm getting on, see, and can't hear so well.'

He lifted his head and shot back, 'None. I said NONE.'

'I thought that's what you said in the first place but I couldn't believe me own ears so I just wanted to confirm it.' Before Micky could stop him, Sam had grabbed him by the throat with an iron-like grip that defied his age and, pushing his face wreathed in anger into his, he snarled, 'We offer our punters a game of chance, Micky, you are offering them no chance. In fact, what you are doing is stealing off them. Your father would be turning in his grave if he knew what you were up to. He was one of the most honest men I have ever met. If it wasn't for the respect I have for your mother I'd have you off my fair now and, I tell you this, I'd make sure other fairs were warned about what you get up to so it wouldn't be easy for you to get a pitch anywhere else in a hurry. Now, at least ten of the ducks should be winners, so sort it now, lad. Be warned I shall be regularly checking – or my sons will be – and you'll never know when. And, another thing, if I ever see your mother sitting like she is looking like she's waiting for the grim reaper to call on her, then I shall personally make sure she's well looked after here with us, but you'll be long gone. From now on I want to see her with her happy smile making the punters laugh with that funny banter of hers and happy around the fair otherwise too. Is that clear?'

When Micky didn't answer him, he shouted, 'I SAID, IS THAT CLEAR?'

Micky vigorously nodded his head. 'Yes, Mr Grundy. Yes it is.'

Sam released his hold on him. 'Good. Now see to them ducks but first hand me that rag doll.'

Micky flashed a look at the big doll hanging in pride of place amongst the other prizes of cheap fluffy toys and plastic bags with goldfish swimming inside them hanging from the circular domed roof of the stall and on the support column in the middle, amongst the numerous flashing colourful lights, before bringing his eyes back to look confusedly at Sam. 'Why d'yer want that? It's our big prize for anyone who hooks three winning ducks in a row.'

Sam smiled mockingly. 'That you made sure no one had any chance of winning ... any of your prizes in fact. Just hand it over or I'll get it myself.'

Micky ducked back through the small door in the skirt of the stall, grabbed the doll, then leaned over the water trough and, in a begrudging manner, passed it to Sam. Sam shot him a look that said: 'I'll be watching you' before he stepped back over to the still-sobbing little girl and, patting her on her head, said, 'I think this dolly needs a home and I heard you'd like to give her one.'

While the child's mother looked on, stunned, the little girl lifted her head and as soon as her eyes settled on the doll, her tears miraculously dried to beam with a happiness that matched the smile her lips were displaying. As her eager arms stretched out to take the coveted doll from Sam's hands, she uttered, 'She's mine to keep. Honestly, mister?'

'You won her fair and square, lass. The man who runs the stall made a mistake and you did hook a winning duck.'

She clutched the doll lovingly to her chest and looked up at her mother. 'Can we take Ermentrude home and show her to Daddy?'

Her mother smiled tenderly down at her. 'Yes, of course, love.' She then said gratefully to Sam, 'Thank you so much.' Grabbing her daughter's hand, they went off, soon to be swallowed up in the crowds.

Before he carried on with his walk around, Sam looked at his pocket watch, secured to his waistcoat by a thick gold chain. It was a prized treasure his father had given him on his twenty-first birthday, that his own father had given him on his. It was just coming up to ten past nine. Not long now before he was with the woman who had come to mean such a lot to him, who he hoped was going to give him the answer he so wanted to hear when he put his question to her.

A short distance away, Suzie was taking a break from helping her parents on their toy and bric-a-brac stall, smoking a cigarette at the back of it. Her thoughts were whirling, heart thumping in anticipation of what was in store for her once she had finished work that night. She'd told Donny an old friend from one of the fairs her parents had worked with before they'd come to Grundy's had married an outsider from Barnsley who Suzie had bumped into when she had visited Grundy's fair earlier that evening. Her husband was away working at the moment with his job as a lorry driver and the old friend – according to Suzie – had invited her to come and see her when she finished work so they could have a catch-up together over a bottle of wine. She was welcome to stay the night – as long as Donny didn't mind, of course. Good-natured Donny was pleased his wife was going to spend time re-acquainting herself with a long-lost friend, although not so happy she was spending the night as he would miss her.

Had Donny known where his wife was really going and who she intended to spend the night with, he would have been totally devastated.

The previous Monday morning Suzie had travelled to the same row of shops that, a couple of hours before, Gem and Velda had visited. She usually went shopping with a couple of other young married women that she was friendly with, but that morning she was not in the mood for anyone else's company. Despite being ever on the lookout to find herself a man to better her life with, she had been utterly disappointed not to even get a whiff of a possible contender and was starting to feel despondent that she would be stuck for the rest of her life with a boring husband that she was fond of but didn't remotely love in a way a woman should the man she married, with no better future facing her than the one she had with him now. She was worried that all her future held was living in a caravan with the most basic of amenities, having to work long hours for the few shillings a week her parents gave her for her labours, to supplement the income her husband earned labouring for his parents on their ride, to feed and clothe them both. They had little to spare for any luxuries or social life.

As she had been about to leave for her shopping trip her father, knowing where she was going, had asked her to place a bet for him on a dead cert at the bookie's. Suzie had no love for her father. He put gambling and drinking before his family and it was the reason she had grown up with six of them living in a cramped, disintegrating two-person van, wearing cast-offs. Many times the only food they had to eat was what her mother had managed to cadge off other members of the community they were living amongst at the time. They rarely had money to buy fuel for the heater or lamps and Suzie constantly felt the shame and embarrassment of it all. It was this which had ignited the flame in her that when she grew up she was going to do all it took to get the best life she could for herself. This morning she was feeling so low that she couldn't be bothered to admonish her father for throwing yet more money down the drain at the expense of her mother going without and so she just snatched it off him, along with the slip of paper with the nag's name on.

Suzie was a smoker herself but even she gagged when she took a breath of the cigarette-filled air when she first entered the shop. It was full of groups of shabby-looking men milling around waiting for their races to begin, relayed to them over the radio speaker high on a wall, or venting their anger for bets they had just lost, trying to conjure up excuses to give their wives for their empty pockets. Having fought her way to the counter, ignoring the extremely suggestive remarks she received from various men as she did so, and whilst giving the dodgy-looking man beside her a dark glare for pushing up too close against her for her liking, she slapped the note with the horse's name, along with two half crowns, on the counter and said tersely to the counter assistant, 'Half crown each way and can you make it quick so I can get out of this hellhole before I choke to death.'

As the man took the note and money he responded, 'Wish all my customers were as good to look at as you. Fancy a drink in the back office, if you're not in too much of a rush to get off?'

She was about to tell the bookmaker just what he could do with his drink when she stopped short, clamping shut her mouth. She had expected to be greeted by a hard-faced, loudly dressed man, the same sort that she had on numerous occasions seen her father placing his bets with in the array of bookies he had dragged her inside, so she was shocked to see that this man was young, in his early thirties. He was dressed very smartly in a fashionable dark blue suit and crisp white shirt and his looks were the sort that made her legs go weak. A shiver of anticipation travelled down her spine and, hiding her hand with her wedding ring on it from him, she smiled winningly and told him that, for him, she did have a few minutes to spare for a drink.

His name was Larry Bickerstaff and she quickly gleaned from him that he was the owner of three thriving bookies in the town, had his own house, sports car and holidayed abroad twice a year. Most importantly, he was unattached. Larry was everything she had been on the lookout for; someone who could give her the kind of life she craved. From that moment, her life with Donny was already fading into the background as she planned her future with Larry. Through her expert conniving and powers of manipulation, she had managed to spend time with him several times since first meeting him that Monday morning. She had been intimate with him on several occasions too. Tonight he was taking her out for dinner and dancing, then she was staying the night with him in his house. She had formulated a plan of how she would install herself in that house when the time came for the fair to pack up and move to their next venue in seven days' time.

Larry believed Suzie to be a single woman herself who was just here in Barnsley for two weeks to visit her friend whose parents owned the visiting fair and who she helped out when needed. Back in her fictitious home town of Carlisle, she lived in her own flat, albeit it being rented. She was an orphan, her parents having died when she was young, and she had been raised in a children's home. She was a personal secretary for an accountant. Larry would be a pushover for her. Already he was smitten – couldn't keep his hands off her.

Stubbing out her cigarette, she glanced at her wristwatch. Just over an hour to go and she would be heading off for a night of passion. He didn't know it yet, but Larry was going to give her the future she'd promised herself.

Over on the dodgems, with his hand hovering over the controls and humming along with Bill Haley and the Comets' 'Rock Around the Clock' that was blasting out, Solly watched the riders manoeuvring the gaily coloured toy-town-like cars around. He took a glance at his wristwatch as he brought the ride to an end and the vehicles slowed to a stop. The riders began to clamber their way out and the next punters scrambled excitedly in. It was coming up for nine-thirty. He smiled to himself. Finding out that his two sons were going out after work tonight and his father informing him that he wouldn't be having supper with them this evening either as he had other plans – which he declined to enlighten Solly about, leaving him filled with intrigue about just what his elderly father could possibly be up to – meant that himself and Gem would be on their own. It had been a while since he'd showed her how much he loved and appreciated her, and tonight he planned to. As soon as the last stragglers left, he'd secured the dodgems for the night, then made sure no one else needed his help around the fair, the fun could begin. He'd already arranged with a gaff lad to fetch fish and chips and deliver them to his van along with the bottle of wine and bunch of flowers he'd gotten one of the women fair workers to bring him back from their shopping trip earlier. He intended to head straight to their van to have the table set and the wine cooling in a bucket of cold water to surprise Gem with as soon as she came in; her believing she still wasn't finished for the night as she had supper to cook and clear away, then ready the van for rising the next morning. He couldn't wait to see that lovely face of hers light up when she saw her surprise.

Bill Haley had finished rocking around the clock by now and the gaff lad in charge of keeping the music playing had chosen 'Cool Water' by Frankie Laine and the Mellomen. Once all the punters were seated and Solly had started off their ride, he looked across towards the waltzers that his brother was in charge of and the pleasure that had been flooding through him at the thought of the special time ahead with his wife left him to be replaced with sadness. He sighed. Had the relationship he had with his brother been different, Solly would have invited him, along with a girlfriend if he had one, to join him and Gem tonight; to share their meal with a glass or two of wine or beer, have some laughs playing cards. Gem would have liked that as she loved company.

He was still as much at a loss as he had been over twenty years ago when his brother, one he had shared as close a relationship as ever brothers could, suddenly changed overnight from the fun-loving, good-natured nineteen-year-old he had been into a surly, distant stranger. What he did in his spare time, Solly had no idea; if he went out, stayed in alone, entertained anyone he'd met whilst working or out and about in whatever place they were playing in. He never joined in with any family occasion, nor any Grundy community social get-togethers. He kept himself very much to himself. All his family had been bewildered by the sudden change in him and nothing they had done to try and restore Sonny to his old self had worked. But then, how could it when they had no idea what caused it in the first place. Even all these years later, Solly still missed the closeness he had shared with Sonny. He never stopped hoping that the old Sonny would somehow miraculously resurface and the relationship return to what it once had been. Otherwise, Solly wasn't looking forward to what the future could hold when the time came for Sonny to replace their father in charge of the fair. As he was now, Sonny was not an easy man to get on with; he treated everyone he had dealings with in the same indifferent and intolerant manner. It was if he saw everyone as being beneath him. As a boss therefore... Solly was deeply concerned what life would be like for himself and the community.

A loud scream jerked Solly out of his troubled thoughts. His head spun around in the direction it had come from. A gaff lad was sitting in the middle of the track, face wreathed in agony, clutching his arm to his chest. The cars still whizzed around him and on suddenly spotting a human obstacle in their path, the panic-struck drivers desperately did their utmost to steer their vehicles away from the stricken young man. As he dodged between the cars over to the lad to help, Solly didn't need to ask him how he'd come to land as he had. Showing off to the pretty girls amongst the drivers, he'd jumped from the back of one moving car to another, misjudged, and landed heavily on the metal plate track. The pain he looked like he was in possibly meant his arm was broken, but hopefully it was just a sprain.

Otherwise the lad would need to be taken to hospital and if Solly couldn't find anyone else that could drive that was free to take him, he'd have to do the deed himself. He prayed he could or else his planned romantic time with his wife looked to be in jeopardy; there was no telling when another time like this would come along again.

In the operating room of the waltzers, one foot propped up on the small counter, Sonny looked at his wristwatch. It was just after nine-thirty. Not long to go now. He had got himself through the doors of a private drinking club and had been going there for the last three nights. He had ingratiated himself with a group of local businessmen, them believing he was also a businessman. His story as usual was that he was in Barnsley seeking suitable showroom premises to expand his elite car business. He'd even had business cards printed now. One of the men he had met was holding a cocktail party, to which plenty of his business associates were invited. Sonny wasn't stupid. The man was only cosying up to him in order to secure himself a large discount off a vehicle he might buy from Sonny in the future as payback for introducing him to potential new customers. He was full of glee that the pompous man had absolutely no idea that he'd just invited the sort he saw as scum into his own home to help himself to his chef-prepared rich food, to consume large quantities of his fine wines and liquors and to smoke his expensive Cuban cigars.

When his plans for the future came to fruition,

Sonny planned to visit Belinda. Dressed in his handmade clothes, gold rings on his fingers, a wad of bank notes bulging in his pocket, he would arrive at her door in his luxury car so she could see with her own eyes, hear from his own lips, the grave mistake she had made when she had chosen to believe her own kind's lies about fairfolk when she refused his proposal. He would also make her aware there would be no redemption for her with Sonny due to the callous way she had turned him down. He vehemently hoped that her life, since he had last seen her, had not gone well. He hoped she was impoverished and in a miserable marriage so his revenge would be all the sweeter.

There was a tap on the door and his head jerked up to see a woman standing there. She was in her late thirties, not bad-looking in a trashy way; brunette hair backcombed high in a fashionable beehive, tight-fitting dress hugging the curves of her hourglass figure. He had noticed she had been at the fair for the last couple of nights; she had ridden on the ride he had been operating at the time. It was obvious to Sonny the woman fancied a bit of fun with him of the carnal kind; he was a good-looking, sexy man – he was well aware of that – so who could blame her? As her attempts to catch his eye had failed up to now, she was clearly taking matters into her own hands. Sonny had no doubt that, were he to oblige her, her time with him would be kept secret; a thrill to look back on when she was old and grey. Based on past experience, should she ever see him in the street afterwards, she would either totally ignore him or sneer disgustedly as she crossed the road out of his way, same as most of her type did.

Reaching over, he opened the door and said nonchalantly to her, 'Yeah? What can I do for you?'

Leaning provocatively on the door frame, she ran her tongue over her lips and said seductively, 'I'm sure you know fine well what you can do for me without me having to tell you?'

He slowly travelled his eyes up and down her body before he brought them back to rest on hers and, in a mocking voice, he told her, 'I wouldn't touch you with a barge pole, lady. Don't like the thought of what I might catch off a tramp like you. The way to get off the ride is that way.' He pointed over her shoulder.

Her face screwed up with anger. 'Why you ... you ... bastard. Call me a tramp when you're nothing but a dirty, robbing, gyppo. You ... you...'

Before she could finish her tirade he had jumped up, hands on her shoulders, and he was pushing her away from the door. 'Fuck off my ride before I throw you off. Go and prostitute yourself with someone who ain't fussy where they dip their wick. I am and, as I've already told you, it ain't with a common slut like you.' With that, he pushed her back against a stationary waltzer carriage and pulled shut the operating room door. Taking his place back on the stool with one leg propped up on the counter, he proceeded to roll himself another cigarette, his thoughts returning to focus on what the evening ahead held for him.

In the pay booth of the Tunnel of Love, Gem was

so lost in her thoughts that her sister-in-law, Fran Grundy, widow of her husband's eldest brother, Joshua, who had died in the war, literally had to bellow in her ear before she got Gem's attention.

'I left Rosa and Nita in charge while I went to powder my nose, so just popped in on my way back to see how you are,' Fran told her. 'You were miles away.'

'I was just watching that girl over there.' Gem pointed a finger in the direction of the waltzers.

Fran looked out of the pay booth window in the direction Gem was indicating. She could see numerous girls of varying ages coming and going or hanging around on the steps awaiting their turns. 'Which one?' she asked.

'That one in the blue slacks and beige jacket.'

Fran spotted her and studied her for a moment. The girl looked harmless to her, not doing anything untoward, she was just leaning against a post smoking a cigarette. 'What about her?'

'I'm sure she's watching me?'

Fran, a matronly, homely, attractive woman in her late forties, was wearing a worn-looking fur hat pulled over her short, dark, tightly home-permed hair. She was wearing an A-line skirt and hand-knitted jumper with a woollen coat over the top as the night had turned chilly. She squinted over at the young woman in question. 'She does keep looking over this way but it doesn't look like she's watching you in particular, to me. I'd say she's more got her eye on Phil the gaff lad. Do you know her?'

Gem shook her head. 'From this distance it's hard to see her properly but, as far as I know, I've never seen her before in my life. She might not be watching me right this minute but I swear she has been.' Gem then forgot about her as a more important matter popped into her mind. 'How did your date with Jonny go last night? I like him, Fran. He seems the gentle giant sort to me. He reminds me of the film star Stanley Baxter; tall, muscular and brooding. He'd certainly protect you if you were in a sticky situation. Solly speaks very highly of him, too. Jonny's not hidden the fact that he's had a fancy for you since he came to work for Sam so I'm glad you finally agreed to give him a chance. You've had a couple of dates with him now, haven't you?'

Fran mused thoughtfully. 'He reminds me more of Sean Connery, only not quite so dark-haired and, of course, he's not Scottish but from Huddersfield. Still, I do feel very protected when I'm with him and he treats me very well.'

Gem eagerly asked, 'So, do you think this might become serious between you both?'

Fran sighed. 'It would be nice to have myself a man again and the more I'm with Jonny the more I'm getting to like him, but ... well ... I feel I'm being disloyal to Josh. The girls don't know about us yet and I have no idea how they'll feel about me replacing their father with another man.'

Gem told her sternly, 'I know you two had a really good marriage but he's dead, has been for over ten years. Josh was a good man and if he was still here, he'd be telling you that you've mourned him long enough and to grab some happiness while you can.'

Fran looked thoughtful for a moment before

she smiled and said, 'Yes, he would. Before he went off that last time, he told me that if he didn't come back I was to find myself and the girls someone to look after us and to be happy. When he didn't, finding myself another man ... well ... that was the last thing on my mind. I coped by throwing myself into raising the girls and trying to make up to them for the loss of their father, as you know, but now they're grown up and don't need me as much, I'm on my own a lot. I really feel I'm ready to share my life with another man, someone like Jonny who makes me feel special. Still, as I said, I can't shake off this feeling of being unloyal to Josh.'

Gem affectionately patted her arm. 'Josh will always have a special place in your heart, Fran. He was your first love and the father of your children. But he's no longer here to hold you in his arms and comfort you in bed, but Jonny is. It might not work out between you both, but at least give it a proper chance. It might turn out that you're as happy with Jonny as you were with Josh.'

Fran thought on this for a moment before a slow smile spread across her face. 'Yes, you're right. I'm meeting Jonny after we finish up tonight for a drink and a game of cards with Ivy and Bert and some of the others if they fancy joining us and, if that goes well, I'll ask him to come and have dinner with us on Sunday, see how the girls take to him.' She then glanced at her watch. 'I need to get back. The girls are going out tonight with your Jimmy and Robbie and a few of their other friends so I've told them that, as soon as the last ride is finished, they can scoot off to get themselves ready and leave me to close down.'

'Enjoy yourself tonight and don't forget to pop in and see me tomorrow to tell me how it went.'

'I won't,' Fran said as she left the tiny booth and shut the door behind her.

Gem saw the signal the gaff lad gave her announcing that he was ready for her to start off the ride. Having done the deed, her eyes then strayed over again to where the young woman had been standing. The girl was gone. Maybe Fran had been right and it wasn't herself, after all, the girl had been watching but Phil. He was a good-looking young man, after all. She stifled a yawn. She was tired tonight, would like nothing more than to arrive back at her van, find a cup of tea waiting for her, and then crawl into bed. Her work wasn't finished for today yet. Her sons might not want feeding as they were going out but her husband and father-in-law would and the clearing up still needed to be done afterwards.

Donny wasn't particularly looking forward to finishing work that night and spending the rest of it alone, although he did genuinely hope that his wife enjoyed herself. He would see to any chores; there was bound to be some clearing up to do. Clothes would be left all over the bed as Suzie sorted through what to wear and take with her for her overnight stay. There'd be pots to wash, a pile of washing in the basket, the floor to sweep. Suzie was lax when it came to anything domestic and his mother was always nagging him that he should be far less tolerant of her; make her do what wives were supposed to and that was to take responsibility of all their husband's needs, not just in the bedroom. But Suzie had the ability to render him useless when it came to him showing her that he was not happy with her in any way. It always saw him ending up apologising to her and feeling guilty for being unreasonable and challenging her in the first place. He wasn't stupid enough to know that Suzie took advantage of his good nature but, when all was said and done, his wife was everything to him. He couldn't love her any more than he did; nothing was more important to him than her happiness. If that mean he was deemed as being under her thumb by the rest of the Grundy community because he helped her in what was deemed as women's work around their home, then so be it.

He made his way through the living van area towards his own, extending a genial goodnight to fellow community members coming or going as they secured down for the night or were sitting outside having a last drink and cigarette. Velda was sitting outside hers and, as he passed, he made to wish her a goodnight but then noticed she had company in the guise of the boss himself, Sam Grundy. They were both deep in conversation together. He often saw them enjoying time together as he was on his way home. The boss and the fortune-teller had been good friends for a long time. He wondered if they would ever become more than that? He supposed at their age though they were too old for such things as romance. He respectfully crept past in an effort not to disturb them. Ren's van was behind

Velda's and in his endeavour to avoid any contact with her he then veered his path to slink into the shadows of the vans opposite, just in case Ren should be outside hers and an awkward situation arise between them.

He was still reeling from the shock of learning how the woman he had been such close friends with for all of his life, had trusted implicitly with his innermost secrets, admired and thought so highly of, in return thought so disparagingly of him. That she thought him an imbecile to ridicule behind his back to other members of their community. He was surprised that none of his other friends, people he believed he had a good relationship with, had even hinted a warning to him.

He suddenly stopped short and looked over towards Ren's van as the voices from those gathered outside reached his ears. There were the two Grundy boys, Jimmy and Robbie, their cousins Rosa and Nita and several others, all dressed up ready to go out. Ren was looking very pretty in a full blue skirt with several net underskirts underneath, a white Peter-Pan-collared blouse and a short blue cardigan with flowers embroidered in an assortment of colours running down the front. He remembered then that they were all going to a party tonight. The invite had come from a local girl Jimmy had met earlier that week and been seeing since. Her friend was having the party in her flat and on Jimmy asking if he could bring some friends along, her response had been: Of course! The more the merrier and records, food and booze were welcome also. Unaware of what Donny had learned about Ren's true feelings for him and his own decision to estrange himself from her now, Jimmy had sought him out earlier that day and asked if he and Suzie were going to join them. Donny would dearly have loved to accept, despite the fact that he would possibly get in trouble with Suzie when she found out he was going to a party without her, even though she was out enjoying herself without him. But as Ren would be going he had made his excuses, aware he'd never be able to relax and enjoy himself. So it was with a heavy heart that he carried on making his way to his own van, letting himself inside to spend the evening by himself, passing the time tackling undone chores.

Chapter Ten

Velda leaned over and gave Sam an affectionate pat on his arm. 'I'm glad that's all sorted and you can put it behind you now.'

He nodded. 'So am I. It's been causing me a headache for weeks and I really appreciate you listening to me rattle on about it. I finally came to my decision and I can now rest easy when my time comes.'

She chuckled. 'Well, not yet for a while at any rate or who else will I share a nightcap with? I'm so glad I was able to help.'

He eyed her awkwardly for a moment before he ventured, 'Well, I wanted to talk to you about that, you being my friend I mean. You see...' He paused for a moment to take several deep breaths and gather his wits in an effort to say words to Velda he'd wanted to for a while now. In the meantime Velda's own heart was thumping as she knew the moment that she had been dreading had arrived. Her own thoughts tumbled to remind herself of the words she had already formulated in which to respond to him without damaging in any way the relationship they already shared. She was only drinking tea but she quickly poured herself a small whiskey and swallowed it to afford her some Dutch courage to deal with what was to come. Sam continued, '...I... Well, you've become more than a friend to me, Velda, much more. I've, er, well...'

She put her hand on his knee by way of stopping him going any further and although her emotions were raging internally, she managed to speak evenly. 'Sam ... I care for you too, very much. I'd like nothing more than for us to become much more to each other.' How much she wished for that, longed for it, but through matters beyond her control it was something that could never happen.

Before she could say any more though, Sam had grabbed her hand, was holding it tenderly between his gnarled ones and was excitedly blurting, 'We'll be so happy together, me and you, I know we will. It was dark days for me when my Nell died. Thought it was the end of the world for me. I don't need to tell you that though do I, Velda, as you helped me through those terrible days. But as I got to know you, saw what a wonderful woman you were, I began to see that it wasn't the end of the world for me after all, that there was a woman that I could be just as happy with as I was with Nell. You made me see I did have a future without her, Velda. I'm just so happy that you feel the same way about me as I do you. Now, if there's anything you want to do to the van before you move in...'

Sheer panic was racing through Velda and, holding up her free hand in a warning gesture, she interjected, 'Sam, please, stop.'

He eyed her, confused. 'Why? What's wrong? Oh, I'm going too quick. You want us to court for a bit first before we...'

'No, no, it's not that.' She pulled her hand free from his to wring both of hers together and, face wreathed in grief, told him, 'Sam, I do care for you as much as I could any man, but I can't be with you.'

He gawped, taken aback. 'Can't? Why?'

She was very aware of how much it had taken a man like Sam to bare his soul to her like he was and she hated lying to him but, regardless, she had no choice. 'Because ... well because my conscience won't let me.'

He looked bewildered. 'Conscience? I don't understand? We're both free... You are free aren't you, Velda, not got some husband–'

'No, no, of course I haven't.'

'Well what's this about your conscience not letting you be with me then?'

'Nell was a good friend to me, Sam, you know she was. I thought the world of her and, regardless of the fact that she's no longer with us, if I got together with you I would feel I was betraying her. She would always be standing between us, Sam, so it would never work. You understand, don't you?'

He shook his head, befuddled. 'Can't say as I do. Nell was a generous woman. Last thing she would want is for me to spend the rest of my life mourning her and if I found someone else I could be happy with, I know I'd have her blessing.'

Should Nell have known Velda's secret she would most definitely not be giving her beloved husband her blessing to pursue a relationship with her. 'I dare say she would be, Sam, but I just can't. As I told you, I'd feel I was betraying her. What we have together is so precious to me, you must believe that, and I don't want to do anything that would risk causing any harm to it.' Although she had gone over in her mind several times what she was going to say to Sam, saying it out loud was proving so distressing for her that, by way of ending this situation she said, 'Would you mind if we called it a night, Sam? Been a long day today and I've a few things I need to do before I go to bed. If the weather is fine I'll see you for your nightcap tomorrow night?' she hopefully added.

Sam hadn't been expecting this outcome; he had thought Velda would be very welcoming towards his proposal and they would start planning their future together. He had been looking forward to having her by his side as his companion, someone to share his daily life with, cuddle up to in his lonely bed but, regardless, there was a part of him that did – in a way – appreciate her reasons for not wanting to take their relationship further. Maybe, given time, she might change her mind. He could only hope so anyway. He flashed her a forced smile. 'Yes, love, you see to your chores and get yourself to bed. And, of course, if the weather is fine, I'll see you tomorrow night as usual.'

She forlornly watched him go, glad in a way the situation that had been hanging over her for a few weeks now was finally over but so very sad the outcome could not have been different.

As it was, Solly did not have to take the errant gaff lad to the hospital. He had broken his arm but Solly managed to get one of the labourers to accompany him in a Grundy lorry so he was able to witness the look of pure joy on his wife's face when she arrived home to find him waiting for her, brandishing a bunch of flowers and glass of wine, with the table set and the food that would fill the empty plates keeping hot in the oven.

As Gem laid her knife and fork down on an empty plate a while later, she looked tenderly over at her companion. 'That was such a lovely thought, Solly, thank you. The flowers are beautiful and the wine is going down a treat. I am such a lucky woman to have you.'

'Yes you are,' he said jocularly, then added soberly, 'But not as lucky as me to have you.' He watched her start to clear the table and raised his hand to stop her. 'Leave the clearing up to me. Go and relax on the sofa with your wine.' He then added with a twinkle in his eyes and meaning in his voice, 'Or go and get yourself into bed and I'll be with you in two ticks.'

She downed the remains of her wine, got up and said, 'Make it one tick. I'll be waiting. Eh, and don't let on to your dad you arranged supper tonight and cleared up afterwards or he'll be having a go at me for not being a proper showman's wife to you.'

She made to go into the bedroom but was stopped by the door opening and Sam arriving. He looked subdued and snapped gruffly, 'Saw your lights were still on so came to see if there was any supper left.'

They both individually thought: *So much for having a few hours of romantic time to ourselves.*

Solly frowned at his father. 'I thought you had other arrangements tonight?'

Sam grunted. 'My meeting didn't last as long as I thought it was going to.'

Gem was back at the table now, collecting the dirty plates together. She knew her father-in-law well enough to know he was very upset about something. She wondered what it could possibly be over. He'd certainly seemed in good spirits when he had had dinner with them earlier and, as far as she was aware, no incidents had happened at the fair tonight to upset him. 'We had fish and chips tonight and I'm afraid there's none left but I could fry you up some bacon for a sandwich?' she told him.

He went and eased himself down on the sofa. 'No, don't bother, not really that hungry. I'll have a drop of that wine if there's any left in the bottle or a finger of whiskey would be preferable.'

Solly went to a cupboard to fetch the whiskey. 'Didn't you have your nightcap with Velda tonight then after your meeting finished early?'

It was a moment before Sam replied dismissively, 'Just a quick one. She was tired and had a few things to do before she went to bed.' Then he growled, 'What's with all the questions? It's like being in the middle of a Spanish Inquisition.'

Gem looked sharply at him. So could that be the reason for Sam's bad mood? Had he finally unburdened his feelings to Velda in the hope of igniting a proper relationship with her, but she had refused him? She was only surmising, basing her assumption on Sam's behaviour of late in respect of Velda and her own conversation with the older woman during their shopping trip, but it seemed the only answer she could think of for Sam's abrasive reaction. Gem still couldn't understand why Velda wasn't at all receptive to giving a closer relationship with Sam a trial at the very least as the pair did get on so well together. Nothing ventured, nothing gained, was Gem's opinion. She did hope, though, Sam got over his disappointment sooner rather than later. He wasn't exactly the life and soul of the party kind as it was, so when upset over anything he tended to take it out on those closest to him.

As Gem set the table for breakfast, Solly did his best to have a conversation over nothing in particular with his father, but Sam was being very uncommunicative, only grunting any response he decided to give to something Solly said and, finally, much to both his son and daughter-in-law's relief, he finished his drink, declined another and, without a by your leave, left.

As soon as he closed the door behind him, Solly

let out a huge sigh of relief. 'I know he's my dad but, God, am I glad to see the back of him. Some mood he was in tonight, far grumpier than normal. I wonder who or what has upset him? Anyway, thankfully he didn't stay that long and it'll still be a while before the lads come home, so that means we've still the van to ourselves.' He winked at her suggestively.

Gem flashed a look around to satisfy herself all was tidy and ready for rising the next morning, only noticing that one task remained undone before she replied, equally as suggestively, 'I'll be all ready and waiting for you.'

Solly hurriedly attended to the last task, desperate to join his wife in bed. He smoothed out the newspaper the fish and chips had been wrapped in and folded it into quarters. He was just about to fold it once more to make it a size to fit comfortably on top of a larger pile they kept for using as toilet paper when a head and shoulders photograph of a woman caught his eye and he stopped to study it. The woman seemed vaguely familiar to him. The photograph was not a very clear one, it was grainy in parts, and looked like it had been taken by an amateur photographer, possibly as part of a larger group as the head of the woman seemed to have been cut out and enlarged. Solly's level of reading wasn't much higher than just the basics, him having learned simple words whilst his sons were doing their lessons with their mother and what he had picked up over time, but intrigue made him try and read the article accompanying the photograph.

He managed to sound out the name of the

woman in the photograph as Emily Dunn. His face screwed up thoughtfully. That name seemed familiar to him too but again, like the face, he couldn't place it. He did recognise the name of the town the woman came from. It was the same one as the last town the fair had played in. The woman must have come to the fair whilst they were there and gone on a ride he was manning at the time and that was why her face seemed familiar to him. He was unable to make out any of the words of the rest of the article except for one which was the word POLICE. This woman was wanted by the police for some reason. He wondered what for? This was one of the times that he regretted that he couldn't read proficiently. He would remain ignorant as to why this woman was of interest to the authorities. He finished folding up the newspaper, put it away with the rest and, with all thoughts of the missing woman gone from his mind, hurried off to join his wife.

Ren, Robbie and Jimmy and the rest of the group of friends had to ask directions several times before they found the address of the flat where the party was being held. It was in a street of old, large Victorian villas that had all been converted into six flats each. As they walked down the street it was apparent which flat the party was being held in as Winifred Atwell's 'Let's Have A Ding Dong' was blaring out of a first-floor window and several teenagers were sitting on the window ledge, smoking cigarettes and drinking whatever it was from a variety of receptacles from tin cups to dubiously obtained pub glasses.

As they arrived, a girl called jocularly down to them, 'Can't come up unless you've brought booze with you.'

It was Jimmy that called back, 'Beer and cider do?'

'Very nicely. And so will you,' she said.

Robbie nudged him in his ribs and joked, 'Seems you'll have two fighting over you tonight, Brother, that girl in the window and the one that invited you to the party in the first place.'

Jimmy elbowed him back. 'Nothing new there then, me having woman fighting over me. Hazards of being good-looking. Come on, let's get in and have ourselves a good time.'

The fairground friends had to climb over young men and women, chatting and drinking, sitting on the stairs leading up to the flat and then they eased themselves through a gaggle more on the small landing at the top. Inside, the one-bedroom flat was heaving with at least thirty more dancing in a space created in the large living room by moving the furniture up against the walls. There was flirting and snogging on shabby sofas and armchairs and youngsters milling around, chatting. On a table by a wall was an Airline portable record player, blasting out, and a mixed pile of 78 and 45rpm records, mostly from the latest hit parade. In the kitchen people were replenishing drinks, eating sausage rolls and crisps, chatting and kissing. The bedroom was occupied by a pile of coats and a couple hidden underneath them. The atmosphere was lively and inviting, a good time being had by all. They were welcoming new arrivals, no matter what colour, race or religion they were.

A while later, Ren, mellowed by the couple of drinks she had consumed, was on the top of the fire escape off the kitchen with another girl of her own age, happily answering her barrage of questions about life for those that lived and worked for a travelling fair. Ren couldn't wait to grill her about her life living in a house and work in an office of a local factory. Nita and Rosa had both found themselves partners they each had a fancy for and were dancing in the living room with them. Robbie was in the kitchen having a genial but heated discussion with several other males on the topic of football. The girl who had invited Jimmy to the party was sitting on his knee in an armchair in the living room and the pair were oblivious to anything else that was going on around them. The rest of the fairground group were enjoying themselves too, mingling and dancing with other locals.

Then, suddenly, the girl on Jimmy's knee gave a yelp and, next he knew, she was no longer on his lap. Bemused as to what had just occurred, his eyes popped open and his head jerked up to see three youths looking murderously down at him. All three were dressed alike, Teddy Boy style, in draped coats with black velvet collars and cuffs, drainpipe trousers and narrow ties. One of the youths' suit was in red, one electric blue, the other light grey; they had black crêpe-soled shoes on their feet and hair piled high in a DA style. The Teddy Boy in the red suit had a tight hold of the long hair of the girl Jimmy had been canoodling with, almost pulling it out by its roots. Face wreathed in agony, she was pleading with him to let her go. Some of the party-goers nearby, on recognising the newcomers, had huddled together and were looking fearfully over at them.

The Teddy Boy in the red suit roared, 'You're dead, mate. She's my girl you've been–'

Before he could finish, the girl he was roughly manhandling screamed, 'I ain't your girl. I'm no one's girl. I go with who I choose. Every girl that you get to go out with you is too scared to say no, but I ain't scared of you, Les Pocock. Not you or the rest of your thugs, I ain't. Now get that through your thick head and let me go.'

Yanking her hair, making her yelp out in pain again, he pushed his face into hers and menacingly hissed, 'Get it through your thick head, Di. If I say you're my girl then you are until I decide otherwise. Got it.'

Jimmy had jumped up from the chair by now and was facing them. 'You heard what Di said. She's not your girl. Now let her go.'

Les laughed scornfully, eyeing Jimmy like he was something he would scrape off his shoe. 'Or what? Fancy dying tonight, do yer? Who are you anyway? I ain't seen you around these parts before.'

Before Jimmy could respond, the lad in the blue suit piped up, 'He's from the fairground, Les. I recognise him from when I was there last Friday. He was on the dodgems.'

Les's face screwed up furiously. He shook Di and bellowed, 'Did you know he was fairground scum?'

'Yes, yes!' she cried. 'I invited Jimmy and his friends to Mandy's party. And he's not scum. Don't call him that. Now let me go, Les, you're hurting me.'

He shook her frenziedly again. 'I'll fucking kill you, you slut. Letting this filthy, thieving gyppo maul you.'

Fury erupted through Jimmy then. 'We're not thieving gypsies, we're showmen, you ignorant cretin.' He balled his fists and, in no uncertain terms, warned Les, 'Now let Di go, you bloody bully. I won't warn you again.'

Les laughed. 'Or what, *gyppo?*' He released his hold of Di, shoving her forcefully away from him. She toppled backwards into the armchair Jimmy had just leapt out of and, to Jimmy's horror, he then reached into his pocket and pulled out a switch blade, flicked it open and brandished it in Jimmy's direction. 'I'd fuck off, mate, before you find out what it feels like to have this...'

He got no further as he felt a weight land on his back and the knife flew from his hand to skitter across the floor, landing out of sight, under the table with the records and player on. He screamed as he felt his own hair being yanked out by its roots. He wailed, 'Not me hair. Don't touch me hair.'

'You'll have none left if you don't clear off yourself and leave Jimmy and Di alone,' a voice shouted in his ear.

Les lurched around, to find his two cronies, only to see them cowering together as they watched the proceedings. He screamed at them, 'You fucking useless idiots! Get this ... this ... off my back.' He then started to swing backwards and forwards in an attempt to dislodge the person clinging to it.

His two mates made to help him but then several of the male party-goers jumped on them to hold them back. As the cowards they were, they didn't need much restraining; seemed quite relieved that they were being, in fact.

Jimmy's eyes, meanwhile, were darting backwards and forwards as Les frantically spun around, desperately trying to remove the person from his back so he could retaliate. The body on his back finally flew off to land heavily on the floor by the door. Fearing what was coming then for Les's attacker, Jimmy made a dive for Les to stop him, but missed. Les, meanwhile, had clenched his fist and was about to land it forcefully on the face of his attacker but, to Jimmy's surprise although not as much as it was to Les himself, a fist seemed to come out of nowhere to land squarely on his chin. It sent Les flying backwards to land across the knees of a shocked couple on the sofa.

Through the doorway then came the rest of the body the fist belonged to. 'Bloody hell that hurt,' moaned Robbie, rubbing his smarting, bruised knuckles.

Ren then scrambled up from the floor, giving herself a brush down and said ruefully, 'Hopefully they might think twice before they gatecrash a party again.'

Jimmy shot back, 'That was a daft thing you did, Ren. You could have got hurt.' He was at her side now, looking down at her in deep concern.

'You're not hurt, are you?'

She grinned up at him. 'I'm not, but I wouldn't care if I was. I'm not about to let that bully get away with throwing his weight around without putting up a fight.'

Di was at Ren's side now, impressed. 'That was so brave of you.'

Ren waved a dismissive hand. 'Ah, it was nothing. Dealt with far bigger bully boys than them at the fair and lived to tell the tale.'

Jimmy went over and slapped Robbie on his back. 'Sparring with the boxers paid off, Brother. That was some mean left hook. In the nick of time too,' he added suddenly, having a vision of the flick knife heading towards him.

Still rubbing his smarting knuckles, Robbie told his brother, 'It was a right hook I used but, yeah, I have learned a thing or two from our boxers, thank God. It came in handy tonight.'

Di arrived then and said to Robbie, 'Come in the kitchen and I'll find something to put on that hand. First though, there's some rubbish I need to get rid of.' She turned and glared at Les, now coming to from his punch in a heap on the floor after the couple had pushed him there off their knees. 'You and your *nancy* boys get yourselves out of here and don't come back. And just so we're clear. I am not your woman, never have been, never will be. The thought makes me feel sick. Now stick that in your pipe and smoke it. Oh, and a bit of advice. I'd lie low for a while if I was you, Les Pocock, as you're going to be a laughing stock once it gets around that you were bettered by a woman half your size.' She inclined her head towards Ren. 'Not such a big man after all, are you?'

Everyone was laughing and jeering at him and with the shame of being made to look a fool in front of all these people as well as his two henchmen hanging heavily on him, Les scrambled up from the floor. As he pushed past the gathering near the door, he glared thunderously at them all but it was Jimmy's ear he growled into, 'You and the rest of the fairground scumbags will be sorry you crossed me.'

Grabbing his two friends, he pushed them both roughly out of the door and followed them.

Seconds later, a young woman stood in the doorway with a young man in tow who, for the last hour, she had been with under the pile of coats in the bedroom. They both looked somewhat dishevelled. Grinning, she slurred, 'Great party. So glad I decided to throw it. First one I've ever thrown there's never been any trouble.'

She couldn't understand why the rest of the room started laughing. It was only Jimmy that wasn't though. Les Pocock's parting words were still ringing in his ears. He hoped they were hollow ones!

The party atmosphere returned and it was getting on for nearly three in the morning when the fairground friends reluctantly decided they had better get back to the fair, even though the party was still in full swing. They all had work in the morning, whereas the rest of the party-goers could spend the day in bed if they wanted. They had all made new friends though who they would hopefully meet up with again before the fair moved on again next Sunday and they'd definitely look up when they came back again next year.

The journey back to the fair took them through the peripheries of the town centre and, by the time they had reached those streets, having already danced for the last few hours, Ren was feeling fatigued and she was starting to lag a little behind them. One of the premises they were passing had low window ledges and she took a moment to sit on one to rest, mindful not to let her friends out of her sight and she risk losing her way home. This time of a night the streets were deserted, the fairground crowd the only ones seeming to be inhabiting them, so she was surprised when a door in a three-storey building opposite opened and a man and woman came out. Before the door shut behind them, from what she observed inside, it looked to her like the place was a private club of some sort. The woman was all over the man, embarrassingly so, although he didn't appear to mind, and both were obviously the worse for drink. Ren herself was, too, but she wasn't too inebriated for it to strike her that the woman somehow seemed familiar to her, very familiar in fact. She was the mirror image of Donny's wife Suzie. By the time the couple turned into the street and headed away from Ren, Ren was positive the woman *was* Suzie. She would know that spiteful, nasty woman anywhere. But then she reasoned with herself it couldn't be, could it? Suzie with another man when she was married to Donny? Besides, it was the early hours of Sunday morning and Suzie would be in bed with Donny, snuggled up, asleep. It was the consumption of drink she had had playing tricks on her eyes, it had to be.

Just then she felt a hand on her shoulder and she jumped, eyes darting up to see who had accosted her, relieved to see it was Robbie grinning drunkenly down at her. He slurred, 'We noticed you were missing and I was elected to come back to find you.' Realising his little friend was tired, Robbie, despite her protests, hauled her to her feet then up onto his shoulders and she couldn't help but shriek out in laughter as he ran back, with her clinging on for dear life, with her hands clasped around his forehead, to re-join their friends.

Les Pocock sat on his sagging bed, slapping a length of thick chain he was holding in one hand rhythmically against his other palm, his face screwed up murderously. Not only was he furious that the girl he considered his own property had chosen a fairground worker above him, those scum from the fairground had got the better of him and, worse, one of them was a freak of a woman half his size. The other members of his gang would get to hear about this, that was if they hadn't already, and his role as leader could be in question. He couldn't have that. He was the big man in his world, the name of Les Pocock revered, and he meant to keep it that way. Besides, he had told that lowlife gypsy who had stolen Di off him that he would be sorry he had crossed Les Pocock and he was damned sure he was going to honour that threat and, in turn, redeem himself as the leader of the gang.

Going over to his bedroom door he opened it and called out, 'Finished sorting me suit out yet, Ma? If not, get a move on as I'm going out again.' He had a gang to round up to do his bidding, to make sure those fairfolk rued the day they came to Barnsley.

Chapter Eleven

No matter how little sleep was gotten the night before by some members of the Grundy community, no matter how acute their hangovers, all the fairground folk were up and about the following Sunday morning at the crack of dawn. They beavered away over their allotted tasks, all ensuring that the maintenance jobs that had been put off until more time could be attributed to them, such as painting and repairs, as well as the usual daily ride safety checks were done to Sam Grundy's high standards. Only then would time for leisure begin.

With the sound of church bells ringing in the distance, eight women were sitting in a circle outside a caravan, shelling peas into bowls for each of their respective families' Sunday dinners. They had already cleaned and polished their living accommodations, seen to any washing and, after dinner, there was a huge pile of ironing yet to do. So, although what they were doing now was work of a kind, it was easy and enjoyable and a chance to socialise. Four of the women were in their seventies, two of them widows, the other three in their forties; two were married to showmen, one to an all-round labourer and driver and the youngest woman in the group was a teenager lending her mother a hand. The four older women were reminiscing about the past.

'Nearly had a riot on our hands,' Betty Smith was saying in her aged, cracked voice. 'Well, I mean, it wasn't fair was it? Most of the punters were pedalling their hearts out on the velocipede and the rest were just sitting back enjoying the ride and putting no effort into it at all. Course, I am going back to the 1890s now, before we had generators to power the rides. Clever man he was, who came up with the idea for the velocipede.'

Fourteen-year-old Kitty Pope hadn't a clue what Betty was talking about. 'Just what was the velocipede, Mrs Smith?'

Betty was only too delighted to explain to her. 'It was bicycles fixed to a roundabout, connected to some sort of pulley contraption underneath. Once the riders started to pedal, it would move them round, how quickly depended on how fast they all pedalled together.'

'Sounds fun,' said Kitty, putting peas she had just released from their pod into the bowl on her mother's lap.

Sadie Mickleton piped up, 'Not that the rides aren't fun these days but there was something magical about the times when steam engines powered them. My granddad had steam yachts, called *Lusitania* and *Mauretania* after the huge ships, that used to swing really high back and forth. My dad had a switchback ride where all the carriages were carved like Venetian gondolas, painted in gold with red velvet seats. When you rode around in them you felt just like a princess.' Her old, rheumy eyes glazed distantly as past memories resurfaced. 'Oh, it was summat so it was. Me as a young girl riding on those great stream tractors as we drove them through the town we'd come to play in to let the locals know we'd arrived. Like a carnival itself it was, all the tractors painted in their bright colours pulling the rides and living vans behind them, the locals waving and cheering as we passed and us waving back, throwing free tickets to some which there was always a mad scramble for. When we arrive in a town now and do our arrival parade down the high street it's not quite the same to me as it was back then. I know the lorries are all painted up and we still all wave from the cabs and backs and those walking alongside hand out leaflets and the free ride tickets, but lorries don't quite cause the same excitement as those huge steam-powered tractors did, in my opinion.'

Gem nodded in understanding. 'Yes, I remember my father taking me to a stream tractor rally when I was a little girl and, as you say, there was something magical about riding in one. You were so high up you felt you could see the whole world. The man who owned the tractor let me pull the whistle. Whoop, whoop!' she mimicked. 'I can still hear the noise the whistle made now and see the billows of steam coming out of it when I pulled the chain. The whistle had a tin cap on the top of it and holes in the sides that made the sound when the steam blew through it and, to me, it looked like the drawings of the Tin Man in the book I had called *The Wizard of Oz.*'

Betty couldn't read so had no idea what Gem was referring to. 'I often wonder what happened to those two steam tractors me dad and granddad owned. Probably rotting in some farmer's barn somewhere I expect, as no one uses them nowadays, do they?'

Fran, who was sitting next to Gem, asked the old lady, 'Did your dad sell the tractors then, when we went over to generators? Bet you were sad to see them go from what you've told us.'

She nodded. 'I was sad to see them go, yes. Mam had no choice as she couldn't run the rides herself when me dad was killed, with us kids all still very young then and with her having Granny to look after as well. Granddad was dead himself when it happened, so all we had was Mam to look after us all.'

'Oh, your father was killed. I didn't know that, Betty. How did it happen?' Gem asked her.

'He was fixing one of the tractors, putting on a new belt when he shouted something to the lad that was helping him who thought he'd said for him to start it up and so he did and the belt caught Dad up in it when it started to whirl around. Obviously that wasn't what my dad did shout to him but what it was we'll never know. Anyway, it was horrible … chopped to pieces he was and scattered all ways. We owed money on the rides and by the time Mam paid off all that was owing by selling the rides she'd just enough money to bury him and buy the darts stall, which is what the family is still running today.'

'A great uncle of mine had a similar fate,' spoke up Tilda Pope, Kitty's mother. 'He was larking about though at the time, showing off to a girl he had a fancy for by trying to climb up on the canopy while the tractor was still moving. He slipped off and was crushed to death when one of the wheels went over him. Lads still lark about and get hurt, killed even, these days only it's the lorries they do it on not the steam tractors. Anyway, I meant to thank you for the bit of cake you sent over to me yesterday, Betty. Lovely it was.'

Betty smiled. 'My pleasure. Can't lay claim to making it meself as my wrists aren't up to whisking up butter and sugar together any longer so I bought it from that grocery shop down the road. Not bad for shop-bought, was it? That reminds me, Gem, what on earth is up with Big Sam lately? I mean, he can be grumpy on the happiest of days but yesterday I asked him if he'd like a piece of the cake as he was passing my van and he didn't even answer me.'

Gem thought she had a good idea but family business was kept in the family. She did hope though that Sam got over his disappointment with Velda soon as she couldn't deny his grouchy mood was getting on all his family's nerves and, from what Betty had just said, affecting his workers too. She responded lightly, 'He probably never heard you, Betty. I've been suspecting for a while he's going deaf. He is over seventy after all.'

One of the other younger women spoke up. 'Well he heard me alright when I asked him yesterday if I could pay our stall rent late cos I had to get some new shoes for my Billy as there's more holes in the bottom of the ones he has than shoe leather. Do you know what the old bugger said to me? "We didn't have shoes at all when I was a kid and it didn't do me any harm. Rent's due tonight." And then he just walked away.'

Gem secretly felt that Sam had been a little harsh with the young woman as she would have allowed her to be late paying her rent in the circumstances but then, in fairness to Sam, if it got around that he had allowed one stallholder to be late paying their pitch rent then they would all try it on and his authority as boss would be undermined. She said, 'Well, with respect to Sam, if everyone was late with their rent he wouldn't be able to pay his bills to keep the fair running and we'd all be up the swanny without a paddle.'

As a member of the family, Fran was very aware that this conversation would be uncomfortable for her sister-in-law so thought it best to put a stop to it. She announced, 'That sounds like some of the men coming back so if any of yours are amongst them, ladies, they'll be wanting their dinner. I've enough peas to do us, so I'd best go and check how my meat is doing. Got a nice piece of mutton from that butcher down the road and he was kind enough to bung me some beef fat to render down for dripping so my Yorkshire pudding will be the bee's knees today, cooked in that. Not often a flattie gives us something for nothing, is it?'

Gem looked at Fran excitedly and whispered so the others couldn't hear, 'Oh yes, Jonny is coming to dinner today, isn't he? I hope it goes well.'

Fran went to respond but was stopped by

Eunice Sidebottom, one of the other older woman, saying, 'You've got Jonny Hiddles coming for his dinner with you today, haven't you, Fran?'

Fran gawped, shocked. 'How did you know that?'

She shrugged. 'Don't know who told me.' She looked at her neighbour. 'Was it you, Betty?'

'No, it's news to me. Glad for you though, Fran. That Jonny seems a nice man. Helped me a few times without me having to ask and always very pleasant, I've found him. 'Bout time you had some happiness, long time ago now you lost your Josh and no one mourned the loss of a husband more than you did, Fran. You could pick far worse than Jonny, to my mind.'

Gem was trying not to laugh at the look on her sister-in-law's face that her private life wasn't, it seemed, as private as she had thought it was.

Fran bristled. 'Glad I've got your approval, Betty. I'll make a point of letting you all know how it goes. Better hearing it from the horse's mouth than exaggerated through the mouths of several others.'

She made to rise when the peace was suddenly shattered by loud, angry shouts and the bashing of metal against metal. They all automatically looked in the direction of the fairground where it was coming from, although the living vans were blocking their view.

'What the hell is going–' Gem was cut short as louder crashing noises, of denting metal and splintering wood, and angrier shouts resounded. She jumped up from her chair, unmindful of spilling the bowl of peas off her lap and, with the others following behind her, ran off towards the main fairground. As she squeezed herself between two stalls and entered the arena, the sight that met her froze her rigid. A swarm of Teddy Boys, at least thirty of them, armed with thick lengths of chain, lump hammers, axes, long knives and other assorted dangerous-looking implements, were rampaging around smashing at anything in their wake. The half dozen fairground men who had still been working away inside the main fairground when the gang had first arrived and begun their rampage of destruction had armed themselves with whatever was to hand and were chasing them around, hell-bent on stopping them. A few feet away one of the fairground men was lying out cold on the ground, a gash on his head pouring with blood.

Gem spun around and shouted to the women behind her, 'Go and get the rest of the men and, Kitty, run to the telephone box and call the police, tell them what's happening and to get here quick and send an ambulance too.'

Gem made to spin back around but Fran caught her arm. 'Where are you going? You can't go in there, you could get hurt ... killed!'

'Vic Gallows has been hurt. It could be ages before an ambulance gets here so I have to see what I can do for him.'

Fran knew there would be no changing of her sister-in-law's mind once she had made it up, so she didn't waste time trying. 'I'll fetch my first-aid kit,' she called out as she ran back to her living van.

Unmindful of her own safety, Gem ran into the

fairground and over to Vic, dropping down beside him. Despite the mayhem that was going on around her, she calmly assured the injured man, 'It's alright, Vic, Fran's gone to fetch her first-aid box and the ambulance will be here soon.' But she was talking to herself as the man was out cold. She lifted her head and looked dazedly around at the battle raging around her. Teddy Boys were smashing everything in their wake, a handful of fairground men trying to stop them. Then her blood ran cold as she saw a figure race past her armed with a metal pole. It was Solly. She watched in horror as he encountered a Teddy Boy armed with a metal chain, him swinging back his arm intending to maim her husband with it but, thank God, Solly was too quick for him. Before he could thrash the chain into him, Solly had brought the metal pole he was brandishing hard against his accoster's legs, sending him buckling to the ground screaming in pain from a possible broken leg or legs. Then all hell really broke loose as the rest of the fairground men got the summons from the women and, now armed with their own makeshift weapons, swarmed into the main fairground. Then, to her horror, behind them came the fairground women, old and young alike, all brandishing rolling pins, heavy-based saucepans and whatever else they could lay their hands on. Amongst them were Ren and Velda and her nieces, Nita and Rosa.

Fran arrived back then with her medical kit. 'Take care of Vic,' Gem told her as she jumped upright and grabbed the large spanner Vic had been holding when he was attacked.

'What do you think you're doing?' a terrified Fran cried out.

But Gem was already out of earshot and in the thick of battle.

Thirty or so thugs, armed with weapons, terrorising defenceless locals into doing their bidding was an entirely different matter to the same thugs threatening the livelihoods of fairground folk and Les Pocock was soon to realise that he had picked on the wrong group of people.

Forty-five minutes after the rampage began, a dozen or so policemen piled out of a Black Maria at the entrance to the fairground to find all but one of the Teddy Boys, looking very dishevelled and subdued and many needing hospital treatment, banded together in a group by the carousel, surrounded by a very angry circle of fairground men and women clearly prepared to do anything necessary to prevent any of them escaping.

In light of what had happened the previous night at the party, Jimmy had no doubt Les Pocock was the leader of this gang and thus the instigator of this attack on the fairground, fulfilling his promise to Jimmy that he would be sorry he had crossed him. But why then wasn't he amongst the gang of captured thugs? No army would go into battle without their leader?

He looked around him. His gut instincts told him that Les was still in the fairground, hiding somewhere, watching for his chance to escape and leaving the rest of his gang to face the music. Utter disgust for the man surged inside him. He played the big man but, deep down, he was no more than a coward. But Les Pocock wasn't going to escape scot-free if he could help it.

Jimmy's guess was that Les would be hiding somewhere in the living van area, aware that only the very elderly, tiny or infirm would be there at the moment as all the rest were in the fairground. Hoping he was right, he slipped through a slim gap between two stalls and secreted himself behind a van. He then poked his head around the front and took a look around. He could see no sign of Les Pocock. He did notice though that several of the vans that he could see from his position had damage to them. It seemed that some of Les Pocock's gang had entered the living van area during their rampage.

He crept around the front of the van and then dashed the short distance over to the next, looked around that and again saw no sign of his quarry. He kept repeating this until finally he spotted him, looking extremely panic-stricken and shaking in fear, squatting at the back end of Donny and Suzie's van, constantly peeping around on the lookout for the chance, Jimmy assessed, to move nearer to the boundary hedge where he could forge a way through and then flee across the fields to freedom. That was his intention but Jimmy's plan was to do whatever it took to prevent him.

He crept around to the front of the van he was himself secreted behind, which was next to Donny and Suzie's, then across to the front of Donny and Suzie's van. Once safely there and praying Pocock hadn't moved in the meantime, he crept to the back and, heart pumping madly in his chest, peeped around to look. Les was still there but it was apparent that he was about to make a move to the van next door. That van was right next to the boundary hedge and, should a space big enough for Pocock to wriggle though present itself, Jimmy would have little chance of bringing the man to justice for the part he had played in the trashing of the fairground, so it was now or never. Silently taking a deep breath, he jumped from out of the side of the van and then leapt across the distance of the front, landing full force on top of his quarry. Les was so shocked by this unexpected attack, having no idea he was being watched, that he was momentarily struck rigid.

Before Pocock could gather his wits and retaliate, Jimmy quickly straddled him, pinning his arms down with his knees, and with fury raging inside punched him square on his chin. 'That's for what you've done to us fairfolk today,' he fumed. Then he balled his fist again and gave him another. 'And that's for all the other people you and your gang have terrorised in the past and for Di too.' He then got up and, with an iron grip, grabbed hold of a now-limp Pocock and dragged him through the living van area and on into the main fair area where the police were still rounding the rest of the gang up. He took Pocock to the man who looked to be in charge. 'His name is Les Pocock and he's the leader of the gang. He was trying to make a getaway.'

Inspector Stibbins, a stocky man in his forties, eyed Les with derision, suspecting that the nasty-looking purple bruises beginning to form on his chin hadn't been caused whilst he had been running around causing havoc with the rest of his gang but were courtesy of the young man that had brought him to him now. Stibbins' only regret was that it wasn't himself that had given the malicious man the beating he fully deserved for all the suffering he'd brought to others during his reign of terror in the town. He smiled smugly at Les. 'Ah, Pocock. At last. Can't wriggle your way out of this one.' He then addressed a constable close by. 'Put this lowlife in the van with the rest.' When the constable was leading Pocock to the Black Maria, Stibbins said to Jimmy. 'We've been after Pocock for a long time but never managed to pin anything on him. He's behind lots of crime in the area, him and his band of thugs. He'd have got out of this if you hadn't stopped him.' He slapped Jimmy on his shoulder. 'Well done, young man.'

Solly then arrived, looking worriedly at his son. 'Where have you been?' he demanded. 'Your mother and me have been frantic since we couldn't find you, we worried you were lying hurt somewhere or worse.'

Inspector Stibbins spoke up. 'You've a son to be proud of, Mr Grundy. He's done a job for us that we couldn't by nabbing Pocock. He's a nasty piece of work and that's a fact. Our streets will be all the safer now he's off them and for a good long time if the judge has any sense.' He then looked around at the carnage Les and his gang had caused during their rampage. 'Doesn't look like me and my family will be coming to the fair tomorrow night as we'd planned. The kids will be disappointed.'

Solly assured him, 'No, they won't, inspector. If

we all have to work with no rest until opening time tomorrow, the fair will open.'

'Then I'll look forward to seeing you all again under better circumstances when I bring the wife and kids.'

After the police had departed, the fairfolk looked around in utter dismay and disbelief. Stalls had been smashed and most of the rides had some level of damage to them. They all hoped it looked worse than it actually was but, regardless, much work was needed to restore it all, along with the worry of the cost which owners would all individually have to find to put right their stalls and rides. With profits providing livings not luxuries or much leftover to put by for savings, that would not be an easy thing to do. Eight men and two women belonging to the Grundy community, besides Vic Gallows, received injuries that needed hospital treatment but thankfully none suffered anything more serious than cuts needing stitches and bruises and, in Vic's case, concussion.

Big Sam gathered them all together and addressed them in his usual no-nonsense manner. 'Right, we've got just over twenty-four hours to get the fair back to straights and ready for opening tomorrow at two, so let's not waste any time.'

Gem addressed the women. 'We'll pool all our food and have one big dinner for all of us. Are you all alright with that?'

No one said they weren't. At times like these everyone pulled together, even the children. As the men set to in the fairground, the women went off to make sure they were well fed and the children were commandeered to run errands and help where possible.

None of the fairfolk were at all happy about the amount of work that faced them but none were as unhappy as Sonny was. He had planned a relaxing day, so the thought of now having to carrying on working, and hard physical labour at that, repairing all the damage those stupid cretins had caused, wasn't on his agenda whatsoever. But even for a clever manipulator as Sonny was, this was a situation he couldn't get out of as his father and brother were bound to spot his absence, should he shirk his duty. Every member of the Grundy community was expected to do their bit in times like these, no exceptions. Sonny's only consolation was that in the not-too-distant future, any labour of the physical kind would be a thing of the past for him as he'd have the money to pay others to do it.

Chapter Twelve

Velda had heard that several of the living vans had been damaged by the Teddy Boys but it wasn't until she returned a while later from the fairground to check her own accommodation that she realised two of the support poles had been broken, the striped tent fabric ripped in places and the two red-and-green-painted front wheels of her van had been hit with such force by a lump hammer that they were buckled so that the van was unstable. Until repaired, it was not possible for it to be lived in.

As she was staring at it, worried about what she was going to do accommodation-wise, Gem came by. She was labouring under the weight of a huge cauldron-sized iron pot filled with gravy that one of the women had prepared for their collective Sunday dinner. She was going to put it with the rest of the food that was being laid out on long trestle tables that had been set out further down in the living van area. Witnessing Velda in such distress, she put the steaming pot down on the ground and put her arm around the big woman's shoulders.

'Soon have it back to rights, love, and as good as new. We didn't escape either. Several of Sam's rides were damaged and a couple of the dodgem cars are complete write-offs, but all our living vans escaped those louts' attention, thank goodness. But don't you worry, Velda, whatever help you need, you'll get. You can't live in your van until the wheels are fixed, though, so in the meantime you can come and stay with us. I hope you won't mind the sofa but I'll make it as comfortable as I can for you. One condition, mind, I shall expect a free tarot reading,' she quipped in the hope of lightening the situation. Not that she ever would have a reading with Velda. It was the last thing she wanted. Velda had a gift for seeing into the past and present of those whose cards she was reading and Gem had a secret she wanted keeping that way.

Velda looked at her, panic-stricken, and blustered, 'No, no, you're full already with your family. I'll be fine, honestly. I really appreciate you offering though. I can fix up a makeshift tent meanwhile.'

Gem frowned at her, bemused. Why would coming to stop with her for a short time land Velda in such a tizzy? She had thought her offer would have been jumped at; a proper home to stay in against a cold, draughty tent until her van was fixed. She must have misunderstood; it was her way of showing that she didn't like the thought of imposing on them. 'I'm not having you sleep in a tent for the next couple of days, Velda. No disrespect meant, but you're not exactly a teenager. It still gets very chilly at night. You could end up with pneumonia. You're coming to stay with us and that's final. I'll send one of the youngsters to crawl inside the van and fetch out what you need, some clothes or whatever to do you meantime.'

Ren had been lucky. Her stall and living van had escaped the eyes of the marauders so with no repairs of her own to see to, she was helping the Miller family repair their Hit The Moving Target stall which, at the moment, was minus its canopy. The props holding it up had been smashed through and the mechanism that moved the targets along that the punters tried to hit with the three balls their sixpence bought had received some damage.

Despite Donny ending their friendship, it still didn't stop her being worried for him. How could she suddenly stop loving a man she had for so long? So, before she had even checked on her property, she surreptitiously went in search of him. She was gratified to spot him looking no worse for wear, in discussions with his parents over repairs to their stall which had received minor damage. As she turned to go to check her own, a memory returned from the previous night of the woman coming out of the club draped over a man, them both the worse for drink, who had resembled Donny's wife Suzie so closely. As she progressed through the fairground to check on Donny's welfare, she passed Suzie's parents' stall which had only received minor damage but she saw no sign of Suzie herself offering to lend them a hand. Maybe, though, she was helping the other women prepare the meal.

And then, as she was heading back to check on her own stall, Ren had seen her. She was walking brazenly through the stalls carrying a small suitcase, having obviously stayed out the night somewhere. What was most noticeable to Ren was that Suzie was wearing the same coat and shoes that she had seen her double wearing the previous night, coming out of the club draped over the man she was with. Looking like someone was one thing but wearing the same clothes too? The woman she had seen with the man had been Suzie after all.

Her thoughts tumbled then. Suzie must have excused herself a night away from her husband, telling him it was a girlfriend she was visiting, because she couldn't see Donny agreeing to her going out with another man. Suzie was cheating on Donny; there was no other explanation for what Ren had observed last night. How could Suzie do that to such a lovely man as Donny? He treated her like she was the most precious gift in the world and he absolutely adored her. If it was possible for a heart to weep, hers was weeping now. She felt so much sorrow for the man she loved more than life itself being treated so badly by his wife. It had almost destroyed her to watch and hear Donny pledge his love, body and worldly goods for life to another woman but her consolation had been that Donny was happy. But the thought of what this would do to him, she couldn't bear. This would destroy him.

But what could she do? She could confront Suzie. Tell her she knew what she'd been up to and warn her that if she didn't curb her ways then she would tell Donny. But then Suzie would just deny it. And, besides, Ren had no proof to support her accusation. This was just so awful. All she could hope was that this was just a one-time adultery on Suzie's part. The fair was moving on in six days' time, the town they were playing in next was twenty miles away, so Suzie would not be in a position to continue assignations with the man Ren had seen her with last night anyway.

Donny, unashamedly, did not hold back any of his emotions in showing his wife how glad he was to have her back. Suzie, in turn, gave an Oscar performance showing her husband how much she had missed him. To show him just how much she cared for him, she told him that she had planned a surprise for him on Saturday next. He had tried to wheedle a clue out of her as to what it could be but she had stuck firm; a surprise wouldn't be a surprise if he knew what it was. Had he had any idea just what the surprise his wife had in store for him was, Donny would be totally shattered.

In the early hours of the following morning Sonny laid down the hand of cards with a satisfied flap. 'Royal flush. Unless anyone can beat that then I think the pot is mine.'

The other five men around the table all threw their own hands in then with an amount of disgust. Stabbing out the nub end of his cigar into an overflowing ashtray, one exclaimed, 'Fucking hell, Goodman, you haven't won hardly a hand all night and then land the pot. You're not Irish, are you?'

As he scooped up the pile of notes and coins, roughly four hundred pounds in total, small change for the other players but a king's ransom to Sonny, he said, 'I'd offer you a chance to win it back but it's getting on for three and I've a nine o'clock meeting.'

'Tomorrow night then. Here, same time,' another man said as he swallowed back the dregs of whiskey from the bottom of a tumbler, then refilled his glass from the near-empty bottle on the table.

'I can't. You've cleaned me out tonight,' said another man.

'Yeah, me too,' said another.

'I'm heading back home tomorrow, so I can't,' said the third.

'Then it's just us three,' said the man with the cigar.

Sonny nodded. 'Fine with me.'

The room the game was being held in that Sonny had wangled himself a chair at was in the basement of a disused warehouse on the banks of the canal. Sonny scraped back his chair against the splintered wooden floor, stood up, went over to the coatstand by the door, a relic of when the warehouse used to be a thriving operation, unhooked his coat and pulled it on, then returned back to the table. 'Same time, same place tomorrow night then.' As he stuffed his winnings into his inside pocket, he addressed the table, 'Been a pleasure, gentlemen.'

With that, he turned and left.

As soon as he left the building, he ran hell for leather down the weed-strewn rutted tow path towards the humpback bridge, steps at the side leading up to a road that would take him back into town, not slowing down until he arrived there in case the men he had just relieved of their money decided to come after him to reclaim it. The game had come in the nick of time for him as his finances had been running worryingly low as he'd been rather extravagant of late. Four hundred pounds would buy him a new topcoat, a couple of quality suits, three pairs of leather shoes, replenish his array of expensive aftershaves and still leave enough over to fund his fun for the next few weeks at least, should another game not come his way in the meantime.

Sonny had known as soon as he'd sat down at the table in the shabby room that two of the men around the table were card sharps. They clearly both believed Sonny was like the other three men;

just businessmen having themselves some fun. They had no idea there was a third sharp at the table, the third being himself. Sonny had learned his tricks whilst growing up in the fairground from an array of experts who had made their living fleecing people out of their money with their packs of cards. Sonny had bided his time, letting the sharps believe that they were controlling the game, until the pot was of a substantial enough amount, then gone in for the kill and walked away with the lot. He had no intention of returning for a repeat tomorrow night. Now the men were warned, should he win the pot again it would probably end in violence, him receiving the worst of it and no money in his pocket for his troubles. Therefore, when he didn't turn up tomorrow night, the men would come looking for him. It was extremely doubtful they would think to seek him in the fairground or recognise him out of his Raymond Goodman disguise but, regardless, it would be prudent of him to lie low until he was a safe distance away in the next town the fair was heading for as a precautionary measure.

The next night, at just after eleven, Sonny had just shut the door of his living van and flicked on the lights, intending to pour himself a nightcap, relax back in his chair and listen to some late evening music on the wireless, when he felt a thwack on the back of his head, then everything blacked out. When his vision swam back into focus, he found himself slumped in his armchair and it took him a moment to realise that a man was sitting in the chair opposite and another man, tall and broad with the battered face of an ex-boxer, was standing by the side of him, glaring at him menacingly.

The man sitting cross-legged in the chair was small, no more than five foot five, barrel-shaped, aged in his sixties and with receding grey hair. He was dressed smartly in a grey suit and tie, a dark overcoat draped around his shoulders. First impressions were that he was the kindly grandfather sort but then his eyes told Sonny that he certainly wasn't. They were cold, hard; the sort that warned whoever looked into them he was not a man to cross if you valued your life.

Only for a second did Sonny wonder why a man like him was paying him a visit but then his stomach lurched as it struck him forcefully that those two sharps last night weren't working for themselves but were in the pay of this man, who obviously wasn't at all happy that his men had returned, unable to hand him his cut of their spoils. Those two sharps had played a good part, not giving Sonny any clue they weren't playing for themselves but on behalf of a much larger outfit. A crooked game was one thing, but an organised crime one where only the criminals left the table with any money in their pockets, and the rest of the players with physical damage to them when money they had won had been taken forcefully back from them, Sonny would never have gotten involved in. What he couldn't understand though was why those sharps had let him walk away with that pot last night and not relieved him of it there and then. It seemed he was about to find out.

Rubbing his smarting head, Sonny demanded,

'Who the hell are you?'

The man smiled and said evenly, 'Well, you're not who you say you are, are you? Raymond Goodman. Does he actually exist?'

Sonny eyed him warily. 'What do you want?'

'The four hundred you fleeced off my men last night for a start.'

Sonny snapped, 'I won that fair and square.'

'Hardly. My men are pros, but whatever tricks you used they hadn't come across before.'

'So I take it you're here to collect. Why didn't your men just have me jumped last night and relieved of it?'

'Normally they would have, but you led them to believe there were richer spoils to be had so they decided to follow you to see which hotel you were staying in, to then return in the morning and clean you out before you returned from your meeting.' He paused for a moment to light a fat cigar and blow a large plume of foul-smelling smoke into the air. 'Only they were quite surprised when it wasn't some posh hotel you returned to, but here.' He took a slow look around the living van before bringing steely hard eyes back to rest on Sonny. 'Not exactly the Ritz, is it?'

Sonny shuffled in his seat. It was one thing himself invading flatties' homes, enjoying their hospitality whilst knowing they would have him hung, drawn and quartered should they discover just what member of society they were inviting in, but outsiders invading his home, knowing exactly who he was and how they felt about his likes, was another matter. This man was the sort that wouldn't lose a wink of sleep should he decide to make an example of Sonny, leaving him fighting for his life or, worse, dead. 'Look, no argument from me, I'll get you the money. If I'd have known it was a professional game I would have steered clear. I expect you're a busy man and have more important places to be.'

The man held his hand up. 'Not so fast. I never discuss business without a drink. Jonathon, do the honours.'

The brute's name was *Jonathon!* Had Sonny not been so frightened, he would have laughed. A bottle of cognac was on a shelf in the kitchen area, along with a couple of glasses. 'Business? What business could you have with me except to get your money? As you can see, I'm just a fair worker.'

The man leaned forward and eyed Sonny darkly. 'Did you not listen to me? I said I do not talk business without a drink.'

It was only his boss Jonathon got a drink for and, despite the fact he could desperately do with one, Sonny felt it prudent to stay put.

Drink in hand, the man took a gulp, swilling it around his mouth before he swallowed it. 'Not a bad drop. Obviously you do well for yourself. Now, that business I referred to. There are times I need a safe place for keeping certain items for a length of time, somewhere the filth wouldn't think to search.'

Sonny eyed the man quizzically. 'This is a travelling fair, we're never in the same place for longer than a week, a fortnight at the most. I can't see how that would...'

The man's eyes darkened thunderously and he

smashed a fist hard down on the arm of the chair, making Sonny jump. 'The reason I'm who I am and you're just a pleb is because I've got brains. A fair is the perfect cover because you do move around. The police believe we like to keep our loot where we can keep our eye on it so wouldn't dream of thinking we'd ever let it out of our sight. But I won't have any trouble worrying over my goods being out of my sight until I come to collect when I'm ready to as they'll be kept very safe and secure, won't they?'

He was leaving Sonny in no doubt that should anything that was left in his safekeeping not be available when it came time to collect, just what would happen to him. 'Yes, yes, course they will be, Mr er...'

The man sat back and smiled as he took another sip of his drink and a draw from his cigar. 'Glad we understand each other. I want a list of the places the fair is playing in for the rest of the season and where it holes up over winter. Just expect a visit from a representative of mine at any time, understand.'

Sonny didn't like this state of affairs one little bit. What if the police did get wind of this arrangement? But then, as matters stood, it seemed he wasn't in any position to refuse. 'What do I get out of it?'

He flashed his gold tooth at Sonny with a smile. 'You'll get your cut when the goods are handed over to my representative.'

Sonny supposed that was something. 'And what about last night's winnings?'

He thought on that for a moment before he responded, 'Well, whatever way you did it, you won it. I'll just take the same cut as I would have done from those two clots had you not outwitted them. Half.'

Sonny had thought he'd end up with nothing for all his troubles so half was better than he'd hoped for. He looked over at Jonathon, then back at the man in the chair. 'Alright if I go and fetch your share?'

'Go with him, Jonathon.'

The man and his minder left straight after Sonny had handed him his money and his parting words to him were that someone would be in touch very soon.

A while later Sonny had finished the whole bottle of cognac that had been almost three-quarters full before the crime boss and his henchman had arrived. He couldn't believe what he'd gone and got himself involved in. Pinching a wallet, cash lying around or thieving some jewellery he could pawn from someone's house he'd gotten himself invited into was one thing. Sonny suspected that the man wanted him to hide items of great value, high on Wanted lists by police. He had no choice in this matter though, it was do as the man said or risk ending up in a concrete coffin on a building site.

But just where would he hide the man's goods? The hiding place would have to be inside his van as far too many people had access to anywhere else in the fair. But where was he going to find a place inside his van to hide goods? Bleary-eyed, he slowly looked around before his eyes came to rest on the arch leading into his bedroom. Then a slow smile kinked his lips. He knew just the perfect place to hide the man's goods and, should they be uncovered in the meantime, it wouldn't be him that paid the price.

Chapter Thirteen

Gem had taken it upon herself to drop by Ren's at some point every day to check on her. Ren seemed her usual chirpy self but her eyes held a sadness in them that told Gem she was still suffering the loss of her dear friend and far from over it yet. Now she knew of her plight, Gem wished she could do something to help the lovely, fun-loving little woman get over her loss but knew from experience that emotional pain caused by the loss of a someone precious was not something that happened overnight; it could take months, years in fact. Besides, she couldn't openly say or do anything as she was not supposed to know. All Gem could hope for was that by calling regularly to see her, Ren would know that she might not have the love of the man she wanted but, regardless, there were people who cared very much for her.

Having bought a quarter of boiled sweets from Ren's stall to suck on while she updated the accounts, Gem was about to return to her van when she spotted Col. He was acting very suspiciously, seeming to be sneaking his way out of the fairground. Lessons were still in progress so he should be in the school tent. She called over to him. At hearing her voice, he froze mid step before slowly turning around to look across at her with an extremely guilty look on his face.

Going over to him she looked down at him quizzically. 'Why aren't you in school, Col?' Then a horrifying thought struck her. 'Oh, you're not running away are you? You only told me the other day how happy you are with Iris and Bert. Is that not true then, are you so unhappy with them you've decided to run away?'

He gawped mortifiedly at Gem and urgently blurted, 'No, no, I ain't running away, 'onest I'm not. I am so very happy, Mrs Grundy. Mam and Dad are the best mam and dad I could ever have ... well except for...' He didn't need to tell Gem his own dead mother and father. He frenziedly blurted, 'I'll go straight back to school, I promise, but you won't tell me mam and dad will you what yer caught me doing only they'll be cross with me and think I'm not a good boy and want rid of me.' Tears came then to his eyes and he started to cry, absolutely distraught at the thought.

She knelt down before him and took his hands and earnestly told him, 'Col, Iris and Bert love you as much as they would had you been born to them. Iris was only telling me the other day that neither her or Bert could imagine their lives now without you in it. They would be upset of you sneaking away from lessons and punish you for it but never get rid of you, you must never think that.' She then asked him quizzically, 'Just where were you sneaking off to, Col?'

He sniffed back snot as he wiped tears away

with the back of his hand. 'It's mam's birthday today and I've been doing errands for people to earn money to buy her a box of chocolates and was going to pick some wild flowers for her from the fields on my way back from the shop. I have to go straight home after school to do my chores and if I told Mam I wanted to go to the shops she'd want to know what for and wouldn't let me go on my own anyway, so the only way I could buy her present without her knowing was to sneak out of lessons. I asked Miss Dunn if I could go to the toilet.'

Gem was sniffing back her own tears by now. 'Then you'd better hurry to the shops and get back as quick as you can. Miss Dunn is bound to ask what has taken you so long so tell her that on the way back you bumped into me and I kept you talking.' She smiled warmly at him. 'Iris is going to love her surprise birthday present from you.'

A look of delight split his face. 'Ahh, thanks, Mrs Grundy.'

'Here, before you go have a sweet,' she said, offering the bag out to him. He didn't need asking twice.

She watched him run happily off towards the entrance. If Iris had any doubt on just how much she meant to Col then in a very short time she was going to have that dispelled. Such a likeable young lad he was and Gem knew that come time he was going to become a greatly valued member of their community.

She was just about to resume her way back to her van to update the account books when she then saw a large group of women, middle-aged and elderly, streaming through the fair entrance that Cal had had just dashed through. Her heart sank and she heaved a frustrated sigh. Over her twenty years with the fair she had seen many bands of women such as these descend upon them to protest for what they claimed was the rise in local crime, noise and disorderly conduct, caused by the fair being in their vicinity. Any moment now, Gem expected the women to brandish their placards and start causing havoc. She was just thankful they had chosen a Wednesday afternoon on which to make their protest as it was the quietest time of the week so had fewer people's enjoyment to spoil and less loss of earnings for the fairfolk. She knew she was no match for a gang of angry women but, regardless, she needed to try and stop them from what they were about to do, spoiling the fun of the people that were here. She wished she could summon Solly; he was good in situations like this. He had a way with him that calmed volatile people down and defused explosive situations such as this one now potentially was. He wasn't on site though, he was off in the town collecting leaflets and posters from the printers to send off with a couple of the older fairground children to hand around and put up in shops in their next port of call. Then he was to buy parts to fix two rides that were still out of commission after the raid by the Teddy Boys. He was also going to collect Velda's wheels from the wheelwright which had been ordered when it became apparent that her own two were beyond repair. Sam had been known to fuel these protests with his own anger that the mob dared to attempt to hound them out with their outrageous claims, so fetching him wasn't a good idea. Nor did Sonny have the temperament to soothe women on the warpath. So she was the only member of the family to tackle this situation at the moment.

Putting the bag of sweets into her pocket, she went over to waylay them. She addressed the woman who seemed to be in charge; a large, formidable, matronly woman with a bulldog face with hairs on her chin. She was dressed in a brown tweed suit, brogues on her feet and her greying hair was cut into a short, unflattering bob just below her ears. Gem, though, was somewhat perplexed as the women appeared be in a state of excitement against what she thought would be angry.

Gem said politely, 'Can I help you.'

She shot Gem a surprised look before she responded matter-of-factly, 'I don't think so, young lady. We are all quite capable of managing this on our own.' She turned to the rest of her group and clapped her hands several times to get all their attention. 'Are we ready then, ladies?'

Before any could respond, Gem blurted, 'Look, there's no need for this. There are people here enjoying themselves and you'll spoil their afternoon if you do.'

The women all looked at her, bewildered. The leader of them folded her arms underneath her vast bosom and sternly demanded, 'Do what exactly? Just what is it that you think we've all come here to do?'

'To protest about the fair being here.'

The woman stared at her for a moment then, to her shock, she burst out laughing. A deep, horsey *haw-haw-haw.* She turned to the rest of the women. 'Did you hear that, girls? This young lady thinks we're all here to protest against the fair.' To deepen Gem's shock, they all laughed together then. The leader turned back to Gem and told her, 'We're here, my dear, to enjoy ourselves at the fair, not protest against it. It's been years since any of us have actually had the chance to have fun on the rides, play on the stalls and just enjoy ourselves without children or grandchildren pestering the life out of us. Usually it's us watching them have all the fun. We're all members of the WVS, the North Barnsley branch. I'm the chairwoman. When one of our members at a meeting a few weeks back mentioned Grundy's was due and that she'd be taking her grandchildren and that she couldn't remember the last time she actually had some fun herself at the fair without having the responsibility of children or grandchildren to watch over, that got us all saying the same thing. So we unanimously voted that instead of having our annual spring outing at a country garden or suchlike, we'd have an afternoon at the fair instead. So here we are. Now, if you don't mind, dear, we are wasting time. Please excuse us.'

With a huge smile on her face Gem then watched as thirty or so middle-aged and elderly ladies dispersed. Some headed in the direction of the gallopers, some for the House of Fun, some over to the side stalls and others to Ren's stall to buy their candy floss, sweets and ice creams to eat while they decided what to have a go on first.

Gem was so very relieved that the women had not come to do what she had suspected. She would have liked nothing more than to be a bystander and observe these usually upright woman shrieking and laughing like schoolgirls on the rides, but her own work beckoned. Sam would be wanting his financial update imminently and if she hadn't updated the accounts she wouldn't be able to give it to him.

She was heading towards her van when she spotted Emily Dunn. She was supposed to be teaching the children wasn't she? Seemed Col wasn't the only one sneaking out of lessons today. She stopped dead, wondering just what the woman was doing. She seemed to be lurking by one of the stalls, closely watching four of the WVS women giggling like schoolgirls as they tried to shoot the targets on the shooting range. Gem wondered if she knew the women and was waiting her moment to make herself known to them without interrupting their enjoyment. But then she saw Emily turn her attentions to another group of the women taking a turn on the Roll-A-Penny stall. It was then that the look on Emily Dunn's face registered. Such longing that she had never witnessed before in anyone. Emily Dunn didn't know those women; she was wishing she was one of them.

She went over and laid a hand gently on her arm by way of letting her know she was there without startling her. 'Hello, Miss Dunn. Can't deny that those women are enjoying themselves.'

The older woman sighed. 'Yes, yes they certainly are.' A worried look then clouded her face and she blustered, 'I shouldn't be here watching them. The children have been so good and all did well in a spelling test I gave them this morning, so I decided they deserved a treat. I asked Sadie Middleton if she would sit with them for a short time while I fetch a bag of sweets from the sweet stall, but then I saw the women and got side tracked I'm afraid.'

'Those women belong to the WVS and they've come to have some fun. When I first saw them arrive I worried they were here to protest. Oh, whoops! That woman on the carousel is laughing so hard she nearly fell off. Oh, and look, that women on the rifle range can certainly shoot as she's won the large teddy. She must have hit three bull's eyes in a row to have done. One of her grandchildren is certainly going to be pleased with their granny when she gives them it. Which is your favourite ride, Miss Dunn? I have to say that mine is the dodgems but then I do have rather a soft spot for the gallopers as Solly proposed to me when we were both riding on them.'

She replied hesitantly, 'Oh, I er ... don't have a favourite.' She then added, wistfully, 'They all look such fun, don't they?'

Gem eyed her sharply. By her tone of voice and what she had said, she could only mean one thing. Emily Dunn couldn't have a favourite ride as she never been on any. Gem couldn't believe that she had met a living soul that hadn't experienced the thrill and excitement of a visit to the fair! But by the way she spoke and conducted herself, Gem assumed her background to have been a poor one. Well, this was something that was in Gem's power to put right. Sam would just have to wait for his financial update; this couldn't as far as she was concerned.

'Do you know, Miss Dunn, I might work on the fair but I can't remember when I actually had myself some fun in it. No time like the present. What would you like to go on first?'

Emily looked agog at her companion. 'What, me go on the rides!' A look of pure excitement lit her face for a moment but then quickly faded. 'Oh, but I told Mrs Middleton I'd only be gone a few minutes, so I need to buy those sweets and get back.'

'I'm sure Sadie will be fine looking after the children for a while,' Gem assured her.

'You are sure she will? Oh, then I very much would like to have a go on a ride. I'd better fetch my purse.'

Gem chuckled. 'One of the perks of working for a fair is that you get to ride on anything you like for free. Now, which one would you like to try first?'

The gleam in her eyes shone beacon-like and her voice was loaded with utter joy when she said, 'Oh, the carousel, please.'

As they ate dinner that evening, Gem relayed the events of her afternoon to the others around the table. 'I can't believe that Miss Dunn had never in her life been on a fair ride until now.'

'Miss Dunn,' said Solly thoughtfully as he forked a portion of sausage and mash into his mouth.

'Emily Dunn, our school teacher,' Gem reminded him.

'Oh, yes, of course she is, I remember now.' He lapsed into thought again and mused, 'Funny though, I've read that name somewhere recently.' He then looked meaningfully at his two sons. 'Before you tell me I can't read, I can a little and I know I have read that name somewhere, just can't remember where at the moment. This gravy is delicious, Velda.'

The older woman smiled, pleased. 'Glad you like it. There's plenty more.'

'I appreciate you cooking tonight,' Gem told her.

'Least I could do towards repaying you for putting me up while my van is being fixed. The men will have the wheels back on by tomorrow morning ready for me to move back in, Solly?'

He nodded. 'It's all been organised. Your van will be as good as new.'

Gem looked at their guest affectionately. It wasn't until after she had extended her invitation to Velda that she worried that, although they got on well as friends, living together in such a small space as the living van was could be difficult and prove more of a trial than a pleasure. But she had no need to worry. Velda had been a thorough joy to have around. The woman had been extremely considerate, always insisting on taking a back seat when there was a clamber for the bathroom in the morning and waiting until everyone else, had retired for the night before she did herself; she always tidied away her bedding of a morning and never left any of her personal items around. She insisted on helping Gem with the housework and preparing the meals, but never in such a way as to undermine Gem's position as the mistress of the house. Gem had enjoyed having another woman on hand to talk to, appreciated her help around the van and would miss her company when she left. She decided to tell the woman her feelings.

Velda smiled warmly at her, leaned over and patted her hand. 'Me too. All of you, I will miss. I'd forgotten what it was like to be part of a family and I have thoroughly enjoyed it.' Her words were said in all truthfulness. Each member of this close-knit family had opened their arms and welcomed her in, had done all they could to make her feel at home. They had respected her privacy, a matter that had worried her the most over coming to stay as she deeply guarded it. To her shock, that was what she would miss most when she left; being part of a family. She wasn't looking forward to going back to living on her own as much as she had thought she would be.

The next morning, at just after eight, Gem was putting on her coat to ward off the chill for the short trip over to her father-in-law's living van, where he was waiting for her to update him on the fair's financial situation. Solly, Jimmy and Robbie had already left to start work, leaving just herself and Velda. The older woman was filling the cast-iron slipper bath with boiling water, taking advantage of the fact that the Grundys had a bathroom, albeit a rudimentary one; the water from the bath, when released, ran out of the plug hole and through a pipe straight into the ground. She didn't, so a soak in a proper bath, not a shallow tin one, was a luxury.

'This one should do it,' she said to Gem as, dressed in her flowing robe-like dressing gown, she hauled the iron cauldron-type pot off the stove and made a hopefully final journey to the bathroom with it. When she returned, she put the pot back on the stove and refilled it with water ready for when hot water was needed and remarked to Gem, 'Bit early for a meeting with Sam, isn't it? Even people who work in offices don't start until eight-thirty.'

Gem sighed. 'It's payback for me not having the figures for him yesterday afternoon because I chose to have some fun on the fair with Miss Dunn. That's why I had to stay here to do the accounts last night instead of being in the pay booth of the Fun House and had to get Solly to find cover for me. He's just being cantankerous, that's all. He's letting me know that, when all's said and done, he's the boss and when he says jump we jump. He's been extra grumpy since...' She suddenly clamped shut her mouth, realising she was about to say, since she suspected Velda had turned down his advances to her.

'Since when, dear?' she prompted her.

She blew out her cheeks. 'Oh, since ... er ... can't remember. For a while, anyway. You must have noticed he's been grumpier than usual for the past couple of weeks as you have a nightcap with him most nights.'

Velda felt that Sam had accepted her reason for her not wanting to change their friendship exceptionally well and he treated her just the same as he had before his approach to her, but from what

Gem was telling her, it seemed he hadn't taken it as well as she had thought and was taking his disappointment out on his family. She felt remiss for that but, regardless, that was beyond her control. 'Can't say that I have. He's been his normal self with me.'

'I'd best get off or he'll be docking my wages if I keep him waiting. Not that I get any wages for what I do, it's just expected of me as Solly's wife. I'll be about an hour. By that time you'll have finished your bath and maybe we could have a coffee together before you pack your stuff? You can be all settled back in before the fair opens at two.'

Velda looked pleased at the suggestion. 'A coffee with you will be lovely. I'll look forward to it.'

Gem had hardly reached halfway between her own van and her father-in-law's when she suddenly stopped and slapped her hand to her forehead, loudly tutting and annoyed at herself. She couldn't update Sam on financial affairs when she hadn't got the accounts books with her, which she had left on the kitchen table. She retraced her steps and, back at her own van, let herself in, not bothering to announce her return to Velda as she thought her to be in the bath enjoying her hot soak.

A minute or so previous, stripped for her bath and with one foot raised, preparing to get in the inviting hot water, Velda realised that she had forgotten to bring her towel in with her to dry herself off with. It was at the side of the sofa, stored neatly away with the rest of her belongings. She had collected her toiletries so was cross with herself for not remembering the towel too. She had the van to herself though so no need to put on her dressing gown whilst she nipped out of the tiny bathroom into the living area to fetch it. She was halfway into the lounge when Gemma walked in. For both women it was like time stood still as they both stood, staring frozenly at each other. Then, after what seemed like an age, both gathered their wits simultaneously, Gem to cover her eyes with a hand whilst exclaiming, 'Oh, my God!'

Velda cried out, mortified, 'Oh, Gem... Gem... I... I...' She leapt into the bathroom, grabbed her dressing gown, pulled it on, then dashed back out again to stand before Gemma, grab hold of her arms and frenziedly plead, 'Please, Gem, please let me explain.'

Gem dropped her hand to glare stupefied at the older woman. 'What is there to explain? You've lied to us, fooled us for all these years. You're a *MAN!* How could you do this to us? Why?'

She vehemently blurted, 'Because I *am* a woman, Gem. I might not have the body of a woman but I'm just as much a woman as you are. Don't look at me like that, please. Before you judge me, before you tell me to go, please hear me out first. Please, Gem, please?'

Gem stared at the person she knew only as a woman called Velda. She felt that she ought to afford her the courtesy to explain the reasons behind the deception. She said, stonily, 'I have to tell you that, at the moment, I don't know what I feel ... disgust ... revulsion ... confusion ... and other things I can't find the words right now for.

I can't promise I'll feel any different after I hear what you have to tell me, but I will listen.'

Velda sagged gratefully and uttered, 'Thank you.' She sank down on the sofa, pulling her gown tightly around her as though seeking comfort from it. After Gem had sat down in the armchair opposite, she took a deep breath and began, 'Right from when I can remember I didn't feel right about myself, that something was wrong, only I didn't know what. As a very young child, three or four perhaps, when I was on my own I would take off my clothes and look at myself in the mirror. I can remember feeling that what I was seeing wasn't what I should be, only I didn't know what it should be, just not what I was. Sounds stupid, I know, but that's the best way I can describe how I felt about myself then. I was the youngest of three brothers and I knew I was different to them somehow. When they played with their toy cars, football in the street, all the sorts of stuff boys did, I wanted to be with the girls, playing with them and their dolls and doing other girly things with them. It was dresses I wanted to be wearing not trousers. I wanted my hair long so I could have it in pigtails and pony-tails, pretty ribbons at the ends. My mother thought it was just a stage I was going through and would grow out of it but my father was having none of it and neither were my brothers. They teased me mercilessly. I was a nancy, a cissy. Because the other boys used to rib them over me, my brothers would beat me when my parents weren't around. Most nights, every night in fact, I'd cry myself to sleep. My father had always believed there was something medically wrong with me and, finally, he took me to the doctor. He was a crusty old Scotsman and he told my father that I was just being rebellious and to beat it out of me with a stick. So whenever I was caught doing anything that wasn't considered what boys did, I was thrashed black and blue. Then, finally, my mother got fed up with the neighbours telling her I wasn't normal, sniggering that she'd given birth to something unnatural. At her wits' end she decided I was mentally unstable as she couldn't think of any other reason why I acted as I did. She threatened that if I didn't start behaving like I should, then she'd have me sent away to the lunatic asylum and they would give me electric shock treatment. And, if that didn't work, a lobotomy to repair what was wrong with my brain. I'd heard of those places and I was terrified. So I squashed all my feelings of wanting to be with the girls, dress like them, play the games they did, and forced myself to join the boys, play their games; be tough and rough like they were. I hated it, hated myself. Each day was purgatory for me but I kept up my act for fear of what would happen to me if I didn't.

'It wasn't until I was about thirteen years old that I met a woman ... who I thought was a woman ... who told me just what I was and, for me, that day was like a weight had been lifted, as I finally understood what was going on with me. My mother had sent me on an errand to collect a dress from the dressmaker she had been using for years. When I arrived in her shop the dressmaker, Mrs Golders was her name, told me to wait in the sewing room as she was in the middle of a fitting and as soon as she was finished she would see to me. She told me to help myself to milk and biscuits and there were some comics I would find that she kept for customers' children to keep them occupied whilst she dealt with their mothers. She would be about half an hour, she told me. I helped myself to milk and biscuits, found the comics, and I was just about to sit down and wait for Mrs Golders to return when I noticed the dress. It was hanging on a rack with others, but this dress was different. I had never seen anything so beautiful. It was a party dress for a young girl of about my age. It was made from the most fine material that sort of shimmered in the sunlight coming through the window. It was white with many net skirts underneath and a wide red band around the middle that tied in a large bow at the back and the ends hung right down to the scalloped hem. It was like the dress was screaming at me to try it on and the need for me to do that was far too great for me to resist. Only a few minutes had passed since Mrs Golders had told me she'd be about half an hour, so I had plenty of time.'

Velda's eyes glazed distantly over as she re-lived such a pivotal moment in her life. 'The dress fitted me like it had been especially made for me. As I looked at myself in the mirror it was like I was seeing myself for the first time; as I should be seeing myself. Looking pretty in a dress. I was so consumed with my reflection that I didn't know anyone else had come into the room until I felt a light touch of a hand on my shoulder and Mrs

Golders said, "You look beautiful, dear, but that dress was made especially for another little girl for her birthday and she'll be very upset if it's not in perfect condition when she comes in with her mother tomorrow to collect it. I've other dresses you can try on if..." I never let her finish, I screamed at her that I was only larking about putting on the dress, terrified she'd tell my mother what she'd caught me doing but she took me by my shoulders and shook me hard until I'd calmed down and then said quietly to me, "I know one of my own kind when I meet one. Now, carefully take off the dress and hang it back up, then wait here until I come back and we'll have a talk." I had no idea what she meant about knowing one of her kind when she met one. There was something in her manner though that told me not to be frightened and to wait for her to hear what she had to say to me.

'It seemed ages before she returned and, during that time, I'd built myself up into a terrible panic. I was so worried she was just stalling me so she could summon my mother and any minute she would come charging in and have me carted off to the asylum for what Mrs Golders had caught me doing. I was on the verge of running off but then Mrs Golders came back and, to my relief, she was alone. She could see what state I was in. She sat down next to me, took my hands and told me not to be frightened as she wasn't going to tell my parents and that she understood why I had done what I did. She said she had known since I was a little boy that I was the same as she was. I still didn't understand what she meant: that I was the same as she was. She was a woman, she looked like my mother, dressed like her, wore her hair in a similar style and smelt like she did and I'd no reason not to believe she wasn't a woman. But she had a way with her that just made me want to listen to what she was telling me. She told me she had so very much wanted to talk to my mother about me, who she could tell was struggling to understand why I behaved as I did but to do that would mean her divulging her own secret about herself and then being hounded out by those that didn't understand or accept her for what she was. She told me that hardly a living soul is born perfect, that nearly everyone has something about them that isn't perfect. Some babies are born without one of their limbs, with something wrong with their brain, some with a nature that makes them fall in love with others of their own sex and some in the wrong bodies altogether. They have the body of a female but brains that think and behave like a male. We aren't mentally ill but just how Mother Nature had made us.'

Velda was desperately worried about how Gem was taking this information. Was she disgusted, horrified or beginning to understand what Velda's life had been like for her through a quirk of nature? She daren't look at Gem to find out for fear she would see that look of revulsion that she had done her best to avoid for all these years she had known her by keeping this secret to herself.

She went on: 'It was like everything fell into place for me then. The relief was enormous. Mrs Golders went on to tell me that, unfortunately, very few people understand this and when people don't understand something they are frightened of it. Until the time comes that people do understand then we have no choice but to hide what we are from them or our lives be made a misery. She told me that she had had a terrible time as a child, what she suffered was almost the very same that I had. Like she had, I had two choices. I could continue to live a lie for the rest of my life as a man or be true to myself and live as the woman I really was, which is what she had decided to do. I was not in a position to make that decision now so, until I was, the best advice she could give me was to live a lie and that way at least have harmony with my family and those around me. When the time came, my decision wasn't going to be an easy one to make. If I decided to live as a man I would be going against all my own female instincts and have the constant battle of making out I was something I wasn't. If I chose to live as the woman I truly was then it would mean divorcing myself from my family, who would never accept me as a woman, and making a life for myself where no one knew me. It also meant that it was unlikely that I would ever meet anyone who would want a relationship with me so would never have a family of my own.

'Any friends I had would need to be kept in the dark for fear of losing them or divulging my secret and then me being hounded out. I'd have to start all over again somewhere new. Mrs Golders was right. Even at my age I realised that, when it came to me to decide my future, it was not going to be easy. Mrs Golders solemnly told me that she would never speak to my mother of what had transpired between us. She made me promise to remember that she would always be there for me and that, should I find life a struggle, I could always wait until after the business was closed and go to her shop where I would be at liberty to dress as I wanted and have free rein over her make-up and wigs. Over the next few years I took that offer up many times and being able, for a short time at least, to become the person I really was helped me cope. We became become very close, did Mrs Golders and I, and I know she looked forward to my visits as much as I did.

'I was nineteen when I knew the time had come to make my decision over my future. I'd gotten to the stage that I just couldn't live the lie I was any more and the thought of living like I was for the rest of my life filled me with dread. My two brothers were both married by this time and my parents were strongly hinting that I didn't seem to be making any effort towards finding myself a wife. My mother was starting to invite the daughters of friends and neighbours around; it was so awkward for me and the girl involved. Over the years I had collected together clothes of my own; dresses, skirts, blouses, brassieres that were padded to give me a chest, a couple of wigs, shoes, handbags... All the things I needed to change my appearance to what it should look like to me. I was slim back then, with a good head of hair, and I wasn't particularly very hairy anywhere else; I only needed to shave a couple of times a week. I do have big hands and feet, but then so do other women. I might be blowing my own trumpet, but when I was all dressed up I made a good-looking woman back then. I would have fooled even my mother had she met me in the street. Not so much these days as, over the years, I have put on weight.

'Anyway, I decided to make a new start. I had a little money I'd managed to save from my wage as an assistant in a hardware store, not much, but enough to last a few weeks if I was careful. So after telling Mrs Golders what I was doing, thanking her for her friendship and all she had done for me, I left a note for my parents explaining why I was leaving, feeling it better to tell them the truth than leave them in the dark. I then caught a train to London. I got on that train as a man and got off as a woman. Why I picked London I've no idea but it was as good as any place to start my new life as a woman in.

'It was late in the evening when I came out of the station, not having a clue where to start finding myself a bed for the night. I put down my case and looked up and down the street, wondering which best way to head. I noticed a woman was watching me. By the way she was acting and dressed, I knew she was a prostitute. She started to walk over to me and I was scared that she thought I was a prostitute too and was going to tackle me to move off her pitch. I snatched up my case and began to hurry off but she caught up with me and told me that I had looked so lost and lonely and reminded her of how she was when she first arrived in the city that she just had to come and ask me if I needed any help. At that moment, I didn't care what she did for her living,

I was just so grateful to have the offer. I told her I was looking to make a new life here but first needed a bed for the night and that I had no idea where to start looking. Sophia, that was her name she told me, said that if I didn't mind a lumpy sofa I could stay with her and her other flatmates. I almost fell on her in gratitude.

'I stayed with Sophia and Elsie, sleeping on their sofa for over a week, and during that time they introduced me to a number of their other friends. And what a mishmash of people they were; other prostitutes, homosexuals who earned their living as drag artists in the clubs, strippers and also people who did ordinary jobs in the banks and offices in the city. What a welcoming group of people they were. Whether Sophia, Elsie, or any of the other people I was now friendly with guessed I wasn't the woman I said I was, they never let on in all the time I mixed amongst them. I suppose they all had their own secrets.

'Some nights after the shows ended and Sophia and Elsie had finished their work for the night they would meet up with some of those friends in their flats, take drink and food and insist I came along. One of the women I met at one of these get-togethers was middle-aged woman who earned her living as a fortune teller. Rosie Lee, she called herself. I never did find out what her real name was. She had a spare room which she was willing to rent out to me if I wanted, as long as I was quiet when she had people in to do their readings. I had already managed to get myself a job as a waitress in a cafe which was just a walk away from Rosie Lee's flat and she seemed nice enough.

'I stayed with Rosie for two years, we really got on well together. She hadn't had an easy life. Had been married to an abusive husband and, as soon as her kids had left home, she left him. She had no idea where she was going but somehow ended up in London. Rosie was lucky as she'd always had a gift for fortune-telling. Her mother and grandmother had had it too and she used to tell her neighbours' and friends' fortunes, so she decided to use that gift to make her living in London. When we were alone in the evenings as she'd no clients, she took to teaching me how to read the tarot, then palms, the crystal ball and how to hone in on my sixth sense. I found I was rather good at it all and Rosie thought so too. Finally, I started to try my hand at doing it myself on the other waitresses at work and was surprised how accurate I was. Never got it right all the time, no clairvoyant can truthfully claim that, but seven times out of ten at least. I never charged any money though, just did it for the pleasure of trying to help people who needed it.

'Then I came home from work one night, aware that Rosie was going to be expecting a client shortly after so was prepared for a quick change and then going around to visit a friend, but I found the flat empty. All Rosie's stuff was gone and there was a note for me propped up on the mantle. It seemed that a man had been asking around the area about Rosie; from the description it was her husband and, terrified what he would do to her should he catch up with her, she had no alternative but to make a quick escape. She didn't say where she was going or whether she would be back. She was sorry to land this on me without any notice. That left me in quite a dilemma. The flat was in Rosie's name and I was only the lodger so had no right to stay there without her. I couldn't afford the rent myself, even if the landlord allowed me to stay. Even for a small, pokey room, the rents in London were extortionate. I knew there was no point going to my friends for help as none of them had any room for me unfortunately. Sophia and Elsie had another stray staying on their sofa at that time, so I had no alternative but to leave myself.

'I had no idea where to go. Then I remembered that, when I was a child, my parents took me and my brothers to the seaside and there had been a fortune teller on the promenade who had a queue of people waiting to see her. It was spring now, I had the summer in front of me, so wondered if I could make a living for myself telling fortunes on the seafront. I could try, at least. So I headed for the nearest seaside town, which was Southend. I didn't fare well there. There were already several fortune tellers operating on the front. I then tried several other seaside towns and found the same so I wondered if I'd be best to try towns further up north. Every town I tried I had no luck until I arrived in Scarborough. I was overjoyed to find that there had been a clairvoyant plying her trade there for years in a small hut on the parade but hadn't shown that season and no one knew why. So my turning up was most fortunate. I stayed for the rest of the summer. Holidaymakers seemed happy with my readings and a few of the locals came to see me regularly. I managed to get cheap lodgings with a widow. Because I lived quite frugally, I did manage to put some money aside but not enough to keep me on over the winter when the season finished. There were no jobs going as anything to do with the summer trade was shut down and the locals who worked in those summer jobs had snapped up anything going over the winter. It seemed I had no alternative but to try and find work away from the coast. The thought of lugging my belongings on trains and buses from town to town while I travelled around to find work as I had done when I had left London and landed in Scarborough didn't appeal, so I decided to use some of my savings on a little Ford Popular. A garage on the corner of the street where my lodgings were was selling it quite cheaply.

'The nearest big town was Leeds. Hopefully I would get some sort of work there, a place to live at least for the winter, give me time to decide what to do next. As I drove through a small market town, I decided to stop for something to eat. That's when I saw a poster for a travelling fair stuck on the door of the cafe I was about to go in. The fair was Grundy's. I hadn't been to a fair for many years and the urge to do so was so strong that I abandoned my meal and went to the fair instead.

'It was early afternoon but still teeming with people when I arrived and, as I wandered around, it wasn't the crowds enjoying themselves that caught my attention but the fairfolk themselves. I saw the way they got on together, bantering between themselves, arguing, helping each other out, and it reminded me so much of the mish-mash of people I'd been amongst in London, that I was missing so terribly. I could imagine them all looking out for each other and sharing their lives. It was strange but I felt like I had arrived home, that this was the place that I was supposed to be. The urge I was feeling to become part of the fairfolk family was overwhelming. There didn't seem to be a fortune teller already that I could see, so if I could only persuade the owner to take me on...' She heaved a deep sigh. 'You know the rest, Gem. Thankfully, Sam did agree to give me a trial.'

Velda did then pluck up the courage to look at Gem. 'Of course I constantly had the worry that someone would look at me too closely and guess my secret but, thankfully, no one ever did and, not once in the thirty years I have been with Grundy's have I ever openly deceived any of you. Everyone accepted me for a woman from the moment I arrived and so did you when you first came. You've never had cause to question I wasn't since. Not meaning to be vain but, as I told you earlier, I was good-looking when I was younger and I had a few men come on strong to me. I never took them on, even just to have a date with any of them, as to me that would have been me being deceptive; them believing they were dating a woman when in fact I was a man. That doesn't mean to say I didn't want to... I would have loved to have felt a man's strong arms around me, his kiss on my lips, but that was one of the prices I had to pay for living my life as I was. That was why I have never led Sam on. I love that man,

Gem, with all my heart. Have done since I met him, even though he was already married to the love of his life and very happy with her. We can't help who we fall in love with, can we? To hear Sam ask me what he did the other night was my wildest dream come true but I quashed it, made sure his hope of any relationship with me was well and truly nipped in the bud. It was probably the hardest thing I have ever had to do. I really wanted to grab him and tell him how much he meant to me. Witnessing the pain in his eyes at my rejection broke my heart. It is said that we should grab happiness when we can but, in this case, that wouldn't have been fair to Sam to use him like that, knowing the pain and heartache he would suffer when the truth of my situation did come out. Let alone what it would mean for me, because I would have to leave Grundy's, wouldn't I?'

She paused for a moment then, worriedly wringing her hands and with tears of deep distress glinting her eyes, uttered, 'I so regret what you saw and the shock it must be for you. Please know how very sorry I am. Sometimes, dear, life can be cruel and for those it's been cruel to, well, all they can do is make the best of it. That's all I have done, is make the best of my life and tried not to hurt anyone. I could ask you to keep my secret but that would be unfair of me and my morals wouldn't allow me to ask another to lie on my behalf anyway. If you give me a couple of hours to get dressed, pack up and hitch my van to my Land Rover to make my leave before you tell people what you found out about me this morning, I would appreciate it.'

Gem's thoughts were tumbling as she watched Velda get up, fetch her clothes from where they were neatly stored at the side of the sofa and then disappear into the tiny bathroom, pulling the curtain across behind her. She bowed her head and clasped her hands tightly together. The utter disgust she had felt earlier at what she had seen and the implications of it had slowly dissipated as she had listened to Velda's story unfolding. All she felt now was an overwhelming sadness for the life that Velda had been forced to live through no fault of her own. She couldn't imagine what it must have been like for her, was still like for her in fact, to have the body of a man and yet everything else about her be female. It was hard for her to understand, she doubted she ever fully would. She herself was proud of her body. When no one was around, vain of her or not, she liked to stand before a mirror and admire as well as find criticism in the parts she didn't like about it, so she couldn't envisage how it must be for Velda to look at herself and feel neither admiration or dislike for her body but vehemently hate what she was viewing, feeling it alien to her.

She lifted her head and looked over at the curtain drawn across the alcove into the bathroom, visualising the person behind dressing themselves. Regardless of what she had seen earlier, she still saw Velda as a woman. Velda was right that in all the twenty-odd years she had known her, never once had she had cause to question who she was. What would become of Velda if she did divulge what she knew about her? Velda had no blood family to accept her back into their fold, no other friends to aid her, so nothing but a lonely existence would face her as, once word got around on the fairground grapevine, no other fair community would accept her amongst them. She wasn't a young woman any longer either, so starting again wouldn't be easy.

Gem wrestled with her conscience. But now she knew what she did, would she not be deceiving others by keeping this from them? Then Gem remembered her own secret and the reasons she had kept it to herself for fear of the damage it could do not only to those it affected but to herself as well, should it be discovered. Wasn't she then being hypocritical in damning Velda for keeping her secret when she herself was guilty of doing just the same? And when all was said and done, was she herself prepared to wreck the life of this kindly, wise woman who had never harmed her or anyone else she knew in all the years she had known her? Could she live with herself afterwards if she did? She knew she couldn't. So what if she locked what she'd seen away in the back of her mind and never thought of it again? She could do that for this dear woman's sake, couldn't she?

The curtain on the bathroom alcove was pulled back and Velda emerged then, carrying her dressing gown. Gem had never seen her look so wretched. Immediately she got up and went over to her, laying a hand on hers and smiling at her kindly. Velda looked back at her warily, wondering just what it was that Gem was about to say to her. 'As far as I'm concerned, this morning never happened. I never came back and saw what I did. You are and always will be a woman to me and one I care for very much. We will never speak of this again.'

Velda gawped at her, utterly astounded. 'You mean this, Gem? You would do this for me? Oh, I ... I ... don't know how I can ever thank you.'

Gem smiled, broader. 'I'm being selfish. If you left who would I go shopping with, moan about Solly with, ask another woman's advice on any problems I had? I would miss you and so would everyone else in the Grundy community. Will the bathwater still be hot?'

Velda frowned, bewildered. 'Er ... yes, it should be.'

'Then go and enjoy having a soak in it and when I come back from updating Sam we'll have that coffee together before you collect your things and return to your own van.'

Chapter Fourteen

'Who was the bloke?'

Sonny jumped at the unexpected voice of his brother, hastily secreting the small package the man had given him into his back pocket as he nonchalantly responded, 'What bloke?'

Solly bristled. 'You know damned well what bloke I'm talking about. The one who was just leaving as I arrived?'

'Oh, him.' Sonny shrugged. 'Just asking if we'd

any work going. I told him to look for Dad as he's the one who hires and fires. Did you want something?'

Solly was frowning, bothered. He distinctly got the impression that his brother was lying to him. The man didn't look the sort to be looking for casual work in a fair. Too well dressed and he was acting furtively, in Solly's opinion. As for Sonny, he too was acting a little jumpy; as someone would when they'd be caught doing something they shouldn't. He hoped that Sonny wasn't up to no good with the man. Even if he wasn't and his business with the man was all above board, it wasn't likely that Sonny would tell him. It had been many years since his brother had confided in him. Nearly twenty years ago now. 'Eh? Oh, yes. It's Dad's birthday on Monday, so we're having a surprise get-together after the fair closes. Just family and a few of dad's close friends.'

Sonny looked unimpressed and grunted, 'You always have a surprise birthday do for Dad so some surprise that will be to him. Anyway, it's only Saturday, we've a move from here to Skipton to get through tomorrow, so why are you telling me now?'

Solly responded evenly, 'Does it really matter when I tell you as I doubt you'll come anyway. Can't remember the last time you graced us with your presence at a family do. Gem goes to a lot of trouble to make them special. It wouldn't hurt you to show your face this time. Dad isn't getting any younger. I know he's a tough old bugger and hopefully has got many more years in him yet, but there's no telling how many more of these dos we'll be arranging for him.'

He looked at Solly for a moment before he muttered, 'Yeah, okay, I'll be there. Now, if you don't mind, the tannoy system is playing up on this ride and I need to sort it before we open at two.'

As Solly walked away he was under no illusion that Sonny would break a twenty-year habit and come to the party. Gem had asked him to invite Sonny and that's what he'd done.

Sonny watched him go, breathing a sigh of relief. For a moment he worried that Solly had actually seen the exchange that had taken place between himself and his visitor but he would have said so if he had. This was the first package that had been placed in his safekeeping, which he would hide away later when he knew the coast was clear. He wondered how much his pay would amount to when someone turned up to collect it? Hopefully hiding these illicit goods for 'Bossman' might turn out to be quite lucrative. Bossman's courier had already handed him a five-pound note when he'd handed him the package with more to come when it was collected. That made him wonder just what the worth was of the contents? Had to be considerable as even just his part payment of five pounds was more than some men earned in a week.

Over at her parents' stall Suzie was trying to hide her excitement from her parents. Today was the day her new future was going to start. She couldn't wait to leave all this behind, to live in a nice house with all modern conveniences, a car to take her out in, a generous allowance for her to spend on what she wished, holidays abroad in fancy hotels and a fabulous social life in the best restaurants and clubs in town. Donny had left to start work before her this morning and, as soon as he had departed, she had hurriedly packed her belongings and hidden them at the back of the van ready to collect and make her getaway later when no one would see her as they were all busy on the rides and stalls.

The first he would know about her leaving him was when he found the note she had written him when he came back at dinnertime. She had only told him the basics, no details of where she was going and who with as the last thing she wanted was for him to come looking for her. She didn't care a jot how upset he'd be when he discovered the truth. As far as Suzie was concerned, Donny had just been a stepping stone towards getting the life she wanted for herself. The man who was going to provide this fabulous new future for her didn't actually have any idea he was yet, but she knew how smitten he was with her. He had made that very plain during the times they had made love, in fact constantly paying her compliments when they were together and bemoaning the fact that the two-week visit to see her fairground friend was far too short. He had said he would miss her when she went home, so she was only taking matters into her own hands to grant him his wish that she didn't leave him, wasn't she?

She couldn't believe how much she had to thank her father for being solely responsible for her meeting the man of her dreams. His compulsive gambling had cost the family dearly, at times seen them go hungry and cold but, had he not had his habit, she wouldn't have gone into the bookies two weeks ago and met her saviour. Fate certainly had been looking after her that day.

She took a quick glance at her watch. Time to make a move. This was probably the last time she would see her parents. Did that bother her? No. Not at all. She despised her father for his selfishness and bullying and loathed her mother in equal measure for not protecting herself or her children.

She addressed her mother, 'I've got a headache, Mam, so I'm just going back to my van to have a couple of pills.'

The weary-looking, middle-aged, shabbily dressed woman who looked at least twenty years older than her forty-two years shot a worried look at her daughter. Not out of concern for her, although she was, but more for the fact that she knew that once Suzie left, her husband would start bullying money from her. It was money she needed to buy food and necessities that he used to fund his lunchtime session at the nearest pub and a visit to the bookies before the fair opened at two. With Suzie not around to stop him from helping himself out of her handbag, she was no match for him. She flustered, 'Oh, no need, love, I've a bottle of aspro in my handbag. I'll get them for you.'

'It's alright, Mam, I want the privy as well.' She leaned over and pecked her cheek. 'Take care of yourself.'

Suzie's mother watched her leave, frowning and

bewildered. That was an odd thing for her daughter to say to her considering she was only going to be away for no more than a few minutes?

Meanwhile, Solly was on his way to the fair entrance with several coloured lightbulbs to replace ones that he had noticed had blown earlier that morning. As he passed by Ren's stall he called, 'Morning, Ren.'

The response that he got from her to his greeting was, 'Oh, bugger. Oh, sod it. Oh, damn.'

He stopped his pace to stare over at her, mystified. 'Anything wrong, Ren?'

She heaved a despondent sigh. 'I'll say there is. Bloody rats or mice have got into my last three sacks of sugar. I don't know how they managed it as the sacks were locked in the cupboard at the side of my candy-floss machine.' She disappeared from Solly's view behind the candy-floss machine for a moment before she reappeared again, an angry scowl on her face. 'They've gnawed a hole in the back of the cupboard and that's how they got in.'

Solly looked at his watch as he stepped over to her. 'The wholesaler shuts at twelve on a Saturday and it's now coming up to half eleven so you'll never get there in time, even if I got Dickie Bickers to drive you who thinks our lorries are racing cars. You'll have to replace the sugar from the grocer down the road.'

'And pay through the nose for it,' she grumbled. 'Bang goes any profit I might have made today.'

'The Irish have a saying for times like this. Sod's law. I'll get one of the lads to repair that hole for you. I'd take you myself to the grocer's but I've a few jobs to see to before opening. Just bear with me a minute and I'll find–' He stopped short as, out of the corner of his eye, he spotted Donny talking to one of the stallholders. He called to him, 'Donny, you busy for the next half hour?'

He called back, 'Not particularly, boss. I've done all my jobs so was going around to see what help anyone else needed before I head back to my van for dinner. Just asked Harry here, but he says he's fine.'

Harry Oldershaw, a rotund, jolly man in his late forties wearing a loud checked suit and trilby hat on his completely football-shaped bald head, who owned the Mighty Striker stall, jovially called over to Solly, 'Apart from the fact that me poor feet could do with a massage, but as Donny ain't a bonny young lassie, then he doesn't quite fit the bill. Oi, but don't tell the missus or she'll have me guts for garters.'

Sonny chuckled at Harry's quip before he called back over to Donny, 'I've a job for you.'

Ren realised just what that job was and urgently insisted, 'Oh, no need to bother Donny, Mr Grundy. I can manage this myself. A walk will do me good.' Ren didn't drive. Not that she wouldn't like to learn and have the independence a vehicle of her own would bring her, it was simply that she was too small for her feet to reach the pedals.

'Struggling down that country lane lugging big bags of sugar and in this hot weather. You think I'm going to let you do that?' Solly looked appalled. Just then, Donny joined them. Much to Ren's upset, he didn't even look at her let alone acknowledge her presence. 'You won't mind will you, Donny?'

'Mind what, boss?'

'Driving Ren to the grocer down the road to buy some sugar. Rats have made a meal of all she had left to make the candy floss with.'

He shuffled uncomfortably on his feet. After what he learned about her from his wife, he preferred not to have to spend a second in the woman's company, let alone at least half an hour, but then he didn't see how he could get out of it, so lied, 'Er ... no, no, course not.'

The half a mile or so walk to the shops from the fairground took roughly twenty minutes so driving in a lorry took less than five, but to the two estranged occupants in the lorry cab, bouncing up and down as the wheels hit the ruts in the rough country road, the journey seemed like hours.

It was very apparent to Ren that Donny hadn't at all wanted to drive her to the shops and just how uncomfortable he was in her company. He sat, staring straight ahead out of the window, his body taut. He didn't speak one word to her. She hadn't tried as she hadn't wanted to purposely cause herself hurt with the likely rebuff she would get from him. Considering how close they had used to be, as close as any friends could possibly be without any romance between them, Ren was bewildered as to why Donny couldn't even look at her now. What had she done that was so bad this state of affairs had resulted? By the time they did arrive at the shops, she couldn't contain herself any longer. She respected the fact that Donny had decided, after all these years, to end their friendship but the least he could do was give her a reason for doing so. Having an opportunity like this to get him to explain himself might not come along again for a very long time, if ever in fact. It was now or never.

As he turned off the engine she shifted her body on the long front bench seat to face him and, before she lost her nerve, blurted, 'Why are you being like this with me, Donny? We've been such good friends since we were babies. What have I done that's so bad you can't even look at me now? Considering we were such good friends, I deserve to be told.'

He was looking straight out of the window, not looking directly at her, when he responded, 'I know, Ren.'

She frowned, bewildered. 'Know what?'

Face screwed up darkly, he spun his head to look at her and blared out, 'How you really feel about me, that's what I know.'

She gasped, astounded. Donny knew that she loved him, worshipped the ground he walked on! She shuddered. Judging by the look on his face, the very thought was disgusting to him. So was that why he didn't want to be around her, as knowing she loved him was so abhorrent to him? She implored him, 'Look, I never meant you to find out. I never told anyone, so how on earth...'

'Liar!' he spat at her. 'You told anyone who'd listen. Thank God Suzie decided to tell me what you were saying about me behind my back or you'd still be making a complete fool of me while I was none the wiser, believing you were my best friend.'

She was gawping at him, astounded. 'I've no idea what you're talking about, Donny.'

He sneered at her. 'Yes you do. Making fun of me behind my back.'

She gasped, stunned, and spoke emphatically and with an amount of indignance, 'I have never done any such thing. If I am guilty of talking behind your back it was only to sing your praises.'

He glared at her. 'So calling me an imbecile, an idiot, ridiculing me all the time, is singing my praises, is it?'

She was too shocked by what he was accusing her of to be relieved at the fact that it wasn't, after all, that she loved him that he was proclaiming he knew. 'What!' she exclaimed, horrified. 'I have never called you any such thing. I swear on my life I haven't. Who would tell you such terrible things?'

'Suzie did. She hated hurting me but she couldn't keep her mouth shut any longer, me not knowing how you really felt and treating me like you were. Going to try and convince me Suzie's lying, are you?'

'If that's what she's told you, then yes I am.'

'She's my wife, she wouldn't. Anyway, why would she have need to?'

Apart from the fact that she didn't like the fact that her husband had a close relationship with another woman, despite the fact that woman was no threat to her on a romantic level, Ren had no idea. She wanted to tell Donny how badly his wife treated her when no one was around and that she had good reason to believe that she was playing around behind his back, but couldn't bring herself to hurt him and he might think she was making it up to excuse away what Suzie was accusing her of. Over Donny's shoulders, through the driver's door window, it was then that Ren noticed someone heading over to the bookie's. 'Why don't we ask her now?' She pointed out of the window.

Donny turned and looked in the direction Ren was pointing to see his wife heading into the betting shop. Her father must have persuaded her to place a bet for him. But why was she lugging a couple of suitcases and her vanity case with her?

By the time Donny got out of the lorry, Ren was scrambling out after him. She wanted Suzie to look her in the eyes when she tried to worm her way out of the lies she had told her husband. Suzie had disappeared inside the shop and they followed after her.

Inside the small office behind the counter the man behind the desk, which was piled high with paperwork he'd been dealing with before his visitor had unexpectedly arrived, was looking at Suzie, agog. 'What are you doing here? Bernie knows he's not supposed to send anyone back here without getting my say-so first, especially if I've got the safe open. The amount of money we take here, to have it at hand for them to snatch and run off with... I'll be having words with him. Anyway, I thought we were meeting tonight after you finish helping your friend at the fairground for a last evening together before you go home to Carlisle tomorrow.'

She shot him a winning smile and, before he

could stop her, she had gone to his desk, swung him around in his seat and sat on his knee, running her fingers tenderly down the side of his face. She said seductively to him, 'That's it, Bobby, I'm not going home.' She cupped his chin and kissed his lips. 'I know how devastated you were going to be when I was gone. You've kept telling me how much you love me and will miss me. So now you don't have to. I made some telephone calls this morning and gave up my job and flat. We can be married as soon as you like. If you give me your keys, I'll go and settle myself into your house and be waiting for you when you come home.' She left him in no doubt just where she would be waiting for him.

'Haven't you forgotten something, Suzie. That you're married to me.'

The unexpected voice made the pair in the chair look over to the door.

Still reeling from Suzie's announcement, Bobby was unable to react at that moment to yet another unannounced intrusion into his office. Suzie jumped up from his knees and, for a moment, stared at her husband, panic-struck. Then anger at his appearance and the prospect of all her hard work being scuppered reared up and she angrily demanded, 'What are you doing here? Are you following me?' She then spotted Ren. 'And what's she doing here?'

Bobby found his voice then and angrily cried, 'You never told me you were married.'

She spun to face him. 'There was no point as my marriage is over.'

Although he felt like this was a nightmare he

was in the middle of, Donny shot at her, 'And you didn't bother to tell me it was?'

'I left you a letter.'

'A letter! Is that all I am worth to you? I don't understand. You never gave me any hint that you weren't happy with me.'

She sneered. 'Happy! I was as miserable as sin. Did you never think to question why someone like me, with my looks, would settle for a boring ordinary-looking bloke like you who could only offer me a caravan to live in. I'm worth more than that, much more.'

'So why did you marry me then?'

'Because you were a better bet at the time than living with my parents.'

He felt like someone was ripping his heart out and wringing it tightly. 'So you've never loved me,' he uttered.

Her reply was blunt. 'No. Couldn't care less about you if you want the truth.'

Ren couldn't believe what she was hearing. Her heart was breaking for Donny. Regardless, she wanted answers to another matter. 'If you've never loved Donny and didn't care about him, then why cause trouble between me and him by telling him those lies you made up about me? Why break up our friendship?'

She smirked. 'Because I wasn't prepared for him to realise that I wasn't the one he really loved and should be married to and risk him leaving me until I didn't have need of him any more.'

Donny gawped at her. 'What on earth are you talking about? There's no one else.'

She sniggered, looking at him like he was the

village idiot. 'I needn't have bothered breaking you two apart as you're too thick to know who you really love.'

Bobby then found his voice and asked her, 'And what makes you think I meant what I said when I told you I loved you, Suzie? You must have told your husband lots of times you loved him and obviously never meant it.'

She looked at him, frozen, as the truth dawned on her. She gasped. 'You're telling me you lied to me! Why, you bastard.'

He laughed. 'The pot calling the kettle black. You're not the only one who lies to get what they want.'

'What's it like getting a taste of your own medicine, Suzie,' Ren shot at her.

Suzie spun to face her, glaring at her menacingly. 'You shut your mouth, you fucking freak.'

'Oi, don't speak to Ren like that, Suzie,' Donny snapped.

She shot back, 'And why should I have doubted that you would jump to her defence against me.'

'Because she's my friend and I won't have anyone speak to her like that.'

She smirked. 'Just a friend, eh?' Then her situation with the man she had pinned all her hopes on for her better future overwhelmed her and she spun back to face him and pleaded, 'I know you don't mean what you said, Bobby. You do love me. You're just angry I never told you I was married. You know I love you with all my heart. That's the honest truth, on my life it is. I'll be a good wife to you. I'll make sure you never want for anything. We're meant to be together. I'm sorry you found out about my marriage like this. I was going to tell you, honest I was. I'll get one of those quickie divorces.'

Bobby rose from his chair, placed his hands on her shoulders, fixed his eyes on hers and, in no uncertain terms, told her, 'I do want to get married, Suzie. Only when I meet the right woman though, not a slut like you. All you were to me was a bit of fun. It didn't take me long to work out what you were truly after when you realised I wasn't just a handsome face but owned several betting shops and had done very well for myself out of them. Thought you'd just have to bat your eyelashes and I'd be putty in your hands. Well, that might have worked on chump over there, who was stupid enough to marry you, but not me, lady. That life of Riley you thought I'd give you, well, I will give that to some woman but, as I've already told you, that won't be you. I have to say, though, that you're not bad in bed, I will give you that. Certainly know what a man wants so that he's desperate for more. That and only that is why I've been seeing you for the last two weeks. It certainly wasn't for your scintillating conversation or your knowledge on anything more than what Marilyn Monroe or Jane Russell is up to according to the latest Hollywood gossip in those trashy magazines you read or what the latest fashion in hairstyles is.' He then dropped his hands and addressed Donny, 'I feel sorry for you, mate, being stuck with the likes of her for a wife. If you've any sense you'll get shot as quick as you can. Now, will you please all leave my office as I have work to do.' He then added to Suzie, 'Don't forget your stuff. I don't want you having any reason to come back here.' He then called out, 'Bernie, come in here, I want a word with you.'

Suzie stared at Bobby, stupefied, as her dreams lay shattered around her.

All Ren's thoughts were on Donny. She turned her head to address him but, to her shock, the space he had been standing in was empty. She dashed outside but, to her dismay, saw no sign of him or the lorry. Before she could start to panic, Suzie arrived out of the betting shop dragging her luggage along with her.

As soon as she saw Ren the utter misery her face had been wreathed in changed to fury. Dropping her luggage she leapt over to Ren, slapped her hard on her face, whilst screaming furiously out, 'You bitch. You bloody bitch. This is all your doing. You've wrecked everything. I'll kill you, I will. Bobby was going to give me the life I've always wanted ... the life I deserved and you've ruined it. You've been spying on me, you must have or how did you know to bring Donny here this morning and confront me in Bobby's office?'

Ignoring the pain from her smarting cheek, Ren glared darkly up at her nemesis and told her in no uncertain terms, 'Hit me again and I'll give you as good back, Suzie. For your information, I haven't been spying on you. I've better things to do with my time. If you need to find blame for Donny and me catching you out in your disgusting plan then it was down to mice.' If the situation hadn't been so tense then Ren would have laughed at the look of abject confusion on Suzie's face at what she'd just told her. 'It's you that's wrecked your own life through your own greed. Nothing is ever good enough for women like you. Even if me and Donny hadn't happened to have been here today and Bobby hadn't been bright enough to see you for what you are, your relationship with him wouldn't have lasted long as the life he was giving you soon wouldn't have been enough and you'd have been on the lookout for someone else that could give you more. I hope you rot in hell for what you've done to Donny but I bet you won't lose one night's sleep over it because the only person you care about is yourself.' She then sneered disgustedly at her. 'You know you won't have an easy time of it back at Grundy's after it becomes common knowledge what you did as, despite what you think about Donny, the rest of us think very well of him, so I'd lie low for a good long time if I was you. Go and stay with a friend for a bit away from the fairground ... that's if you have any, that is.'

Suzie snorted, 'Don't tell me you care what happens to me?'

'Then I won't, because I don't. I dare say though, whatever you do next, you'll end up smelling of roses. Your sort always do.'

Suzie raised herself up to her full height and stuck her chin in the air. 'You're right, I will. You see if I don't. As for that stupid idiot I married, well you're welcome to him.' She maliciously smirked, stabbed Ren hard in her shoulder and spat, 'Do you think I had no idea how you really feel about him? I used to laugh myself silly at the way you'd look at him when you thought no one was looking with those cow eyes of yours. On my wedding day as I was saying my vows I was giggling to myself cos I knew that you were in the congregation wishing with all your heart that it was you standing in my place. Well, as I said, as I've no longer any use for him, you're welcome to my cast-off. Of course, that's as long as he's desperate enough to be willing to be seen out with a freak like you on his arm after having someone as gorgeous as me.' She laughed before she turned from Ren and, still with her head held high, collected her luggage and stalked off in the direction of town.

Ren sighed heavily. She could have been gloating with pleasure over witnessing Suzie's downfall but all she felt was a deep sadness for how Donny must be feeling and her need to find him and offer him her support through this terrible time. A woman coming towards her weighed down with a bag of shopping was a reminder to her of why she had come here in the first place. With no transport at her disposal she would, after all, have to lug the heavy sacks of sugar back to the fair. Had Solly not offered Donny's services as a driver she had been going to borrow a barrow to wheel the sacks back to the fairground. Much to her relief though Ernest Flinders, the grocer, was feeling kindly disposed towards the fairfolk who had considerably upped his profits these last two weeks since they had arrived. Selling three sacks of sugar in one go, a quantity that would usually take him several weeks, made him even more kindly disposed towards them. He offered to leave his wife in charge while he personally drove Ren and her purchases back to the fairground.

As soon as Ren had stored the sacks of sugar safely away in the now extra-reinforced cupboard next to the candy-floss machine, she went in search of Donny. She was very worried not to see any sight of him or the lorry. It appeared that he hadn't come back after he'd left the bookies. She wasn't quite sure what to do but thought she would wait a while. He was probably parked up in some layby somewhere, trying to get his head around what Suzie had done to him. She wished she was with him to offer him her support but, as she wasn't, all she could do was hope he was alright. When he hadn't arrived back by the time the fair closed that night, she was worried sick about him and felt it only right she tell his parents.

His parents were as distraught to find out what Suzie had done to him as Ren was and his fuming mother wasted no time in going to tackle Suzie's parents over their daughter's despicable behaviour towards her son. Ren didn't witness that exchange but heard afterwards that bitter words were thrown at each other and the rift took a long time to heal.

It was Gem that Ren told what had happened to Donny and who then passed the information on to Solly. Solly then told his father for his instruction as to what he wanted to do about the lorry. As Solly knew he would be, his father was far too concerned for Donny's welfare to be worried about him taking off with one of their vehicles. As a man who prided himself on being a good judge of character, Sam was angry with himself that he had seen no sign of Suzie's true nature, believing that she was a caring and willing young woman, same as everyone else had done ... except for Ren.

The whole community prayed that Donny would return safe and sound when he was good and ready. He knew where the fair was due next so would know where to find them.

Chapter Fifteen

The move from Barnsley to a huge disused factory car park in the middle of Skipton, where the council had relocated the fair after the site they had played on for over fifty years had new houses built on it, didn't go anywhere near as smoothly as the one to Barnsley had. The good weather turned stormy and the fairfolk had to brace themselves against the wind and rain to dismantle all the rides and stalls and load them securely onto the lorries; the field became a quagmire, vehicles getting stuck fast in the churned-up mud and much time was lost having to tow them out. As it was a new site they were heading to, several members of the community misunderstood the directions Sam gave them and individually got lost, ending up miles from where they should be. They had started to unload before their mistake was realised. On arriving at the new site, Sam was to find that the council employee responsible had forgotten to turn the water and electricity supply on, so they had to rely solely on their oil-powered generators until first thing Monday morning when the council offices would open.

To worsen matters, two drivers decided to have a bet as to who could arrive at the new destination first. Consequently, racing at speed to pass each other on winding country roads between Barnsley and Skipton, one lorry had to swerve to avoid a collision with an oncoming car and landed in a ditch. It took several hours to locate a local farmer willing to forgo his Sunday dinner to tow the lorry out with his tractor ... for a price, of course, so the bet cost them both dearly. It was even worse for the two men; they had no choice but to admit to their tomfoolery as, during the crash, several items on the back of the lorry were damaged as well as the vehicle itself. The men were instantly sent packing by Sam. He turned a blind eye to fun, but not stupidity. Antics such as the men had gotten up to not only put lives at risk and proved very costly but didn't do the fair's reputation any good at all.

So it was touch and go whether the fair would be ready to open at two o'clock on the Monday after-noon, but through everyone's combined efforts, at one fifty-five the lights were switched on, music began blasting out of the numerous speakers, and all the rides and stalls were manned, ready for the hordes to descend.

Earlier that Monday morning, the labourer as-signed to erect the school tent found that during transit the tent had been amongst the load that had been on the back of the lorry that ended up in the ditch; one of the support posts had been broken. The man, a recent recruit to the Grundy's workforce, was no carpenter. In fact, he was proving not much good at any task he was given and he was lazy too, so Sam was on the verge of letting him go. The other labourers that had the skills to fix it were otherwise occupied and would be for a long time yet, so Solly volunteered to fix or replace it. He erected the tent himself as soon as he had finished the job he was on. It did mean there was no school that morning, much to the delight of the pupils who found sneaking off to explore the old disused factory far more interesting, even though they had all been warned to steer clear of it.

It wasn't until the afternoon when the fair was up and running that Solly got around to dealing with the tent.

Before he did, he sought out his wife. She was in the pay booth of the House of Fun and was so consumed with her own thoughts that she did not hear the first tap on the window. She heard the second, as it was a loud rap with his fist.

She jumped and looked out at him crossly. 'No need to bang so loudly. You nearly broke the glass,' she scolded him.

'You looked far away when I got here. Nothing the matter, is it?'

She looked at him blankly for a moment. She wasn't sure. Just before Solly had arrived, she could have sworn she had spotted a young woman over by the carousel watching her, the same woman she had seen watching her in the last place they had been before they had moved here.

That venue had been twenty miles away. It wasn't unusual for people to travel miles to have themselves some fun at the fair but unusual when they had so recently. But then the woman hadn't seemed to be having herself any fun, just standing watching Gem until she had spotted that Gem was watching her in return. She then hurried off out of sight. Gem mentally shook herself. Maybe it wasn't the same woman, just someone who looked like her. 'No, nothing at all. Just a bit tired like everyone else is today. It was a long day for us all yesterday. Have you had time to fix the school tent yet? The sooner the better as, twice this morning, the kids have had to be herded out of the old factory. I doubt they'll go back in again though after the warning they got that, if they do, they'll be made to go to lessons seven days a week instead of five. At least when they're all at their lessons they aren't at liberty to get up to stuff they shouldn't be.'

'I'm just off to do it.'

She looked at him as if to say, *Well, why aren't you then?*

He looked sheepish. 'It's just that I can't remember the name of the teacher. You know I've never have been that great with names and I've only met the woman once in the two weeks she's been with us, when you introduced me in passing when she first came here.'

'It's Miss Dunn. Emily.'

'Ah, I remember now.' Then a thought struck him. Why was it that name seemed familiar to him but not in connection with the fair's school? At that moment he couldn't think why. 'I'll get to it and tell Miss Dunn when it's all done. See you later.'

The pole was repairable and didn't take long to fix. As soon as he had gotten the tent erected, he went to Emily's van to tell her that she could resume her duties. The neat-looking older woman beamed on seeing who her caller was. 'Ah, Mr Grundy. It is Mr Grundy, isn't it? Gem's husband, or is my memory playing tricks on me?' It was then she realised he was looking at her strangely. 'Is anything the matter?'

As soon as she had opened the door and he had seen her face, the memory stirred of seeing that same face in a photograph recently. First her name had seemed familiar to him and now her face, but somehow not connected with her being here at the fair or to do with the school. He wished he could remember why her name had seemed familiar and where he'd recently seen a photograph of her. 'Oh, er ... no, no, everything is fine. I've just come to tell you that the tent is fixed.'

She looked pleased. 'That is good news. I shall go and round the children up. I understand they've been running their parents ragged this morning. They'll be pleased even if the children are not, thinking they would be getting the whole day off. Thank you, Mr Grundy.'

He had heard many of the children's parents singing this woman's praises, along with Gem. In the short time she had been teaching the children to read, Gem had told him that some of them were already demanding their parents buy them books from the second-hand shop so they could escape into the exciting fictitious worlds Miss Dunn introduced them to when she read to them. She seemed a genuinely nice person who really cared. Gem was right to put up a fight with his father to take her on so that the next generation of Grundy fairfolk were not going to have to struggle like his generation had done, and those before him, without the ability to read and write. They would certainly know far more about the outside world than he or his likes did. There were so many things that he would like to know that he could have read about had he been able to read.

As he left her he again wished he could remember why her name had seemed so familiar to him and just where he had seen a likeness of her, but then all his thoughts of Emily Dunn left him as a gaff lad collared him to ask what ride he was being expected to help on that afternoon.

They had just finished their evening meal, Sam had already left and Gem was clearing away. As soon as she finished, she had to take up her duty that night of manning the helter-skelter with Nita, her niece. Solly, Jimmy and Robbie were readying themselves to go and relieve gaff lads on three rides so they could have their evening meal before the evening hordes descended. Jimmy said to his father, 'I need to go to the privy before I go back to work so you both go ahead without me.'

'Right you are. Oh, you'll need to take some more newspaper with you as I used the last sheet when I was in there earlier.'

Jimmy said to his mother, 'Got any squares already cut, Mam?'

'No. Just rip some paper up for now and I'll cut some up properly later. You know where I keep the sheets. I know there's some as your father folded a newspaper up the other night and put it in the drawer.'

Something then triggered in Solly's brain, like a bulb being switched on. Newspaper. Photograph. Emily Dunn. That was where he had seen her name and photograph. He called urgently to his son, 'Don't take any of that newspaper until I've had a look at it first.'

'Why?' his wife asked him, bemused.

'Because I need to check something.' He went to the drawer and took out the pile of newspaper sheets Gem saved for use as toilet paper, scanning each sheet until he came to the one he was after. He then proclaimed, 'There it is.' He picked up the sheet and held it out to show Gem. 'That's a picture of Miss Dunn. It's not a good photo, but it's her, else I need glasses. I couldn't read the whole article but I managed to make out her name and the word police.'

As she took the page of newspaper, Gem said, bothered, 'Emily Dunn is in trouble with the police, I don't believe it!' As she studied the photograph and read the accompanying article, she looked increasingly worried. 'The Skipton police are asking if anyone has seen her and, if so, to get in touch with them. I wonder why they want to interview her?'

'She's wanted for murder,' offered Jimmy.

Gem scolded him. 'Don't be silly. Miss Dunn is no murderer.'

'She might have smothered her mother for her inheritance for all you know,' said Robbie.

'You read too many novels, Son,' said his father. Then he said to his wife, 'But the police don't want to speak to anyone without any reason, Gem. You were wondering why a woman like her would want to give up her life to come and travel with us, so maybe now we know that she's using us to hide from the police. She probably didn't reckon on any of us spotting a police alert out for her in the newspaper. Most of us can't read anyway, so she maybe thought the chances weren't high of that happening.'

'Mmm. But I just can't imagine Miss Dunn doing anything she shouldn't. She's such a sweet, kind lady.'

'I have to say, I felt the same about her myself when I was speaking to her this morning but maybe the sweet old lady bit is just an act. We all thought Suzie was a nice girl and didn't think for a minute she was capable of doing what she has to Donny,' Solly reminded her.

Gem heaved a troubled sigh. What if Emily Dunn was just acting a part like Suzie had been and wasn't really the sweet older woman they all thought she was but a conniving, deceitful criminal trying to escape justice from her heinous crimes? 'I suppose we ought to tell your father and ask him what he wants to do?'

Robbie said, 'Have you forgotten that Granddad has gone to meet an old chum of his in a pub in town and won't be back until late?'

'Oh, yes, Herbie Dockers. He was the blacksmith we used to shoe the horses' shoes when we still had them before we got the lorries. He would also see to any ironwork we needed when we came here. No doubt Dad'll be the worse for drink when he does roll home,' said Solly. 'He left me in charge.' He raked a hand through his thatch of hair. 'If the police find out that we knew we have a criminal here and didn't tell them, that could mean big trouble for us. We need to tell them.'

Panic swamped Sonny when, stretching his legs outside the small operating booth in the middle of the Sky Chairs ride, he spotted Solly with a policeman weaving his way over towards him. He was terrified that, somehow, the authorities had found out that he was hiding illicit goods on behalf of a possible known criminal. His relief was therefore enormous when he saw Solly and the policeman then change direction and head over into the living van area. Whoever the policeman was after was, thankfully, not him. But then should his arrangement with Bossman have come to the authorities' attention they could strip him naked, search his van and anywhere else associated with him personally from top to bottom, and they wouldn't find anything anyway. He'd been too clever in selecting his hiding place to allow that to happen.

A while after that, Gem was sitting on one of the two small armchairs in front of the wood stove in Emily's small, one-bedroomed living van. She was looking at the older woman sitting in the other chair, mortified. 'We didn't have any choice but to tell the police you were here after

Solly seeing the article in the newspaper.'

Sitting next to her, Emily smiled in understanding and patted her hand. 'You certainly didn't have any choice, my dear. How could you turn a blind eye to possibly having a criminal hiding in your midst? Absolutely not, you couldn't. Had I known the police were looking for me, I would immediately have ... turned myself in.' She issued a chuckle. 'I can imagine you thinking I was a murderer, or something equally as bad, that I was hoping the police would never think to look for me living in a fair. What really surprises me is that my neighbour in the flat downstairs, Mrs Cross, was worried enough about my sudden departure that she thought something suspicious had happened to me so reported it to the police. She and her husband had only moved in three months before, they were out working all day, and I only saw Mrs Cross a couple of times. I wasn't really that acquainted with her so I never thought to tell her of my plans to leave. I have no family, you see, so the only person I did inform was the landlord and that was by letter which I left on the mantle for him to find when he called to collect the rent. I didn't give him any details of what my future plans were, just my notice to quit along with the rent until the end of the month. It all happened so quickly you see, having my offer to teach the children accepted and then the fair leaving two days later on the Sunday. So it was only two days to get everything organised to join you.'

Gem smiled at her and returned the affectionate pat on the hand. 'And we're so glad you did.

After all the trouble in the past we've had with teachers making the children's lives a misery and not really ever teaching them anything, to actually have a teacher that wants to travel with us and teach the children... Well, I couldn't quite believe you giving up a job in a proper school, living in a house and leaving all your friends and family beh–' Gem's voice trailed off as, to her shock, she saw that Emily's face had paled and she was staring back at Gem. Gem demanded, 'What is it, Miss Dunn? What have I just said?'

'Well, er ... just that you think I'm a qualified teacher.'

She frowned at her, bewildered. 'Well, you are, aren't you?'

She shook her head. 'No. No, I'm not. It was always my ambition to be, dreamed of since I can remember, but circumstances put a stop to it. My father was a very clever man, always wanted to be a doctor. While he did his training, my mother supported him by working all sorts of jobs, all the hours God sends. He came top of his class when he graduated, could have got himself a well-paid job in a hospital or with a private surgery, but he wanted to help the people who needed him most. So he set up in a poor area of Barnsley that had never had a doctor living there before. My mother fully supported his decision; she was a very caring woman.

'They wanted a large family but, unfortunately, I was to be the only one for them. They were wonderful parents. Trouble was, he was too kindly and found it difficult to charge for his services to people he knew couldn't afford it and so our standard of living suffered until we were nearly as poor as the people he administered to. We might not have had much in the material sense but love was in abundance. My father hoped that I would follow him into the medical profession but fully supported my desire to be a teacher, both my parents did. My mother used to tell me stories of when I was young and used to line up my teddies and dolls and pretend they were my pupils. I worked really hard at school and won a scholarship to a college in Newcastle to study to be a teacher of English and History. But, two weeks before I was set to start the course, my father unexpectedly died from a heart attack.' There was a glint of tears in her eyes as she re-lived memories that were clearly painful to her. 'It was such a shock, one minute he was in his surgery administering to a patient whilst my mother was in the kitchen making him tea to drink before he went out on his rounds and the next, the patient was screaming out that my father had collapsed. We were told later that he died before he hit the floor. It was a terrible time for us both, but for my mother losing the love of her life, without any warning, sent her spiralling into a deep decline, like she had died too.

'I hoped she might start to come out of her depression after the funeral but, in fact, she got worse. Life didn't seem to have any meaning for her any longer. I had no choice but to give up my dreams of going to college to become a teacher as I couldn't leave her on her own to fend for herself, she wasn't capable. Also, the house we lived in with the surgery attached was only rented so we had to leave that to make way for the new doctor coming in to take Father's place. Thankfully I managed to find us a small flat that I could afford the rent on from a job I got myself in an office. The flat I've just left, in fact.

'My mother never did really improve. I only managed to get her out for a walk a handful of times; she acquired a fear of open spaces and only felt safe when she was inside the flat. She would do simple tasks, like cook a meal for when I got home after work and do some light housework when she felt up to it, but most of the time she would just sit in a chair by the window staring out. I always suspected she wasn't looking at the view but re-living memories in her mind of times with my father.

'I did have the opportunity to marry once. Horace Stevens. He worked for the same company I did at the time. Handsome, he was. I was very much in love with him. He was nice and kind like my father had been but, unfortunately, his kindness never stretched to having my mother live with us when we married. I couldn't bring myself to put her in a home so Horace went on to marry another woman and they had six children together. Mother lived to be eighty-nine and died six years ago. I miss her terribly, of course I do, but finally she's back where she belongs; by my father's side.

'It was not long after she died that I saw the job advertised for a clerk for a school. It was the nearest I was going to get to actually being a teacher working in a school. I applied and, to my delight, I got it. I thoroughly enjoyed working there. As well as taking care of all the office work I also helped supervise the children having their lunch and at playtimes in the playground. Miss Gilcrest was a firm teacher but she was kind to the children. That was why I was shocked at the way she treated the fairground children when the fair arrived in town. She ranted that it was so unfair of the authorities, expecting her to accommodate such illiterates who lived such unsanitary lives, and she worried that the local children would catch some dreadful disease from them. She obviously saw them as no better than vermin to be fumigated out of her school and she certainly did that, didn't she, by the way she treated them. All children, to me, no matter where they come from, what colour they are or what religion, have the right to an education. There was little I could do about it though. If I voiced my opinions to Miss Gilcrest, she was in the position to sack me. I am not ashamed to admit I saw the fairground children making their bid for freedom and I did nothing it about it. They were better out of that school as far as I was concerned. I just happened to be heading back inside after supervising the children during their dinnertime play when you arrived, Mrs Grundy. I overheard the conversation between you and Miss Gilcrest. I wanted to cheer and congratulate you for berating her for how despicably she had treated the children. But then it got me to thinking that, although I wasn't qualified myself, I had been well educated and had learned enough from working at the school to see how lessons were constructed, that maybe I could offer to teach the children. And, selfish of me it may seem, it might also fulfil my dream to be a teacher after all. I only had another year or so until I retired and the thought of having nothing to fill my time with filled me with dread. Basically I'm alone in the world; I never really had a chance to have a social life and make friends as all my spare time was taken up looking after Mother so the prospect of becoming part of a close community and making friends was very appealing to me. That is why I approached you with my offer.' She paused then and looked at Gem remorsefully. 'I am just so very sorry that I never made it clear to you that I wasn't actually a qualified teacher. I would still very much like to continue doing what I am, but I completely understand if you want me to leave and find someone who is qualified.'

Gem had been deeply touched by Emily Dunn's story. She had seen it as a way of fulfilling a life-long dream of becoming a teacher but, far more importantly, to her it had also been her desire to impart her knowledge to those that lacked it. She might not be a qualified teacher but, in the short time she had been with them, she had taught more to those under her charge than they had ever learned at any outsiders' school they had attended. And they had enjoyed themselves too, through the methods Emily Dunn used to teach. Also, she had fitted very well into the community, Gem hearing nothing but praise for her from other members. Besides, if Sam should get to hear of this slip-up she had made, he would remind her of it for the rest of his life, at any opportunity; that a true-blooded show woman would never have made such a blunder, even though it was the sort of mistake anyone from any walk of life could have made in the circumstances. Sam would conveniently forget that, over his time as fair owner, he had himself taken on many workers that turned out not to have the skills they proclaimed they had. And there was the fact that if Emily Dunn left, the task of teaching the children would fall to her again! Gem would shackle Emily to the tent if she had to to keep her here as the community's teacher.

'You'll leave over my dead body,' she emphatically informed Emily Dunn with meaning. 'I should not have assumed that you were a qualified teacher when you first approached me with your offer, so the blame is mine. You might not have a piece of paper stating that you've passed your teaching exams, but you've proved to be a far better teacher to our children than any other teacher has.'

Emily smiled broadly in relief. 'Thank you. I know I've only been with you all such a short space of time but I already feel I belong here. I'm very fond of the children already and very much want to see them flourish, so the thought of going back to my old life and the future that awaited me...'

Gem leaned over and gave the woman a warm hug. 'Well throw those thoughts away because that's not going to happen.' She released her hold on Emily and took a look around her van. 'You've made it very homely in here.'

She smiled. 'It's surprising how quickly you get used to not having so much space. I was rather claustrophobic for the first couple of nights and it took me time to remember that if I needed light I didn't flick on a switch but lit the oil lamps. I've learned to cook on a wood stove not a gas oven but I don't have all the housework I used to in the flat and this van is far cosier in the evening when I sit reading my books or listening to my crystal wireless set.' She chuckled. 'Mind you, I don't get that much time to read with all the callers. Parents are often sending their children to ask if I need any help fetching my water or collecting wood for the stove or the mothers come themselves with samples of their baking. I shall be fat soon. People are very kind.'

Yes they were, especially keeping an eye out for the older members of the community, thought Gem. 'You know you can call on us for anything,' she reminded her.

'You made that very clear when I first arrived and I won't hesitate to, should I need to.' She paused for a moment. It was apparent that she had something she wanted to say to Gem but was unsure whether to.

'Is anything the matter?' Gem asked her.

'No, no, not at all. It's just that I would dearly like to repay the kindness everyone has shown to me. I can bake but my efforts aren't anywhere near as good as the other women here so I wouldn't insult them with it and, besides, I've hardly mastered how to cook a meal on the wood stove yet so haven't attempted to bake anything. But I was wondering if I could offer to teach any of them that wanted to to read and write. Run adult classes or individually teach them when they can fit it in with their work. My quandary is that I don't wish to insult these dear people by reminding them of their inabilities and them thinking that I feel myself superior to them by offering to teach them, if you understand me, Mrs Grundy.'

She did. People could very, very sensitive when it came down to their failings. 'I think it's a great idea of yours. I have an idea how we can tackle this. When you decide to start the adult classes up, I'll get Solly to come to you for lessons. Once word gets around that the son of the owner is learning to read and write then others will feel that if he can so can they.' Though just how Solly would react to the fact that his wife had promised that he would go back to school without asking him first! Once she got it through to him that it was to encourage others to better their lives then he would see the wisdom of her offering his services. Wouldn't he?

Emily replied, 'Yes, I can see that would work. I'll get some lessons prepared in readiness and let you know when I'm ready to begin them.' Then a thought suddenly struck her and she exclaimed, 'Oh dear, where are my manners? Would you like a cup of tea, Mrs Grundy? And I do have a couple of Mrs Sparrow's scones that she had her daughter bring over for me last night but, as I'd already had a piece of apple pie from Mrs Jackson for my pudding, I didn't manage to eat them.'

She really ought to relieve whoever it was Solly had assigned to help Nita on the helter-skelter whilst they waited for the police to arrive after informing them that a person of interest to them was working at the fair and deal with the aftermath, but Mrs Sparrow's scones were legendary. So light and tasty. She had a secret ingredient that she wouldn't tell anyone, no matter how much they tried to bribe her. She didn't often give them away, so she must look on Emily Dunn very favourably to have given her two. No way Gem could resist the chance of one. She enthusiastically accepted Emily's offer.

Chapter Sixteen

'I'm really bothered about her. She might come across all bright and chirpy but I know she's deeply worried about Donny. I thought he'd be back with us by now but he's been gone for four days and not a word has been heard from him. His poor mother is beside herself too.'

Gem was sitting with Velda outside her van, having elevenses with her. Several other women had been with them too; each had individually departed back to their own vans to resume their housework, including Ren. Both women were now watching the back of her as she walked back into the fairground to finish readying her stall for the afternoon session.

Gem sighed. 'She'd make a good actress as she's good at playing a part, is our Ren. It's not like we can offer her any support ourselves is it, as she has no idea we'd realised... Well, you did and told me ... her real feelings for Donny.'

Velda then sighed heavily too. 'If she'd only open up to us we could offer her that comfort but, as I said when I took you into my confidence over this, I feel she's got it into her head that we'd all feel sorry for her for being in love with a man that sees her as nothing more than a friend, so she suffers in silence. Anyway, now the others have gone, can I ask what it is that is playing on your mind?'

Gem gawped at her, wondering how she knew. But then, of course, with her sixth sense she would. 'Can't hide our feelings from you, can we, Velda.'

She smiled. 'Afraid not. Anyway, had the other women not been so involved with how the romance is going between Jonny and your sister-in-law ... which I'm pleased to see is going very well ... then they, like me, would have noticed you're not your usual chatty self today.'

Gem grimaced. 'If I tell you why, you'll only think I'm paranoid.'

'I'd never think that of you, Gem. If something is bothering you, there'll be good reason for it.'

'Well I'm not so sure there is. Is thinking someone's watching you good reason to be worried?'

Velda frowned at her quizzically. 'What makes you think someone is?'

'Just that I'm sure I've seen the same girl on three separate occasions now, seeming to be taking more than an interest in me, that's all. The first time was in Barnsley and the other two times were here in Skipton. The most recent time, in fact, was last night after I left Miss Dunn and went back to take over charge of the helter-skelter. She was lurking by the Tunnel of Love.'

Velda laughed, her deep, throaty chuckle. 'I can't believe you thought Miss Dunn could be a murderer hiding out in the fair from the police.'

She laughed. 'Robbie first put the idea into our heads. He's always had a vivid imagination. A man came to work for us for one season, really nice chap he was who wouldn't have hurt a fly. I can't remember his name now, but he only had one eye as he'd lost his other in the war. Robbie was convinced he wanted to pinch one of his to replace his lost one with so he wouldn't go near him. Screamed in terror, in fact, and clung to my skirts whenever he caught sight of the man. Thankfully the man was the understanding sort, knew that he must look frightening to kids and didn't take offence, but still it was embarrassing. Anyway, the police don't want to speak to people for no reason so you can't blame us for thinking it was because Miss Dunn had done something she shouldn't have.'

'She's a nice woman. She seems to be settling in very well with us all.'

Gem leaned over and patted her hand. 'So are you a nice woman.'

A warm glow rushed through Velda. She knew this was Gem's way of reaffirming to her that a woman was how she saw her despite knowing different and that her secret was never in danger of being divulged. 'Thank you, dear,' she said with meaning. 'So, back to your worry about the young woman you feel is watching you. Do you know her?'

She shook her head. 'Never seen her before in

my life... Well, until the first time I caught her watching me that is. Last night I made to tackle her over it but when she saw I was preparing to approach her, she scarpered. I did have a quick search for her, not for long as I'd left Nita on her own and had to get back, but I couldn't see her anywhere.'

'Mmm. Well, the fact that she didn't want to talk to you is strange, I have to say, if she'd nothing to hide. That's if she really is interested in you for some reason, that is.'

'You think I am making a mountain out of a molehill?'

'No, not at all. It might be a coincidence that every time you've spotted this woman she just happened to be looking your way.'

'Oh, yes, I see what you mean.'

'I don't think it's that odd that you've seen this woman three times now at the fair as some people, youngsters especially, come every night whilst it's playing in their town and some will travel miles to visit too.'

'Yes, that's true. I went every night after I met Solly. Of course, my parents being the type they were, had no idea I'd gone once, let alone six nights on a trot, them believing I was doing my homework at my friend's house at the time. Of course a friend they had vetted first for her suitability and approved of me having. Oh, yes, of course, it's probably one of the men that work for us she's got her eye on.' She smiled at Velda. 'I *am* making too much of this, I can see that now.'

'This stew is lovely,' said Solly.

Gem smiled, pleased. 'Well, thankfully, the butcher isn't against fairfolk patronising his shop and didn't try and fob me off with an old piece of mutton, which some of them do. He gave me a nice cut from a fresh supply he'd just had in.'

'Maybe he fancied you, Mam. You're not a bad-looking woman. For your age, that is,' piped up Jimmy through a forkful of food.

Solly shot a look at her. 'That butcher better not have a fancy for you or he'll have me to deal with.'

She chuckled. 'I've only got eyes for you, husband dear. Anyway, I can assure you he has a very nice wife working with him in the shop. And, Jimmy, thanks for the compliment about me not being bad-looking but you could have left it at that and not reminded me that I am getting on. Food alright for you, Robbie? You're a bit quieter than you usually are.'

'Yeah, it's fine, Mam, ta. I was just thinking of something that one of the gaff lads told me earlier.'

'Oh, what's that?' his father asked him.

'Well ... just that some woman was asking him questions about Mam.'

Gem's head shot up. 'What woman was asking questions about me? What did she look like? And what sort of questions was she asking him?'

He shrugged. 'Just how old you were and if he knew what town you came from. Jerry couldn't tell her as he didn't know that much about you as he only came to work for Grundy's in April.' He didn't give his mother chance to quiz him further as he hurriedly forked the last bit of food into his mouth and scraped back his chair. 'I've got to get back to work as I've not finished checking all the seat bolts are tight on the big wheel yet.'

'Wait for me. I haven't finished touching up the paint on the nose of one of the carousel horses,' said Jimmy, he too gobbling down the remains of his meal and then hurriedly getting up.

'You'd both better get a move on as it's only an hour until we open.' As the two boys left, Solly then turned to Gem. 'So what's with this woman asking questions about you?'

With a worried frown creasing her brow, she got up and began stacking dirty dishes. 'I'm none the wiser than you are. All I can tell you is that I've seen a woman recently I thought was watching me. Three separate times in fact. I talked to Velda about it this morning and, until Robbie told us just now what he did, I thought I was being fanciful and she wasn't really watching me at all. Now, I–' She was cut short by a knock on the door. It was a loud rap, the sort that was more of an angry summons than a polite tap. As she was already standing up, she automatically went to answer it.

She was surprised to find a young woman facing her, the same young woman who had just been the topic of her and Solly's conversation. She was about the same height as Gem and slim, dressed very fashionably in a fine-knit crew-necked jumper in a baby pink colour that was tucked into a pair of black pants. An oatmeal-coloured box jacket was over the top and black pumps on her feet. Her dark brown hair was cut in an Audrey Hepburn urchin style, feathering around her pretty face. Gem judged her age to be around twenty-two or -three. 'You!' she exclaimed in surprise. 'You're the one I've seen watching me and, I've just learned, asking questions about me too.'

To Gem's shock, the young woman rudely pushed past her and on into the van, where she spun to face her. In a tone of voice loaded with utter disgust for the person she was addressing, she spat, 'Because I wanted to make sure I'd got the right woman before I confronted you.'

Gem recoiled, bemused. 'Confront me over what?'

Solly was on his feet now and making his way over to the two women. 'Who are you?' he demanded of the young woman.

She fixed angry eyes on Gem and demanded, 'You don't recognise me? Nothing about me that seems familiar to you at all?'

She shook her head. 'No. Should it? I've never met you before.'

She sardonically hissed, 'Oh, haven't you? You sure about that?'

Gem was becoming angry herself now at this young woman's uninvited, rude intrusion into her home, at her offensive and sarcastic manner. 'Listen, young lady, I have no idea who you are or why you're here and I don't appreciate your rudeness either...'

Before she could say any more, the other woman cried, 'And I don't appreciate being thrown away like a piece of garbage, like I was nothing. You have two sons and you kept them, didn't you, so why not me?'

Gem gawped at her. 'What! What on earth are you going on about?'

Solly spoke up. 'I don't know what your game is but I think you should go before I make you.'

She blared at him, 'I'll go as soon as I get answers.'

'Answers to what?'

She smirked and hissed, 'As if you didn't know.' Then, stabbing a finger in her chest, said, 'Did you think you would hand me over and that would be it? You'd washed your hands of me and could forget and carry on like I had never existed. Well I did exist and I deserve to know why you did what you did.'

Gem was looking even more mystified. 'Did what I did?' she uttered, confused. Then, slowly, the realisation of who this woman was suddenly exploded inside her like a bomb blast. Her face paled ashen and her whole body sagged. She had believed her secret was safe, would never be exposed. She felt like the ground was opening up beneath her, that she was falling into a cavernous hole, the walls collapsing in on her as she tumbled downwards and was finding it difficult to breathe. She gasped for air before she cried, 'Oh my God, you're alive! But I was told you had died.'

'Gem, what are you going on about?' a bewildered Solly demanded as the young woman looked on, stunned, trying to digest what Gem had just claimed.

'Oh, Solly, I never told you because I didn't want to cause you the pain I knew it would.'

He stared at her before the truth hit him and he blurted, 'You had a baby before we got married and you never told me?'

'I agonised over it, Solly, but I felt it was best

not to.'

'Was it mine?' he demanded.

'Of course it was yours,' she cried, insulted that he would even consider otherwise. 'There has never been any other man in my life but you.'

'He's my father!'

They both spun their heads to look over at the young woman, momentarily having forgotten she was there.

'Yes, he is.'

The woman glared at Solly for a moment whilst she digested this and then found her voice again. 'What did you mean, you were told I was dead when I was born?'

'I was. You died because the cord was around your neck and it strangled you.' With no warning all Gem's maternal feelings flooded to overwhelm her. She might not know this girl, had not known of her existence until moments ago, had not had a good-enough look at her yet to see anything of herself in her or of Solly either but, regardless, there was an all-consuming need for Gem to hold her in her arms. She wanted to tell her that although she had believed she had died at birth that, regardless, her love for her had never died, that she had mourned her loss every second of her life since. But now wasn't the time. The girl was angry, confused, desperately needing to know the truth of why her mother hadn't kept her. In her words, had thrown her away like she was garbage. Solly, too, she could tell, was also fighting with a mixture of emotions ... outrage and mystification that his wife had given birth to their child yet never mentioned a word of it to him during their twenty-one years of marriage. She helplessly stared from one to the other, unsure where to start her explanations to them both to answer their individual questions. The only thing to do was to tell them both her story and vehemently hope it vindicated her in their eyes as to how this state of affairs had come about.

She made her way over to her armchair and sank down in it, tightly clasping her hands in her lap. Once she saw they both had seated themselves too, she took a deep breath and began. 'I was thirteen at the time and, without my parents' knowledge, I visited the fair one afternoon when it came to town. My parents were the very strict sort; they saw fairs as places of danger to a young girl like me so, unless I was accompanied by one of them or an adult at least, I was banned from going. My father owned his own business, making lenses for glasses. We lived in a gabled house in a good area of Harrogate and he could afford to send his three daughters to a private girls' school. He was very proud of the fact that he was a Mason. My mother was on the local council, chairwoman of the local branch of the WVS and she did a lot of charity work too. Both my parents were very well thought of in our community.

'I was their eldest child. I was not the sort of daughter that disobeyed my parents but I did have a rebellious streak and when my best friend suggested we sneak off to the fair behind both our parents' backs, the excitement was too hard for me to resist.' She paused for a moment and deeply sighed. 'I wasn't to know then that that decision would change my life for ever.

'There are those that scoff at the notion of love at first sight, but I am living proof that it does exist. The instant I looked into Solly's eyes as he helped strap me and my friend into one of the waltzer cars, it was like I was sitting on a cloud, blasts of fireworks exploding around me. Solly told me the same had happened to him when he saw me.' Solly nodded his head as confirmation of her claim. 'For the rest of the week we spent as much time as we could together. I felt no guilt in deceiving my parents; I was too much in love, too desperate to be with Solly to care about anything else. The last night before the fair moved on was terrible for both of us, knowing it would be a year before we saw each other again. One year felt like a million to us both. We knew it was so very wrong of us but, at the time, it felt so right that we made love together. When the fair went away and took Solly with it, it was like my life was on hold; nothing meant anything any more to me. I missed him so dreadfully. When he went away, part of me went with him. I was upset that I didn't even have a photograph of him to look at and kiss each night before I went to sleep, I only had my memories of him to keep me going. I bought a calendar which I hid in my drawer in my bedside cabinet and, every night before I went to sleep, I would take it out and cross off the day.

'It was so hard for me to appear my normal cheery self in front of my parents but I had to as the last thing I wanted was for them to question me as to why I was so down. I couldn't tell them why or all hell would have broken loose; that I was mourning for a boy who worked at the fair. Of course I worried that Solly would meet someone else in the meantime and forget all about me. My friend didn't hold back in reminding me that fairground boys were famed for being the love 'em and leave 'em type, so all I could hope was that I was right about him, that he'd meant what he had said to me; that he loved me and would be loyal to me during the year we were apart.

'In my naivety of such things, I had no idea I was pregnant. It was my mother that told me. I had not long turned fourteen, a month before in fact. I can remember that day clearly. It was four months after the fair had moved on, early August, and I was in my bedroom with my mother sorting out clothes to take with us on our annual holiday to the Lake District. I had started my periods the year before and they were still not what you could call regular so the fact that I had missed a couple hadn't worried me at all. I was trying on a dress, my mother telling me it had been big on me last year so should fit me well by now, but I couldn't get it over my stomach. My mother tugged and pulled but she couldn't either. Finally we gave up and as I stood in my underwear waiting for her to give me something else to try on, that was when she noticed the mound of my stomach. Having had three children herself, she knew a pregnant daughter when she saw one.

'To say my mother was beside herself was putting it mildly. She didn't rant and rave, she wasn't the type, but you knew when she was angry and my mother was incensed. All she could think about was what the neighbours would say; how having one of her daughters have an illegitimate child would affect her and my father's reputation as pillars of the community. When she forced me to tell her who the father was, well, her reaction was pure outrage. How could her well-bred daughter give herself to the likes of a gypsy? I tried to tell her that Solly was a showman. Showmen worked hard for their living and were honourable people, but she was having none of it. To her, people that travelled were the dregs of the earth. She tried to make me admit that Solly had forced himself on me; it was obvious that that would make things better for her somehow, rather than the fact that I had willingly given myself to him. But I wouldn't, no matter how hard she tried. She told me not to even consider that she would allow me to keep the baby. As soon as it was born, it would be adopted. I was in a total state of shock, but as it slowly sank in that I was carrying a baby, even though I was very young, I wanted it so badly. A love grew right then for the life that you and I, Solly, had created that was growing inside me. I don't know how I found the courage to stand up to my mother but I told her that this baby was mine and I was going to keep it. I said that I knew the baby's father would stand by me and we would raise it together. All she said to me was, "If that's the way you want it." Well, I took that to mean that after all she had said that, as a mother herself, she accepted that I wanted to keep the baby and would support me and Solly raising it. Help us by way of some money to buy a van to live in at the fair, something like that. How stupid I was.'

She paused for a moment to wipe a tear from her eye before she went on. 'But now I know she never had any intention of letting me keep my baby, as that was when she must have decided on her plan that she was going to arrange for it to be adopted and tell me that it had died. She forbade me to even attempt to get in touch with you, Solly, and tell you about this. I wanted to, believe me, desperately so. You had a right to know you were going to be a father and there was a hope in me that maybe your family would help us too. After all, the baby was their grandchild. But I had no idea where the fair was at the time or any idea how to find out, so I couldn't let you know.

'My father too was furious, he could hardly bring himself to look at me and he only talked to me when he couldn't avoid it. I thought he would come round once his grandchild was born. They still went on holiday that year but I didn't go with them. They told everyone that I had gone to stay with a sick spinster aunt to help nurse her and when the school term started I would attend a school nearby until my aunt had no need of my help any longer. Really though, I was with an old widow in a cottage in the country, miles from anywhere. My mother had found out that she made her living from looking after pregnant women who wanted the fact they were having a baby kept secret. She helped arrange adoptions too. But she had no reason to arrange one for me as I was keeping my baby and me and its father were going to raise it together.

'My time with the woman wasn't so bad. She was a kindly old biddy and she looked after me well. There was another woman there when I was too. She was older than me, in her twenties. She too was unmarried and her parents also didn't want the stigma of having an illegitimate grandchild. So they did the same as my parents and arranged for her to stay out of sight and have the baby adopted. Eloise, that was her name, was happy about that as she didn't want the baby. She had fallen pregnant after having too much to drink one night and couldn't even remember the father's name. She certainly didn't want that one mistake to ruin her life. I couldn't understand how she could not want her baby and hoped for the baby's sake that she would change her mind when it was born. Whether she did I do not know as her baby was due after mine. We spent most of our time taking long walks in the countryside when the weather was fine and Mrs Lovitt taught me to knit so I could make a layette for my baby. We also helped with our share of the housework. To say I was content and looking forward to my baby arriving … well, I was. Very much so, because soon after the birth the fair was due back for its annual visit, Solly would be back, and we'd be a family together.'

To now realise that at the time she had been obliviously planning her future life with her baby and Solly, that her mother had already made sure that was never going to happen, was causing Gem such great distress she was finding it difficult to carry on. Still, this was no time to break down as she had a story to finish that two people were not only desperate to hear, but had every right to.

She forced herself to continue, 'As soon as it

was apparent to Mrs Lovitt I was going into labour she sent for my mother. Although I know she was so cross with me for getting myself pregnant and especially over who I had by, and was also greatly annoyed by my defying her wish to have the baby adopted and raising it myself, she was very kind to me during my labour. She bathed my head, held my hand and spoke soothing words to me. Although I was in a great deal of pain, I do remember thinking at the time that this behaviour by her was most unusual as my mother is not at all the demonstrative type. This will sound extremely nasty of me, but I do wonder now if this was her way of helping the birth go smoothly as the parents that Mrs Lovitt had helped her find wouldn't want a less-than-perfect baby and the last thing my mother wanted was that on her hands to deal with if they refused to take it for any reason.

'The labour seemed to go on for ever to me but it only actually lasted another four hours after my mother arrived. As soon as the baby was born, I wanted to hold it, look into its face and tell it I loved it, but Mrs Lovitt immediately wrapped it tightly in a blanket and took it away. It was my mother that broke the news to me that the baby had been born dead from the cord wrapped around its neck.' Gem could not help the tears that flooded then. 'I was ... oh, I can't describe the pain of being told my baby was dead. It was utterly unbearable. I was absolutely inconsolable. I demanded to see the baby as I wanted to say my goodbyes to it, but my mother insisted it was best I didn't. She wouldn't tell me whether it was a boy or girl either, said it was better I didn't know. She said the baby wasn't meant to be and it was best for me now to put this behind me and get on with my life. When we went home I was to keep up the story that I had been away helping my sick aunt as, if the truth got out that I had had a baby at fourteen years of age and especially that the father was a fairground worker, others would make my life a misery. I'd be labelled a slut and the private school I was attending would not accept me back, nor would any other school take me either, and my education would suffer. My future would too.'

She paused again to wipe her wet face with the back of her hand before she went on, 'I can't believe now that all the time my mother was telling me my baby was dead, the new parents must have been downstairs getting my baby ready to take home with them.' She then furiously blurted, 'How could any woman who calls herself a mother tell her own daughter such wicked lies, deceive her so despicably, and all because she was worried about what people would say if she had a daughter who'd had an illegitimate baby? My mother deserves to rot in hell for what she has done to me ... to all three of us. Denying us being together for her own selfish reasons. My father, too.'

She paused yet again to take breath for a moment whilst she tried to compose herself and, once she had, she went on, 'By the time the fair came back to town, of course I hadn't seen you for a year, Solly, and I didn't know whether you still felt the same about me. As it was, my mother found out when the fair was due to arrive and made sure that I wouldn't get to come and see you, if that's what I intended to do. For the whole week it was there she arranged for me to be picked up from school and I would be locked in my room for the rest of the night. She excused what she was doing by telling me it was for my own good. It never entered her head that there was a drainpipe outside my bedroom window with thick ivy growing next to it which I could use to make my escape. If there hadn't, I would still have gotten out somehow, as I was determined to see you, Solly. Thankfully Mother was out most nights attending some council or her women's group meetings, my father was always locked in his study working and, once I knew Mother had left the house, I would shimmy down the pipe and make sure I was back in my room before she got home.

'I was terrified the first time I came to see you, Solly. I didn't know what to expect after us not having set eyes on each other for a year but as soon as we saw each other we fell into each other's arms. It was obvious our feelings for each other hadn't changed one little bit, if anything had grown stronger. I was so deliriously happy. I meant to tell you about the baby, had it all planned what I was going to say to break it to you as gently as I could, but just when I was about to it struck me just what pain this would cause you, to know that I had gone through all that and you not there to help me through it. The pain of losing a child is like no other pain. It never leaves you either. You just learn how to live with it. You are constantly wondering what life would have been like had the child lived, what they would have looked like, been like as a person. I didn't want you suffering that pain every second of your life like I was, Solly. Not when I was suffering enough for us both. So that's why I never told you.' She lifted her head and looked over at him then before she remorsefully uttered, 'I just hope you can forgive me.'

She waited for a sign from him that he did but she couldn't see his face as he was sitting with his head bowed now, shoulders slumped. It was plain for her to see that this revelation, that he had a daughter he'd known nothing about, was difficult to come to terms with. So she turned her attentions to their daughter then, who had sat in stony silence all through Gem's story and implored her, 'You were not thrown away like rubbish. I might have been young but I would have given up everything to be your mother. Solly, I know, would have too. We would have raised three children together, not two, but because of my mother we never got the chance. I know you don't know me, but I swear on my life that every word I have told you has been the truth.'

The young girl looked blankly at her for what seemed like an age before she said quietly, 'I do believe you.'

Gem then looked again at her husband for any sign that he did too but he was still sitting, head bowed, slumped forward like he was frozen in time.

At her daughter's confirmation that she believed her story, Gem's whole body sagged in relief.

Again an overwhelming need to throw herself on her daughter and hug her, proclaim her love for her, flooded her being, but Gem sensed that she was far from ready at this moment for such an intimate display of affection from her and so instead she quietly asked her, 'Have you had a good life? What were your parents like? Your name? We don't know your name!'

She took a deep breath before she responded. 'Jennifer. Jenny. Yes, I have had a good life. My parents were good people. I couldn't have wished for better. I was their only child. They were both very loving and kind. There was always lots of laughter. My father worked in a busy newsagent's, well, he managed it really as the owner had several shops and wasn't around very often. My mother helped in the shop when she wasn't busy looking after us. I did too, when I was old enough. I used to love weighing out sweets on a Saturday morning to the queue of kids that came into the shop with their pocket money. We weren't well-off, as such, but we lived in a nice flat about the shop and my parents did their best to make sure I wanted for nothing. My father died ten years ago. Suddenly, it was. Natural causes. He'd been in two wars fighting for his country and had worked long hours in the shop, sometimes sixteen a day, and the doctor's opinion was that it had all taken its toll on him. He was only fifty-two. I was fourteen at the time. It was a bad time for me and Mum. But we got through it together. Of course that meant a new manager for the shop and Mum and me had to leave the flat.

'Mum found a little two-up, two-down terrace

that she could afford on her wage from a job she got herself as a factory machinist. It wasn't in the best of areas but Mum made it homely for us both. When I left school, I went to work in the office as a junior in the factory Mum worked in. I went to night school to learn shorthand and typing and worked my way up to be the factory manager's secretary.

'I had no idea I was adopted until just before my mother died three months ago. She was ill for about a year before she died. Stomach cancer. I nursed her as best I could. It broke my heart to watch this once big, jolly woman slowly waste away to skin and bone. She was only days away from dying when I was sitting by her bed reading to her one night and she suddenly took my hand and said she had something to tell me. It was something she should have a long time ago but it was just that the time had never seemed right. If she didn't do it now, she might never get the chance. That's when I found out I was adopted. Both my parents had dearly wanted children but after years of trying and nothing happening they decided to adopt. By that time, though, they were both coming up for forty and were told they were too old. They were devastated and resigned themselves to the fact that they would never have children but then my mother heard about private adoption. After making a lot of enquiries, she found a woman who arranged them. I assumed money was involved but my mother never mentioned that. She went to see the woman and, to her pure joy, the woman told my mother she would put her on her list.

'She said the wait for the summons from Mrs Lovitt ... that was the name of the woman arranging the adoption ... to tell them she had a baby for them seemed like an eternity. They had made a nursery for the baby and each night my mum would go in there and sit in the rocking chair imagining cuddling her baby in her arms and how this baby was going to complete their lives. She told me that the moment I was put in her arms she felt an overwhelming love for me as much as she would have done if she had given birth to me herself. My father felt the same too.

'They were both so grateful to the woman who had given this precious gift to them they asked if it was possible they could pay a visit to her, who they knew was upstairs in the house, to thank her, assure her that they would be good parents to me. They were told that wasn't possible but the message would be passed on. She then told me that all she was told of my mother was that she was an unmarried woman and it wasn't possible for her to raise her child. They did manage to find out something else though. While they were preparing to leave for home with me, Mrs Lovitt left the room for a moment to deal with the mother of the woman who had just given birth to me; she'd come down to ask for a pot of tea. Mrs Lovitt forgot to shut the door properly so they could hear her and the other woman talking. Mrs Lovitt addressed the other woman as Mrs Garvey and Mrs Garvey was telling Mrs Lovitt that she wanted her to pack up her daughter's belongings for her as quick as she could as she didn't want to miss the train back to Harrogate. Mrs Lovitt told her that her daughter should at least be allowed to rest until tomorrow, but Mrs Garvey was insistent that she was well enough to travel. Mrs Lovitt then asked her if she wanted her to include the baby clothes that Gemma had made for the baby but the answer was no as they wanted no reminders at all of it. So all she could tell me about the woman that gave birth to me was that her name was Gemma Garvey and that she came from Harrogate, but at least I knew something.'

Her face scowled darkly then. 'To find out after twenty-two years that the woman I believed was my mother wasn't, that some other woman had given birth to me who didn't want me, wanted no reminder of me at all, knocked the stuffing out of me. I felt like all my life had been one big lie. I wasn't who I thought I was. I desperately wanted to find this woman who had given me away and tell her what I thought of her for what she had done. But then the woman who had raised me, who I dearly loved, was dying and out of respect for her I put this all to the back of my mind and concentrated on making her remaining days as comfortable as I could for her. A week later she died.'

Gem was feeling acutely jealous, furious and cheated that another woman and man had nurtured and raised her daughter when it should have been her and Solly. But at least the people who had raised their daughter had been good to her, given her the best life they could. That was something indeed to be thankful for.

'Once the funeral was over, I was determined to find out what I could about my real mother. I didn't want anything from her, nothing at all to do with her in fact, but I did need to know why she gave me up. I know she wasn't married and it would have been a struggle but other unmarried mothers keep their children, so why didn't she me? At least try before she gave me away. If her mother could pay for her to be cared for by a woman while she was pregnant and to arrange my adoption, then she wasn't from a poor family so she surely could have afforded to keep me. I wanted to look her in the eye and hear from her own mouth her excuses and then have the pleasure of telling her what I thought of her.

'At work we have telephone directories for every town we do business with and one was for Harrogate. I borrowed it to take home with me. I had realised that my mother was probably married by now and would have changed her name, but I thought it worth a try. There were a few other Garveys listed with different first initials but there were five with the first initial of G so I thought they might be worth a try first as one of them might be Gemma or, if not those, one might be a relative. Next day I called them from work when my boss was out of the office. The first four I called, one didn't answer but the other three were single men.

'The fifth call though was answered by the wife of a Mr George Garvey but again they didn't have a daughter called Gemma. As I was just about to tell her I was sorry to have bothered her, she told me to hold on a moment as although they weren't the Garveys I was looking for, her husband did have a second cousin; Wilfred Garvey. The cousins had never been close, moved in different circles in fact. Wilfred had his own successful business and her own husband was just a factory worker. His cousins were the sort of people who thought themselves too good to mix with sorts they felt below their station, relations or not. But if she remembered correctly, Wilfred had a daughter called Gemma or it could have been Gina or Jasmine, she wasn't sure, but felt it was worth me enquiring. She told me she believed they lived in a big house and the name of the road she thought it was on, then wished me well in finding my old school friend after having lost touch with her, as that was what I'd told her was my reason for telephoning. I immediately looked in the telephone directory for Wilfred Garvey or W. Garvey but there wasn't any listed. I called Directory Enquiries but was told that number was ex-directory so they wouldn't give it to me. The only thing I could do to find out if they were the Garveys I was looking for was to go and visit them in person. I had the name of the road they lived on, so finding which house they lived in shouldn't be difficult.'

She paused for a moment as her face darkened angrily. 'I couldn't believe how nice the house was. It was huge, at least four bedrooms I guessed, and had a big garage at the side for two cars at least. There was a short drive leading up to the house and the garden was immaculate, not a blade of grass out of place. An old man was working in it. I asked him if I had the right house for a Mr and Mrs Garvey and he told me I had and that Mr Garvey was out but Mrs Garvey was in.

'I was expecting a really old lady to answer the door considering she had a twenty-two-year-old granddaughter, so was shocked that she could only have been in her late fifties. I didn't think it was my grandmother at first until I told her I was looking for a Mrs Garvey and she told me that she was Mrs Garvey. She was very polite to me at first. I think she thought I was collecting for the church bazaar or something. As soon as I told her who I was and that I believed that her daughter Gemma could be my mother, her whole manner changed and she looked at me like I was something she would scrape off her shoe. She poked me hard in my shoulder and told me that she'd made it clear when I was adopted that the family wanted nothing to do with me ever and to remove myself from her premises and never come back. She told me if that if I didn't, she would call the police and have me arrested for harassing her. She then slammed the door on me. So that was it. That nasty woman left me in no doubt that I was never going to find out why my mother had given me away. And her my grandmother too. I was devastated.

'As I was walking back down the street, though, I felt a tap on my shoulder. It was the man I'd seen working in the garden. He looked a little jumpy, said he needed to be quick for fear of Mrs Garvey seeing him. He went on to say that he couldn't help but overhear our conversation and felt it was shameful the way Mrs Garvey had spoken to me. He had worked for the Garveys for over thirty years keeping up their garden and seeing to odd jobs around the house. He had known Gemma. He said she was a nice girl; always stopped and had a chat with him when she came home from school if he was working in the garden even though he knew her mother had warned her not to fraternise with the staff. When she was about fifteen though, she suddenly left home. He'd no idea why as the family were very tight-lipped on the matter. He had seen her again though, quite a few times in fact and very recently too. He'd never approached her in case Mrs Garvey got to find out and sacked him.

'The first time he'd seen Gemma was when the fair came, about a year after she'd left home. She was taking the money for one of the kiddies' rides. Every year since he had seen her, working on different rides each time. He and his wife always took their children to the fair, then the grand-children. He noticed she was wearing a wedding ring and the next time he saw her she was preg-nant. He didn't see her for a couple of years after that but the next time he did, she was pregnant again and had a little boy with her. I asked if he knew the name of the travelling fair and he told me it was Grundy's. The fair wasn't due there for another couple of months for their annual visit but he felt sure that if I made enquiries I would find out where they were just now. I thanked him for his trouble and the information he'd given me and told him that that's what I'd do. I'd ring all the councils and find out where the fair was. After a few calls that's how I found out it was in Barnsley. But after what the gardener had told me, I was furious. What kind of woman would hand over her baby, then give up the good life she had to go and live in squalor with gypsies, marry one and then have more children. She must be a monster. Certainly had no conscience anyway.'

'But now you know different, that I'm not a monster?'

Jenny looked at her for a moment before slowly nodding her head. 'Yes ... yes, I do.' Then, to Gem's shock, she jumped up. 'I have to go.'

Gem jumped up too, imploring her, 'No, no, please, you can't leave yet. We have so much to talk about. You have two brothers to–'

She raised her hands in warning for Gem to stop. 'I need time to get used to all this. You have to realise I came here hating you, expecting to find ... well, as I said, a monster. I was ready to rip into you and make you feel guilty for what you'd done; if ever I could make a woman like I thought you were feel guilty that was. Now to find out that it was my grandmother that's responsible...'

Her voice trailed off and she spun on her heel. Before Gem could stop her, she had run out of the van.

Gem made to chase after her but thought better of it. Her daughter had told her she needed time to get her thoughts around what she had learned today and Gem should honour her wish. She sank back down in the chair, buried her head in her hands and the tears came then; great fat ones of sorrow, loss and despair, but intermingled were those of joy to have discovered that her child had not died at birth after all but was alive and well. She felt an arm around her shoulder and lifted her tear-stained face to see Solly perched on the arm of the chair looking sadly down on her. 'Do you think she'll come back?' she uttered chokingly to him.

'Once she's come to terms with all this, hopefully she will. We need time too, Gem, to digest this. When I got up this morning I was the father of two sons but, hours later, I now find I have a daughter as well. Three children I have, not two. Same for you too.' He heaved a deep sigh. 'I am angry with you, Gem, for not telling me about this. I understand why you didn't, I do really, you were only trying to protect me. Even so, I had a right to know. It's killing me to know that you've been mourning the loss of our child by yourself when I should have been able to comfort you.'

She sniffed. 'Yes, I realise that now. I am so sorry, Solly, really I am.'

He squeezed her shoulder and kissed the top of her head. 'I know you are. There's nothing else you've kept from me, is there?'

'No, absolutely not,' she cried vehemently. 'Just this and only this.'

'Then let's keep it that way. I never want any more surprises like the one I've had today.' He looked at her quizzically as she wiped her face with a sodden handkerchief and stood up. 'You're not thinking of going back to work right now? You've just had one hell of a shock, Gem, and need time to take it all in. We need to decide how we're going to tell the boys they have a sister. How they are going to take this, God only knows.'

'I have someone I need to see.'

'Who?' Then his face screwed up thunderously.

'No, Gem, you're not going to see her. What's the point?'

'Like our daughter, I need to look her in the eye and have her tell me why she did what she did. It wasn't just that she had our child adopted behind our backs, but to tell me she was dead. I want to hear how she justifies that.'

'I'm going with you then.'

She shook her head. 'No, Solly. I remember the one and only time you met my mother and I will not allow you to go through that again. I need to do this on my own.'

At the time, Gem had cursed Solly for making her learn to drive. She had often been tasked with driving a heavy old bone-shaking Leyland lorry loaded with fair rides and paraphernalia down winding pot-holed country lanes, worried that she'd end up in a ditch. But, at this moment, she was grateful for Solly's patience in teaching her as it meant she didn't have to catch trains and buses to reach her destination.

As soon as she pulled the ageing lorry to a stop in the driveway of her destination, only a foot or so away from the steps leading up to the front door, a middle-aged woman immaculately dressed in a tweed skirt and blue twinset, grey hair expertly coiled high on her head, appeared out of the door. Her face was wreathed in fury and she was waving an angry hand at her. 'Get that ramshackle contraption off my driveway!'

Gem's anger and hurt over her mother's betrayal of her had built to fever pitch and she flung open the door, clambered out of the cabin onto the gravel driveway and, feet planted firmly apart, fixed icy eyes on the woman. 'No welcome home then for the prodigal daughter, eh, Mother? Well there isn't because you don't recognise me, do you? But then why would you, as you haven't seen me for over twenty years.'

If she was shocked at her eldest daughter's unexpected appearance then she didn't show it. Only her eyes moved when she looked Gem over before she spoke. 'Look at you, dressed like a common street labourer and driving a lorry, for God's sake. I take it then that you're still living with those tinkers. If not, you certainly look like you are.'

Gem knew that she wasn't exactly dressed in the best of clothes, but she was clean and tidy. But she could have kicked herself for the fact that, in her haste to leave the fairground, she had grabbed what she thought was her own jacket from one of the hooks by the van door and put it on without realising that it was Solly's old work coat which was covered in oil and several sizes too big for her. Her mother was being her usual arrogant self. 'Yes, I am still living with those ... what you insist on calling gypsies even though you know they're not but show people. I am very happy, couldn't be more so. Solly has been a wonderful husband to me and we have two strapping, well-mannered, intelligent sons.'

Her face still a blank mask, her mother said dismissively, 'That's of no interest to me. I told you when you left this house, never to return unless you came to your senses. You obviously haven't so, as far as I am concerned, we have nothing to say to each other.'

'Oh, we have plenty to talk about, Mother,' she shot furiously at her. 'I came to tell you I had a visitor today. I expect that you won't be shocked who it was because she came to see you, looking for me, and you slammed the door in her face. How could you treat your own granddaughter so disgustingly, Mother? But I got the shock of my life when she knocked on my door because, you see, I was told by you she was dead.'

Mrs Garvey eyed Gem with complete disdain. 'By rights she shouldn't have been conceived in the first place, had you not been such a harlot.'

Gem was clenching and unclenching her fists in an effort to control her boiling anger. She took a deep breath before she responded, 'I was no harlot. I was in love and Solly loved me. What we did ... yes, it was wrong, we were too young, but my baby was conceived through love. I wanted to keep it and all through my pregnancy you made me believe that you were going to allow me to, never a hint at what you really intended for it once it was born. You wanting nothing to do with me and my baby was your choice, Mother. I know for a fact that Solly's mother and father would have been angry with us, but they wouldn't have had the baby adopted behind our backs. They would have helped us take care of it. Been doting grandparents. But you never gave them the chance to be. You never gave *me* the chance to be a mother to that child. You even did worse than that, Mother, didn't you? You told me my baby was dead and you did that so I'd never go looking for her. You didn't want to risk me finding her and bringing her home and the fact that your daughter had a baby at such a young age coming out that way; all your friends, neighbours and cronies getting to hear. That was all you cared about, wasn't it? What other people would think of you. You deprived me and Solly of being parents to our baby just so your reputations as upright citizens wouldn't be damaged.' She glared at her thunderously. 'Do you feel any guilt, remorse for all the pain you have caused? Not just to me and Solly, but to our daughter who believes we didn't want her? Who believes we threw her away like she was a bit of rubbish.'

There was no hesitation when she bluntly answered, 'No, why should I? Your father and I had worked hard to build our good name in the town and I wasn't about to let a daughter of mine ruin it. Did you give your father and I any thought at all when you opened your legs and let that scum have his way with you?'

Gem's lips tightened as she shook her head at her. 'I should hate you, hope you rot in hell for what you did, but I feel nothing for you at all. When I came here, I think deep down I was hoping that you'd be sorry for what you had done and we could somehow make amends. How stupid was I to hope for that? I feel no connection with you at all. I'm just glad I got away from you when I did so you couldn't rule my life and steer it the way you wanted it to go, instead of what I wanted for myself. I have no doubt my sisters didn't have much choice who they married as you would have seen to it that the men they chose were the type you approved of. I dread to think what kind of man you'd have made me marry and what kind of life I would be living now had I not stood up to you and married the man I loved. Don't worry, I'll never bother you again. There is nothing here for me. I miss my sisters, I wish they'd come to see me, but I doubt they will dare for fear of crossing you.'

Without even a farewell in any guise, she then spun on her heel, kicking up gravel in her wake, and climbed back inside the lorry. She backed it out of the drive and drove off, not even looking back to see whether her mother was watching her go or not. She didn't care. She just wanted to put distance between her and that selfish woman. She was having difficulty believing the fact that they were closely related; in her, Gem could see nothing of herself.

Back at the fairground, Solly was desperately waiting for her to return and he pounced on her before she even managed to get out of the cab, demanding of her, 'Are you alright? I've been worried sick about you since you went. I hope your mother treated you better than the last time you saw her.'

She gave a wan smile. 'She hasn't changed, Solly. I'm glad I didn't let you come with me. Let's just say I won't be going to visit her again. Now I want to just forget about it.' She eyed him then, searchingly. 'I don't suppose...'

Knowing what she was going to ask, he cut her short. 'No, love, she's not. You'll just have to be patient. I'm sure she'll come back when she's good and ready.'

She wanly smiled. 'I do so hope so.'

He put his arms around her and pulled her

close. 'I've asked the boys to come straight home after the fair closes tonight as we'd like to talk to them. We can't keep this from them, Gem, they need to know they have a sister. And when Jenny does come back we'll all welcome her into the family with open arms. Shall I ask my father to be there too?'

It gave her hope that Jenny would come back. She nodded. 'Jenny is his granddaughter, so of course. Right, well, I have two sons to feed and their father and grandfather as well, so I'd best get on with it.' *Hopefully soon that will be three children,* she thought.

Intrigued as to why their father had said he and their mother had something to tell them, both Jimmy and Robbie were trying to deduce just what it was about. After several lame guesses they both decided that their mother was pregnant again. They weren't sure about a baby keeping them awake at night and all those smelly, dirty nappies but, regardless, both were quite excited about the prospect of welcoming a new member into the family. Both being male, they hoped it was a boy.

Sam, Jimmy and Robbie all sat in stunned silence whilst Gem and Solly told them what had been going on. Once the shock wore off a little, they all three decided they couldn't wait to meet their older sister and granddaughter, respectively.

They were all equally furious to learn of the part Gem's mother had played in their sister being adopted against her mother's wishes and it took much warning from Solly and Gem for them not to visit her to vent their fury for denying them the joy of having her in their lives. As Gem instilled in them, the past was gone and couldn't be changed, it was the future they needed to focus on.

Sam's birthday party was usually a raucous affair. Since Nell's death, Gem had taken over the arrangements, holding the event in and outside of their living van. Most of the community would attend. Even if not able to stay the course, they would at least pop by for a drink and bite to eat, have a dance to whoever had been commandeered to play their fiddle or accordion. Most would suffer from their overindulgence the next day. This year's birthday party was the same riotous affair as all the rest had been; the attending community certainly enjoying themselves. For the Grundy family themselves there was a cloud hanging over it. Two clouds, in fact.

They all might have appeared to be enjoying the proceedings as much as the rest were, but the fact was they weren't. The first reason was that, as usual, Sonny didn't make an appearance, not even to show his face. It was much to the family's disappointment, but especially for Sam himself who had been hoping, as he did every year, that this year Sonny would deign to come.

The other reason was that, although they didn't know her, hadn't known of her existence a matter of days before, the family all felt that, regardless, Jenny should be here with them and it wasn't right that she wasn't.

Unbeknown to his family, who believed he was secreted inside his own van whilst the party was going on, Sonny was in fact several miles away. He was entertaining a woman he had met a couple of nights before at the bar in a classy hotel. Her wealthy husband was away on business as they had hours of strenuous sex in his bed in their four-bedroomed house in an affluent area of town. As she slept afterwards, Sonny helped himself to any jewellery he could sell on and the cash lying around before making his escape before she woke.

Chapter Seventeen

Velda wasn't easily shocked, but Gem's story had shocked her – to her core. They were both sitting outside her van, sharing a pot of tea. Usually at this time of night it would be Sam she would be entertaining but tonight he had gone to bed early, given his advancing years, the amount of drink and lack of sleep he'd had the night before at his birthday party. Aware of this, Gem had taken it upon herself to talk to her friend in private to fill her in on recent happenings.

After she had finished, Velda sighed and reached out a meaty hand to give Gem's an affectionate pat. 'I thought I was past being shocked by what some people will do to make sure things go the way they want them to, but what your mother did to keep her and your father's standing in the community untarnished was pure wickedness. At least all is not lost though. You might have missed out on the first twenty-odd years of your daughter's life but you have the rest of her future to spend with her.'

'So you think she will come back?'

Velda smiled warmly and gave Gem's hand another pat. 'I don't need my powers to tell you that. Of course she will. Her life has just been turned upside down and, like she said, she needs time to get used to it all. Once she has, she'll want to get to know her real family and hopefully be part of it. I can imagine the wait is agony for you, having already missed out on so much of her life already, but you'll have to find the patience. I have to say that I am worried I'm losing my touch. I never got any vibes from you that you were harbouring such a secret. I usually sense something even though I don't know quite what it is.'

Gem heaved a huge sigh. 'I had to bury it deep. I was frightened of Solly sensing something was wrong with me and demanding to know what it was, then he'd suffer the loss as much as I was. Especially on her birthday. That day was always particularly difficult for me.'

'I can appreciate it was. Well, instead of that day being a sad one for you, in the future you'll be throwing a party for her and it will be a happy one.' She lapsed into silence for a moment before she said, 'I don't think your mother's going to be very happy soon.'

Gem frowned at her. 'Why?'

'Well it's my guess that, very shortly, the whole town is going to know that she's not the charitable woman she makes out she is. And your father isn't going to look very good either. She might think that no one knows what she did except for you, but there is someone else, isn't there? Her gardener. He possibly felt sorry for his employer when her young daughter ran away from home to marry a fairground worker, as he must have thought that's what you had done when he saw you those times the fair came to town. But after overhearing the conversation between your mother and Jenny, he obviously realised that you must have had a baby before you ran away that your mother forced you to give up and there was no compassion in her for that daughter when she turned up wanting to find her mother. She didn't need to have anything to do with her herself, but the least she could have done was tell Jenny where to find you. To witness his employer, one who portrays herself to be above reproach, acting so appallingly... Well, he might not be able to keep that to himself, might unburden himself to his wife and if the wife is the gossipy sort...'

Gem gawped. 'Oh! Oh dear. I wouldn't like to be her when what she did gets around. She'll never be able to hold her head up in public again.'

'Life has a funny way of repaying those for selfish, cruel acts. I have a feeling your mother is about to get payback for hers.' Just then she noticed a shadowy figure come out of a van, close by, and head off towards the main fairground. It was Ren.

Velda wondered where she was going at this time of night and, if she wasn't mistaken, she was carrying something. She hoped it wasn't a bottle of spirits to drown her sorrows with. She did notice that, last night at Sam's party, she was the worse for it by the time she left. She heaved a sigh. 'It's about time life gave Ren the happiness *she* deserves. She's demented with worry for Donny. I just so wish he'd come back; at least if only to put her mind at rest he's alright. And his poor mother. All of us, in fact, we're all worried about him.'

Gem said, 'He's been gone nearly a fortnight now and no word from him at all. I hope he hasn't done anything stupid. He was besotted with Suzie. Are you sensing anything?'

'I can't trust my feelings over this, Gem. I think a lot of Donny and see Ren like a daughter, so I can't tell whether my powers are telling me that he's alright where he is and he'll be back safe when he's ready or if it's just wishful thinking. Like all of us, all I can do is pray for his safe return.'

Over in the fairground, in the near pitch darkness, a thoroughly miserable Ren groped her way through the rides looming dark and sinister above her, like huge dormant beasts waiting to pounce on their prey. She wasn't quite sure where she was heading, but the inside of her small van was stifling and claustrophobic on this warm night and she needed air. She was on the search for somewhere isolated where she risked no one disturbing her. She wanted to have a good few gulps out of the bottle of wine she had brought with her, then maybe once it had worked its magic, she would get some sleep.

As the days had gone by and her worries for Donny's safety had increased, she wouldn't have slept at all if she hadn't used drink by way of helping her. At least when she was working, her mind was occupied. But once she was on her own, her thoughts were free to run riot. And roam freely they did; she imagined him in all sorts of worrying situations ... living rough on the streets, in hospital after suffering a critical accident... She knew other members of the community were just as worried about him as she was but they didn't love him, couldn't possibly, as much as she did herself.

The big wheel suddenly appeared before her and she thought this as good a place as any in which to sit and consume her medicinal beverage. Ducking under the chain barricade, she made her way to the bottom seat and eased herself onto it backwards until her bottom hit the back. Being so small, her legs didn't dangle over the front but stuck out in front of her. Once settled, she pulled the cork out and took a large gulp. As she swallowed, she looked skywards. It was cloudless tonight, no moon at all and out of a jet black background millions of stars twinkled. She remembered herself as a child believing in fairies, dragons and wizards who cast magic spells and stars that granted wishes. She would pick the one she felt was the brightest and make her wish. Those wishes had always been granted, but then they were childhood ones. Ones she always spoke out loud to make sure the stars could hear, and only for a new teddy or dress, so it was more than likely that her mother had heard. Could she wish on a star? She took another long swig from the bottle, letting the comforting liquid trickle slowly down her throat. What the hell; nothing ventured, nothing gained. Stupid of her or not, she would make that wish. Anything to bring Donny back home safe and sound was worth a try to her.

It was the star Sirius that was shining the brightest to her. She opened her mouth to begin making her wish but instead jumped in alarm as she felt the pressure of the seat go down beside her. She spun her head to see who it was. She recoiled in shock, then blinked several times just to make sure she wasn't seeing things. Then, just to confirm they were real, she reached out to touch their arm. Her fingers touched solid matter and, now convinced that the person beside her was definitely alive and breathing, she uttered, 'Donny!' Then, unable to stop herself, she cried out, 'Oh, Donny, it's really you!' Her relief and pure joy looking into the face of the man she adored with all her heart was indescribable. She wouldn't need to use drink to get her to sleep any longer. From now on she'd sleep like a baby knowing he was, at last, home safe and sound. She threw her arms around him, hugging him bearlike. 'You've no idea how worried I've been about you. I've hardly slept since you went off and no word from you since.' Then it struck her with force that her zealousness to see him was far more than just a friend would show to another, so she quickly released her hold on him and awkwardly blustered, 'Well everyone has been worried about you, not just me. Your mother is beside herself.' Despite being desperate to know the answers, she tried to sound casual when she asked, 'You are alright, aren't you? Where have you been all this time?'

He seemed distracted, something was obviously

preying on his mind, and he said shortly, 'I'm fine. Well, I am now. Wasn't when I left, far from it.'

She looked at him in sympathy and said softly, 'I'm so sorry for what Suzie did to you. She didn't deserve you, Donny.' His face was in shadow and it was hard for her to tell whether he was still suffering the pain of his recent betrayal, still trying to come to terms with it, or if he had accepted the situation and was on the road to recovery? Had he lost weight? She could understand if he had. What he had been through was enough to cause anyone to lose their appetite. From what she could tell though, he seemed well in himself. She was a little disconcerted as he did appear to be a little on edge, nervy in her company, and she wondered why as it wasn't like he didn't know her inside out. After all, he knew her nearly as well as he knew himself, and there was no reason that she could think of why he would feel anxious with her. Then she remembered that for several weeks prior to his leaving, they had been estranged thanks to Suzie's lies about her. He was probably feeling guilty for believing her lies that he now knew weren't true. He knew Ren didn't hold grudges and so she hoped his visit to tell her he was back was a sign that now Suzie wasn't around to poison their friendship any longer, he wanted it to return to how it had been before she had driven her wedge between them.

'Your mother must have been overjoyed to see you? Your dad as well?'

'I haven't seen either of them yet.'

She thought that strange. Surely it was his parents he would have automatically sought out first to put their minds at rest that he was back in one piece.

'I was coming to see you and saw you coming out of your van and heading into the fairground, so I followed you.'

She smiled at him warmly. 'I'm glad you did. Well, I expect you'll be wanting to see your parents so you can let them know too.' Intrigue then made her ask, 'Before you go though, just where have you been?'

'One of the gaff lads that used to work for us that I got friendly with left us to work for the fair in Bridlington. I went to see if he still worked there and he did and let me stay with him in his van. It was a bit cramped, as three other lads were staying in it too, but it was a roof over my head and it gave me time to get my head around all this.' He paused for a moment to take breath before he continued, 'Suzie said some things to me...'

She cut in. 'Terrible things, Donny, and she was just being spiteful, so you mustn't take them to heart. She was just saying those things as an excuse to do what she did.'

'Not all the things she said were her being spiteful, Ren. Some of them were the truth about me. One of things she said about me though, I couldn't understand ... that I was too thick to realise who I really loved and should have married. I loved her, so I did marry the woman I should have, didn't I? But then I got to thinking that I was only young, fifteen, when Suzie came along, that I didn't really understand what proper love was then. I was besotted with her, couldn't believe that a woman like her would pick me as her boyfriend when she could have had any man she wanted. Then, before I knew it, we were married. If I knew then what I do now I'd have seen that we hadn't got much in common, didn't see eye to eye on lots of things and we never talked, not really, unless it was about something that Suzie wanted to talk about. Time on my own to think has made me see there's a big difference between infatuation and real love. But that wasn't all I realised. While the others were at work and I was alone in the van, it suddenly struck me that it wasn't actually Suzie I was thinking of most and missing like hell, wishing she was with me, helping me through all this. I was missing the way she always managed to cheer me up when I was feeling down; always made me laugh with her funny ways and the things she said. Lots of other things about her too that I loved. Suzie was right. I *was* too thick to see that it was her I loved and should have married, not Suzie. That's if she feels the same about me. I know she likes me, I know she cares about me by the way she's always been with me, but love...' He slapped his hand against his forehead and exclaimed angrily, 'It hurts so much and it's embarrassing to know that you've been stupid enough to let someone use you like Suzie used me. It was hard for me to come back and face everyone here, but I knew if I didn't come back then I'd never see the woman I really love again and I couldn't bear that. So I came back to find out if there's any chance with her. I just hope

I haven't left it too late.'

As she was listening to him, her heart was sinking, knowing that she was going to have to go through the excruciating pain of watching the man she loved marrying another woman as she had done when he'd married Suzie, forcing herself to keep a smile on her face. In truth she wanted to beg Donny to marry her instead. Maybe on the day he married this woman he was now proclaiming was his real true love, his soulmate, it would be best she made an excuse not to be there. But then how could she do that to him; she was his best friend, after all, and best friends supported each other through everything, not just what they handpicked.

She tried to work out just who this woman was that he did really love? There were quite a few women of their age in the community. Could it be Beryl Evans? She was very pretty but then she'd only ever had eyes for Davie Jimson and the pair had been courting for years, were getting married as soon as Davie had enough money to buy his own stall or ride to support them on, so it couldn't be her. Charmaine Kitchen? No, definitely not. Donny wouldn't look at a girl who had slept with most of the single men, and some married ones, in the community and outside of it too. Olive Ilkey? Before she could explore the possibility that it might be Olive, she realised that Donny was still speaking and she hadn't been listening.

She apologised to him. 'Sorry, what did you say?'

'I asked if I've got any chance, Ren?'

He was asking his best friend her advice for fear

of making a fool of himself. She leaned over, patted his hand and, resolutely, said, 'Of course you've got a chance with her. She'd be daft if she doesn't snap you up. You'll never know though until you ask her, will you?'

Acute misery washed over her and she knew that, any minute, she was going to cry. Not in front of Donny or he'd want to know why. She needed to get back to her van and grieve in private over what might have been but never would. She started to ease herself off the seat but he stopped her by grabbing her arm and demanding, 'Where are you going?'

'Well, you'll be wanting to get off and go see this woman and find out if she feels the same about you. It's late but she might still be up. I need to get back. I've clothes to iron for work tomorrow.'

He looked at her imploringly. 'That woman I'm talking about is you, Ren. It's you I love. Always have. It took Suzie's home truths to make me realise that. I do have something to thank her for, after all. I know I don't deserve you after the way I treated you. Deep down, I knew it couldn't possibly be true that you would talk about me behind my back like Suzie claimed you did. But she was my wife and I couldn't think of any reason why she would make up such horrible things about you, so I believed her. I should have known better. You haven't got a malicious bone in your body, Ren.' He then beseeched her, 'Can you forgive me? Please say you will. I really do love you. I can't imagine my life without you in it ... not just as a friend, but as my wife. As soon as I get a divorce, that is.'

She was struck utterly speechless. The words she was hearing from his own mouth she had longed to hear for as long as she could remember. Now she actually was, she was having difficulty believing them. She knew Donny well enough though to know that he was not the type of man who said anything if he didn't mean it. She should tell him how much he meant to her too, how deep her love for him ran, how it broke her heart when he married Suzie, that to become his wife was her wildest dream come true, but in her shock – that he felt the same as she did about him – all she could manage was, 'You'd better see about getting that divorce then.'

Donny being such a well liked and respected member of the Grundy community, his return back into the fold was well received. His family were overjoyed to see him so happy and content with the woman they had always believed he should marry. The wedding was going to be a truly special event. All the fairfolk would make sure of that.

Chapter Eighteen

It was the end of September. The Grundy fairfolk had dismantled the rides and stalls and rebuilt them again twelve times since they had left Skipton. It was Sunday afternoon and they had just arrived in Hexham, a small market town, south of the river Tyne.

Gem was feeling hot, tired and irritable. The move to Hexham from Penrith, their last port of call, a distance of forty miles, had not gone smoothly. Penrith was on the west side of the Pennines, the row of mountains known to all as the backbone of England. Despite the stunning views, the roads were both steep and narrow. Mud on the road caused one lorry to skid, it then having to be towed out of the thick grassy moorland verge by another. To do so, both vehicles first had to be offloaded of their cargo, then reloaded back on again. More time was lost from vehicles being delayed by sheep on the road. One unfortunate sheep did end up on the back of the lorry, having been accidentally hit; the perpetrator being of the mind that it was better to provide his family with several good dinners than leaving it to rot. A lorry got a puncture and, thanks to an unseen pothole, a living van became detached from the vehicle pulling it. The driver behind only just managed to swerve out of its way before it veered onto the moorland to bump up and down over it for several yards until it came to an abrupt stop, finally tipping over onto its side.

Thankfully none of the Grundy community were physically hurt during any of these mishaps but repairing damage to the vehicles involved was not going to be cheap and would eat into the profits of those affected; the winter months would not be so comfortable unless they could make up their shortfall before the season came to an end at the end of November. Jimmy, his mother as passenger, was driving a Scammell Pioneer low-loader that was ferrying their living van in a convoy of ten others. The vehicles were the last to leave the site in Penrith, half an hour later than intended due to one member of the convoy having mislaid his lorry keys which he finally found in a puddle of water, having dropped them out of his pocket whilst he was having a last check that the cargo was secure. Gem was getting worried about them making up the lost time en route, worried that if they didn't she would be behind schedule in the cooking of the huge meal to feed all the workers that she was in charge of over in Hexham.

Unfortunately for Gem, though, they were not going to make up the lost time but would lose even more. The convoy she and Jimmy were travelling in, them being last in the line of in fact, was the same one that the caravan was in that hit the pothole which caused the tow bar connecting it to the ramshackle Land Rover to snap. The vehicles in front had carried on, not realising what had happened behind them, so it was up to the two vehicles behind to help. Consequently, by the time Gem and Jimmy arrived at Hexham and Solly, Jimmy and Robbie had offloaded the living van off the back of the low-loader, secured it, fired up the generator and gotten the fire in the stove ablaze, the delay in making a start on the meal was now over three hours behind. The fair-folk men, labouring away constructing the fair rides and stalls, were all ravenous by now, breakfast being a long-distant memory, and with no sign of their next meal yet, tempers were beginning to fray as a result. The women, aware of this and worried about arguments or, worse, fights breaking out between their hungry men, were doing their best to hasten the meal along.

Children were severely warned to stay out of trouble and play together. Several women were in their own vans making a variety of puddings for afters, whilst at Gem's van others were sitting outside in a circle on an assortment of chairs they'd brought along with them, peeling mounds of potatoes to be boiled for mashing. Others were scrubbing carrots and chopping turnips. Several other women were erecting trestle tables, pushing them together to make one long row in a space nearby. Inside Gem's van, two women were keeping an eye on two massive cauldrons of oxtail and vegetable stew bubbling away on top of the stove, making sure the contents didn't burn. Gem herself was at her kitchen table using a large pudding bowl to mix a vast amount of flour, suet and salt together to make dumplings. She had already made twelve loaves of soda bread which were cooling on the windowsill, when Robbie burst in.

'Mam, where's that box of toy cars I had as a kid? You didn't throw them away, did you? I hope not.'

She looked at him blankly as she spooned cold water into the dumpling mix, careful not to overdo it which would make the dumplings hard. 'Box of toy cars?' she repeated quizzically.

'You remember, I collected them when I was little and by the time I grew out of playing with them I'd got at least forty.'

She twigged then. 'Yes, yes, I remember. You used to take one of the cars to bed with you and cuddle it like you would a teddy.' She then said agitatedly, 'But why are you mithering me about those cars now when you can see how busy I am?'

'It's just that I promised Lol Fisher's lad, Matty, that he could play with them if he stops pestering his dad. He's being a right little bugger, keeps pinching tools and running off with them, seems to think it's funny that his dad has to chase him to get them back, even though Lol has warned him he'll murder him if he doesn't stop it. I think he will murder him if he doesn't, Lol's that fired up. We're already behind erecting the fair with half the men getting here late and a murder will put us even further behind. We'll never have it all done before we open tomorrow. I warned Matty to behave himself while I get the box of cars and he promised me he would but I'm worried he won't be able to control himself and start playing up his dad again, so I need to find the box quick and get back.'

Had Gem not been feeling so pressured herself to get the meal finished, she would have laughed at Robbie's comment. She said tersely, 'Well, yes, that's a good idea giving Matty your box of old cars to play with to get him to stop annoying his dad, but why are you mithering me about it?'

'Well, as I said, I don't know where the box of cars is. Can you remember where you would have stored them? I've already looked under Jimmy's bottom bunk and it's not there.'

She sighed as she stopped what she was doing to try to remember where she had stored the box of cars. Then it struck her. 'I remember seeing it now inside the hidey-hole under me and your dad's bed when we moved some stuff around to make space to hide Col. If it's not there I don't know where it could be. Now, leave me be to get on with my work or the men will never be fed. Oi, and make sure you leave the bedroom as you find it!'

In his hurry, Robbie yanked off the bedclothes, then the mattress, heaping them by the curtained wardrobe, then felt inside for the small knob of wood in the corner. Once found, he pulled up the piece of wood that formed part of the base of the bed but also concealed the hidden space underneath. To his dismay the space was filled with all sorts of items, some his mother had kept for sentimental reasons, but most of it he could not fathom why. Especially the old clothes of his and his brother, long ago grown out of, and a burnt orange glass punch bowl and twelve cups that hung from hooks off the rim of the bowl, a wedding present from a now-dead aunt of his father's that he knew his mother hated and had never used. But under that lot somewhere was the box he was after.

He began pulling out the clothes first. In his haste to get to whatever was hidden beneath them, he did not notice that, as he yanked out an old jumper that he'd been six years of age the last time he had worn it, from out of the folds a small oilskin-wrapped package flew out, to sail over his shoulder and land inside one of his mother's well-worn wellingtons, standing erect in the bottom of the wardrobe beside other pairs of her shoes.

Robbie had absolutely no idea that what he had unwittingly just done was going to ignite a chain of events that would have a catastrophic effect on his family and change their lives for ever.

Having finally unearthed the wooden box that held his prized collection of metal toy vehicles, Robbie put the box aside whilst he returned everything back to how it had been before he disturbed it. As soon as he had finished, armed with the box of toys, he raced back to the fairground to present it to Matty, hoping he hadn't been too long and his father had carried out his threat on him!

The meal was finally ready and, having had their bellies filled with their womenfolk's tasty, nourishing food, good tempers were restored amongst the men. They returned to labour away for many more long hours preparing the fair for opening the following afternoon, leaving the women with the monumental task of clearing up.

Chapter Nineteen

Sonny never knew when one of Bossman's henchmen would appear to either drop off a package or collect one. Most important for Sonny was that the dues he paid for their safekeeping were beginning to build up to a good sum. Plus, as soon as he inherited it, he would be able to add the proceeds of the sale of the fair to fund his new business with; the first of a chain of exclusive nightclubs. He was now becoming more and more excited about the prospect of this wonderful new life he was going to have and he was getting frustrated as to when he would be in a position to make a start on it. It was, though, coming up to winter, his father was seventy-one years of age now and people of his maturity didn't cope so well with the bitter weather. So hopefully, with a bit of luck, his father would catch something nasty and that would speed up his passing into the hereafter, clearing the way for Sonny's new life to begin.

The arrangement with Bossman was that these visits were always to be timed mid-evening, when the fair community were busy making money from the hordes, so it would leave him free to either collect or hide the packages without fear of anyone seeing him. Of course there was always someone about in the living area, mostly the senior members of the community too old to work on the rides and stalls any longer who were the ones minding the children while they slept, or workers themselves travelling back and forth to their vans for some reason, so he still had to be vigilant.

Tonight his visitor was a tall man dressed in a long brown mackintosh over a smart suit with a brown fedora hat pulled down over his brow. Sonny was in charge of operating the Mont Blanc ride which was a large, circular contraption that had long jointed arms with cars suspended from the ends of each that splayed out from the central core to rise high in the air as the engine spun it round. He first noticed the man when the ride had stopped, people were clambering out of the cars and new riders getting in. He was leaning against a support pillar on the wooden steps leading up to the ride, his head bent as he lit a cigarette. His cigarette lit, he flashed a glance over at Sonny, sitting in the small operating booth in the middle of the ride. The nod of his head informed Sonny he would be waiting for him in the designated meeting place. That was Sonny's living van where he would inform him whether he was dropping a package off or had come to collect one already in Sonny's possession. Telling one of his helpers that he was taking a break for a few minutes, Sonny went off to meet the man.

The man was already inside his van when he arrived. He was brusque and to the point. He had come to collect the package that had been left with Sonny several weeks ago whilst the fair had been playing near Bradford. He was the ruthless, cold type that would shoot first then ask questions later, not the sort to mess with at all. Anxious to be rid of him, Sonny hurried off to collect the package.

Darkness had descended about an hour before on that September night and, as he sneaked his way through the shadows to the huddle of forty or so living vans towards his destination, he had twice to press himself into the side of a van for fear of being seen by members of the community. Thankfully he arrived without detection. If he had been seen there would be questions asked why he was entering a particular van when none of the residents were at home; he never visited when they were. With cat-like swiftness, he ascended the steps at the front of the van and slunk inside. He switched on the torch he had brought with him and shone it around. Four people lived in this van but it was far cleaner and tidier than the van he lived in. His brother, though, didn't have to see to his own housework as he'd someone to do it for him. As he would have done had she not been brainwashed into believing all fairfolk were filthy vagabonds.

He moved into the bedroom. Positioning the torch on a shelf in Solly's curtained-off wardrobe so that the light from it shone directly at the bottom of the bed, he yanked off the covers, then the mattress before lifting out the section of board concealing the hidden space underneath. It was the perfect place to hide Bossman's illicit goods as he knew that rarely did Gem or Solly have cause to look here themselves. Should the goods somehow be discovered by the police, it wouldn't be him that was arrested for being in possession of stolen goods but his brother.

On top of a pile of clothes was an old jumper his nephew Robbie had worn when he was a youngster. Why Gem should keep clothes her sons had long ago grown out of was beyond his comprehension. Women were mysterious creatures sometimes. He carefully unfolded the jumper. He stared down at it, stupefied. The small oilskin packet that he had secreted inside it a few weeks ago wasn't there! Had it somehow slipped out? Maybe it had been jolted out during one of the moves? He grabbed the torch and shone the beam around the inside of the storage space, paying particular attention to any little cavity not filled by any stored items where the package might have slipped into. Still he could see no sign of the package. Where on earth was it?

A niggle of worry ignited in the pit of his stomach. Whatever was in that package had to be very valuable to the boss and he daren't think how that man waiting back in his van for him to return with it would react if he arrived empty-handed. He had to find that package, he just had to. It had to be inside the hidey-hole, it was just that he had missed it. He went to make a start on taking everything out when a sound reached his ears. Was that someone coming in the van? His heart thumped wildly when he heard another noise. Someone was in the kitchen. Thankfully, both room separator curtains were pulled across so he couldn't be seen but if whoever it was came in here they definitely would. He couldn't be found in here doing what he was, as what excuse could he give that would be believable? He just prayed the man waiting back at his van would believe him that he had mislaid the package and needed more time to find it. If he didn't... As quickly and quietly as he could, he replaced everything as it had been before he'd arrived, then climbed over the bed trying to straighten the covers as best he could behind him. He climbed out of the window and dropped down to the ground on the other side. As tall as he was, he could just manage to reach the window to push it shut. As he sneaked around to the front, he took a peek inside the window at the front showing into the kitchen area. He could see Robbie, looking in a wall cupboard for something ... a plaster as he'd cut his finger ... and silently cursed him for returning at that time to put a stop to what he'd been doing.

Sam was bone weary. He'd had a long day and all he wanted to do was have a nightcap and go to bed. He didn't think he even had the energy in him to hold a conversation with his dear friend Velda whilst he drank that nightcap, so tonight he planned to have it on his own in bed, that's if he could manage to keep his eyes open for long enough to drink it. There had been a time, not that long ago in fact, when he could have worked like a navvy all day and still have it in him to drink, chat and dance into the early hours of the morning and rise bright as a lark at the crack of dawn the next day to tackle another full day of work. Now his age was showing itself and those days of hard labour and long nights of socialising were well beyond him. But he still had plenty of years left in him yet and although he might not have the stamina he once did have, he was determined to live his life to the full as much as his ageing body would allow him to.

He had hoped that would have been with Velda by his side, now he had come to terms with losing his beloved Nell. He had been utterly devastated by her turning down his proposal to take their relationship further. His visions of them sitting side by side in armchairs by the fire on a dark winter's night chatting about the day's events before they retired to bed had vanished like a puff of smoke, but when he had gotten over his disappointment and really thought about Velda's reasons for not going ahead, he did appreciate they were valid. He was now happy that she had decided they should just remain friends. In truth, he did have the best of both worlds. His daughter-in-law saw to all his domestic needs and Velda was there for him whenever he felt the need for the company of a woman.

Today he had driven eighty miles to another travelling fair on the outskirts of Sunderland where he'd made prior arrangements with one of the ride owners who was selling his ride as he was retiring to live in a bungalow on the west coast, leaving both Solly and Sonny caretakers of the business so as not to cause discord between them for the short time he was away. Regardless, he was aware that if any of the community had a problem it would be the approachable Solly they would turn to rather than face short shrift from Sonny. Sam couldn't see the old showman selling the ride having a happy retirement living in one place all the time and he suspected that it was his wife who had pushed him into it. It wouldn't surprise him if they only lasted a year or two in the bungalow before the lure of life on the open road proved too much to resist and they were back living amongst their own fairfolk community again. Once a traveller always a traveller to him.

As soon as he'd spotted the ride advertised in the *World's Fair* weekly newspaper, his interest had been sparked. He was always on the lookout for affordable rides to expand the business with, keep the punters coming in. The ride was called the Dive Bomber. Twin cars were mounted on a vertical rotating arm, spinning on their own axis to give riders the sensation of diving and looping. The ride was over ten years old but had been well maintained and was being sold at a very good price. When he had discussed it with Solly, it had been his opinion that it was well worth going to see. He was right; it had been. On the spot Sam had made the decision to buy it. Of course, Sam had haggled hard with the owner and was very pleased with himself to have agreed a much-reduced price than what it had been advertised at. He wouldn't take possession of it until the end of the season which was in just over a month's time and had made arrangements for a date to have it collected. Any repairs or repainting needed could then be done while they were laid up over the winter months and the ride would be in pristine condition ready to join the rest of the rides when the new season began next March.

Despite his fatigue, Sam was in good spirits when he arrived back in Hexham at just after nine that evening.

As he eased his creaking body out of the vehicle and had a good stretch, the level of noise coming from over in the main fair arena told him that a good crowd had come in tonight and his spirits rose even higher. As he made to go into his van it struck him that despite his need to get to bed it would be remiss of him if he didn't first inform his family he was back safely from his jaunt as he knew they'd be concerned. Solly was the best person to inform as he would then tell Gem who then wouldn't waste good food on making him supper he wasn't going to eat. Then he'd let Sonny know too. He doubted very much Sonny would be bothered one way or the other. He tried to remember what ride Solly was in charge of tonight. The dodgems? Waltzers? Sky planes? It was one of those anyway. Those rides were all spaced apart from each other and to visit each until he found the one Solly was working would mean him having to battle his way through the crowds which didn't appeal to him with his back aching so badly after his drive there and back to Sunderland. He did remember that Sonny was on the Mont Blanc tonight which was sited closer to the living van area than the others, so he changed his mind and decided to inform Sonny of his safe return and ask him to dispatch off one of his gaff lads to find Solly and tell him. Aided by his walking stick, he hobbled off.

Arriving at the Mont Blanc ride he was furious to find that Sonny wasn't there, only two gaff lads running it. Not only that but having told the lads he was just slipping away for five minutes, according to them, Sonny had now been gone for over twenty. Sonny was very aware of his father's feelings on leaving gaff lads unsupervised during busy times. What if an accident happened or the ride broke down? Slipping away for five minutes to pay an urgent visit to the toilet or grab a drink was acceptable, but being away for over twenty was another. He'd better have a good reason for his absence or Sam would not be at all impressed. Had he not been his son, he would have instantly dismissed him for such a serious misdemeanour. Therefore he would have to think of a suitable punishment that fitted his crime so he would think twice before he did it again, along with a severe warning that, son or no son, if there was ever a repeat then he'd be demoted to the role of labourer with no responsibilities and a lot less wage. The thought of the humiliation alone should be more than enough to do the trick, knowing his father well enough to know that he would carry out his threat. He secretly hoped that Sonny did have good excuse for sloping off – that he'd suddenly taken ill? Despite his difficult relationship with him, brought about by Sonny himself, Sam did love him very much. He hated the thought of their fragile relationship being eroded any further by losing his trust in Sonny to fulfil his responsibilities in a manner expected and having to watch him like a hawk in future to make sure he did.

He would try the obvious place to find him first. His living van. As usual, Sonny had parked it as far away from the other vans as he could. Sam himself, the same as the rest of the fairground community, had always needed to feel close to those he lived amongst; it afforded a feeling of security. Sonny's need to isolate himself from the rest of the community he had never understood. As soon as the van came into view, Sam could see a light was on in the living room area and there was a silhouette of a man behind the closed curtains. Sonny was at home then? But what was he doing, just standing there, seeming to be doing nothing that Sam could tell, when he should be at work? He hobbled over to the steps and, as soon as he had let himself in, he immediately blurted, 'What the hell are you playing at, Sonny? Leaving the gaff lads to it while–' He stopped short in shock to see he was not addressing his son but a complete stranger. 'Who the hell are you?' Then the obvious answer struck him. He did look far too well dressed for a common burglar and he couldn't see any sign of the bag the man would need to carry away his spoils in, but what else could he be doing here in his son's van on his own? He raised his stick, and charged as fast as he could over to the man whilst crying out, 'Caught you red-handed, you thieving bast–'

Sam's attack on the man was brought to an abrupt end as the man snatched up a heavy overflowing glass ashtray and, with the butts and ash flying out of it like confetti, brought the heavy object with force down in the middle of Sam's forehead. Sam was dead before he hit the floor.

Moments later an empty-handed Sonny arrived, terrified at what faced him when he informed the man that he couldn't find the package. He was stunned to see the man brushing cigarette ash and butts off his coat and out of his hair, wondering how he had come to be covered in them. Then he spotted the body of his father lying face down on the floor near the man's feet. He raced over to him, falling down beside him. 'Dad! DAD!' He didn't need to check for a pulse as it was obvious his father was dead. He jerked his head around to look up at the man. 'You killed my dad, you fucking bastard! Why? Why would you do that? He was just a harmless old man.'

'Self-defence. Now, give me the package. You've already kept me waiting long enough.'

Sonny was still reeling from the shock of his father's death but the man's demands swept all that aside as fear for what the man would do to him once he told him what he was about to flooded through him. Jumping up, he stepped backwards, wanting to put as much distance between him and the man as the limited space in his van would allow, whilst blurting, 'I can't find it. It must have got wedged in something during one of our moves. I need more time for a proper look. Honestly, you've got to believe me. But anyway you've just killed my dad...'

Before he could say another word the man had lunged over to Sonny and, with an iron fist, grabbed him around the neck and pulled him up until his face was only a couple of inches from his own. In no uncertain terms he then hissed, 'Shop me to the police and it'll be two funerals your family will be arranging, not just one. I'll be back for the package another time but if you don't hand it over then...' He paused for a second before he meaningfully added, 'How you die won't be as quick and painless as your father did. Understand?'

Solly did. The man thrust him away and made his leave. Solly sank to his knees. He had wished his father dead so he could claim his inheritance, but not like this, not before his proper time. His grief, however, was short-lived. His father was dead; he had been an old man, had had a good life and might have died from natural causes very shortly anyway. *He* was still a young man, however, and very much alive with a good future ahead of him. That's what he needed to concentrate on now ... making sure he stayed alive so he could enjoy that future. And he wasn't prepared to die before he had achieved what had been eating away at him to do for the last twenty years.

His thoughts whirled. Finding the package could wait for now. Bossman's henchman wouldn't risk returning for it for at least a couple of days so he didn't run the risk of bumping into the police whilst they were in the fairground investigating the death of the man he'd just killed. The package must still be hidden in the storage space under his brother and sister-in-law's bed, it was just that during his search he hadn't discovered its whereabouts. He would the next time he looked. It was how he was going to deal with his father's death that was his immediate concern.

His father had been killed in his van with an ashtray that belonged to him, that would only have his fingerprints on it as the murderer had been wearing gloves. So, as matters stood, he would be the only suspect and it would be him that was hung for it. His thoughts raced again and it struck him that the only way out of this for him that he could see was that he needed to make his father's death look accidental. Fairgrounds were full of hazards for the men that worked on them, so accidents were not uncommon. But how did he make his father's death look like one, enough to convince the police that that was how he'd died?

He jumped up from the floor and began pacing up and down as his thoughts continued to whirl. Nothing plausible presented itself to him. He was at the point where he actually thought he could physically feel the hangman's noose around his neck when, like a thunderbolt, a memory from years ago crept into his mind. He'd been about ten at the time when one of his father's labourers had been helping to erect the helter-skelter. The skeleton of it had been constructed and the slide encircling it was in place. The labourer on the small landing at the top of the slide, where those about to slide down would sit on a mat before they pushed themselves off down the steep incline, had been about to secure the last of the barrier boards in place running down the side of the slide, when he had suddenly lost his balance and toppled through the empty space that he had been just about to fill. He fell forty foot or so. His death had been recorded as accidental. The same as his own father's would be because that was how he also was going to have appeared to have died.

He would have to wait until it was dark but, if he moved his father's body and placed it face down on the ground immediately below the last top board of the skelter, his father's death could not possibly be deemed as being caused by anything else other than him having accidentally fallen from the top. What an old man like him had been doing at the top of the helter-skelter late at night in the first place was anyone's guess. Once Sonny had done that, all that was left for him to do in case the police did come calling, was to make sure that there was nothing to show that his father had been in his van.

But just as he was feeling pleased with himself for his clever plan to distance himself from his father's death, a glaring problem struck. The police or attending doctor would question why there was no blood on the ground. He looked over at his father's body and his eyes settled themselves on the pool of blood surrounding his head that had started to congeal around the edges, the rest in the middle of the puddle still liquid. The solution was simple. If he scooped up as much as he could, he could pour it on the ground before he positioned his father's head face down on top of it.

Sonny could find no further flaws in his plan, so as far as he was concerned it was perfect. All that remained for him to do once he had executed it was act as shocked and upset when his father's body was discovered as everyone else.

Chapter Twenty

It was a young lad that was to find Sam's lifeless body at just after seven the next morning when taking the family dog out to do its business. The family were distraught when informed of Sam's death. Then, once word travelled, the whole Grundy community sank into a state of mourning. Sam had been a much-beloved ringmaster and his loss would be deeply felt.

The fact that he'd appeared not to have arrived home last night hadn't unduly concerned Solly or Gem, as they'd assumed he'd decided to stay up in Sunderland and have a few drinks with some old friends of his. That he had returned and not informed them, had come to be at the top of the skelter then lost his balance and fallen off it to his death, was a complete and utter mystery that no one in the community could fathom. No one had seen Sam arrive back last night, so could offer no information to aid the police with their investigation. No sign of any foul play was found when an inspection of the top of the skelter was made, and the crush to the front of his skull was confirmed to them by the doctor as consistent with him having fallen such a long way. After questioning, the family told the police that Sam had no reason whatsoever to end his own life. In fact, he had been excited at the prospect of expanding his business with the purchase of the new ride he had gone to see in Sunderland that day. After only being on the scene for less than two hours, the police informed the family they were satisfied that, for reasons only known to Sam himself, he had decided to go to the top of the Skelter and whilst there had lost his balance and fallen over the side. His death was accidental and the post mortem carried out later confirmed this.

Sonny was not now going to die from hanging through being blamed for a murder he didn't commit but he still could by other methods and far more painful ones if he didn't find that package, and quick. The return of Bossman to collect the package could be imminent.

The first opportunity he had to revisit the hiding place was later that afternoon, which he managed to engineer. Despite the family's grief, the business needed to be kept running as well as a funeral arranged. Seeing a way to get his brother and his wife away from the van for a couple of hours, Sonny suggested that Gem and Solly would be the best ones to arrange the funeral as they had been on better terms with their father than he had and would know more about how he would have wanted his funeral. They agreed. They decided that they would also arrange for an announcement of Sam's death to be put in the *World's Fair* births, deaths and marriages section, so that everyone in the fairground community who had known him could attend the funeral if they so wished.

Sonny assured his brother that while they were away dealing with these matters, himself, Jimmy and Robbie would take care of everything else. Regardless of his own grief at the unexpected and sudden death of his beloved father, Solly could not fail to notice that Sonny seemed to have had a change of personality all of a sudden, appearing to be as grief-struck at his father's death as he himself was. Still, if it had taken his father's death to make him realise just what he had been missing out on for all these years family-wise, then one good thing would have come out of it as far as Solly was concerned. He warmed to the thought that, finally, it looked like he was getting his brother back and they could become as close as they had been before Sonny had changed.

Sonny let half an hour go by to be sure that Gem and Solly would by then be safely engaged making the arrangements with the undertaker for his father's funeral, and his nephews working, before going back inside his brother's van to find the package. He wasn't concerned now about any of the other members of the community seeing him go into the van as they would have known he had been in there all morning closeted with his family, grieving together. They would think he was still dealing with matters pertaining to that. Besides, they would all be more concerned that once Sonny took over the reins of the business, as fairground tradition dictated, nothing would change for them and Sonny would continue on in the same way as his father had. Little did they know that there would be no fair for them to be worried about.

Inside the bedroom, he had just grabbed hold of the bedcovers, preparing to pull them off, when he heard someone come in the van. It must be Robbie or Jimmy come back to fetch something. They would have no need to come into their parents' bedroom. If he remained quiet, they wouldn't know he was here. But then a horrifying thought struck. Both room-sectioning curtains weren't shut and whoever was in the van would only have to look in this direction and they would see him. Praying that they hadn't and that he could slip inside one of the wardrobes to hide himself, he slowly turned around to check and, to his horror, saw Solly looking quizzically at him from over in the living room. Acting as though he hadn't at all been caught red-handed doing something he shouldn't be, he casually let go of the covers and made his way back into the living room area to stand before Solly and casually ask, 'What are you doing back so soon?'

'When we got to the undertaker's he was busy with other people and had another appointment straight after to go out to visit another client, so we're going back later. More to the point, what are you doing in my bedroom? You were about to search for something inside our hiding place, that is very obvious to me, Sonny. Just what are you after?' Then he thought he knew just what. 'Dad's will. Oh, God, now I know why you've been so helpful. You wanted us out of the way so you could get your hands on it. And here was me thinking you'd realised that you'd missed your family for all these years and wanted to be part of us again.' He disgustedly shook his head. 'Couldn't you wait until after the funeral, at the official will reading, to claim your inheritance? Already made an appointment with a solicitor, have you?'

Sonny would rather he did think that was why he was in his bedroom and not for the reason he really was. 'That's about the size of it.'

Solly glared darkly at him. 'Well, you've wasted your time because the will's not here. I suspect Dad would have kept a copy of it and put it with his other papers in his van somewhere.'

Sonny smirked. 'I've waited a long time to claim my inheritance and, as soon as I do, the business is all mine to do what the hell I like with. Well, except for a ride as that is traditionally what the second son gets. If Dad hasn't stated exactly the ride he'd left you, I will be generous and let you have your pick.'

Solly was frowning, bemused. 'What do you mean by that? That once the business is yours, you can do what you like with it?'

Sonny looked at his brother for a moment before he responded, 'Well, you're going to find out sooner or later so you might as well know now. I'm selling up and using the money to build my own business. It will be far more successful than this poxy fair is.'

Solly gawped at him. 'But you can't, Sonny. What about me and Gem and our children, what will we do if you sell the fair? And not just us, but all the people that work for us? Dad worked all hours to build the business to what it is today. For his children he did that, Sonny, so he'd leave us with something worth having to make sure we were well provided for. How could you do this to him?'

Sonny snorted in derision. 'The fair means nothing to me nor do any of the people that work for it. I couldn't give a damn what happens to you all. I've been biding my time for years for Dad to die so I can get away from you all and now my patience has paid off.'

'What have we ever done to make you despise us like this?' Solly bewilderedly demanded of him.

The chance to offload feelings he'd kept to himself for so many years was too great for Sonny to resist. He blared, 'You know that outsiders see us as scum, are only ever willing to mix with us when they're at the fair, using us to have their fun. Yet you all still pander to them, doff your cap at them when they pass you by, turn the other cheek when any of them spit at us in the streets. Mam lied to me. She told me that outsiders treated us like that because they were jealous of us, of the way we lived, but that's not true. I was nineteen when I fell in love with an outsider. She was stunning to look at, fun to be with, everything about her was all I wanted in a woman. I adored her, would have died for her to save her. It took me all my courage to ask her to marry me. She laughed in my face, told me that apart from the fact that her parents would disown her and none of her friends would talk to her again, that she would never lower herself to marry a thieving gypsy. She said she wouldn't be seen dead in the street with me, the only thing she saw me good enough for was a bit of fun, but it had to be somewhere private where no one could see her with me for fear of the shame and embarrassment of any of her lot finding out she'd letting a traveller have sex with her. Oh, she was nice enough to say I was the best she'd had in that way, I'll give her that.

'But the joke of all that was that it was her that was beneath me, that it was me that would be lowering myself marrying her. She lived in a pokey two-up, two-down terrace with her parents in a slum. Her father was a drunken wastrel and they all survived on what her mother earned as a cleaner and the board money her kids who were at work gave her. She had a dead-end job herself as a machinist for a factory. Yet I was the son of a man who owned his own business. I hated you then, Solly, because I don't know how you managed it, but you married an outsider. She'd defied her parents to be with you, didn't care what all the other outsiders would think of her. Yes, I admit it, I was jealous of you because you obviously had something special about you that I didn't have, something that made Gem turn her back on her family and the life she had to be with you.'

He started pacing up and down, arms flaying about in an angry manner. 'If I hadn't been anything to do with the fair, Belinda would have married me and we'd have been happy together. I wanted to run away from the fair and everything associated with it, to make a fresh start where no one knew me, invent a new background for myself so no one would ever look at me like scum any more as they did once they knew I was a fair-ground worker. But I had no money and the only work I was skilled to do was all to do with the fair. So I was stuck with it. How I managed to be civil to outsiders who came to the fair from then on, I'll never know. But after what Belinda did what she did to me, I promised myself I'd never let any woman treat me like that again and I never have. I also vowed I was going to pay back as many outsiders as I could for the way they treated me.

'It took me a while to come up with my idea. It wasn't perfect as I really wanted them all to know what I'd done to them but that wasn't possible without me giving myself away and them getting the police on me, so my revenge on them would be my secret. That's why I distanced myself from you all, because I didn't want anyone, especially my family, finding out what I was doing and reporting me to the police. I bought myself some good clothes, changed my appearance so even you wouldn't have recognised me if you passed me in the street. I was Raymond Goodman, luxury car dealer in the area looking for premises to expand my business. I got myself invited into wealthy people's homes, those idiots believing they were making a new business contact who they'd be making money out of, when really it was me that was fleecing them and making fools of them too.

'I drank their fine wines, ate their rich food, had my way with their woman and stole anything I could from them I felt worth selling on for decent money. The night before last I was relieving the wife of a local councillor of any jewellery that I felt was worth a bob or two at a pawn shop and of any cash she had lying about, as she was sleeping in her marital bed after we'd had rampant sex. What I would have given to have seen her face, her husband's face, everyone's face who I've taken for a ride in the past, when they eventually find out that the suave, wealthy businessman they invited into their homes and lavishly entertained believing that I was going to be useful to them in helping them line their own pocket, when they find out that I was in fact nothing more than a fairground worker.' He stopped his pacing to grin triumphantly at his brother. 'You see, Solly, very soon your brother won't be a filthy fairground worker any longer but rich and famous. King of the Nightclubs, that's what I'll be known as. A while ago I came up with a better way to get my revenge on outsiders.

'I was in a club, a high-class joint; a couple of drinks and a plate of food in that place cost more than some men earned in a week. I found out that there was a waiting list of wealthy people desperate to become a member of it so they could be seen there by all the rest of the rich and famous in their town. They'd do anything it took to get their hands on that membership. The barman who was telling me all of this said that they would try and bribe the owner with weekends at their place in the country, a private box at the races. It was rumoured that women would even sleep with him, they were that desperate. And do you know who the owner was? A little fat Greek or Turkish immigrant. The sort of man that normally those wealthy people wouldn't dream of mixing in the same circle with. If he lay dying in the street, they'd step over him with their noses stuck in the air pretending they hadn't seen him. But those same people were treating that little ugly gnome of a man, who could speak only broken English, like he was a God to them, hanging on his every word. I could tell that they all detested that they were having to pretend to like that man, but they had no choice to though, had they, or else they risked him taking their membership of his club off them. How humiliating would that have been for them when their other rich friends and wealthy neighbours found out they weren't seen as being good enough to be members of his club.

'That got me to thinking that if I was the owner of that club, then it would be me they were all kowtowing down to, treating *me* like I was royalty, pandering to all my whims, just so they could keep socialising with the other rich and famous cronies inside my club. So that's what I'm going to do with the money I make from the fair when I sell it. I'm going to open an exclusive night club, eventually a string of them in fact, that the cream of society will flock to because they will be the only place anyone of any worth is wanting to be seen socialising in.

'My clubs, though, are going to be a lot more classy that that foreign immigrant's. I'm going to have it designed to feel like you are entering a palace. It will be plush and luxurious, the best of everything. The bar will be stocked with every drink available to be served in sparkling cut-glass glasses. Only the very best entertainers will be dancing and singing for my guests; a handpicked top-class chef cooking the food; properly trained waiters and waitresses pandering to the punters' every whim. Apart from the floor shows, there will be a gambling room, another for a classy type of strip show, and other rooms for people who want privacy to entertain their guests in. The profits from that club will finance the start of the rest of them.

'To everyone, though, I will just be known as Mr Smith. Where I've come from, how I got my money to start my business off with, will remain my secret. Then, once my clubs are the talk of every town I have one in, people from other areas willing to travel miles to have a night out in, newspaper photographers waiting outside all night for a chance to catch the rich and famous coming and going, a waiting list for membership for each of the clubs as long as my arm, *then* and only *then* will it be the time for everyone to know that the person they have been sucking up to, begging to be allowed membership to my clubs, is just a dirty, thieving traveller. Now isn't that just the perfect revenge for all those snobs who think they're better than me; me knowing that they all secretly despise me yet having to treat me with the utmost courtesy and respect or else they won't be allowed inside my clubs.'

His face turned ugly then as he darkly hissed, 'But there's one person above all else whose face I'm determined to see with my own eyes when she finds out just what she gave up when she turned down my proposal. I will hire a private detective to find out where Belinda lives now and then, dressed in my Savile Row suit, handmade leather shoes, a wad of cash bulging in the pocket of my cashmere coat, I will visit her in my chauffeur-driven Rolls-Royce, so I can tell her in person, let her see for herself, just what kind of life she gave up the chance of having. And just because she saw me as being beneath her. But the best part is that, before I leave, I'm going to hand her a ten-shilling note and tell her it's payment for the sex she let me have with her all those years ago.

'So now you know just why I turned against you all, all those years ago, and my plans for the fair. If I was you, I'd start looking for another fair to work for because, very shortly, this one won't belong to Grundy's any more. Oh, and as I'm the owner now, find someone else to cover my work because my days of working for this fair are over.'

With that he spun on his heels and strode out of the van, leaving an utterly speechless Solly staring blankly after him.

Several moments later, Gem arrived. As she began taking off her jacket she was saying, 'Velda is very upset over Sam's death. She was very fond of him. It's good she's got a queue of people at her tent to keep her mind off it. I told her I'd go and have a cup of tea with her when she finishes work tonight as we couldn't really talk that much, knowing the punters were waiting outside for their readings. Anyway, we've time for a cuppa ourselves before we have to go back for our appointment with...' Her voice trailed off as she then noticed the look on her husband's face. She demanded of him, 'Solly, what on earth has happened while I've been to see Velda? Something has, I can tell by your face.' When he didn't respond she went over and shook his arm. 'Solly, Solly, what is it?'

He finally uttered, 'Sonny has just told me he's selling the fair as soon as it's in his name.'

It was her turn to look shocked. 'What! Oh please tell me that this is some kind of bad joke Sonny is playing on us, Solly. Haven't we got enough on our plates with your father's death without his idea of having himself some fun. It *is* a joke, isn't it?'

He shook his head. 'He was perfectly serious when he told me.'

'No, surely you misunderstood him.' She went over to the kitchen table and sank down in a chair, then looked up at her husband in utter befuddlement. 'Why would he sell the fair? This is all our livelihoods, not just Sonny's and ours but all of the people who work for us. What does he think is going to happen to us if he sells the business? Your father built it up to what it is now so he could leave his sons with a good business to provide a living for them, not for Sonny to sell it.'

Solly pulled a chair out at the table and sat down too. 'That's what I told him too, Gem. But Sonny doesn't care about that. He doesn't care about any of us. He wants the money from the sale of the fair to open a nightclub with. Not just any old nightclub, but one wealthy people will pay a fortune just to have membership of and treat him like he's God for fear he'll take their membership off them. He intends to eventually own a string of them.' He then proceeded to relate to Gem all that Sonny had told him of his reasons behind his scheme.

When he had finished she blew out her cheeks and heavily sighed as she ran a hand through her hair. 'Let me get this straight... Sonny fell in love when he was nineteen with an outsider who turned him down, nastily I admit. And he's let what she did fester inside him for all these years to the extent that he believes all outsiders feel like she did about us fairground people and so has made it his mission to make as many of them as he can pay. This defies belief, it really does. I wish that Sonny would have come and talked to me when that ... Belinda ... did you say her name was ... turned him down. I could have made him realise that the reason she turned him down wasn't because of what her family and the rest of them would say about her, it was because she didn't love him enough to marry him and live the life he was offering her.' She let out a long exhale of breath before she went on. 'I can understand why Sonny didn't want any of us to know what the woman did to him at the time. He'd have been so hurt and humiliated, embarrassed, especially with you, Solly, and very jealous of the fact that I was an outsider who had turned my back on my family to marry you but the woman he wanted to marry wasn't prepared to.' She shook her head, sadly. 'I can't say I agree with what he's been doing to make himself feel better but I can understand the satisfaction of getting his own back on them. There's been so many times I've wanted to feel the pleasure of slapping the face of someone who's been nasty to me when they've found out I belong to the fairground; spat in the street at me; been told by people they don't want dirty lowlifes like us in their community. I wanted the satisfaction too of seeing their faces when I told them that I was in fact from a decent family, that my father was a businessman who could afford to send me and my sister to private school, but I never did anything because I would be lowering myself to their level then, wouldn't I?

'His idea for these clubs, though. I can't deny that it all sounds a great idea. If Sonny did get them off the ground, get the sort of people he wants as members into them, then he could end up being fabulously rich, far better off than what he would be as a ringmaster. I've read about clubs in London where some people pay extortionate sums to become members because they're seen as *the* places to be seen in. But, Solly, I don't believe though that this is all about Sonny just wanting to become rich and revered so no one ever dare look at him like he was something they'd scrape off their shoes.'

'What is it really in aid of, then?'

'It's all about his need to get his revenge on Belinda for what she did to him all those years ago. That's what it is.'

Solly was looking at her, stunned. 'But I can't believe that my brother is prepared to put his family and all the rest of the fairfolk on the streets just to get his own back on that one woman?'

'Well, it's festered away inside him for so long that it's consumed him, stopped him thinking straight. We need to get through to him, Solly, that he doesn't need to go to the lengths he's prepared to to make Belinda sorry for what she did to him. Just for her to see that he's done well for himself and that she could have had a better life with him than the one she's got would be enough to have her regretting that she turned him down for the rest of her life. Sonny is the owner of a successful business now and could still go and see her looking the part in a smart suit, driving a Rolls-Royce, his wallet bulging with a wad of money. She doesn't need to know that the suit is hired and the car too, or the money in his wallet is actually for bills we need to pay, does she? We just need to make him see that the satisfaction he'll get from that will be just as great as it would be if he really was the owner of a string of nightclubs, but he wouldn't then have to live with the guilt of ruining all the lives he has to to achieve that. Deep down, the old Sonny that cares about his family and the rest of the Grundy community must still be there, somewhere. We just have to try and reach it.'

Solly gnawed on his lips. 'I hope we can.'

Gem was afraid it might be too late. Sonny had been planning how he would get his revenge on Belinda for years, so he might not be at all receptive to what they had to say. He might be hell-bent on doing it his way, no matter what the cost. Regardless, she said, 'I hope so too, for all our sakes. We'll go together to see him as soon as we get back from our meeting with the undertaker.'

Chapter Twenty-One

Lurking out of sight behind a living van, Sonny had a good view of his brother's as he bided his time waiting for the occupants to once again leave for their appointment with the undertaker. Again checking that both his nephews were otherwise occupied, he let himself into Solly and Gem's van. He had no real care any longer whether anyone came back and found him now that everything was out in the open; he wasn't leaving this van until he had that package in his hand.

Yanking the bedclothes off the bed, he began his meticulous search. A half an hour later, he fell to his knees in despair and cradled his head in his hands. The package was nowhere to be found. The only thing he could think of was that the package must have fallen out somehow during one of their moves and been left on a road somewhere for someone else to find, or in a ditch.

The fear of God came over him then. What on earth was he going to do? Even if Bossman's henchman believed his story over how the package came to be lost, what the contents had been worth in monetary terms, they would look to him to recompense them with. He had no doubt that would be a considerable amount. Even if he could persuade them to accept payment from him in replacement of the lost goods, where on earth was he going to get that kind of money from? His plans for his future shattered into pieces as the money he had meant to use to fund that would now have to be spent saving his life. The fair had to be worth thirty or forty thousand at least, considering his father owned all the large rides and including the value of the age-old charter for the fair to play in numerous towns and cities around the Midlands and North of England. Not to mention the long-standing agreements with landowners and farmers to hold the fair on their land. A larger concern would seize the chance to take a fair like Grundy's off his hands to expand their own. Surely the contents of the package couldn't be worth more than the fair was? All he had to do was persuade Bossman to give him the time to sell the fair before he got his money. He prayed he would. But then a thought struck him. Bossman wouldn't just take his word for it that he was now owner of the fair and it was his right to sell it if he wanted. He would know that his father was dead; the thug that had been responsible would have passed that news on to him when he had reported back to him after his visit last night, but he would demand proof that he was his father's actual heir before he would agree to give him the time Sonny needed to raise the money he was owed. He would need to find his father's will. Solly had said a copy of it would be in his father's van amongst his papers. With no thought to the mess he was leaving behind, he jumped up to go and find it.

Sonny hadn't been inside this van for years and, as he stepped inside, it was like the years melted away. It was as if nothing had changed; it was just how he remembered it. Any minute, he expected his mother to come bustling through to offer him tea and something to eat. The smell was just as he remembered it too. Of his father's favourite type of pipe tobacco. Shoving these memories aside, he began his search for his father's papers. He finally found what he was looking for in an old wooden box on a shelf in his curtained wardrobe. Under various other documents and old letters Sonny found a long white envelope. Without further ado, he tore it open, pulled out the sheaf of typewritten paper inside, and unfolded them. Sonny's ability to read mirrored that of Solly's but he didn't need to read all the document, just the part of most interest to him. His own name as his father's heir. The shock he got to see that it wasn't his name but Solly's – that his father had stated his brother as main beneficiary – had him howl out in fury. He then noticed a letter with his name on it that had been underneath the one containing his father's will. Snatching it up he ripped it open, pulled out the letter inside and tried to read what it said. Most of it he couldn't, but enough of the words to get the gist. His father believed that Solly would make a better ringmaster than he would. His rage then mounted to fever pitch as he furiously screwed the letter up and threw it across the room and, whilst still clutching the copy of the will, he stomped angrily around the small space at the bottom of the bed. 'How could you do this to me, you bastard. How could you? I'm your eldest son, it's me you should have left the fair to. You think Solly's a better man than me, that's the truth of it. That's what you were telling me in that letter you left me. Thought I would understand and forgive you for choosing him over me? Well, I fucking don't. A ride. Oh, you left me a ride. How good of you. What the fucking hell am I supposed to raise the money I need with just that. I hope you rot in hell–'

He was cut short by an old lady, her aged face wreathed in worry. 'What's the matter, Sonny? I heard the shouting and thought someone was being murdered in here.'

He spun to face the old crone and screamed at her, 'If he was still alive I would be committing murder for what he's done to me.' He then pushed her out of the way as he stormed out, leaving her staring agog after him.

With nothing to bargain for his life with now, he had to be away from here, as far away as he could be. He had to find somewhere to hide where he would never be found. Bossman had made it clear that he wasn't the kind of man to be made a fool of and then turn a blind eye. He would make it his mission to hunt him down and make an example of him, he had no doubt about that.

As he returned to his own van to pack up his belongings and make his hurried getaway in one of the fair's lorries, he rued the day he had got himself an invite to that game of cards that had resulted in him getting involved with the types of people he was now fleeing for his life from. From now on he would have to live the rest of his life constantly looking over his shoulder; the future he had planned for himself now unachievable and just a fanciful dream. That one stupid mistake had cost him everything, but it was his chance to finally get his revenge on Belinda that he regretted the most.

The visit to the undertaker's was a harrowing experience for Gem and Solly. They hadn't been expecting to be arranging a funeral for Sam for many years yet. In respect of Sam's status it would be a grand traditional showman's affair. A black carriage with two black horses, black plumes on their heads, to ferry Sam's mahogany brass-handled coffin from the entrance of the fair to the local church.

Until then he would be lying-in-state in his living van for those of the community who wished to to pay their respects to him. On the day of the funeral there would be six fairground pall-bearers: Solly, Sonny, Jimmy and Robbie and the other two yet to be decided. The pall-bearers would carry Sam's coffin from the living van via a route through all the stalls and rides in the main fair area to the waiting carriage and then again from the church down the aisle. Hymns and order of service were decided upon and Solly told the undertaker that he would talk to his older brother over which one of them would be giving the eulogy. The main details dealt with, the undertaker then suggested several halls big enough to hold the amount of mourners that they would be expecting at the wake afterwards and caterers for the food.

At the back of both their minds was their desire to persuade Sonny to put a stop to his plan of selling the fair and leaving them all in a very precarious situation and instead seeing the wisdom of the one that Gem was going to put to him.

As soon as they arrived back, they wasted no time in going to see Sonny. It was the old lady that had gone into Sam's van to enquire what all the noise was about who told them that Sonny wasn't home when they went to knock on his van door. She told them what had happened earlier, of going into Sam's van to find out what all the angry shouting was about and finding it was Sonny and then after as she had been sitting outside her van peeling potatoes for chips for her family's supper when she had seen him, looking like he had the weight of the world on his shoulders, piling luggage into one of the lorries, then driving off in it like a maniac. She hadn't seen him since.

They thanked her for the information, then let themselves inside his van, both of them deeply bemused as to why Sonny had departed in such a hurry when surely it would have been better for him to stick around until at least the solicitor had dealt with the paperwork of getting the business transferred to him. As Solly went into Sonny's bedroom, Gem curiously looked around the living area. It looked like a bull had charged through it. Her eyes then fell on a crumpled sheaf of papers lying at her feet. Picking them up, she smoothed them out and started to read the words written on it.

As she was trying to digest just what she was reading, Solly then arrived in the living area. 'He's took all his stuff. Doesn't look like he's coming back.'

She prised her eyes off the document and lifted her head to look at him, her eyes shining in relief. 'I have your father's will. It was on the floor. The fair isn't Sonny's to sell. Your father left it to you.'

Solly stared back at her. 'What! Dad made me his heir? But tradition…'

She interjected, 'Obviously your father decided not to observe the rules of fairground tradition when it came to deciding which son he thought would make the best ringmaster to replace him when he died. He might have loved Sonny, but Sam was far from daft or blind. We all knew that Sonny only did what he had to and if anyone had any problems that only the family could deal with, Sonny was the last one they'd turn to as they all knew he'd only pass them back to one of us. Maybe he did suspect that Sonny might decide that he didn't want to be ringmaster anyway and sell it. Whatever, thank God, he decided to make you his heir and not Sonny as this means he can't sell the fair and we have no need to worry any more about what's going to happen to us all.'

His shoulders then sagged in relief. 'Yes, yes it does, doesn't it?' He then sank down on the arm of Sonny's armchair and said, 'I can't imagine how Sonny must be feeling.'

'Oh, to hell with that, Solly. He doesn't deserve your sympathy considering what his plans were.'

He nodded. 'Yes, you're right. But he's still my brother and I love him. When he does come back, I will make sure he's well looked after.'

She smiled adoringly at him. 'He doesn't deserve a brother like you. You're far too kind for your own good sometimes. But that's just one of the things I love about you.' She folded up the will and pushed it into her skirt pocket. They could read the rest of it later. She took his arm. 'Come on, I'm parched and you must be too. I need a cuppa. With something in it a bit stronger after the day we've had. I think you should arrange for others to cover for both of us tonight, the boys too if they'd like, as I'd doubt anyone would expect us to work tonight.'

As if they hadn't had enough shocks that day, yet another awaited them when they got back to their van. It was Gem that was to go into the bedroom to change out of her good clothes she had dressed in for her visit to the undertaker's for more casual ones, and discover the mess Sonny had left behind after his fruitless search for the elusive package he had been desperate to find.

'Solly, we've had burglars!'

He immediately shot through to join her, both staring in dismay at the piled-up bedding and mattress blocking access to Solly's wardrobe and at the strewn-about items that had been stored neatly in the storage space.

'What do you think has been stolen?'

She shrugged. 'I have no idea if anything has. I can't remember half the stuff that was in here as it's been there that long. There was nothing of any real value, that I do know.'

Then a thought struck Solly. 'Oh, I think I know who's done this. It was Sonny. I told you this morning that I caught him about to clear the bed so he could look in the hidey-hole; I assumed for Dad's will. I told him we hadn't got it. If it was anywhere, it was more than likely amongst Dad's papers, but he couldn't have believed me and while we've been out looked anyway.'

She heaved a sigh and snapped, 'Well, the least he could have done was put everything back as he'd found it. Give me a hand straightening it up, love, then I'll mash us both a cuppa.'

Both Jimmy and Robbie turned down the offer of a night off. They would sooner work to keep their minds busy. The news that their grandfather had made their father his heir and he was now the new ringmaster they were to keep to themselves, out of respect, until after their grandfather's funeral.

When she knew Velda would be in her van preparing her evening meal before she went back to work for the night, Gem paid her a visit.

She sat Gem down in the one and only comfortable chair she had, pulling out a kitchen chair to settle her large body on before enquiring of the younger woman, 'How are you bearing up, love?'

She gave a wan smile. 'Solly's beside himself. It's breaking my heart watching him breaking his heart, but all I can do is be there for him and support him the best I can. The boys have taken it hard. Fran, Nita and Rosa too. My relationship with Sam wasn't what you could call a close father- and daughter-in-law relationship. He never forgave me for being an outsider, never missed a chance to remind me of that with his barbed comments which used to irritate me to hell, so I shan't miss those. I do know though that, deep down, he was fond of me. I will miss him. It surprises me to realise how much I will.'

She then looked at Velda. 'But it's you I should be asking that, Velda. How are you bearing up? Sam was the love of your life. I can't imagine how hard it is for you not to show how much you're grieving for him, only being able to properly when you're on your own.'

She leaned over and affectionately patted her hand. 'Well, that's how it is and I have to get on with it. I remember saying to you once that life can be very cruel sometimes and this is one of those times.' Then her face screwed up. 'Try as I might, I just can't understand what he was doing on top of the skelter in the first place.'

'No one can, Velda, including the police. It's something only Sam knows himself. Anyway, I didn't want to disturb you having your meal but just came to tell you that Solly and I have a lot to talk about so I won't be along later after the fair closes to have a cuppa with you after all.'

'Don't worry. Ren, I have no doubt, will be over as soon as I get back from finishing work tonight, like she does every night. I expect she'll be itching to see to anything I need her to do for me then get off to be with Donny. It's such a joy seeing her so happy, not before time either. She never believed this state of affairs would ever happen and she doesn't want to miss a moment longer than she has to without Donny by her side. Anyway, I totally understand you and Solly will have such a lot to discuss. It must have come as some shock to Solly to learn that Sam had made him his heir instead of his brother.' She then knew by Gem's face that this was news to her and blurted, 'Oh, I'm sorry you didn't know ... haven't you read

Sam's will yet?'

'Er ... yes, yes we did, this afternoon.' Although she was close friends with Velda she didn't think Solly would appreciate it becoming common knowledge what Sonny had planned for them all once he'd got his hands on the business. Not that Velda would have told anyone should Gem have taken her into her confidence anyway. 'I'm shocked that you knew though. We haven't told anyone yet, except for the boys of course. Felt it's not right to until after Sam is buried.' Then a thought struck. 'Yes, but of course, you two had become very close and he talked to you, didn't he, about which son would make the better one to leave in charge of the fair?'

She nodded. 'It was something that bothered him very much. He loved Sonny but felt that Solly would make a far better ringmaster than Sonny would. He struggled with his conscience and you know what a stickler he was for abiding by showmen's traditions. I did suggest he left it to them in equal shares so they ran it between them but, in the end, he felt he had no choice but to make Solly his sole heir. To Sam's mind he was the one that had all the qualities to keep the business prospering and the community happy, whereas Sonny didn't. Solly shared the same vision for the fair's future, whereas he had no idea what Sonny's was as he never talked to his father, except in passing. Sam had worked for the type of bosses he worried Sonny would turn out to be and it was not a pleasant experience. And he knows Solly will look after his brother. He did write a letter explaining to Sonny why he had done what he had. Has he read it yet? Hopefully it will make him understand what difficulties his father had in making his decision and why he finally decided what to do. I hope he can forgive him for it.'

'Sonny's left, Velda. We've no idea where he's gone or when he's coming back. We think it's because he's so angry over what his father did and also it will be humiliating for him when it finally comes out who the new ringmaster is. The community will know then that he was pushed aside in his younger brother's favour. Since Joshua died he's always believed that, one day, it will be him that is the new owner.'

'Mmm. Well, maybe it's best for Solly that he has gone off. Solly can get on with running the fair as he wishes without his brother's shadow hanging over him.'

Gem frowned, bothered. 'It's a huge responsibility that Solly wasn't prepared to have.'

'Oh, Gem, dear, Solly was virtually running the fair alongside his father anyway. Sam started taking more of a back seat a couple of years ago when his arthritis really started slowing him down. And it wasn't Sonny that worked alongside your father, them two sitting together, discussing matters and making decisions that would affect us all; it was Solly. Sonny was only doing as little as he felt he could get away with. I always got the feeling from Sonny that he didn't really care about the fair, only worked here because that was the only life he knew and could earn his living from. I wouldn't have put it past him to be making plans to sell the fair as soon as he got it and to live on the proceeds, not a thought to any of the rest of us.'

Gem thought, *Velda has no idea how accurate she is.*

Velda then went on to ask Gem if she had had any contact from Jenny, which she knew Gem was so very desperate for. She knew she wanted to start getting to know the daughter she had had no idea she had. She was desperate for her to take her rightful place amongst her real family. Velda knew Sam had been very much looking forward to meeting and getting to know her, and she felt it was just so very sad and such a shame that Jenny would never now have the privilege of discovering just what a character and wonderful human being her grandfather had been.

Gem got up. 'I'll come and see you tomorrow and tell you about the funeral arrangements. You'll be with us, Velda. Sitting up front. I told Solly I thought you should be with us as you and Sam were such close friends, but me and you know the real reason I feel you should be. It's only because of your situation you weren't able to be together as a proper couple.'

There were tears of deep gratitude in her eyes when she uttered, 'Thank you, Gem.'

Solly and Gem were to learn the real reason behind Sonny's hurried getaway later that evening. Gem had returned from her visit to Velda to find Solly quietly crying to himself in the armchair. Without a word she went over to him, put her arm around him and pulled him close by way of showing him her love and support for his loss.

After making him eat some food and pouring

them both a medicinal whiskey each, at just after nine o'clock they were sitting together, side by side on the sofa, holding hands as they finished reading Sam's will. Apart from small bequests to long-standing, loyal Grundy fairworkers and a memento each for a couple of cronies Sam had known since a young man, Sonny was to pick a ride of his choice. Sam had also left him his old watch and chain his own father had bought him on his twenty-first birthday and half of any cash he had at the time of his death. Gem was very touched that Sam had bequeathed her Nell's old jewellery box which, amongst many pieces of costume jewellery, included her wedding and engagement rings. Knowing how precious these things had been to him, that told her that her father-in-law had been far more fond of her than he had ever let on to her he was. Fran, the widow of his eldest son Joshua, would receive Nell's precious collection of fairground glass, some pieces dating back to before the turn of the century. His four grandchildren, Jimmy, Robbie, Nita and Rosa, would each receive the sum of twenty pounds. Of course he had left nothing to Jenny as, when he had written his will, he hadn't known of her existence and had not had time to rectify that before he met his untimely death.

The will now properly read, they then went over the funeral arrangements together, mentally noting the things they still had to arrange for it. Flowers still needed to be ordered, hall to book, food decided for the wake. Solly would need to try on his one and only suit to check if it still fitted him as he had filled out a little since the last time he had worn it at his mother's funeral five years ago. They were suddenly interrupted by the van door thrusting open and two strange men walked in like they owned the place.

Whilst Gem sat staring at the two intruders, Solly jumped up to angrily exclaim, 'Who the hell are you two?'

It was the older of the two men that responded, 'I'm looking for your brother. I was informed you'll know where he is.'

Solly didn't like the look of his visitors at all. They looked unsavoury to him and he wondered what sort of business Sonny could possibly have with them? 'Well, I don't. He's gone. Went this afternoon while me and my wife were out. Took all his stuff with him. I've no idea when he'll be back. Why do you want to see him?'

The man did not look pleased by this information and demanded, 'Did he give you a package before he left, telling you to keep it safe until someone collected it?'

Bemused, Solly shook his head. 'No. I told you, he was already gone when we arrived back. Now, if you don't mind, I'd like you to leave.'

He fixed his cold, hard eyes at him. 'I'll be the one who decides when I leave.' To Solly's indignation he walked over to the armchair and sat casually down in it, his brute of a companion standing behind it. Resting his elbows on the arms and tenting his fingers, he then warned them both, 'If you're thinking of trying to attract attention, I'd think twice if I was you as my friend here will shoot. Show them I'm not bluffing, Jonathon?' The big man pulled open the left side of his top coat to afford Gem and Solly a view of the gun sticking out of an inside pocket before he let it drop back in place. 'Now sit down,' he ordered Solly.

Gem urged him, 'Do as he says, Solly.'

Solly had already decided that it was wise he did and dropped back down beside her.

The man then said to his companion, 'Drink, Jonathon. Whatever they're drinking will do me fine.' He then told Solly and Gem, 'I don't talk business without a drink in my hand. Helps keep my brain sharp.'

'Business? We have no business with you!' Solly said.

'Your brother did though.' He took the glass of whiskey from Jonathon and took a sip of it. 'Not bad. Not as good as the stuff your brother had, but it'll do.' He settled himself more comfortably in the chair and crossed his legs before he spoke again. 'Your brother and I had an arrangement. He would keep items safe for me. Things, let's say, I didn't want the police knowing I had. He got paid well for his services. Trouble is, it seems that he didn't want to hand over the last package he was looking after. Tried to fob my associate off that he'd temporarily mislaid it and needed more time to find it. Out of the goodness of his heart, he gave your brother the benefit of the doubt. Me, now well, I'm not so easily took for a fool. It was obvious to me that something wasn't right, so that's why I'm here myself. Seems I was right. Your brother was obviously planning to do a runner with the package after taking it upon himself to open it and see what was inside. More than likely thought all his Christmases and birthdays had arrived at once. Only, before he could disappear off, my associate called to collect it.' He paused to take another sip of his drink before continuing, 'What was in that package is worth a lot of money. Not the sort of money I'm willing to write off.'

Starting to worry where this all was leading, Solly said, 'I don't see what this has got to do with me and my wife?'

'We know nothing about any of this, so why are you bothering us with it? Your arrangement was with my brother-in-law,' Gem spoke up.

He eyed Solly icily. 'Lippy, your wife. I'd warn her to shut her mouth unless she's got something to say worth me listening to.'

Solly shot Gem a warning to do as the man said. Then addressed him himself. 'My wife is right though. Your business was with my brother, not with us.'

'Your brother isn't here, so now my business is with you. I like to keep things in the family.'

Solly gawped incredulously at him. 'You're looking to me to pay you the money the goods inside that package are worth?'

'You're not as daft as you look.'

'But ... but ... what sort of money are we talking about?'

'Fifty grand.'

'HOW MUCH?' he cried, astounded.

Gem felt she did have something worthwhile saying then. 'We can't get our hands on money like that, haven't got a hope in hell of ever doing so.'

'Then I suggest you find your brother and get him to hand me my belongings back.'

'But I told you, we have no idea where he is,' Solly reiterated.

'Well you'd better hope that he realises the error of his ways and comes back with the package with nothing missing out of it. But anyway, wherever he is, I have eyes and ears all over the place and once he starts trying to get rid of what's inside that package then he's on borrowed time. Saturday night. If that package is not back in my hands by then, I'll just have to come up with some other way for you to pay me back.'

'What do you mean by that?' Solly asked, warily.

'I'm a fair man, so as it wasn't you personally that double-crossed me then I won't be making you pay in the same way I normally would to someone who had. You can work off your brother's debt.'

He said, stunned, 'We'd never pay all that off if we worked for you for the rest of our lives! And I suppose you mean in the same way that my brother worked for you? Hiding your stolen goods from the police until you find a buyer.'

'A fair's a good place to hide people in too that ... er ... let's say, need to lie low for a while. And there are times I have a use for someone to do little jobs for me that the police wouldn't suspect. Women have a way of getting things done that men don't seem to have the same charm for.'

'What if we refuse to work for you?' Solly asked.

The man said evenly, 'You've surprised me. I didn't take you for a stupid man. When I want something I make it my business to get it. Now, I can be a very patient man, Mr Grundy, but my patience is wearing very thin. I've a buyer for those goods in that package who's not going to hang around for ever. You've got until Saturday. Expect me sometime during the evening. You'd better be here. And, er ... not that I don't trust you, but don't think of having any company as I will have this place checked out before we talk any business.'

He stood up and, without another word, walked out. As he passed by Solly and Gem, following his boss out, his companion again opened the left side of his coat, flashing them another look at the weapon he had concealed inside by way of reminding them his boss meant business.

As the door shut, Solly exclaimed, 'Oh, hell, Gem, what on earth was Sonny thinking of when he got himself involved with the likes of that man? I can't believe that he's been using the fair to earn money hiding illegal goods. Did he not think of just what trouble we would be in if the police had got wind of what he was up to?' A thought struck him. 'When Sonny found out that he wasn't getting his hands on the fair after all, that's when he must have decided he'd help himself to what was in that package and use that to open the club he told us he was planning to. But did he think that man would just let him off with it and not take it out on the family he'd left behind?' He sighed in despair. 'If Dad had found out what Sonny was doing behind his back, he'd have been that mad he'd have throttled him with his own bare hands. What he's doing isn't petty crime, it's major and could have lost Dad his business. When I see him again, I'll kill Sonny myself for putting us in this position.'

Gem said worriedly, 'Oh, Solly, what if Sonny doesn't come back? That man has given us no choice but to work for him. We'll be living the rest of our lives worrying every second of the day that somehow the police will find out what we're doing and we'll end up in jail. But I've got an awful feeling that even if Sonny did came back with the package unopened, that man will still find a way to make us work for him.' She started to cry and blubbered, 'What are we going to do, Solly?'

He looked helplessly at her.

Chapter Twenty-Two

The day of Sam's funeral was a glorious one. A warm early October sun shone down from a bright blue sky, fluffy cotton-wool-looking clouds slowly drifting across it like little sailing ships on a vast ocean. The small church on the outskirts of Hexham was packed with many more fairfolk than either Solly or Gem had been expecting, nearer three hundred to their two. Many were old friends, some distant relatives Sam himself had believed long-ago dead but just the news hadn't reached him; some were people that felt they owed him a debt of gratitude for a past good deed he had done them and a handful just saw Sam's funeral an excuse for a day out with a decent feed and drink at the end of it. Most turned up in their own living vans, starting to arrive late afternoon the day before. Finding space for them all to park was an absolute nightmare. They ended up packed together like sardines in a tin, the rest having to park on nearby waste ground.

The church service was a very dignified affair, a moving tribute to the well-respected man they had come to bury. Many times the vicar had to raise his voice to be heard over the sobbing women; Sam had been quite the ladies' man before he had settled down with his beloved Nell. Solly's eulogy had taken him, along with help from Gem, many hours to compose in his effort to honour a man he felt so very fortune to have been his father. The wake afterwards, in a large hall not far from the church, although starting off very sombrely, as soon as the drink began to flow turned into a raucous affair. The last of the mourners had to be ordered off the premises after twelve o'clock at night so the staff could lock up and go home. The absence of Sonny was a huge talking point amongst the mourners but most seemed to accept Solly's excuse that Sonny was so grief-struck by his father's unexpected death that he couldn't face the funeral and had gone away for a few days.

Despite coping with their own painful emotions, not for one second of that day was it far from Gem and Solly's mind the dire situation they had found themselves in. Neither had come up with any way of finding a way out for them. As they only had two days left before the man returned, they didn't have much hope left that they would and worried that, for the rest of their lives, they would be blackmailed into carrying out illegal work for him. Keeping themselves acting as they normally would in front of their sons, friends and the rest of the community took them every effort. Neither did they feel it right to take any into their confidence. Not even Velda, who Gem confided all her problems in.

It might have been the consumption of drink she had had at the wake but more than likely it was the great amount of pressure she was under that caused Gem to have very little sleep that night. Although Solly was snoring gently beside her, she knew he'd not had much sleep either for the same reason. He had probably not long finally dropped off, in fact.

It was still dark when she awoke the next morning, too dark for her to see the hands of the bedside clock but she judged it to be about six. Knowing she wouldn't get back to sleep she decided to get up and have a cup of tea. She would shortly have needed to be up and about anyway, as very soon people that had travelled to the wake and stayed overnight would be setting off on their journey back to where they had come from and would be expecting her and Solly to be waving them off.

The bed filled the whole space at the front of the van and to get in and out, both she and Solly had to get on at the bottom of the bed and crawl up to the top. Not wanting to wake Solly, she carefully eased the covers aside then, sitting up and bending her legs, eased herself as gently as she could down to the bottom of the bed. At the bottom of the bed she stood up and began to grope her way to the curtain at the entrance and slip through the into the small corridor, where one side was the boys' shared bedroom, the other their bathroom, when she remembered that, due to the lateness of the hour and the inebriated state they were all in last night when they got home, no late-night chores were attended to so there was no fresh water to make the cup of tea with. She would have to go and fetch a bucket from the water pump the council had temporarily erected for them. Which meant she needed to get dressed.

Turning to her right, she groped her way the few steps to her own wardrobe, pulling aside the protective curtain and then felt about for clothes to wear, letting her fingertips tell her which each hanging garment or folded one on the shelves running down the side was that she was feeling. Having found a pair of slacks and a warm jumper, as the mornings were now decisively chilly, as she turned to move away from the wardrobe back further into the room to put them on, her foot caught the side of one of her wellington boots and it toppled over. She realised something had fallen out by the slight thud she heard it make as whatever it was landed on the wooden floor close by. She wondered what it was? As it was too dark to see, she got down on her knees and felt around. Finally her fingertips touched a small package covered in something waxy. She picked it up. The waxy covering was actually oilskin. She frowned in thought. At times she did use various places to hide presents from her family so they wouldn't find them before she was ready to give it to them but she couldn't remember wrapping anything small up in oilskin and putting it inside one of her wellington boots for safekeeping. So if it wasn't her package, then whose was it? Then just whose it must be made her mouth drop open in shock, eyes bulging wide. This must be the package Sonny had been keeping for that odious man. What else could it be? How had it come to be inside her wellington boot though?

'Solly,' she called out in hushed tones so as not to wake her sons. 'Solly. *Solly!* Wake up. Wake up right now!'

A short while later, both were sitting opposite each other at the kitchen table, their arms resting on top of it. Both were leaning forward, their eyes fixed on the small oilskin-wrapped package that sat in the middle. There was no label on it, nothing whatsoever at all to indicate who it belonged to or of what was inside.

After what seemed an age, Gem finally said, 'Do you think it is the package the man is after, Solly? It doesn't look big enough to hold anything that would be worth fifty thousand pounds in it to me.'

He took a deep breath then slowly exhaled it before he answered her, 'Well, it's not mine and you say it's not yours, and the man did describe a small package and this is a small package, isn't it? It has to be, doesn't it? Don't ask me how it got in your welly boot, because I have...' He stopped short as a realisation then flooded to mind. 'Oh, so that's what he was really looking for under our bed. Not Dad's will, but this package. That's where he's been hiding whatever he has for that man. In our hidey-hole. Perfect place, isn't it? How rare is it that we ever have a need to go in there ourselves. It's you that mainly uses it to store things in there that you don't use any longer but are not willing to part with. Maybe when Sonny collected the package to hand it over to whoever came to collect it, in his haste to get in and out without one of us catching him, he couldn't have put it in his pocket properly and it dropped out into your boot as he was putting everything back in place. When the package wasn't in his pocket when he went back to his van to hand it over to the man, Sonny must have thought that it had fallen back into the hidey-hole as he was tidying up after himself so we wouldn't know someone had been in there. It wasn't that Sonny needed more time to hand over the package because he was planning to steal it himself after finding out how much what was inside was worth, it was because he needed more time to get us out of the way so he could get it back out of the hidey-hole where he thought he had dropped it. That must be it, it's got to be.'

She gawped. 'But what if the police had discovered that Sonny was hiding stuff for that gangster and found whatever it was under our bed? The police would have assumed that we were in on it. How could Sonny do that to us?'

Face grim, Solly shook his head. 'I'm beginning to wonder just what Sonny is capable of.'

'Well at least we can hand it over to the man on Saturday and he'll know that Sonny didn't run off with the package but really did mislay it so he didn't double-cross him after all. And he won't be looking to us to replace what he'd thought

Sonny had stolen off him either.'

'Yes, that's a huge relief, I have to say.' He then heaved a worried sigh. 'But as you said before, it doesn't mean he's not going to find another way to blackmail us into replacing Sonny somehow. A man like him doesn't give up a good thing easily.'

Gem's shoulders sagged in despair. 'No, no, he didn't come across to me like a man that would.'

They both lapsed into silence, each lost in their own troubling thoughts. Then snatching up the package and stuffing it into his pocket, Solly scraped back his chair and jumped up. 'The boys are getting up. I need to go out and I don't know how long I'll be.'

She frowned at him. 'Where are you going at this time in the morning?'

He went to her, leaned over and kissed the top of her head. 'I think I've thought of a way to get us out of this situation. I'll tell you everything when I get back.'

'Solly, don't you dare leave me in suspense. Solly!'

But he was gone.

Chapter Twenty-Three

Saturday evening at just before ten o'clock found a highly charged Solly sitting in his armchair by the log burner, drumming anxious fingers on both arms, whilst constantly uncrossing, then re-crossing his legs. The man had said he would be back Saturday evening and to Solly it was now Saturday night, so where was he? He was desperate to get what he was about to do over and done with so he could put Gem out of her misery. She hadn't been at all happy that he had insisted he face those brutes alone. If this all went wrong and matters turned ugly, as there was a great possibility that it would, he would never forgive himself if she got hurt. Then he finally heard the thud of feet ascending the outside steps and fought to look calm and composed before his visitors arrived.

Then there they were, both walking into his van like they owned the place.

Solly went to speak but was silenced by the smaller of the two holding up his hand in warning as, simultaneously, he indicated by a nod of his head for his companion to have a search around the whole van first to check that Solly was indeed on his own like he had warned him to be.

The man first checked the kitchen, a quick glance telling him that there was nowhere possible for anyone to conceal themselves, didn't bother with the living area as it was apparent that they were the only ones in there, then lifted the side of the curtain splitting the living room from what lay beyond and moved out of view. He returned, minutes later, to inform his boss with just a nod of his head that the three of them were the only ones present in the van.

As the man then sat himself down in Gem's armchair opposite Solly, his companion standing at the back of it, Solly again went to speak but was again silenced by a warning hand. 'Short memory it seems you have, Mr Grundy. I told you I don't talk business without a drink in my hand. How I do hate having to repeat myself because people don't listen. Jonathon, do the honours.'

The man now having a drink in his hand, in his need to get this over with, Solly couldn't hold his tongue any longer and blurted, 'You'll be glad to know I found the package. It was in my brother's van behind the clock on the mantle above his wood stove. I can't believe he forgot where he'd put it when your chap called to collect it, but obviously he did. It's not been opened. Anyway, at least you know he didn't double-cross you so he's in the clear.'

If the man was pleased to hear this, he didn't show it. Stonily he responded, 'I'll believe it when I see it.'

Solly immediately jumped up, saying, 'I'll fetch it. Won't be a moment. It's in my bedroom.'

The man told his companion. 'Go with him.'

'You don't trust me,' Solly said as though he was offended, although he'd been expecting this would happen.

'Only a fool trusts anyone but himself. I would have thought that you would realise by now that I'm not a fool.'

The big man followed closely behind Solly as he slipped under the curtain and made his way into the bedroom. The pair of them together almost filled the small space at the bottom of the bed. Solly said to the man, 'The package is in my wardrobe behind you, so if you don't mind moving aside so I can get it?'

The man moved aside and Solly squeezed past

him to retrieve the package from where he had put it earlier; in the middle of a pile of his jumpers. Having got what they came for, they then both returned to the living area. Solly handed the man the package then, without a word, re-took his seat opposite; the man's companion again resumed his position at the back of his boss's chair.

Without a word, the man took an ornate pearl-handled penknife out of his coat pocket, flicked open the blade and proceeded to slit open the package. Sonny was itching to know what was inside that could be worth so much money, but by the way the man was holding it as he inspected the contents, to his disappointment he couldn't see what it was.

Finally the man seemed satisfied all was present and correct and stuffed the package into his coat pocket. He took a sip of his drink first before he said, 'It seems I was wrong about your brother after all.'

Solly made to rise. 'Good. Well if that's all, I'll see–'

'Sit down,' the man ordered him. 'It's me that tells you when I'm ready to leave.' Solly instantly dropped back down into his seat again. The man again took a sip of his drink before he spoke. 'This arrangement I had with your brother. Just because he's not around any longer, doesn't mean I don't see any reason why you can't take his place. Same terms as I had with him. I think you'll find I'm very generous with my employees. Your brother was more than happy with what I paid him.'

Solly took a deep breath in an effort to calm his

jangling nerves before he responded, 'My brother might have been happy with your arrangement, but I'm not my brother and I'm not interested in working for you.'

The man smiled at him, but it was certainly not a friendly one. 'Not your decision to make. You must have realised by now that I am the sort of man that if he wants something he gets it.' His eyes darkened menacingly then and he leaned forward to fix his cold, hard eyes on Solly's. 'Accidents happen, don't they? Be such a shame if a fire started where all your living vans are when everyone is asleep. Jonathon would take great delight in helping to get it going. He's a fetish for setting fires. In fact he has been in jail several times, for arson. Horrible way to die, I should imagine, being burnt to death. Excruciatingly painful and takes a long time too, I should think. And fire spreads quickly too. Before a fire engine could get here, the whole fair is ablaze. And even if you and your family did manage to survive, how are you going to support them with no fair? And not just you, but all those other people that might survive the fire that work for you?'

Solly held up his hands and urgently blurted, 'Okay. Okay. I get the message. I'll do what you want.'

The man smiled. 'Good. Glad to see you're not stupid after all. Well, I hope this is the last time I need to call on you in person now that we've got things straight between us. It'll be one of my employees that you'll be dealing with from now on. In future you won't know when anyone will call on you, it could be any day, but I can tell you that you can expect someone next Tuesday to drop your first package off.'

'Oh, is that when your next job is planned, Mr Morrison? I would be most interested in hearing the details so I can have a welcoming committee waiting for you.'

At the unexpected sound of a strange voice in the room, the man in the chair jumped up to spin around to face the direction the voice came from. His companion spun around too whilst reaching into his inside pocket in an attempt to pull out the gun he had secreted there. He quickly pulled his hand back out on seeing the barrels from two other guns aimed at him.

'Where the fuck did you two come from? Jonathon scoured the place when we first came in and no one else but us three were in this van.'

'I did, Bossman, honestly. I searched everywhere and there was nowhere anyone could hide themselves, except for inside the two wardrobes in the bedroom at the front and there was no one in there when I looked. I made sure all the windows were locked shut too while I was at it so no one could climb in them while we was in here.'

The shorter and older of the two newcomers chuckled, 'Well, that will certainly give you something to puzzle over while you're serving at least twenty years at Her Majesty's pleasure, won't it, Mr Morrison?' Still aiming his gun at him, he walked over to stand next to him. He put his hand in his coat pocket, pulling it back out along with the package Morrison had not long put in there. Knowing his colleague still had his gun trained on the two thugs, he put his own in his pocket and, using both hands, eased open the slit that Morrison had made in it so he could inspect what was hidden inside. At least a dozen clear stones in varying shapes and sizes glittered back at him. He nodded his head several times in satisfaction before he said, 'We always suspected you were behind the robbery of the courier from Holland who was delivering these stones on behalf of his firm to the buyer in Leeds four weeks ago, but we couldn't get enough evidence to prove it. Now we have and you will finally get what you deserve.' He pushed his face into Morrison's and angrily hissed at him, 'That courier, by the way, is still in hospital recovering from what one of your thugs did to him. And I suspect we'll get more evidence once we get a warrant to search your house and office. I don't think it will take much to get matey here singing to us about what he knows about your set-up, either. A promise of some paper and a box of matches to play with should do the trick from what I overheard.' Two other constables then arrived, having been signalled to by Solly that the coast was clear by him opening the curtains, as had been prearranged for him to do. 'Help Sergeant Jones cuff these bastards and get them out of my sight.'

As soon as the men had been manhandled out of the van into one of the two police cars parked out of sight by the edge of the living van area, now alone with Solly, Detective Inspector Marshall, a tall solid man in his early fifties, said to him, 'I bet you could do with a stiff drink?'

Solly nodded. 'A couple. I was terrified of giving myself away before you got all you needed.'

'Well, thanks to you we did and Morrison and his band of merry men won't be at liberty for many years to rob or hurt anyone else or, in your case, blackmail anyone else into working for him. And, if nothing else, some of what they've stolen over the years will be handed back to their rightful owners. Well, I'm just glad to be out of that coffin under your bed as I was starting to get cramp and Jones doesn't seem to take a bath as often as he should, if you get my drift.' The inspector then looked at Solly. 'Clever man who built this van, to include a hiding place like he did that one. I never would have guessed it was there if you hadn't told me about it. Well, that's another favour you've done the law today, Mr Grundy. Now we're aware that vans like this are not always what they seem.'

Not that it was likely but, in the future, if they did find themselves needing to hide something they didn't want the police to discover, it wouldn't be in the hidden space under the bed as, from now on, hidden hiding places under beds would be the first thing they looked for, Solly thought.

The inspector was musing, more to himself than to Solly, 'I wish I had a place like that at home that the wife had no idea about so I could hide whatever I wanted that I didn't want her to know I had.' He then placed his hand on Solly's shoulders and said, 'I know how guilty you must be feeling having to shop your brother to us. I have two brothers and I can't imagine how it would feel if I had to do what you did to one of them. But you had no choice unless you wanted to be at the mercy of Morrison until he decided he'd no need of your services any longer. And I don't need to tell you that, had the police got wind stolen stuff was being hidden by you here, no matter that you were blackmailed into it you would have been in line for a lengthy stay in jail. Whenever you're feeling bad about it, just remember what position your brother left you in when he decided to scarper. We will be searching for him. He's got charges to answer to. If he makes any contact with you in the meantime, try and persuade him it would be in his best interests to turn himself in. Anyway, we'll need you to come down to the station tomorrow and give a statement. Then just keep us informed of where you are so we can contact you when the case comes to trial. I bet your wife is desperate for you to let her know you're safe and I need to get back to the station. Thanks again, Mr Grundy. It's honest men like you we police have a lot to thank for or there'd be a lot more like Morrison free to blight the lives of innocent people instead of rotting in jail where he belongs.'

Moments after the inspector left, Gem breathlessly charged in and immediately accosted her husband, 'Someone told me they'd seen two men in handcuffs being frogmarched towards two police cars. It is that Bossman and his brute, isn't it? Your plan worked? Please tell me it did?'

He smiled as he put his arms around her and pulled her close. 'Worked a treat, love. Just a treat. It all went just as me and the inspector worked it out. The only worry I had was that Morrison ... that's Bossman's name, by the way, or that bear of a chap who's his minder, would hear the inspector and his sergeant getting out of the hidey-hole after we'd left the bedroom. Thankfully, we haven't got any squeaking floorboards to worry about like houses have.'

Her taut body sagged in mortal relief against him. 'I can't believe this nightmare is over and we can sleep peacefully tonight.'

Just then Jimmy and Robbie dived through the door, one after the other. Jimmy exclaimed, 'Is it true, Dad? You're a hero and helped the police collar a well-known criminal and his sidekick? That's what's going around the fair anyway.'

Solly puffed out his chest and grinned proudly. 'Well, hero might be exaggerating a bit, but yes I did.'

The boys both grabbed an arm, each pulling him away from their mother and over to the kitchen table. They pushed him down on a chair, then each took seats next to him.

'Come on then, Dad. We want every little detail!' Jimmy urged him.

'Yes, come on, Dad, spill the beans. I can't wait to hear it all,' Robbie demanded.

Gem laughed. 'I'll put the kettle on.'

Chapter Twenty-Four

Solly threw himself into the chair at the side of his wife and said breathlessly, 'That's got to be it, surely. There can't be any women left I haven't had a dance with.'

Gem chuckled. 'Every woman wants to brag that they've had a dance with the ringmaster at the end-of-season party, Solly. Especially one as handsome as you,' she teased.

He gazed at his wife for a moment, thinking how pretty she looked tonight in a full-skirted white dress patterned all over with large red roses, broad black belt around her trim waist and a lacy red shawl draped around her bare shoulders. She wore red court shoes on her feet and her hair was piled up in a fashionable French roll. 'You know I'm a sucker for a bit of flattery. What are you after?'

'Another drink, please? Just a small one as I'm already feeling tiddly from the three glasses of sherry I had already. The party will go on for hours yet and I don't want to miss any of it from conking out.'

He went off to oblige her, having to fight his way through others milling around to get to the front of the trestle table holding the barrel of beer for the men, bottles of sherry or port for the women and a variety of fizzy drinks or cordial for the children. Solly had paid for it all and it sat beside another trestle that held the food which each family had contributed towards, some bringing plates piled with cheese and cooked ham sandwiches, some sausage rolls, others cakes and trifles. Gem herself had contributed three huge meat pies, a mound of mashed potatoes and several jugs of tasty thick gravy.

As she waited for her husband to return with her drink, her eyes travelled around, for a moment settling themselves on each separate group of people enjoying the social event of the fairfolks' year; much looked-forward to. Early on that afternoon, a group of men had temporarily broken off from their duties in the main fairground for the last time that season, dismantling the rides and stalls, to push a dozen or so of the living vans closer together to make space for the party to be held in. Once that was done and the men returned back to work, a group of women, Gem included, had set to work stringing up lengths of bunting, draping them around the vans surrounding the party space, then placing oil lamps in strategic places to light up the area once the night drew in. It was now just after eight, much food and drink had been consumed and the party was in full swing, everyone enjoying themselves.

At least forty people were dancing together in their own particular style, amongst them her two sons and nieces Nita and Rosa, in a clearing a little ahead of her, to the music provided by old Wilf Griffin. Despite his age of nearly ninety, his fingers were still nimble enough to produce a recognisable tune on his equally as ancient fiddle and, perched on a wooden box beside him, was twenty-nine-year-old Tommy Jaffa, one of the gaff lads, accompanying Wilf on a battered-looking accordion. Then, to Gem's surprise, suddenly everyone stopped dancing and was looking over at the musicians, bemused. She wondered why for a moment, then started laughing as it seemed that Wilf had forgotten what tune he had been playing and had suddenly starting playing a different one to the one his companion was. The mistake rectified, much to an embarrassed Wilf, the music started up again, this time both musicians playing the same tune and the dancing resumed.

On the side of the dance area some other people were singing along to the music, others were talking and a couple of men, obviously the worse for drink, were having a heated discussion which looked to Gem like it might turn into a full-blown argument. When she saw one poke the other hard in his chest, she could see it would need intervention from Solly soon to break it up before either of them got hurt. Suffering a hang-over was one thing but it would not do for any of the men to arrive for work bright and early tomorrow morning suffering from any damage to their limbs preventing them from fully pulling their weight. Work might have stopped so that all could enjoy the party this evening, but there was still a lot to be done tomorrow before the first convoy of lorries could start to transport all the dismantled rides and stalls to their winter rest site in Nottinghamshire, a disused World War Two airfield Sam had persuaded the MOD to allow them to use for the last five years.

She smiled then as she watched several children over at the food table, Col amongst them – Iris and Bert were well aware of what he was doing but good-naturedly turning a blind eye, as this was a time for fun after all – filling their hands and pockets with food and then disappearing under the table to consume it. She then spotted her sister-in-law Fran sitting on one of two chairs outside her van, her head close to Jonny's, both sharing a plate of food. The way things were heading between them, she would predict an engagement announcement from them soon, with a wedding to follow, and she couldn't be more pleased.

She couldn't be more thrilled either for Ren and Donny, who walked past her now, not even noticing her. Or, in fact, anyone else either. They only had eyes for each other. There would be no wedding soon for them; Donny hadn't even begun divorce proceedings because he had no idea where Suzie was. She doubted they were at all bothered though. The obtaining of a piece of paper wasn't going to change how they felt about each other one iota.

It was such a shame though that such a happy ending would never happen for Velda, who she was now looking at sitting in her chair next to Fran and Jonny, a wide smile on her face, foot tapping in time with the music. It would seem to all that looked at her that she was enjoying the party as much as everyone else, but Gem knew that, deep down, she was so very sad that the man who had been the love of her life and had been such a very dear friend to her was no longer around for her to enjoy the company of. Like everyone else close to Sam who was mourning his loss, in time Velda would come to terms with it.

Emily Dunn sat the other side of Velda sipping on a small glass of sherry, tapping a finger against the glass in time with the music as she watched the dancers. She had a look of utter contentment on her aged face. A look that told Gem that she had no regrets whatsoever over her decision to leave her old life behind for a new one with Grundy's and fulfilling a lifetime ambition to impart her knowledge on those who otherwise had great difficulty obtaining it. Once they were settled in their over-winter place she was going to start her adult reading and writing classes. There was a general reluctance amongst the fairfolk to participate mainly through pride or embarrassment and the opinion that they had reached their age without these skills and managed to survive so why bother now. Once it got around that the owner himself was going to be taking them, some minds changed and Gem had no doubt that more would in time. She had been stunned when she had finally plucked up courage to inform Solly that she had volunteered him for Emily's lessons in the hope of encouraging others of the community to, as instead of his annoyance, he had been extremely enthusiastic. It seemed that his inability to read the newspaper article involving Emily and him having to ask others to do the honour for him had not only caused him an amount of shame but served to make him realise just what he was missing out on by not being able to read. And now, presented with the opportunity to and with someone who had the patience to bear with him, unlike his wife, he was more than willing to try. In future, hopefully, it would be Solly informing Robbie about an article he'd read in the newspaper and not the other way around!

Thinking of Solly, a vision of his brother Sonny suddenly came to mind and, for a moment, her good mood left her to be replaced with one of anger as she remembered how he'd put her family and all the livelihoods of the Grundy community in jeopardy. She wondered where he was now. Lying low, afraid to be spotted by either the police or any of Morrison's eyes and ears if he'd no idea that, thanks to his brother, the man had been arrested for his crimes and was now in jail awaiting his trial. Or was he swanning around in full view, unrecognisable in his disguise, using a new name and background he'd invented, building a new life for himself; something he was clearly very adept at, having fooled people for years that he was a successful businessman when, in truth, he was a fairground worker. All those people he had used, abused and stolen from purely to seek vengeance on that woman. Would he be feeling any regret for his actions? She doubted it. She was naturally an extremely forgiving woman, didn't hold grudges, didn't uphold violence, but it would be a very long time before she felt she would ever be able to be in the same company as Sonny again without giving him a piece of her mind.

There was one person though whose company she would give anything to be in. She knew exactly how many weeks, days, hours, minutes and maybe even seconds had passed since she had rushed away telling Gem she needed time to digest the fact that the mother she had believed had thrown her away at her birth, like she had meant nothing to her, hadn't at all. That she had been told by her mother that her baby was dead and had had it adopted. As the days had gone by and Jenny hadn't returned to take her rightful place with her real family, Gem was beginning to worry that Jenny didn't want to and that she would never see her again.

Her thoughts were interrupted by the return of Solly. She smiled at him as she took the glass of sherry off him. As he sat down, he said to her, 'Penny for them?'

'Pardon?'

'Your thoughts. You were miles away just now. I don't need to ask though as I know. Jenny. Come on, love, cheer up. I keep telling you she'll come back when she's ready, I'm positive she will.' He dearly hoped his words of comfort weren't hollow ones. It would break Gem's heart if she didn't. It would break his too. It would also devastate her two brothers who were so looking forward to meeting her and having an older sister around to carrying pranks out on.

Solly was right, she did need to cheer up. Velda, in her wisdom, had once told her that if she willed something to happen hard enough, it would. She had willed Jenny to come back so many times she had lost count. She would pray that Velda was right and very soon she would have willed Jenny back enough times for it to happen. And, besides, this was a party; a special one to celebrate the end of another Grundy season which the owners laid on by way of thanking the community for all their hard work. It wouldn't look good to the rest if the owners didn't look like they were enjoying themselves.

She spun to face him. 'Oh, Solly, I have just realised there is a woman you certainly haven't danced with yet.'

His face fell and he groaned. 'Oh no, Gem. I can't dance any more tonight, I don't think I've got another one in me.'

'She'll be very upset if you don't make the effort.'

His better nature took over. 'Oh, all right then. But this is the last. Who is it?'

'Me,' she said, jumping up and holding out her hand to him.

He grinned at her. 'For you, I'll find the energy for anything you want me to.'

He took her hand and stood up to join her, then looked at her in surprise as she made no effort to go over and join in with the dancers who, at the moment, were failing miserably to dance an Irish jig, most of their attempts resembling more of a Scottish fling, but seemed frozen to the spot.

He asked, 'What's the matter, Gem? I thought you wanted to dance. Have you changed your mind?'

She didn't answer him, so he asked her again. She turned her head to look at him blankly. 'Pardon. Oh, yes, of course I still want to dance. It's just that...'

'Just what?'

As she had stood up to lead her husband onto the dance space she thought she had caught a glimpse of Jenny, over in the distance by the drinks table, talking to someone. It was just a quick glance, very fleeting, before someone had stepped in the way and blocked her view. But then the person had, only seconds later, moved away again and there had been no Jenny behind them, so it must have been her eyes playing tricks on her. In her desperate need to see Jenny she had conjured a vision of her up. She declined to tell Solly for fear he might start to worry that she was going mad.

And then, as she led her husband into the middle of the dancers, she saw her again. This time she knew she wasn't seeing things. It really was Jenny. She was walking towards them, a big smile on her pretty face, a bunch of flowers in one hand, weighed down by a huge suitcase in the other. Velda was right. If you will for something to happen enough times, eventually it will.

Tightening her grip on Solly's hand, much to his bemusement, she launched him off with her to greet their daughter. They had already lost out on the first twenty-two years of her life and she wasn't prepared for them to miss any more of it. The sooner they reached her, the sooner they could gather her into their midst where she truly belonged.

The publishers hope that this book has given you enjoyable reading. Large Print Books are especially designed to be as easy to see and hold as possible. If you wish a complete list of our books please ask at your local library or write directly to:

Magna Large Print Books
Magna House, Long Preston,
Skipton, North Yorkshire.
BD23 4ND